VALLEY OF DEATH

Scott Mariani is the author of the worldwide-acclaimed action-adventure thriller series featuring ex-SAS hero Ben Hope, which has sold millions of copies in Scott's native UK alone and is also translated into over 20 languages. His books have been described as 'James Bond meets Jason Bourne, with a historical twist'. The first Ben Hope book, *The Alchemist's Secret*, spent six straight weeks at #1 on Amazon's Kindle chart, and all the others have been *Sunday Times* bestsellers.

Scott was born in Scotland, studied in Oxford and now lives and writes in a remote setting in rural west Wales. When not writing, he can be found bouncing about the country lanes in an ancient Land Rover, wild camping in the Brecon Beacons or engrossed in his hobbies of astronomy, photography and target shooting (no dead animals involved!).

You can find out more about Scott and his work, and sign up to his exclusive newsletter, on his official website:

www.scottmariani.com

SCOTT MARIANI

Valley of Death

avon.

Published by AVON
A Division of HarperCollins*Publishers* Ltd
1 London Bridge Street
London SE1 9GF

www.harpercollins.co.uk

A Paperback Original 2019

1

First published in Great Britain by HarperCollins*Publishers* 2019

Copyright © Scott Mariani 2019

Scott Mariani asserts the moral right to
be identified as the author of this work

A catalogue record for this book is
available from the British Library

ISBN 978-0-00-823596-3

Set in Minion by Palimpsest Book Production Ltd, Falkirk, Stirlingshire

Printed and bound in Great Britain by
CPI Group (UK) Ltd, Croydon CR0 4YY

MIX
Paper from
responsible sources
FSC™ C007454

VALLEY OF DEATH

PROLOGUE

Kabir removed his pilot's headset and began flipping switches on the Bell Ranger's instrument panels to shut down the rotors. He turned to grin broadly at Sai in the co-pilot seat, then at Manish sitting behind.

'Ready to make history, guys!' he said over the falling pitch of the turbine.

Kabir's two associates beamed back at him. Manish said, 'Let's rock and roll.'

As the helicopter's rotors slowed to a whistling *whip-whip-whip*, the three companions clambered out and jumped down to the rocky ground. It had taken less than an hour from the urban hubbub of their base in New Delhi to reach the remoteness of Hisar District, Haryana, out in the middle of nowhere twenty miles north-west of a once barely-heard-of village called Rakhigarhi.

Kabir stood for a moment and gazed around him at the arid, semi-desert terrain that stretched as far as the eye could see in all directions. Far away beyond the barren escarpment of rocky hills behind him to the north-east lay Punjab, the Land of the Five Rivers; in front of him lay the wide-open semi-desertified plains, arid and rocky with just a few desiccated shrubs and wizened trees scattered here and there and offering no shade. It was mid-September, and the merciless

1

heat of summer was past its worst, but the sun still beat fiercely down, baking the landscape.

Kabir was hardened to the heat, because of the outdoor demands of a job that often took him to difficult and inhospitable places all across the ancient Near East. Unlike his elder brothers, one of whom spent all his time in air-conditioned big-city boardrooms, and the other who, for reasons best known to him, had chosen to live in chilly, rain-sodden Britain. Very strange. Though if it was the life he shared with his beautiful new wife that kept him tied to London, Kabir couldn't entirely blame the guy. She was something, all right. Maybe one day he, too, might be lucky enough to find a woman like her.

For now, though, Kabir's sole devotion was to his work.

Kabir stepped back to the chopper, reached into a cool box behind the passenger seat and pulled out three cans of Coke, one for him and one each for Manish and Sai. His two bright, trusty graduate students were both in their early twenties, only a few years younger than Kabir, who happened to be the youngest professor ever to teach at the Institute of Archaeology in Delhi. With his warm personality and winning smile, he was widely held to be the most popular, too – though he was far too modest to admit it.

Sai rolled the cold can over his brow, then cracked the ring and look a long drink. 'That hit the spot. Thanks, boss.' Sai never called him 'Professor'.

'No littering, please,' Kabir said. 'This is a site of special archaeological interest, remember. Or soon to be.'

'Doesn't bloody look like it right now,' Manish said.

Sai finished the can, crumpled it between his fingers and surveyed it with a thoughtful frown. 'Just think. If I chuck this away among the rocks, four thousand years into the future some guy like us will dig it up and prize it as an ancient relic of our culture, wondering what the hell it can teach him about the long-lost civilisation of the twenty-first century.'

Kabir smiled. 'That's history in action for you. Now let's go and see what we can figure out about the people who lived here four thousand years ago.'

'I don't think they drank Coke,' Manish said.

'Nah, something else killed them off,' Sai joked. 'Question is, what?'

It was one of the puzzles that Kabir had spent his whole career trying to answer, and it was no joke to him. Nor was he the only archaeologist who'd devoted endless hours to solving the mystery, to no avail. He tossed his own empty Coke can back into the cooler, then took out his iPhone and quickly accessed the precious set of password-protected documents stored inside.

Those documents were the single most important thing in his life right now. The originals from which they had been scanned were a set of three old leather-bound journals dating back to the nineteenth century. Not particularly ancient, as archaeological finds went – and yet their chance discovery had been the most significant he'd ever made. And he was hoping that it would lead to an even bigger one.

Outside of Manish and Sai, Kabir trusted virtually no one with his secret. The precious journals themselves were still back in the city, securely locked up in his personal safe while their new custodian travelled out to this arid wilderness, full of excitement and determined to find out if the amazing revelations of their long-dead author were indeed true.

Only time would tell. Sooner rather than later, he hoped. His eagerness to know the truth sometimes bordered on desperation. Yes, it was an obsession. He knew that. But sometimes, he reminded himself, that's what it takes to get the job done.

Shielding his eyes from the sun's glare, Kabir slowly scanned the horizon. The chopper was parked on a rocky plateau from where the ground fell away into a rubble-strewn valley. Heat ripples disturbed the air like tendrils rising from the ground, but he was able to make out the curve of the ancient dry river bed that wound for miles into the far distance. Millennia ago, a mighty waterway had flowed through here, nourishing the land and raising lush vegetation all along its banks. Now it was so parched and dusty that even looking at it made Kabir thirsty for another cold drink.

He looked back at the iPhone and scrolled through the selection of documents until he came to the scan of the hand-drawn map from one of the journals. The hundred and eighty-plus years it had lain undiscovered had done considerable damage. A lot of the pages had been nibbled around the edges by mildew and rodents. Others were so badly faded and water-stained as to be barely legible. Kabir had used specialised computer software to enhance the details, and a UV camera to photograph the worst-affected sections. He'd been pleased with the results. The digitised map now looked as sharp and clear as the day the journal's author had sketched it. The only modification Kabir had made was to insert modern GPS coordinates in place of the original latitude and longitude figures that the author had calculated using the tools of his day, stars and compass.

The map's key feature was the undulating, meandering curve of a river whose line, as Kabir stood there comparing the two, closely resembled that of the dry bed that stretched out in front of him.

'What do you reckon, boss?' Sai, at his shoulder, was gazing at the screen of the iPhone.

4

'I think we might have found it, boys,' Kabir replied. His voice was calm but his heart felt ready to leap out of his chest. He took a couple of deep breaths, then started leading the way down the rocky slope towards the river valley. He ran five miles every day and was as nimble as a mountain goat over the rough terrain. Sai was markedly less so, being overly partial to calorie-laden Delhi street food, and Manish was a city kid too used to level pavements. Slipping and stumbling and causing little rock slides under their feet, they manfully followed their leader down the hillside. By the time they reached the bottom, Kabir was already tracking along the river bed, walking slowly and scanning left and right as though searching for clues.

It was hard to believe that such an arid and inhospitable area could have once been a major centre of one of the largest and most advanced cultures of the ancient world. But that was exactly what it was.

To say that the lost Harappan or Indus Valley Civilisation was Kabir's overriding interest in life would have been a crashing understatement. Long, long ago, over a stretch of time spanning one and a half thousand years during the second and third millennia BCE, the culture had thrived throughout the north-western parts of South Asia. Their empire had been larger than that of Mesopotamia; greater even than that of ancient Egypt or China. It had covered a vast area comprising parts of what were today Afghanistan, Pakistan and north-west India. At its peak, it was thought to support a population of five million inhabitants, which by ancient standards was enormous.

And yet, virtually nothing was known about these people. Nobody even knew what they called themselves, let alone how they organised their society. The most baffling enigma of all was the question of what had finally caused their whole civilisation to crumble and disappear in an astonishingly short time.

For years, it had been widely assumed in the archaeology world that the main centres of the Indus Valley Civilisation had been the excavated cities at Harappa and Mohenjo-Daro, both in Pakistan. This had been a major frustration for archaeologists from India, since tensions between the two nations made it hard for them to travel freely in their neighbouring country. More recently, important finds made at Rakhigarhi in India's Haryana region had radically changed that view. Many historians and archaeologists now believed that the sheer size of the site excavated at Rakhigarhi, and the wealth of incredible, priceless artefacts found under its dusty, rocky ground, pointed to its having once been the capital of the entire civilisation. If that was true, as Kabir fervently wished it was, then it might offer scholars the opportunity to finally start figuring out the secrets of the ancient lost culture.

Exactly what he hoped to find here, all this way from the main Rakhigarhi site, Kabir couldn't say for certain. All his hopes were pinned on the remarkable journals, which described 'a vast treasure most precious to all men on earth'. The man who'd penned those words had been one of the most important explorers of his generation. If his claims were right, Kabir could be standing, literally, on top of the biggest and most valuable archaeological find ever.

Treasure. The excitement he felt at the sound of that word took his breath away.

But even once he found it, getting it out of the ground would be no easy task. Kabir had already made some private, tentative enquiries among his contacts in the Indian government. They were unlikely to agree to fund a new excavation project, but as long as they agreed in principle, Kabir was more than willing to pay for it out of his own pocket. His very own private dig, fully under his own supervision. He calculated that to bring in sufficient manpower and equipment to get things rolling would cost him at least a hundred million rupees, equivalent to about one and a half million American dollars.

Kabir didn't blink at those figures. The benefits of being born into wealth.

Manish and Sai caught up with him and the three of them walked on, following the river bed. Each man was silent, gazing at the rocky ground underfoot and imagining what wonders might be hidden below. It was a heady feeling. Finally, Manish said, 'Wow, boss, you really think it's here somewhere?'

Kabir said nothing. He was gazing into the distance as he walked. His step slowed, then slowed again, and he halted, his eyes still fixed on some faraway point on the rocky horizon to the south-west of the river valley. He frowned. Looked again at the iPhone screen, then studied the horizon once more. Manish and Sai exchanged glances, wondering what the professor had seen. Manish asked, 'What's up?'

Kabir remained quiet for a moment longer, then pointed in the direction he'd been gazing. 'See that range of hills over there?'

Manish and Sai looked. 'Yeah, I see it,' Sai replied. Manish asked, 'What about it?'

Kabir lowered his pointing finger and tapped the iPhone screen with it. He frowned harder. 'It's not here.'

Manish shrugged and said, 'So? Everything else is the same. We must be in the right place.'

Kabir shook his head. 'Those hills have been there since prehistoric times, Manish. They didn't just sprout up in the last two hundred years. Trafford would have drawn them

7

on the map, like he drew everything else. He didn't. Something's wrong.' He was suddenly anxious. He bit his lip and compared the map and the landscape once more.

'But the coordinates led us here,' Sai said. 'They must be right.'

Kabir sighed. 'The coordinates are based on one guy's skill with compass and stars, long before we had pinpoint-accurate navigational technology. There's little margin for error. One tiny slip on Trafford's part and the GPS could take us half a mile off course, or more.'

'So what are you saying?' Manish asked, staring at him.

'I'm saying there's a disparity between the map and this location that I hadn't noticed before.'

Sai said, 'In other words, we're in the wrong bloody place.'

Manish was about to say something when he suddenly froze. 'Hear that?'

Sai said, 'What?'

Now Kabir heard it, too, and turned to look in the direction of the sound.

The approaching vehicle appeared on the ridge above the river valley, some ninety or a hundred yards to the west, the direction of the parked helicopter. Kabir instinctively didn't like the look of it. As he watched, it tipped over the edge of the slope and started bouncing and pattering its way down the hillside towards them, throwing up a dust plume in its wake. It was moving fast. Some kind of rugged four-wheel-drive, like the Nissan Jonga jeeps the Indian Army used to use.

'Who are they, boss?' Sai asked apprehensively.

'No idea. But I think we're about to find out.'

The jeep reached the bottom of the hillside and kept coming straight towards them, lurching and dipping over the rubble. Then it stopped, still a long way off. The terrain on the approach to the river bed was too rough even for an off-roader. The doors opened. Two men climbed out of the front. Three more climbed out of the back. All of them were clutching automatic rifles, but they definitely weren't the Indian Army.

'Dacoits!' Manish yelped.

Sai's jaw dropped open. An expression of pure horror plastered his face. 'Oh, shit.'

Dacoits were bandits, of which there were many gangs across north-west India. They were growing bolder each year, despite the increasingly militarised and notoriously brutal efforts of the police to round them all up. Kabir had read a few days earlier that an armed gang of them had robbed a bank in Haryana. Their sudden appearance was the last thing he'd have expected out here, in the middle of the wilderness. But all the same he now cursed himself for having left his self-defence pistol at home in Delhi. His mouth went dry.

'They must have seen us landing,' Sai said in a hoarse, panicky whisper. 'What are we going to do, boss?' Both he and Manish were looking to their professor as though he could magically get them out of this.

The five men were striding purposefully towards them. Spreading out now. Raising their weapons. Taking aim. Looking like they meant it.

'Run,' Kabir said. 'Just run!'

And then the gunshots began to crack out across the valley.

Chapter 1

Three weeks later

The walls of the single-storey house were several feet thick and extremely well insulated, solidly reinforced on the outside and clad on the inside with thick, sturdy plywood. The house featured several rooms and offered spacious facilities well suited to its purpose.

But it wasn't a dwelling in which anybody would have wanted to live. Not even the mice that inhabited the remote compound's various other sheds and outbuildings would have been tempted to make their nests in its walls. Not considering the activities that went on there.

Yet, the building wasn't empty that autumn afternoon. At the end of a narrow corridor was the main room; and in the middle of that room sat a woman on a wooden chair. She wasn't moving. Her wrists and ankles were lashed tight and her head hung towards her knees, so that her straggly blond hair covered her face. To her right, a kidnapper in torn jeans reclined on a tattered sofa with a shotgun cradled across his lap. To her left, another of the woman's captors stood in a corner.

Nobody spoke. As though waiting for something to happen.

The waiting didn't go on long.

The stunning boom of an explosion shattered the silence and shook the building. Heavy footsteps pounded up the corridor towards the main room. Then its door crashed violently inwards and two men burst inside. One man was slightly taller than the other, but otherwise they were indistinguishable in appearance. They were dressed from head to foot in black, bulked out by their body armour and tactical vests, and their faces were hidden behind masks and goggles. Each carried a semiautomatic pistol, same make, model and calibre, both weapons drawn from their tactical holsters, loaded and ready for action.

The two-man assault team moved with blinding speed as they invaded the room. They ignored the hostage for the moment. Her safety was their priority, which meant dealing with her captors quickly and efficiently before either one could harm her. The taller man unhesitatingly thrust out his weapon to aim at the kidnapper in the corner and engaged him with a double-tap to the chest and a third bullet to the head, the three snapping gunshots coming so fast that they sounded like a burst from a machine gun. No human being alive could have responded, or even flinched, in time to avoid being fatally shot.

The other man in black moved across the room to engage the kidnapper on the sofa. Shouting DROP THE WEAPON DROP THE WEAPON DROP THE WEAPON!

The kidnapper made no move to toss the shotgun. The second assault shooter went to engage him. His finger was on the trigger. Then the room suddenly lit up with a blinding white flash and an explosion twice as loud as the munitions they'd used to breach the door blew the shooter off his feet. He sprawled on his back, unharmed but momentarily stunned. His unfired pistol went sliding across the floor.

The room was full of acrid smoke. The kidnapper in the corner had slumped to the floor, but neither the bound hostage nor her captor on the sofa had moved at all. That was because they were the latest type of life-size, high-density foam 3D humanoid targets that were being used for live-fire hostage rescue and combat training simulations here at the Le Val Tactical Training Centre in Normandy, France. The 'kidnappers' had already been shot more full of holes than French Gruyère in the course of a hundred similar entry drills performed inside the killing house. So had the hostage, more than her fair share. But they'd survive to go through the whole experience another day, and many more.

The taller of the two assault shooters made his weapon safe and clipped it back into its holster, then pulled off his mask and goggles and brushed back the thick blond lock that fell across his brow. His haircut definitely wouldn't have passed muster, back in his SAS days. He walked over to his colleague, who was still trying to scramble to his feet.

Ben Hope held out a gloved hand to help him up. He said, 'Congratulations. You're dead, your team are dead, your hostage is dead. Let's review and start over.'

The second man's name was Yannick Ferreira and he was a counter-terror unit commander with the elite Groupe d'Intervention de la Gendarmerie Nationale or GIGN, here on a refresher course. He'd wanted to hone his skills with the best, and there were none better to train with than the guys at Le Val: Ben himself, his business partner Jeff Dekker, their associate Tuesday Fletcher and their hand-picked team of instructors, all ex-military, all top of their game. Ferreira was pretty good at his job too, but even skilled operators, like world-class athletes, could lose their edge now and then. It was Ben's job to keep them on their toes.

Ferreira said, 'What the hell just happened?'

Ben replied, 'That happened.' He pointed at the floor, where a length of thin wire lay limp across the rough boards where Ferreira had snagged it with his boot.

'A tripwire?'

'You must have missed it, in all the excitement,' Ben said.

The wire was connected to a hidden circuit behind the wall, which when broken activated the non-lethal explosive device right beneath Ferreira's feet. Seven million candlepower and 170 decibels of stunning noise weren't quite the same as being blown apart by a Semtex booby trap, but it certainly got its message across.

'Devil's in the detail, Yannick,' Ben said. 'As we all know, our terrorist friends have no problem blowing themselves to smithereens in order to take us out with them. It can get just a little messy.'

Ferreira shook his head sourly. 'I can't believe you caught me out with a damned flashbang. That was a dirty rotten trick, Ben.'

'Dirty rotten tricks are what you're paying us for,' Ben said. 'How about we stroll back to the house for a coffee, then we can come back and run through it again?'

Chapter 2

'Keep pouring,' Jeff said grimly, holding out his wine glass until Ben had filled it to the brim. Jeff downed half the glass in a single gulp like a man on a mission, and smacked his lips.

'I think I'll get rat-arsed tonight,' he declared.

'Sounds like a brilliant plan,' Tuesday said dryly. 'Don't expect me to carry you back to your hole after you collapse in a heap, though.'

Another busy work day had ended, evening had fallen and the three of them were gathered around the big oak table in the farmhouse kitchen, preparing to demolish a pot of beef and carrot stew that could have fed the French Army and was simmering on the stove. Ben was seated in his usual place by the window, feeling not much less morose than Jeff despite the glass of wine at his elbow, his loyal German shepherd dog Storm curled up at his feet and one of his favourite Gauloises cigarettes between his lips.

While he'd been working with Yannick Ferreira, Jeff and Tuesday had been putting two more of the GIGN guys through their paces on Le Val's firing ranges. Tuesday had been a top-class military sniper before he'd come to join the gang in Normandy. His idea of fun was popping rows of cherry tomatoes at six hundred yards with his custom

Remington 700 rifle, which generally upstaged and occasionally cheesed off their clients. Especially the ones with a tough-guy attitude, who for some reason didn't expect a skinny Jamaican kid who was forever smiling and ebullient to be so deadly once he got behind a rifle.

Ben had warned Tuesday in the past about the showing off. 'We're here to teach them, not embarrass them.' Still, Ferreira's guys hadn't taken it too badly. After class the three trainees had driven off to the nearest town, Valognes, in search of beer and fast food to help soothe their wounded pride and prepare them for another day of humiliation ahead.

Even Tuesday's spirits were dampened by the gloomy atmosphere around the kitchen table. But the glumness of the three friends had nothing to do with the tribulations of their work. The theme of the dinnertime conversation had been women troubles. Tuesday, who appeared to enjoy a stress-free and uncomplicated love life largely because he was always between girlfriends, had nothing to complain about. For both Ben and Jeff, however, it was a different story.

Ben had recently returned from an unexpectedly adventuresome trip to the American Deep South. There, in between dodging bullets and almost getting blown up and eaten by alligators, he'd met and befriended a lady police officer called Jessie Hogan. They had dinner and went to a jazz gig together, and although Jessie made it pretty obvious that she liked Ben, nothing happened between them. Ben drove back to New Orleans and boarded his flight home without so much as a kiss being exchanged.

But that wasn't the impression that Ben's French girl-friend, Sandrine, had formed.

Ben and Sandrine had been together for a few months.

It wasn't love's young dream. Both of them had been hurt before, and it had been a somewhat cautious, reticent start to the relationship before they fell into a comfortable routine. She was a head surgeon at the hospital in Cherbourg, some kilometres away, whose punishing work schedule meant she didn't live at Le Val and only visited now and then. It had been on one such visit, a couple of days ago, when the two of them had been hanging out in the prefabricated office building and Ben had needed to step outside for a few minutes to attend to a delivery of some items for the range complex.

While his back was turned, as luck would have it, an email had landed on his screen: Jessie Hogan, saying what a great time she'd had with him and expressing a strong desire to see him again if he happened to swing by Clovis Parish, Louisiana any time in the future. She'd signed off with a lot of kisses.

Sandrine hadn't taken it too well. Ben had stepped back inside the office to be met with tears and anger. 'So this is what you get up to on your travels, is it?'

Calmly at first, Ben had protested his innocence. But nothing he could say could persuade her, and after a bitter quarrel and a lot of accusations, Sandrine had driven off in a rage. It was Jeff who'd stopped Ben from going after her. Jeff had been right: following a row with a car chase wasn't such a good idea.

Ben hadn't been able to get through to Sandrine on the phone since, and she wasn't responding to emails. He'd decided to give it a few days and drive up to Cherbourg. But it wasn't looking good, and her allegations of infidelity had shaken him to the core. It would never have occurred to him not to trust her, if the situation had been reversed. Maybe he was just naïve when it came to these matters.

'Women,' Jeff said with a snort. His glass was empty again. He motioned for the bottle. Ben slid it across the table, and Jeff grabbed it and topped himself up, clearly intent on polishing off the whole lot before uncorking another. Tuesday rolled his eyes.

'Come on, mate, it's not that bad.'

'Isn't it?'

Jeff's whirlwind love affair with a pretty young primary school teacher called Chantal Mercier had come as a surprise to his friends at the time. The rugged, rough-around-the-edges ex-Special Boat Service commando seemed like the last kind of guy a woman like Chantal would go for. To Ben's even greater amazement, not long afterwards Jeff had announced that he and Chantal were getting engaged. It all seemed to be going full steam ahead. The wedding date was set for later in the year, at the nearby village church in Saint Acaire. Jeff had even been trying to learn French.

But while Ben was in America, a long-simmering dispute between Jeff and his fiancée had finally blown up. Chantal could live with her future husband's military past but couldn't tolerate that he made his living by teaching people how to, in her words, 'kill people'. After much soul-searching, she'd come to the conclusion that she couldn't reconcile his violent and morally corrupt profession with her calling as a teacher of innocent, vulnerable little children. Chantal would have no truck with Jeff's explanations that Le Val was a training facility devoted to teaching the good guys how to protect innocent people from the bad guys, and that all the firearms at the compound were kept strictly secure in an armoured vault, and that the place was about as morally corrupt as a Quaker convention. Adamant, she'd given him an ultimatum: if he wouldn't give up his position at Le Val and let his partner take over his share in the business, then he could wave goodbye to the future he and she had planned together.

Jeff had flatly refused to quit. Whereupon, true to her promise, Chantal had broken off the engagement. The dramatic collapse of their relationship had floored Jeff, and he was still extremely bitter about it. He talked about little else – and Ben got the feeling he was about to start talking about it again now.

'She knew what I did when we got together,' Jeff groaned, staring into his glass. 'What the fuck's wrong with her? Don't answer that, I already know.'

Tuesday looked at Jeff with wide eyes. 'You do?'

'Damn right I do. She's a do-gooder, that's what she is.' Jeff took another gulp of wine and tipped his glass towards Ben. 'Just like what's-her-name. That activist chick Jude runs around with.'

Jude was Ben's grown-up son from a long-ago relationship, now living in Chicago with his girlfriend. Ben wouldn't have described her as a 'chick', but 'do-gooder' was admittedly apt, as was 'activist'.

'Actually,' Ben said, 'things aren't going too well there either. Jude called last night. Looks like they might be splitting, too.'

'There must be something going around,' Tuesday said.

Jeff grunted. 'He should never have hooked up with her in the first place. Let me guess, she finally realised Jude isn't enough of a soy boy commie liberal for her tastes.'

Jeff really wasn't in a good mood tonight.

Ben said, 'Not exactly. She's become a vegan.'

'Oh, please. Give me a break.'

'And apparently she expects Jude to follow suit.'

'What, like, and live on rice and egg noodles?'

'Can't have egg noodles,' Tuesday said.

'Why not?' Jeff asked him.

'Got egg in them,' Tuesday said.

'No kidding. So what?'

'It's exploitation of chickens. Like honey is exploitation of bees.'

Jeff shook his head in disgust. 'Jesus H. Christ. What is it with these food fascists? It's like a disease. It's spreading everywhere.'

'Nah,' Tuesday said. 'It's not a disease, it's psychological. They're stuck in a developmental phase that Freud called the oral stage. The kid learns as a baby that it can manipulate its parents' behaviour by refusing to eat this or that. Basically, it grows up as a control freak, having learned at an early age how to get its own way and be the centre of attention all the time. From their teens they start attaching moral or ideological values to justify using food as a weapon.'

Jeff, whose idea of using food as a weapon was restricted to mess-room grub fights and custard-pie-in-the-face comedy routines, stared at the younger man. Tuesday had a way of coming out with things out of left field, whether it was some obscure quotation, a snippet of poetry or assorted little-known facts.

'Where the hell do you get all this stuff from?' he asked, not for the first time since they'd known each other. 'Fucking *Freud*?'

Tuesday shrugged. 'Brooke got me interested in it. We were talking about psychology last time she was here.'

The name Brooke was one no longer mentioned too often at the table, or for that matter anywhere around the compound at Le Val. It referred to Dr Brooke Marcel, formerly Ben's own fiancée, before things had gone bad there, too. Ben's friends knew that it was a sensitive topic to raise. Likewise, nobody would have dared to mention the fact that the situation with Ben and Sandrine was like history repeating itself. The bullet that had killed the relationship between Ben and Brooke had been the sudden reappearance of an old flame, Roberta Ryder. Nothing had happened there, either, though Brooke hadn't seen it that way. Then again, maybe Ben's failure to turn up for their wedding had had something to do with it.

Tuesday regretted his slip the instant he'd blurted out Brooke's name. He gave Ben a rueful look. 'Sorry. It just came out. Jeff's fault.'

'How's it my fault?' Jeff demanded.

'You asked me. I answered.'

'How was I to know what you were going to come out with? How can anyone know what you'll say next?'

'It's okay,' Ben said, to quell the tensions before Jeff's foul mood made things escalate into a heated debate. 'Don't worry about it.'

All these names from the past, all these lost loves, all these bittersweet memories. Ben sometimes felt as though his whole life path was just a trail of destruction, sadness and remorse. It was little comfort to know he wasn't the only one. He wished that their conversation hadn't taken such a downward turn. Perhaps it was time to open another bottle of wine, or get out the whisky.

Before Ben could decide which, Storm the German shepherd suddenly uncoiled himself from the stone floor at his master's feet, planted himself bolt upright facing the window and began barking loudly. The lights of a vehicle swept the yard outside. There was the sound of a car door.

'Hello, the GIGN boys are back awfully early,' Jeff said, looking at his watch. It was shortly after seven, only just gone dark outside. Nobody had expected Ferreira's crew back until close to midnight, once they'd had their fill of junk food and cheap beer.

'I guess they were less than impressed with the night life in Valognes,' Tuesday said with a wry grin. 'Welcome to the sticks, fellas.'

The GIGN guys drove a monster crew-cab truck with enough lights to fry a rabbit crossing the road. Ben turned to look out of the window. It looked like the headlamps of a regular car outside.

'It's not them.'

Jeff frowned. 'We expecting anyone else?'

Tuesday said, 'Not that I know of.'

Unannounced visitors at this or any time were a rarity at the remote farmhouse, not least because the only entrance to the fenced compound was a gatehouse manned twenty-four-seven by Le Val's security guys, who wouldn't let in any stranger without first radioing ahead to the house to check it was okay.

There was a soft, hesitant knock at the front door. Ben said, 'Let's go and find out who the mystery visitor is.' He stubbed out his Gauloise, rose from the table, walked out of the kitchen and down the oak-panelled hallway. He flipped a switch for the yard lights, then opened the door.

The mystery visitor standing on the doorstep was a woman. Her face was shaded under the brim of a denim baseball cap. The yard lights were bright behind her, silhouetting her shape. Medium height, slender in a sporty, toned kind of way. She was wearing dark jeans and a lightweight leather jacket and had a handbag on a strap around one shoulder. Her auburn hair caught the light as it ruffled in the cool, gentle October evening breeze. Her body language was tense and stiff, as if her being here was more out of obligation than choice.

22

Behind her, a taxicab was parked across the cobbled yard, its motor idling. The courtesy light was on inside and the taxi driver was settling down to read a paper.

But Ben wasn't looking at him. He stared at the woman. He was aware that his mouth had dropped open, but for a few speechless moments couldn't do anything about it.

At last, he was able to find the words. At any rate, one word.

'*Brooke?*'

Chapter 3

The woman made no reply. She stared back at Ben, as though she was as surprised as he was. The moment he'd said it, he realised he was wrong. The way the cap half-shaded her face under the bright glow of the yard lights had tricked him. But the resemblance to Brooke Marcel was stunning nonetheless. The security guys must have been fooled by it too, and just waved her through. In happier times, Brooke had been a very frequent visitor to Le Val and often stayed there for extended periods.

'It's Phoebe,' the woman said, self-consciously. 'Are you Ben? You must be Ben.'

'Yes, I'm Ben Hope,' he replied, somewhat thrown off balance by her presence. 'But who are you? I don't know any Phoebe.'

'Phoebe Kite. Brooke's sister. Sorry, I should have said. I'm a little bit nervous, coming here like this.'

Now it made sense. They'd never met, but Ben suddenly remembered Brooke mentioning an elder sister with whom she was often confused. As the details came back to him, he recalled that Phoebe was some kind of yoga coach – no, a Pilates instructor – who made buckets of money teaching celebrity clients how to tie themselves in knots. Left ankle behind right ear, big toe to tip of nose without bending your knee, that kind of thing.

Phoebe lived in Hampstead or some such jet-setter part of London with her husband Marshall Kite, a millionaire stockbroker and director of a large firm called Kite Investments. Now, him, Ben *had* crossed paths with before, on one memorable occasion. That was another story.

As for why Brooke's sister should have suddenly landed on his doorstep out of the blue, however, Ben was at a total loss. He said, 'There's no need to be nervous.'

'I hope I haven't turned up at a bad time. It's just . . . well, it's—'

'Not at all,' he said, still baffled, then realised that he was keeping her standing on the doorstep. 'Please, won't you come inside.'

He ushered her in the door, catching a whiff of perfume as she passed. Whatever brand the fashionable rich were wearing these days. Ben knew little of these things.

As Ben escorted his visitor up the hallway, Jeff stuck his head through the kitchen door to see what was what, and looked bewildered by the sight of the strange woman in the house. Ben gave him a look that said, 'It's okay, I've got it.' Jeff retreated back inside and shut the door.

Ben led Phoebe Kite towards the living room. It was a part of the house where he spent little time personally, preferring the cosiness of the farmhouse kitchen and its proximity to the wine rack and whisky cupboard. But he sensed that she wanted to talk to him in private. The presence of two other men, especially a slightly inebriated Jeff Dekker, would only make her more edgy. He could feel the tension emanating from her, like a crackle of static electricity in the air.

'This is nice,' she said distractedly as he showed her into the room and flipped on a light switch.

'Please, take a seat,' he said, motioning at the sofa he

never sat on, opposite the big-screen TV he never watched. Idle relaxation wasn't a big part of his lifestyle. 'Can I offer you a drink?'

Under the soft lighting of the living room side lamps, she looked more uncannily like her sister than ever. She perched on the edge of the sofa, eyes downcast, knees and feet together with her hands clasped in her lap and the handbag still looped over her shoulder. Uptight.

She replied, 'No, thank you, I'm fine.'

'What about your taxi outside? You want me to send him away? Wherever it is you have to return to tonight, I'm happy to drive you there myself.'

She made a thin-lipped smile. 'That's very kind. But he can wait.'

'Whatever you prefer.' Ben moved across to an armchair and sat, so as not to stand over her. Back when he'd worked as a freelancer he'd been used to dealing with a lot of extremely, and understandably, nervous clients. He was good at putting them at their ease. He smiled. In his most reassuring tone he said, 'Now, you've clearly come a long way to see me, so I get the impression it must be for an important reason.'

She nodded. 'It is. Terribly important.'

'Then how about you tell me what this is all about?'

Phoebe Kite looked up at him, and for the first time he could see the depth of the distress in her eyes. Green eyes, pure emerald, so much like Brooke's that it was almost painful for Ben to return her gaze.

Phoebe Kite said, 'I need your help.'

When people said that to Ben, it was never a trivial request. In his line of work, it had always tended to mean that something very, very serious and life-threatening had happened.

'I gathered as much. Then what can I do for you?'

26

She shifted in her seat. Covered her mouth and gave a little cough. 'Or perhaps I should say, *we* need your help.'

'We? As in, you and your husband Marshall?'

'No, I'm fine,' she said. 'Marshall's . . . well, he's Marshall. He's always embroiled in some business dispute or other. But we're not in any real trouble. Not your kind of trouble. Sorry, that came out wrong. I meant—'

'I understand. It's okay. But tell me, if this isn't about you—'

'It's about Brooke,' she said in a voice taut with emotion, and Ben felt an icy blade sink all the way through his guts and pin him to the armchair.

'Something's happened to Brooke?' When he said it, the words sounded remote and far away, as though someone else had spoken them. He was suddenly numb.

Phoebe nodded agitatedly and started chewing her lip. Her hands were clasped so tightly in her lap that her fingers were pinched bloodless and white. 'Yes. No. I mean, sort of.'

Ben stared at her and said, 'Sort of what?'

'What I'm trying to say is that something awful has happened. Not to Brooke personally. To her husband.'

Chapter 4

The mixed emotions that flooded through Ben were polarised to opposite extremes. At the same time as the relief melted away the acute terror of something having happened to Brooke, Phoebe's words were a slap in the face that actually made him flinch.

Brooke, married. Even though their relationship had ended a long time ago now, the idea of it was like being whipped by nettles.

The involuntary thought passed through his mind: *Please don't let it be Rupert Shannon.* Long before she and Ben had got together, Brooke had had a brief involvement with the pumped-up, Porsche-driving, self-adoring buffoon who'd managed to push himself up the ranks of the British military thanks to lofty family connections.

If she was back with him, there truly was no God after all.

On the other hand, if something nasty had befallen Rupert Shannon, maybe there was a God, and it was time for Ben to start praying to Him again.

Ben shoved that unworthy thought out of his mind, swallowed hard and said, 'I didn't know she was married.'

Phoebe nodded. 'Oh, yes, for a while now. I think you know her husband. Amal Ray?'

Ben remembered Amal well. He'd been a friend and former neighbour of Brooke's, dating back to when she'd had an apartment in Richmond, Surrey. Amal had been an aspiring playwright who somehow seemed able to maintain a leisured lifestyle, despite having no job and zero theatrical successes to his name. He was likeable in a neurotic sort of way, bookish and nervy, the kind of guy who looked as though he was rushing around even when he was standing still. Ben had always suspected that Amal harboured a secret admiration for Brooke that went beyond the bounds of friendship, though he'd never have imagined it could be reciprocal. He seemed like the last man on earth she'd be drawn to. Brooke, so full of passion, who loved excitement, thrived on the thrill of the challenge and could handle herself in a difficult spot. He couldn't imagine two people more different. The idea of them together was unthinkable.

But Ben wasn't about to let his deeply hurt personal feelings stand in the way of his concern for a friend in trouble. 'What happened?'

'Amal's been kidnapped.'

'Kidnapped?' Ben was genuinely amazed. The idea of innocent people being snatched off the streets or from their homes was hardly anything new to him. For years after quitting the military, he'd worked on the right side of the booming kidnap and ransom industry, liberating victims and dispensing to the bad guys the fate they had coming. He, of all people, knew how widespread and pernicious the abduction trade was.

But the thought of Amal Ray falling victim to it seemed crazy. The guy fitted the profile of a kidnap victim about as well as he filled the bill as a potential life partner for a woman like Brooke.

Phoebe nodded. 'That's why I'm here. Because that's what you do, isn't it? Help people in that sort of situation?'

Ben could have replied, 'Used to do.' Instead he asked, 'When did this happen?'

'Eight days ago.'

'Where, in London?'

'No, in India. That's where he's from.'

'He moved back there?' Brooke, living the married life in India. It was hard to imagine.

'No, they still live in London. Amal was on a trip back to Delhi when it happened.'

'Okay,' Ben said. 'What's the deal? How much are the kidnappers asking for?'

Identifying the motive for the crime, which ninety-nine per cent of the time was financial, was a vital first step. It also offered a reasonable indication that the kidnappers intended to keep their victim alive, at least until they got their hands on the cash. After that, it could go in all kinds of ways. Extremely unpleasant ones, for the victims and their loved ones.

'They're not,' she said.

Ben looked at her. 'You mean there's been no ransom demand? Not a letter, or a phone call, or an email, in eight days?'

She shook her head. 'No contact at all. Nothing.'

Ben pursed his lips, thinking hard. This wasn't just unusual. It was bad. Even worse than the typical kidnap situation. Because it deviated from the set pattern. The longer kidnappers held their victims, the higher the risk of being caught. Plus, they weren't interested in playing nursemaid. They were only in it for quick gains. Hence, things tended to move quickly, with the first ransom demand being issued within twenty-four hours, often less. If families paid up too

30

readily, the first demand was invariably followed by a second, bleeding them for more.

But no ransom demand at all was weird. Ben paused a moment then said, 'So we don't even know why Amal was taken, let alone by whom?'

She shook her head again. 'No, he's simply vanished. Just like Kabir.'

'Kabir?'

'That's right,' she said. 'He's disappeared, too. Three weeks ago. It all started with him.'

'I think you'd better explain. I'm not following.'

Phoebe sighed. 'I'm sorry. It's all so complicated that I can barely keep up with it myself. Kabir is Kabir Ray. Amal's younger brother, an archaeologist in Delhi.'

'And Kabir was kidnapped too?'

'Not exactly. He and two of his work colleagues were attacked. It happened in some remote part of India, miles and miles from anywhere. His colleagues were shot dead.'

This was sounding more serious now, and getting stranger by the second. Ben had a hundred questions, but kept quiet and let her go on.

Phoebe said, 'The local police there think Kabir was killed along with them, but there was no sign of his body, only theirs. After days and days of frantically worrying and hearing nothing new, Amal flew out there himself to try to find out what had happened to his brother – talk to the police, piece together clues or whatever. Next thing, this dreadful kidnapping. A gang of masked men snatched him right off the street and bundled him into a van. Brooke was with him. It happened right in front of her. Poor Brooke. Poor Amal.'

Ben felt his stomach fill with butterflies. 'Was Brooke hurt?'

'No, but it's so awful.' Phoebe plucked a tissue from her pocket and started dabbing at her eyes, which had turned pink and begun streaming tears as she talked. 'I don't know what to make of it. I'm at my wits' end. Mr Hope—'

'You can call me Ben.'

She sniffed, nodded. 'Ben – please say you'll help her find out who did this and bring Amal back to her safe and sound. She's in a terrible state.'

Ben was trying to make sense of all this. A kidnapping with no ransom demand. A deadly shooting in another part of the country. He was thinking reprisals, enemies, someone with a grudge against the family. Or had the brothers been into something that put them in danger?

He asked, 'Do the police see the two disappearances as connected?'

'As far as I know, no. They seem to think bandits were responsible for what happened to Kabir and his friends. That part of India is crawling with them, apparently. But not Delhi. I mean, it's a modern, safe city. Like London.'

Ben looked at her and wondered how anyone could be so disconnected from reality. He said, 'So as far as the authorities are concerned, these are two separate, coincidental events.'

She nodded. 'That's what Mr Prajapati seems to believe, too.'

'Who's Mr Prajapati?'

'He's supposedly the best private investigator in the capital. Brooke employed him to help search for Amal. She doesn't think the police are doing enough.'

'I see.'

Phoebe gazed at him imploringly with her wet, bruised-looking eyes. 'I'm begging you. After all she's told me about you in the past, your military background, your experience

32

with kidnapped children, the amazing things you've done for so many people, I know that if anyone can find out who's behind this horrible thing and bring Amal back home, it's you.'

Chapter 5

Ben leaned back and thought about it for a minute. His past history, both before and after he'd quit the regiment to go freelance, wasn't a subject for open discussion. SAS guys were famously, and justifiably, cagey in the extreme. Partly out of pure habit, partly because they were strictly bound by the Official Secrets Act, and partly to protect themselves and their families from being targeted for reprisal attacks. He didn't like the things he'd done being talked about. But he also knew that Brooke was discreet and would have revealed only the broadest outline of the facts to her sister.

He said, 'Let me get this straight. You're here by your own volition? Brooke didn't send you?'

She appeared flustered by his question. 'I . . . no . . . it was my idea. She doesn't know I'm here. I googled your name and found the Le Val Tactical Training Centre online.'

'You could have saved yourself a trip. We do have email, telephones, all the trappings of modern-day communication technology.'

Phoebe's cheeks flushed red and her gaze dropped towards her lap. 'I was afraid you wouldn't speak to me. I . . . I thought that if I met you face to face, I might have a better chance of getting you to agree to help. Will you?'

'Help, as in, fly out to India?'

She nodded, her face brightening with renewed optimism. 'There's a direct flight from Charles de Gaulle in Paris tonight at eleven.'

He stared at her as if she were crazy. 'You're taking a lot for granted, Mrs Kite. Even if I said yes, Paris is more than a three-hour drive from here. I'd have to down tools and leave right away.'

'I know it's a lot to ask,' she said. 'But Brooke would be so grateful. She's still out there, staying at the Ray family home, isolated in a strange country and having to deal with this nightmare basically all alone.'

'There's also the matter of applying for a travel visa. I wasn't actually planning on taking a trip to India any time soon. It could take days to get the paperwork sorted.'

Phoebe brushed that concern aside. 'I don't think you would need to worry about the red tape. The Rays are an important business family with a lot of money and all the right diplomatic connections to get you into the country, no questions asked.'

'I see. So let's say I agreed. What would I be doing exactly? Working alongside this Mr Prajapati character, the best private detective in Delhi, who seems to have sussed the whole thing out already? How does he feel about the arrangement? Does he even know he's being allocated a new assistant?'

'I understand what you're thinking. You're upset that Brooke hasn't asked you herself.'

Ben shrugged. 'I just think that if she wanted me to get involved, she'd have got in touch directly. She knows where I am.'

'Please don't blame her. She's terribly distraught by all this.'

'I'm sure she is. And she has my deepest sympathies.

But it sounds to me as though she's already dealing with it. It also seems to me that the last thing she needs is me turning up there, unexpected and uninvited, to complicate her situation and bring back a lot of bad feelings. Our relationship isn't exactly as cordial as it used to be. We haven't spoken in a long while, and the last time we did wasn't too pleasant.'

'I'm aware of that. She told me.'

'And the fact that she hired someone else to help with this situation, instead of contacting me, makes it pretty clear where she stands. Wouldn't you agree?'

Crestfallen, Phoebe said in a low voice, 'Then I take it you won't help?'

'It's not my decision to make, Mrs Kite. It was unnecessary for you to come here.'

'I thought . . .'

'I know. You tried. That was a good thing to do.'

'She loved you so much.'

Ben felt a fresh blade of pain pierce his body. 'I loved her. She still matters a great deal to me. All the more reason for not hurting her all over again. She doesn't want me there.'

'What about Amal? Don't you care?'

'Of course I care. I like Amal. But there's nothing I can do for him, except pray it all works out. Which I'm sure it will. If the Ray family are rich, it points to a clear financial motivation for snatching him and there'll be a ransom demand any day now. If they pay up, there's every chance of getting him back without a scratch. It's just a routine business transaction. Happens all the time. The police know what they're doing.'

'Are you sure?'

'Absolutely.'

Most of what he'd just said was a lie. Intended to reassure, but a long way from the dark reality of the kidnap and ransom world. In a high percentage of cases, whether they paid off the crooks or not, families never saw their loved ones alive again. That was Ben's whole reason for having become what he'd called a 'crisis response consultant'. His own ways and means of getting the victims home safe had generally involved the rapid and permanent elimination of the kidnappers, while having as little as possible to do with the bungling efforts of law enforcement officials.

But, as he'd said, this one was out of his hands.

Phoebe looked deflated. She glanced towards the window, through which the lights of the taxi could be seen casting pools of light on the yard cobblestones.

'I suppose I'd better go,' she sighed. 'I can catch the nine o'clock flight back to Heathrow.'

Ben stood up. 'Are you sure you wouldn't like a drink, for the road? You look as though you need one.'

She stood up too. 'That's fine, thanks. I'll have a gin and tonic on the plane. Or perhaps two or three of them. God, I must look a mess.'

'Try and get some rest,' Ben said. 'Brooke, too. I know how tough this must be for her.'

As he was showing her out through the entrance hall, she hesitated, hovered nervously in the doorway and then turned to look at him with a strange expression on her face.

She said, 'I can't leave here without telling you the truth.'

'The truth?'

'She made me promise, you see. But I'd rather betray her trust than go back empty-handed.'

'Promise?'

Phoebe nodded uncomfortably. 'I lied. Brooke did send me to ask for your help. She practically forced me to come and talk to you.'

'But she didn't want me to know, so she made you pretend it was all your idea.'

'She desperately needs you there, Ben. She's just too proud and embarrassed to admit it. But there was nobody else to run to. Prajapati, the private investigator, is even more useless than the police. You're her one and only hope. Her words.'

Ben said nothing.

'One final time. On my knees. For my sister's sake. For Amal's. For all of us. Please, please will you help us?'

Chapter 6

Once Ben had relented and said yes, he had to move fast. As Phoebe departed in the taxi his first job was to break the news to Jeff and Tuesday that something had come up and he had to leave immediately. 'Sorry to leave you in the lurch like this, guys.'

Neither of them could get over Brooke being married, but their concern overrode their surprise. 'What's your take on the kidnap?' Jeff asked. He'd sobered up as sharp as a fighter pilot, his own worries forgotten. His eyes were full of concern.

'The usual,' Ben said, rubbing thumb and fingers together. The universal sign for money.

Jeff raised an eyebrow. 'Writing plays must pay a hell of a lot better than I thought.'

'Family wealth. A lot of it, or so I'm told.'

Tuesday said, 'I can't see Brooke marrying into money. Not her style.'

'No,' Ben agreed. 'That's what I thought, too. Maybe I was wrong about her, but that's not important now. What matters is getting Amal out of this.'

'You want us to come along?' Jeff asked. Ben knew from repeated experience that his friends were both perfectly prepared to drop everything, clients and all, to be at his side in a time of need. But this was a personal thing, and Ben wanted to face it alone.

He shook his head. 'Thanks, but—'

'I get it. Call if you need us, okay?'

Next, Ben threw some clothes and personal items into his old green canvas bag, then spent exactly forty-five seconds under the shower, changed and pulled on his boots and grabbed his bag and jacket, patted the dog and ran out to the barn where he kept his BMW Alpina. It was a fast car, which was very much needed to shave time off his journey to Paris and catch the 23.00 flight. Seconds counted.

Here we go again, he thought as he sped out from the gates of Le Val and accelerated hard away with the BMW's twin beams carving a tunnel into the darkness. It was like a curse. Every time he tried to settle into a steady routine, another crisis would come out of the blue to turn his life upside-down once more. He was worried for Amal, but what troubled him almost as much was the prospect of meeting Brooke under these circumstances. He lit up a cigarette, shoved on a jazz CD and turned the stereo system up full blast to drive that haunting prospect out of his thoughts. The Zoe Rahman Trio, playing 'Red Squirrel'.

He was scorching eastwards along Autoroute 13 at over 150 kilometres an hour, passing Rouen and about halfway to Paris, when his phone rang. He answered it on the hands-free, muting the music.

It was Phoebe. Cherbourg to London was only a thirty-five-minute flight and she was already back in the UK.

'It's all arranged,' she told him. 'You're booked on the flight, first class, naturally. Ticket will be waiting for you when you get there.' She gave him a code number to write down. 'It's a direct flight, no stopovers. You land at Indira

Gandhi International at ten thirty-five tomorrow morning, local time. There'll be a car to pick you up from the airport.'

'And the visa?'

'Just like I told you, not a problem.' It seemed that Amal had an uncle with high-up Indian government connections influential enough to cut through the bureaucracy and open up a magic VIP portal through which Ben could waltz unimpeded. It was his first whiff of the Ray family's status. He suspected it wouldn't be the last.

'You don't know how much this means to Brooke,' Phoebe said.

So much that she can't call me herself, he thought. Again, he had to shove that bad thought out of his head. She probably wasn't looking forward to the meeting any more than he was. 'How's she doing?' he asked.

'Three guesses how she's doing. Her husband's missing. She doesn't know if he's dead or alive. She's a mess.'

It had often struck Ben as curious that so many of the women in his life had the title of 'Dr'. But they were all different kinds of doctors. Dr Roberta Ryder was an American with a biology PhD. Dr Sandrine Lacombe made her living fixing broken bodies and patching up gunshot victims, as she'd done for Jeff Dekker when Ben first met her. While Dr Brooke Marcel had earned her credentials as an expert in psychology, specialising in studying the devastating effects that violent abduction, incarceration and living under constant lethal threat in the most appalling conditions imaginable, for months or even years, could have on the human mind. Nobody understood hostage psychology better. That was how Brooke had come to be employed at Le Val as a visiting lecturer, helping specialist operatives gain insights into the minds of those they might be sent in to rescue.

Brooke also had enough knowledge of the kidnap game

to be all too aware of just how bad it was for its victims. There was a high chance she'd never see Amal again, and she knew it. Little wonder she was a mess.

Ben asked, 'I'm assuming there's still no ransom demand?'

'Nope. Zero contact from these shitty bastards who're holding him. That can't be a good thing, can it?'

Ben chose not to answer that. 'And no more progress reports from the police or the private investigator?'

'If there had been, I would have told you.' Phoebe's tone was snappish. He put it down to stress and didn't blame her for it. She paused, then said in a softer voice, 'Please say you'll get Amal back, Ben.'

It was foolish to make promises in this situation. But he did it anyway. 'I'll get Amal back.' *One way or another. In one piece, or in several.* He kept those dark thoughts to himself as he ended the call.

Ben pushed the car harder into the night. He made it to Charles de Gaulle airport in just over three hours without getting pulled over for speeding, which meant the French traffic police must be slacking on the job. As Phoebe had said, the ticket was ready and waiting for him at the check-in desk. He impatiently whiled away the time before his flight was called, and then he was stretched out on a plush seat in a half-empty first-class section with a glass of single malt scotch, straight, no ice. The benefits of luxury travel. With eight hours ahead of him in which he had nothing much to do except try not to think about meeting Brooke again, the whisky would be the first of several.

After a couple of drinks he ate a light meal from the excellent first-class menu, then had a couple more drinks, then closed his eyes. Still thinking about it. Then again, as long as he was preoccupied with one thing, he couldn't feel so bad about the other.

He fleetingly wondered where Sandrine was at this moment, and what she was doing. Then he wondered how he'd feel if, say, a couple of years into the future, he heard that Sandrine had married some guy and that he, Ben, was now just a distant and semi-forgotten part of her past. He wasn't sure how much it would hurt him. Maybe a little. But not the way he was hurting now. Maybe that was how love was measured, he thought: by how brutally it could rip your heart out and feed it through a blender. By that defin-ition, he knew that he must still feel more than he'd realised for Brooke Marcel.

No, not Brooke Marcel, he corrected himself. She'd be Brooke Ray now.

Brooke Ray.

Shit. Time for another drink. Eight hours was plenty of time to sober up.

Eight hours later and fully sober, Ben stepped out into the hazy Delhi sunshine with his bag on his shoulder and began taking in the sights and colours and smells of India. It was mid-morning, local time, and cooler than he'd expected – only about 30°C and rising as he crossed the tarmac towards the arrivals terminal.

Then again, his expectations were a little vague. He'd travelled the whole world several times around, missing only a few spots, but India nonetheless wasn't a country he knew well. His last visit had been a brief stopover en route to Indonesia, the very same trip that had triggered the end of his relationship with Brooke. It seemed ironic that he was returning here now, under these circumstances.

They say nothing prepares you for the dirt, poverty and chaos of India, but the airport was clean and modern and well organised. Ben passed under a big sign welcoming the new arrivals to the country and was approaching the immigration counter when a well-dressed man with swept-back white hair and a clipped moustache intercepted him with a smile and a handshake, and introduced himself as Vivaan Banerjee of the Indian Foreign Office.

The government man led Ben away from the crowds to a private room, where he made pleasant small talk while checking Ben's identification papers. 'This is just a formality,' he kept insisting as he apologetically asked for signatures on a couple of official documents, and Ben had the strangest feeling of being inducted into some old boys' club. It was another whiff of the Ray family's power and influence. Who needs a travel visa, when you have friends in the right places?

With a flourish Banerjee produced an ink stamp and set about vigorously thumping the signed documents as though there were cockroaches lurking under them. Then he grasped Ben's hand like a long-lost friend and wished him a pleasant stay in India. Ben wondered if Banerjee knew why he was really here, and if that was the reason why the official seemed to be studiously avoiding any mention of the current crisis affecting the Ray family. Maybe now Ben was in the club, the police would be ordered from on high to turn a blind eye if the hunt for Amal got rough.

After he finished with Banerjee, Ben headed for the exit. Phoebe had said there would be a car to pick him up at the airport. As he was walking through the busy lobby, past a life-size statue of two Asiatic elephants penned behind a railing as though they might suddenly rampage and start flattening the public, a young Indian guy picked him out from the crowd and came hurrying over.

'Mr Hope? Delighted to meet you, sir. My name is Prem Sharma. I work for the Ray family. Please, come this way.'

44

Prem was about thirty, slender and handsome, with expressive dark eyes and thick black hair. He wore a light grey suit, nicely tailored, silk shirt, expensive watch, quality handmade shoes. His employers clearly paid him well. He carried Ben's battered canvas bag as diligently as if it had been a Ralph Lauren suitcase and led him outside to a gleaming black Mercedes-Benz S-Class Maybach Pullman limousine longer than some river barges Ben had seen. Yet more evidence of the wealth Brooke had married into.

Prem smiled as he noticed Ben looking at the car. 'Its previous owner was a former president of India,' he explained. 'The most luxurious limousine in all of Delhi, as befits the Ray family's most important guests. It has a twelve-cylinder biturbo engine producing more than six hundred horsepower. Fully armoured, naturally.'

Ben couldn't tell if Prem was just bragging, or trying to sell it to him. 'Naturally. And are we likely to come under attack today?'

Prem replied, 'I would say that is doubtful. But one can never be too careful. In such an event, we would be protected from any kinds of small arms fire and grenade blasts. The vehicle is also sealed against chemical weapon attacks.'

Ben said, 'Handy. But what if they shoot the tyres out?'

'Oh, it will continue to run on four flat tyres for approximately five kilometres,' Prem replied.

'Then it looks like we ought to make it to our destination in one piece,' Ben said. Prem stowed his bag in the vastness of the boot before he smartly walked around to the rear door and held it open for his passenger.

Under different circumstances, Ben might have been faintly amused at being treated like some visiting dignitary. He ignored the offer and opened the front passenger door instead. 'I prefer to ride up front, thanks.'

'As you wish,' Prem replied with a smile, and shut the rear with a soft clunk. Ben settled into the cool, creamy passenger seat, as spacious and comfortable as his first-class armchair on the plane.

So far, it had been an easy trip. The tough part lay just around the corner.

Chapter 7

Prem threw himself behind the wheel of the limousine and fired up the engine, as whisper-quiet as an electric motor and totally insulated from the outside world. Then they were off, and within minutes were carving straight into the hustle and bustle of the vast metropolis that made the hubbub of London, Paris and Moscow seem like ghost towns by comparison. The density of the traffic was insane and the muffled honking of horns all around sounded like distant herds of angry elephants as the huge Maybach nosed its way down wide, leafy boulevards crammed nose to tail with vehicles and narrower streets that were so congested it seemed impossible that the traffic could ever get flowing again. Cyclists, mopeds, pedal rickshaws and little green and yellow tuk-tuk three-wheeler vans were everywhere, weaving among the sea of vehicles and darting across lanes with as little regard for the rules of the road as for their own safety.

If anything, the pavements were even more densely packed. They heaved with a thronging morass of people, people, and more people everywhere. To Ben's eyes it seemed the city's populace must have recovered at least fivefold from the dark days of Indian government population control in the 1970s, when armed troops rounded up citizens in the streets of Delhi for transportation to forced sterilisation camps, with the open approval of Western leaders. Now, the multitude of crowds and sights and colours was almost overpoweringly rich. In the middle of it all were street vendors selling their wares, beggars sitting on steps, street kids running in hordes in search of things to get up to, feral-looking dogs scavenging around for scraps, a crazy kaleidoscope of buzzing urban diversity that was too much to take in at once. The morning sky was shrouded by grey smog that trapped the visibly intensifying heat haze, but the limo's luxurious interior was as cool as an April day at Le Val.

Ben would have happily ridden in silence, but Prem wanted to talk. The car was so silent that he barely needed to raise his voice. 'So you are a friend of the Ray family?'

'I only really know Amal,' Ben said. He added, 'And his wife. I'm here at her invitation, to offer whatever assistance I can at this difficult time.'

'A wonderful lady. So beautiful, so brilliant.' Prem flashed a brief smile at Ben, then shook his head glumly. 'Poor Mr Amal. Poor Mr Kabir. The family are very upset by these tragic happenings.'

'Who are the other family members?'

Prem explained that there was a third brother, the eldest, Samarth Ray, who had taken over the family business from their father. Old Basu, the patriarch, was still alive and now lived with his wife Aparna in a secluded villa outside the city. Both were too elderly and too much in shock over recent events to leave their home. The original family residence in the southern part of Delhi was shared by the three brothers, who had divided it up into three separate apartments. 'But with Mr Amal spending all his time in London and Mr Kabir so often travelling, Mr Samarth and his good lady live there alone mostly.'

'I look forward to meeting Samarth,' Ben said, dropping the obsequious 'Mr'.

'Oh, he is a great and wonderful man. A very, very important member of the business community here in Delhi, patron of the arts, and donates money to many charities.'

'What line of business is he in?'

'The Ray Group has built its empire on commercial real estate and hotels,' Prem replied proudly. 'They own much property in Delhi and elsewhere. Also steel and pharmaceuticals, and a construction division with many government contracts to develop new projects across the city. Mr Samarth is working even harder than ever now, because of the stress of the moment. It is his way of coping. I have two brothers myself. I cannot even imagine something so terrible.'

'And Brooke?'

'Miss Brooke has been staying in her and Mr Amal's apartment within the residence. She is there now, waiting for your arrival. Traffic is not too bad today, so we will be there soon. Maybe forty minu— Oh, look at this damn one.' Prem hit the brakes and had to swerve to avoid a motorbike that had squeezed past the Maybach and darted across their path. The rider, who seemed quite oblivious of how close he'd come to getting wiped out by five tons of car, had a young child riding on the pillion seat, another perched on the rear luggage rack, and a small toddler straddled across the tank in front of him.

'That's one way to get yourself and half your family killed,' Ben observed.

'Oh, life is very cheap in India,' Prem said with a dry smile. 'If you do not already know, you will soon see.'

Soon afterwards, they hit a broader boulevard where the traffic moved more smoothly and there were fewer suicidal motorists. The limo wafted along fast and silently with sweeping lawns and tree-lined canals on either side. 'That is India Gate,' said Prem, pointing. The arched monument towered over Delhi's answer to the Champs-Élysées. 'It was opened in 1931 to commemorate the sacrifices of Indian soldiers. But the government let it become filthy with rubbish. People are animals.'

Life is cheap and people are animals. Ben was getting the inside track. 'I'm so happy to have you as my tour guide, Prem,' he said. But Prem might have missed the sarcasm.

It wasn't long before they left the big boulevards behind and came into a quieter, tree-lined residential area. Prem announced with great pride that this district of the city was the most prestigious and select place to live in all of India. Ben had already figured that out from the number of luxury cars and the impressive white houses he glimpsed tucked away within verdant gardens as they passed. Not a crippled beggar, street kid, stray dog, food stall or tuk-tuk in sight. Even the hazy grey smog seemed to have dissipated.

But such opulence had to be protected from the teeming masses outside. Prem stopped at a private security check-point while guards checked his entry pass before waving the car through. Ben had visited gated communities before, but seldom one where the guards looked like paramilitary troops and carried sawn-off shotguns and submachine guns on open display.

'Only the very richest families can afford to live here,' Prem declared as he moved on at a stately pace through the secluded, shade-dappled streets. 'The Rays have been here since the 1920s, after Mr Basu's father made his first fortune in land deals. He had arrived in Delhi just a few years earlier, with only some coins in his pocket.'

At last, Prem turned the Maybach off the road towards a driveway entrance barred by tall ornamental wrought-iron gates that were topped with spikes. Prem produced a small black remote device from his pocket, like a miniature phone with a ten-digit keypad. He pointed it through the windscreen towards the gates, and Ben saw his index fingertip enter the four-digit sequence 4-1-9-8. Which happened to be the same as the formula number for the Improved Military Rifle brand of smokeless gunpowder favoured by Tuesday at Le Val for brewing up his super-accurate .223 custom handloads.

The gates whirred aside to let them pass. Prem steered the limo up a long paved driveway that curved through what appeared to be a country park, filled with fruit trees and ornamental shrubs and a profusion of exotic flowers of more colours than Ben had names for.

He already had a pretty good idea of how wealthy Amal's family must be, but the sight of the house was the final clincher. It was built on a palatial scale, classically modern and elegant in gleaming white stone with notes of marble here and there, all in the best taste that money could buy. Acres of windows overlooked emerald lawns where peacocks strutted majestically and the jets of sprinklers made rainbows in the sunlight.

'Here we are,' Prem said. 'Welcome to the Ray residence.'

Stepping out of the car it was hard to believe that this tranquil paradise setting was situated right in the beating heart of the most polluted city on earth and the second most populous in Asia after only Tokyo, home to sixteen million people. Prem took Ben's bag from the back of the car and waved him graciously towards the house.

'Come, this way, please. I will take you to see Miss Brooke.'

Chapter 8

Now came the moment Ben had been so nervous about. Prem, whose duties seemed to include being head butler as well as the family chauffeur, led him into the house. Its interior was as cool as the Maybach, airy and sweetly scented by the flowers that filled every corner. The mosaic floors were marble, the art and furnishings were modern and without a doubt supremely expensive. A rich man's dream abode, perhaps, but Ben couldn't understand how anyone could live inside a multi-million-dollar show home.

The house felt empty. Nobody came to meet them as Prem led Ben inside. Ben asked, 'Are Samarth and his wife at home?'

'Oh, he will be at the office now. She is most likely taking a nap at this time of the morning.' Eleven thirty, and the lady of the house was napping. Ben asked no more questions.

The elder brother's private apartment was on the ground floor of the house, occupying what Prem called the west wing. The separate apartments belonging to Amal and Kabir were upstairs, on the first and second floors respectively. Prem escorted Ben up a sweeping marble double staircase with banister rails capped with gilt, then along about six miles of passages floored with handmade oriental rugs, until they reached the part of the house that comprised Amal's personal quarters.

Prem said, 'The apartment has three guest bedrooms. Would you like to inspect them before you choose the one you prefer?'

Ben wasn't sure he wanted to stay in the house. 'We'll talk about my accommodation arrangements later. Where's Brooke?'

As if in reply, Prem stopped at a door. He was about to knock, but before he could announce the visitor's arrival the door opened, and there she stood framed in the entrance. Milky light from tall windows filled the room behind her.

'Hello, Ben.'

'Hello, Brooke. It's been a while,' he said.

'Yes, it has,' she replied.

Her hair had been shorter the last time they'd met. It had grown out again now, and hung in rich auburn curls past her shoulders. She'd lost a little weight and her face seemed more sculpted, if anything looking more attractive than Ben had ever seen her, despite the washed out pallor of her fatigue and the dark shadows under her eyes. She was wearing a loose, sleeveless silk blouse and green satin trousers that matched her irises. She'd been crying.

Ben had known this would be an uncomfortable meeting. It couldn't have been any other way. The atmosphere was heavy with tension. There was a long, awkward silence. Brooke was the one to break it, by saying politely, 'Prem, our visitor might like some refreshments.'

Ben was so focused on Brooke that he'd forgotten Prem was still hovering at his shoulder. He shook his head. 'No, I'm fine.'

'Then you can leave us now, Prem, thank you.'

'I'll take the bag,' Ben said, taking it from Prem's hand.

53

Prem seemed reluctant to go. Ben supposed that he must know, or had guessed, a certain amount about the backstory between them. He might be hoping to see some fireworks if he hung around.

Prem gave a courteous nod, muttered 'If you're sure there is nothing I can do for you,' and took his leave.

They waited until he was gone before they spoke another word. Then waited longer, neither one knowing quite what to say now they were alone together. Ben gazed at her face, so familiar, still sometimes in his dreams. He gazed at the light from the window shining in her hair and the way it silhouetted the curve of her shoulders, and he drank in the well of sadness he could see in her beautiful, tired eyes. They stood just two steps apart, but they might as well have been separated by oceans.

Ben knew the correct and proper thing would be to congratulate her on her marriage. Somehow he just couldn't bring himself to come out with it. Now that their past history had been sealed shut, formally and officially ended, the rekindled memories of their time together came flooding back more wistfully than ever. He could tell she was thinking the same.

Now it was Ben's turn to break the long silence.

'Why?' he said.

She shook her head, not understanding, those two little vertical frown lines appearing above the bridge of her nose the way they did when she was irritated. 'Why?'

'Why?' he repeated.

The frown deepened. 'You mean, why did I marry Amal?' Her tone was defensive. She didn't wait for Ben to answer. 'I married Amal because he's a good and kind man and he loves me, and because he was there for me.'

And he didn't walk out on me literally on the eve of our

wedding, to go off on some crazy mission that could have got him killed. The subtext didn't need to be spelled out. It was there in her eyes. 'And in case you think I married him for his bloody money,' she added, 'I didn't even know about the family wealth until afterwards, the first time we came to India together.'

'It's none of my business why you married Amal. I wasn't asking that.'

She shook her head again. Confused. 'Then why what?'

'Why didn't you call me when this happened? Don't you know I'd have been here in a shot? That I'd throw everything down to help you in whatever way I could?'

Brooke's frown melted. A tear rolled from one eye. She wiped it away quickly with the back of her hand.

'You know why,' she said. 'Phoebe must have told you.'

'I want to hear it from you. Why didn't you come to me?'

'Because it's you, Ben,' she said softly. The sadness in her eyes was making something hot and moist and salty rise up inside him. She added, 'I couldn't, after all the things between us.'

'But you're asking for my help now.'

She nodded and wiped another tear.

'Yes, Ben. Because it's you. You're the only one. I need you to do what you do best. Better than anyone. Find my husband and punish these pieces of shit who've taken him. Do whatever it takes.'

He let out a long breath through his nose, looking at her and thinking of all he'd lost that day he'd walked out on her like that. 'Well, I'm here,' he said. 'And I'm not leaving until we fix this. One way or another. Do you understand? I will do everything I can to make this all right.'

She stepped forward. The ocean between them was suddenly gone. She wrapped her arms around his waist and pressed her face into the hollow of his shoulder, and he could feel the wetness of her tears through his shirt. He tenderly stroked her back. Her hair smelled sweet and fragrant, the same scent that brought back a thousand more memories. He wanted to kiss the top of her head, but stopped himself. He moved his hands to her shoulders and very gently pushed her away from him, breaking the embrace.

'I'm so sorry for what happened,' he said. He could just as easily have been referring to their breakup as to Amal's kidnapping. If Brooke picked up on the ambiguity in his words, she didn't show it.

'It's such a relief to have you here. I've been at my wits' end. I'm going crazy in this place. You've no idea what it's been like.'

Ben said, 'Tell me everything.'

Chapter 9

Brooke invited him inside the room, which was a large living room with various others radiating off it. Amal's personal quarters within the family residence were at least twice the size of her old flat in Richmond, as Ben remembered it. The décor was more classical and old-fashioned than the parts of the house Prem had led him through. Amal had always had good taste in things, Ben had to give him that.

'Come, sit,' she said, motioning to a chaise longue upholstered in satin fleur de lys. 'You want something to drink?'

'I thought it was Prem's job to provide refreshments,' Ben said.

'I only said that to get rid of him. He's a little too nosy for his own good, that one. Cup of tea?'

Ben pulled a face.

'Of course. I forgot, you hate tea.'

'How about coffee?'

'We only have decaf. Amal gets palpitations if he drinks the real stuff.'

'In that case, no thanks.'

'You're right. Tastes like boiled mouse crap, and it's full of dichloromethane. How about a real drink? God knows I need one.' She went over to a decorative cabinet and opened it to reveal the bottles and glasses inside. She slid out a bottle and held it up. 'Laphroaig. Ten years old. Your favourite single malt.'

'You remembered.'

She gave him a sad, tender smile. The little crow's feet that appeared at the corners of her eyes were new, at least to him. Worry lines. 'Ben, there isn't a single detail about our time together that I would ever forget until my dying day.'

He had no idea what to say to that.

He watched as she set a pair of cut crystal tumblers side by side on the pretty cabinet, uncapped the bottle and poured a generous three fingers of scotch into each. When she'd said she needed a drink, she hadn't been joking. She handed him his glass, fell into a soft armchair opposite him and took a long, deep gulp of her drink. It wasn't lunchtime yet and she was attacking the whisky like a trooper. Ben cradled his in his lap, untouched so far. He'd eaten no breakfast on the plane and wanted to keep his head clear.

She studied him for a moment as she savoured her drink. 'You look good, Ben. I hope life is treating you well.'

'Things are fine with me,' he lied. 'You look good too.' Another lie. 'But you need to go easy with the hard stuff.'

'Whatever,' she replied carelessly. 'I don't sleep any more, I can hardly eat a bite. I'm going insane with stress and a couple of drinks is the only thing that makes me feel better.'

'That's my job. We're going to find out who took Amal, and we're going to get him back. Okay?'

She nodded. 'Okay.'

'Now talk to me. Backtrack. Start at the beginning. Every detail you can think of.'

Brooke took a smaller sip of scotch and leaned forward in the armchair with her elbows on her knees, getting her thoughts together. 'Did Phoebe tell you about Kabir?'

'Amal's younger brother. The archaeology professor. She told me that it all started with him.'

Brooke nodded. 'What else did she tell you?'

'That Kabir and his two colleagues were attacked three weeks ago while on a field trip to some remote country area. They were killed. He's missing.'

Brooke gave a sigh. 'More or less, in a nutshell. It happened in north-west India, near a place called Rakhigarhi. It's very remote. They flew there by helicopter.'

'Charter aircraft?'

She shook her head. 'Kabir's own chopper. He's a licensed pilot. Or was.'

'What were they doing there?'

'I'm not quite sure. It's to do with some big archaeological project that he's spent years on. Sai and Manish were two of his graduate students at the Institute. It's not unusual for Kabir to fly out to remote locations for his work, but he always stays in touch with his office. He was supposed to have been back after two days. When he didn't make contact or return, alarm bells started ringing and the local police were called in. The helicopter was found abandoned, raided and stripped of parts. The police discovered the bodies of Sai and Manish a few hundred yards away, but no trace of Kabir himself.'

Ben digested the details, and remembered what Brooke's sister had told him. 'They'd been shot?'

'To pieces, pretty much. According to the police report. They found scores of cartridge cases lying a short distance from the scene.'

'Implying multiple shooters. It doesn't take that much shooting to take down two or three unarmed targets.'

She nodded. 'Using military weapons. The cases were surplus 7.62 NATO stuff.'

'Ex-military,' Ben said. After many years of being issued home-grown copies of the old L1A1 British infantry rifle, the Indian Army had switched to smaller-calibre INSAS weaponry in the eighties. INSAS stood for Indian Small Arms Systems. A backward step, in Ben's opinion, because the L1A1 with its more powerful cartridge had been one of the best combat weapons ever made. The change had caused a flood of decommissioned but still perfectly usable arms to hit the market, a vast amount of which had inevitably ended up in the hands of irregular forces like guerrilla armies, terrorist organisations and criminal gangs all across Asia and eastern Europe. Along with even vaster quantities of the now-obsolete ammunition, crates of which traded hands for a song. Hence, a lot of very trigger-happy killers on the loose. The kind of morons who'd shoot folks to pieces just for the hell of it. If Kabir had encountered a bunch like that, the chances of his survival didn't look too promising.

Ben said, 'Which would tend to support the police's theory that armed bandits were responsible for the attack.'

'That's their take, and they're sticking with it. The man in charge of the investigation over there is a police captain called Jabbar Dada. He calls himself "the dacoit hunter".'

'Dacoit?'

'Outlaws, bandits, gangsters, whatever you want to call them. Apparently that whole region is overrun with marauding criminal gangs. Captain Dada and his police task force are on a mission to wipe them out. Sounds like he's got his hands full. So on the face of it, the bandit theory seemed like a likely explanation.'

'And I gather your Mr Prajapati shares that opinion, too.'

Brooke seemed surprised. 'Phoebe told you about Prateek Prajapati?'

60

'Just that he's supposed to be the best private investigator in Delhi.'

She shrugged. 'So they say. It was Amal who hired him initially.'

Ben asked, 'Why would Amal hire a detective?'

'Because he still wasn't satisfied, and he was frustrated that not enough was being done. He thought that Dada was too eager to run with the bandit theory, instead of trying to come up with proper evidence. If Kabir was shot along with Sai and Manish, why was there no body?'

'How did they account for that?'

'They just assumed that it must have been dragged off by wild animals,' Brooke said. 'Wild dogs, wolves, jackals, maybe even a tiger. Even though the other two bodies hadn't been touched, as far as we knew. It didn't seem to make any sense that some hungry scavenger wouldn't have had a go at them, too. They'd been pecked by vultures, nothing more.'

'Nice.'

'So after endless days of going nuts in London, Amal decided he had to fly out to be here in person, and he jumped on the first plane.'

'You didn't come with him?'

'No, I had a conference I couldn't get out of. I came out to join him a few days later.'

'Did Amal go to Rakhigarhi and visit the spot where it happened?'

Brooke shook her head. 'You know Amal. He wasn't made for roughing it. He freaks out any time he ventures more than ten miles from a major city. He stayed here in Delhi while making a thousand phone calls to Captain Dada's office. Then he went to see Prajapati and employed him to travel out to Rakhigarhi and visit the crime scene on his behalf. Prajapati spoke to the law enforcement officials there and came back satisfied their take on the situation was probably right, and that Kabir had almost certainly been killed along with his two associates, and that it was time to accept it, close the case and move on. Shit happens, basically.'

'Nothing like thorough police work,' Ben said.

'Amal called me that night. He was very upset. He wouldn't accept that his brother was dead. Kept insisting that Kabir must be lying injured somewhere, and the police had just missed it, and they weren't trying hard enough and needed to widen the search. He had a big argument with Samarth about it.'

'The eldest brother.'

'Samarth had already spoken to Captain Dada on the phone and believed he must be right. Amal was furious with him.'

'What about you?' Ben asked. He could see the questions in her eyes.

Brooke clutched her drink in one hand and raised the other in a gesture of helplessness. 'I didn't know what to tell him. The police had searched the whole area and found nothing. Their conclusions seemed to make sense to me too, at the time.'

'At the time,' Ben said. 'But now you're not so sure?'

'Neither are you,' she replied. 'Or you wouldn't be asking me all these questions about Kabir. First one brother goes missing, then the other. It can't be just a coincidence, can it? You see it that way, too, don't you?'

'I'm only trying to build a picture in my mind, Brooke. Maybe it is just a coincidence. Maybe the police are right, and the incident in Rakhigarhi was nothing more than just a tragic case of being in the wrong place at the wrong time, and that we need to look in a totally different place to figure out why this thing has happened to Amal.'

'Or maybe they're wrong,' Brooke said. 'In fact, the more I think about it, the more certain I am that there's more to this.'

Ben looked at her and could see she was resolute. 'Based on what?'

'Based on something Amal said to me, the night those bastards took him.'

Chapter 10

Ben asked, 'What did Amal say to you?'

Brooke fell silent, and her gaze seemed to turn inwards as though she was reimagining the scene from that night. 'When I arrived in Delhi, I'd never seen him so miserable and depressed. He felt like nobody was listening to him, he felt betrayed by Samarth who seemed to just want to accept what the police were saying at face value, and he was frantic at the idea that Kabir was lying somewhere badly hurt and suffering, maybe even dying. I wish I'd never suggested it now, but I had the idea that going out for a meal together that evening might cheer him up. There's a big food district only about twenty minutes' walk from here, with a lot of great restaurants. He was reluctant at first, but then agreed that a walk and a nice dinner out would do him good. We never got there.'

Brooke choked up as she finished speaking, and had to pause for a few moments as she dabbed her eyes. She took another long sip of her scotch. Ben wished she'd stop drinking. She clasped the glass with both hands in her lap and stared at it, shaking her head. Her eyes were pink and brimming again. She was gripping the glass so tightly that Ben was afraid it would break and cut her. 'Oh God, what's going to happen to him?'

'You don't want to focus on those kinds of thoughts,' Ben said. 'You need to believe he's all right.'

She flashed her tearful eyes on him. 'You know perfectly well you're only saying that. Don't try to bullshit me. He's either dead already or he's sitting in some dark hole, absolutely terrified out of his mind. He's not strong, Ben. He'll fall apart under this kind of strain.'

Ben leaned forward and reached out, gently took the glass from her fingers and laid it on the coffee table in front of her. 'So what did he say?' he prompted her softly.

Brooke closed her eyes and let out a long sigh. After a few more moments she was collected enough to resume the story.

'It was as we were walking. It was a lovely evening, cool and peaceful. I'd hoped a stroll would relax him, but he couldn't stop going over and over the whole thing, about how too little was being done to find his brother, and how he was absolutely certain that this wasn't just some random bandit attack as everyone thought. I said to him, "Amal, how can you really be so sure it wasn't?" Like you, I thought maybe the police were actually right and that Amal should listen to Samarth. I couldn't bear to see him torturing himself that way. But then he stopped walking, and he turned to me in the middle of the street, and he looked at me and said, "There's something else about Kabir. Something I know that I haven't told you, or anyone. It changes everything."'

Ben asked, 'Something, like what?'

Brooke slowly shook her head. 'I wish I knew.'

'He didn't say?'

'I could tell he wanted to, but couldn't bring himself to. It was gnawing at him.'

Ben frowned. 'Not even a hint?'

'I only know what little I was able to get out of him. He said that Kabir called him a few days before leaving on his trip, very excited, and confided something really important. Not just your typical run-of-the-mill secret. Something huge.'

'If the trip was related to his work, this archaeological project you said he was working on, then presumably this piece of information relates to that as well?'

'It's a fair assumption.'

'In which case, what are the possibilities?'

Brooke shrugged. 'Archaeologists dig stuff up. Maybe Kabir did, too.'

'A discovery? Of what?'

'I don't know, Ben. You tell me.'

Ben mulled it over for a moment or two, then decided that it was all too vague to even try to speculate about. 'And Amal thought this secret, or discovery, or whatever it is, of Kabir's might have had some bearing on the reason for the attack?'

Brooke nodded. 'That was why he was so convinced it wasn't just some random incident. But whatever it is, Kabir had made him promise not to tell anyone.'

'Not even you? His own wife?' It was hard for Ben to say that last bit.

'That's what I said to him, too. Asked him why he couldn't share it with me, if it was so important. Especially if it meant something about what happened.'

'And his reply?'

'He said to me, "He's my brother, Brooke. Please don't ask me to betray his trust."'

'Okay, fair enough. But why would Amal hold this information back from the police, if it might have shed some different kind of light on the investigation?'

'I asked him the same question. He said a promise was a promise, and that was the end of it.'

'Is Amal normally this stubborn?'

'Look, I know you think of him as just this bookish nerd,' Brooke said.

Ben held up his palms in defence. 'Did I ever call him that?'

'But he has principles. If he felt it was wrong to betray his brother's trust, wild horses couldn't drag it out of him.'

'I'm sure. You'd have to give him a Chinese burn to get him to talk, or twist his earlobe or something.'

She gave him a resentful look. 'That's a low thing to say, Ben.'

'I'm sorry. It might help us, too, if we had any clue what *it* was. You don't have any idea?'

'None.'

'That's just great. Nice to have so much to go on.'

'One thing we can be sure of,' Brooke said. 'Kabir had some kind of big, important secret apparently connected with his trip to Rakhigarhi. And Amal was in on it too. Next thing, both brothers have disappeared, first one and then the other. The confidential information is what connects them.'

'Maybe.'

Her cheeks flushed. 'Not maybe, Ben. Definitely. It means Amal was right. There's more to this than a chance bandit attack. Has to be. And it also has to mean that whatever happened to him is somehow involved with what happened to Kabir. It can't possibly be a coincidence.'

'And all we have to do is find out what this secret was that Kabir made his brother swear never to tell a soul about. Bingo, our first inkling of a lead.'

'If anyone can find out, you can,' she said.

'Do you think he'd have told his other brother?'

'Samarth?'

'If Kabir told him what he told Amal, he might share it with us.'

Brooke thought about it, then shook her head. 'From the way Amal talked, I doubt that Kabir confided in anyone else within the family. The two younger brothers have a closer relationship than with Samarth. He's always kept himself at a distance. There's some tension there.'

'What kind of tension?'

'This is India. Traditions are still very strong here. It had always been understood that all three brothers would enter the family business, take over from their father when he retired, and work together to expand the empire that old Basu had founded. But Amal and Kabir both chose to go their own ways, which caused a certain amount of bad blood between them and Samarth. Their father too, though he's really quite sweet once you get to know him. He's the reason I was able to get you here so fast. A couple of favours were called in from some very high-level people.'

'So I gathered. Let's get back to the events of that evening. You say you never made it to the restaurant. The snatch happened on the walk?'

'Just before we got there. Not long after we'd had that conversation.'

'I think you've been cooped up in this room long enough. Let's get some air. Do you have a car?'

She looked momentarily blank, thrown by the apparent change of subject. 'There's a Jag house car that I use as a runaround. It's down in the garage. Or else we could get Prem to drive us in the Maybach.'

Jaguars. S-Class Pullman limousines. Back when they were

an item, Brooke's drive had been a clapped-out Suzuki jeep. Ben said, 'Let's leave Prem out of it.'

'Where are we going?'

He replied, 'To the food district.'

'I'm not hungry.'

'We're not going there to eat. I want to see the crime scene for myself. You're going to take me to the spot Amal was kidnapped.'

Chapter 11

The sun outside was more intense as midday approached. The air felt as hot and heavy and moist as steam, trapped under the pale sky. Ben's shirt began to stick to his back the moment he left the air-conditioned cool of the house, but despite the heat Brooke had wrapped a light shawl around her bare shoulders. Green and yellow silk, with a paisley pattern. It looked good on her. She carried a small embroidered handbag, or a clutch purse, or whatever woman termed these accessories, on a thin strap. Ethnic fashion wear, probably bought locally for a fraction of what some trendy London boutique would charge. The handbag seemed to hang heavy on its strap. It always mystified Ben what women carried around in those things.

Bees and giant dragonflies buzzed about the flower beds as she led him across the garden and down a path to the Ray residence's garage block, a stretched-out and low open-fronted building painted white to match the house, with exotic ivy growing up its walls. 'I suppose you could call it the family fleet,' she said, showing Ben the row of cars inside under the shade. All lined up neatly facing outwards, all immaculately waxed and polished. Prem had parked the limousine in a space at the end of the row, dwarfing the bright red Ferrari next to it.

'Whose is the flying tomato?' Ben asked. 'Amal's?'

'Amal doesn't drive,' she replied. 'That's Kabir's. The Audi roadster is Prem's. The little yellow Fiat belongs to Esha, Samarth's wife. She doesn't get out much, though.'

'So I gathered. Unlike her husband, who's never at home.'

'He parks his Bentley there,' Brooke said, pointing at an empty space next to the tiny Fiat. 'He's usually home by six or seven, if it's not a busy day at the office. You might get to meet him later.'

The silver Jaguar that Brooke used as general transport occupied the far end of the row. It was the latest F-Pace SUV model, compact and boxy. But its plain-Jane exterior was wrapped around a five-litre supercharged V8 engine. Whatever the Rays owned, it seemingly had to be top of the spec list. By contrast, Esha Ray's choice of a cheap and cheerful Fiat seemed a little out of place.

Ben pointed at it and said, 'Not exactly your typical millionaire's ride.'

Brooke shrugged. 'She used to drive a Porsche 911. She loved that car, but she sold it a few weeks ago. Actually, Samarth made her sell it.'

'Made her?'

'Said the insurance premium was too pricey for a woman's runaround. That's what she told me, anyway.'

'I suppose rich folks don't get that way by spending money unnecessarily,' Ben said.

Brooke shrugged again. 'Whatever. Listen, do you mind driving? I'm a bit light-headed from the whisky.'

'I think I can just about manage that.'

She walked around to the passenger side, on the left like in the UK. A throwback to the olden days of the British Empire. Ben walked around to the driver's side and climbed in behind the wheel. The car smelled brand new. He was glad to be free of Prem, and also glad to have their own transport. He was fast running out of countries where he wasn't banned from booking a rental vehicle. He had absolutely no idea why. Weren't rental companies insured against their property getting shot to pieces, blown up, flattened or sunk in canals?

Brooke got in the passenger side. Her hair brushed his face as they settled in. 'It's keyless,' she said. 'You just press the button.'

Ben had already found it. The Jaguar purred into life, not as whisper-softly as the Maybach, but you couldn't have everything. He pulled out of the garage and started down the driveway, pausing for a peacock that strutted unhurriedly across their path. The gates wafted open for them at the bottom of the drive. Brooke guided him left and down the street. Ben was breathing in her perfume and remembering the last occasion they'd travelled in a car together. It had been back in England, during the short time they'd rented a house in the Jericho district of Oxford. A totally different life, filled with wedding plans and the excitement of the big day looming. Ben had quit Le Val and handed the reins over to Jeff, not intending to return. Those days had been over for him, he'd promised himself and Brooke. Having resumed the theology studies he'd abandoned many years earlier, he'd been looking ahead to a whole new future.

And look at us now, he reflected. Brooke married to someone else, and him back in the same old game as before, with the added twist that he had to help her get her beloved husband back. Life could be strangely ironic at times. His life, especially.

When the armed guards at the gated checkpoint saw Brooke in the Jaguar's passenger seat they waved them through with friendly smiles and barely a glance at her driver.

'It's like living on a bloody military base,' she said bitterly. 'You'd know all about that, I suppose.'

'Just a little bit,' Ben said.

'But at least it's safe. I should never have made him leave home that night. It's all my fault.'

'It happened,' Ben said. 'We can't change it. We can only deal with it.'

'I suppose.'

'So don't beat yourself up.'

'Okay. I'll try.'

'Anyhow, what were you going to do, stay hunkered down behind locked gates forever? If they wanted him, sooner or later they'd have had their chance.'

'They,' she said. 'Whoever *they* are.'

'That's what we're going to figure out.'

'Ben?'

He turned, and saw she was looking at him. 'What?'

'Thanks for being here.'

'It's what I do,' he said.

The twenty-minute route that Brooke and Amal had followed on foot took just three or four by car. Beyond the limits of the serene, upscale residential area they entered a profusion of narrower, humbler and dingier streets crammed to the maximum with activity. Row after row of food stalls and street vendors sprawled over the pavements. Ben fell into line with the slow-moving procession of cars and motor scooters and tuk-tuks that filtered through the jostling crowds of pedestrians. Gangs of children swarmed around the Jaguar, clamouring and waving through the tinted glass.

'We can stop here and walk the rest of the way,' Brooke said. Ben pulled over and wedged the car into a parking space between two stalls. The throng of kids closed around them. As Brooke stepped out she tossed them some coins and said something in Hindi that seemed to please them. The biggest kid grabbed the lion's share of the money and planted himself beside the car like a terrier on guard duty.

'I've been learning a bit of the language,' she explained to Ben, with a shrug that could have been a little self-conscious.

'What did you say to them?'

'That there'd be more rupees if we come back and find the car still in one piece,' she said. 'Come on, it's this way.'

Ben accompanied her through the food market, pressing their way between jostling bodies. The air was intense with the smell of motor fumes mingled with the scents of herbs and exotic spices and aromatic basmati rice and grilled mutton kebab from the vendors up and down the street. The place easily rivalled the grand bazaars of Marrakech, Tehran and Istanbul for sheer buzz and hubbub. Seafood merchants were pulling in scrums of customers for fresh crab and clams and shrimp. There were handicrafts and tourist trinkets and clothes and more exotic varieties of fruit and vegetables than Ben could identify. They passed cafés and small restaurants and musicians and stalls selling mountains of chillies and okra and nuts and teas, all adding to the sensory overload of smells, sounds and colours.

Brooke's fair skin and auburn hair were drawing a lot of looks from men. Hence the shawl that covered her shoulders and protected her from more prying eyes. Ben threw back a few warning glances at the oglers, who quickly looked away. The white knight, protecting the damsel. Who, in this instance, was someone else's damsel. Another painful reminder, but he only had himself to blame.

'It happened down there.' Brooke pointed down a narrow lane to their left, and turned off the main street away from the bustle. Ben followed. There were no stalls along here, and just enough space for a vehicle to squeeze between the crumbly buildings. She stopped and looked uncomfortably around her, then at Ben. 'This is it. The restaurant we wanted to go to is at the bottom of this lane. Needless to say, we didn't get that far.'

'Pretty public spot to pull off a kidnapping,' he commented.

'It's so much busier by day. There was hardly anyone around to witness what happened. And if anyone did, they soon disappeared.'

Ben stood in the middle of the lane and turned a slow three-sixty, scanning details and forming a scene in his mind. He pictured a couple walking. Not a happy pair, because of the troubles weighing on their minds. But things were about to get much worse for them.

He said, 'Okay, describe it to me.'

Chapter 12

Brooke said, 'By the time we got here I was already regretting that I'd dragged him out of the house. We'd walked in silence for the last few minutes. I was annoyed that he wouldn't tell me what Kabir had told him, and I could sense that he was feeling bad about the whole thing. I think he really wanted to share it with me. Maybe he would have, over dinner, or later that evening. But there *was* no later that evening.'

She turned to face back towards the lane entrance. 'The van came from that direction. It turned into the lane, came right for us and screeched to a halt right here.' She pointed at the ground. 'You can still see the tyre marks.'

Ben had already clocked the black stains on the road. Nothing of any great forensic value to discern from those, except that a heavy vehicle had come to an abrupt stop and shed some rubber.

'It happened so fast that neither of us reacted in time. We were caught like a couple of deer in the headlights. Totally defenceless.'

Ben said, 'How many guys?'

'Six, not counting the driver. He stayed behind the wheel while the rest of them jumped out. One from the front passenger seat, two from a sliding door on the side, and the other three from the back. They were all wearing ski masks. All about average height, average build, give or take, except for one who was kind of stumpy, built like a fireplug or a fire hydrant, one of those things. Solid. And very hairy.'

'Hairy?'

'Like an animal. He had tufts of it sticking out from under the neck of his ski mask, and more at the wrists.'

Small and hairy, like an animal. Ben made a mental note of it. Distinguishing features were a good thing to know about.

Brooke said, 'And another of them was much bigger than the rest.'

'How much bigger?'

'A lot. Really big. Probably a foot taller than you. More, even.'

'Come on. Seriously?' Ben was a shade under six feet, not the tallest man in the world by any means, but there weren't many men who towered over him by that kind of margin.

'Seriously. And built super-wide, too. A real hulk. Probably pumped full of steroids.'

Ben made a mental note of that, too. A guy that large would be easy to spot. Maybe not so easy to neutralise, if it came to it. But he could worry about that if and when the situation arose. He said, 'Okay. Go on.'

'They were on us in seconds. Of course, I had no idea what was happening. I thought they were coming for both of us. Muggers, or a rape gang. Forty percent of all the rapes in India happen in Delhi. They beat up the men, hold them down at knifepoint and make them watch as they line up to go to work on the women.' Brooke shuddered. 'But then they made straight for Amal, and I realised that wasn't what they wanted. He was just standing there, like paralysed. I suppose I was too. Two of them grabbed his arms and started dragging him towards the van. He turned to look at me. He was so terrified. He yelled at me to *run, get away.*'

Ben knew that Brooke wouldn't have run, in that situation. She was one of the toughest, bravest women he'd ever met. In unarmed combat training sessions at Le Val she'd been able to hold her own against much stronger and heavier male sparring partners.

She went on, 'Amal's a gentle soul. He's never so much as thrown a punch in his life. But I wasn't about to stand there and let him be snatched off the street like that. I rushed in and collared one of the bastards.'

'The stumpy, hairy one or the massive one?'

'Neither,' she said. 'This one was about medium height, medium build. I punched him in the mouth, and when he went down I yanked his mask off.'

'You saw his face?'

'I can still see it now,' she replied. 'He's an Indian, as you might expect given that we're in India. Swarthy complexion, dark hair, mid-thirties. He was sat there dumped on the ground looking up at me with these big bulging eyes full of hate. He has a missing front tooth.'

Ben made another mental note. *Bulging eyes, missing tooth.* 'Was it already missing, or did you knock it out when you hit him?'

'It was lying on the pavement. I didn't notice it until afterwards. And his mouth was bleeding. So I'd say it was me.'

Ben had to smile in satisfaction at the visual image. He added *bruised lip* to his mental note. That was, assuming he caught up with the kidnappers before the bruising had time to go down. Which he had every intention of doing.

'I picked up the tooth and gave it to the police,' Brooke

said. 'They've still got it, far as I know. I was hoping it'd help to find the guy. Can they DNA teeth?'

Ben nodded. 'Tooth enamel's one of the best sources for DNA samples. But the police in India are known for being way behind on the technology. They don't have any kind of database to match samples with. So I'd be surprised if they turn up anything there, but it was good thinking on your part.'

She gave a sour grunt. 'Fabulous.'

'What happened next?'

Brooke continued the account, glancing here and there as though she was reliving the action all over again. 'Meanwhile the rest of them were dragging Amal closer to the van, right there. He was struggling, but couldn't do a thing. I was screaming at the top of my voice. I could see a few people hanging around, but nobody came to help. I went to grab another of the bastards and pull him off Amal. Then the big hulk I told you about, he lunged towards me and caught me by the arm. Very, very quick for a guy his size. His hand was like a pincer. I tried to put him in a wrist lock, the way you showed me once. Nambudo?'

'Aikido.'

'But he was too strong. He held onto me like he was going to stuff me into the van, too. For a second I was certain they were going to take both of us.'

'You got away?'

'No, they let me go. One seemed to be the gang leader. He yelled in Hindi at the big one, "No! Not the woman, only the man!"'

Ben said, 'That suggests it was definitely a targeted attack. They weren't interested in you, only in Amal.'

'Seems that way to me, too.'

'What did the leader look like?'

'About your height, about your build. Fairly muscular, but lean with it.'

As relieved as he was by the fact, Ben found it strange that they hadn't taken her too. What kidnapper wouldn't benefit from capturing two hostages for the price of one? But then, this whole case was strange. The lack of a ransom demand was the most disconcerting thing of all.

Brooke went on, 'So the big bastard let go of my arm and shoved me away so hard I fell over. Everything spilled out of my handbag. He must have thought I was going to snatch up my phone and snap a picture of him and his buddies, because he stamped on it and smashed it to pieces. Meanwhile, the one I'd knocked down was getting to his feet, and they had Amal in the back of the van. I started running over to try to do more to help him, but then two of them pulled out pistols and pointed them in my face. They looked as if they meant it. I was afraid they were going to shoot me. What else could I do? I backed off.'

'You did the right thing, Brooke. There was nothing more you could have done.'

'You'd have done more.'

'Don't be so sure about that.'

'I know you would, Ben. You'd have taken those weapons off them and rammed them down their throats, sideways. You wouldn't have let them take him.'

'Sometimes you have to let it go. Happens to the best.'

'I failed.'

'You need to get that out of your head,' he said. 'Because you're right, they probably would have shot you. And then you'd be dead. And if you were dead, there'd have been nobody to call in my help. And Amal would have been on his own. No winners in that situation.'

She smiled weakly. 'Maybe you're right.'

'Plus, it would upset me just a little if you were dead.'

'Thanks. Still, whatever happens, I won't make that mistake ever again.' She reached across her side for the little embroidered handbag and unzipped it. She dipped her hand inside and came out with something that made Ben's eyebrows rise. Now he knew why the bag had looked heavy on its strap.

'Where the hell did you get that?'

The pistol was a Browning Hi-Power, almost identical to the one Ben kept at the armoury at Le Val. One of his all-time favourite personal defence weapons, for its ruggedness, balance and deadly effectiveness. Nine-millimetre Parabellum. Thirteen-round magazine capacity, plus one in the chamber. All steel, the way guns used to be.

'It's Kabir's,' she said. 'He keeps it in a bedside drawer at the house, for personal protection. Showed it to me once, much to Amal's disapproval. He hates guns.'

'That figures.' Ben didn't hate them, even though he knew too well what they could do. Nor did he love them, and he mistrusted people who did. In his way of thinking, they were simply tools. Ones to be treated with great caution and respect. Sadly, they often weren't.

'After the kidnapping, I sneaked in there and borrowed it. I should have done it sooner. If only I'd had it with me that night, things might have gone differently. But carrying it makes me feel more comfortable.'

Ben took it from her hand and examined it. It was old and scuffed, but well maintained and smelling of fresh oil. The magazine was fully loaded up. Nine-millimetre full metal jackets, the cartridge rims marked with the head stamp of the Indian government's Ordnance Factories Board. Military ammo. Not available to civilians. Ben wondered where Kabir had managed to procure this kind of hardware from.

He said, 'Might have gone differently for Kabir, too, if he'd taken it on his trip.'

He went to hand the pistol back to Brooke, but she waved it away. 'You hold onto it. You can handle it better than I can.'

'I'm hoping I won't need it.'

'What's that saying you told me once? Better to have it and not need it than to need it and not have it. It's a truth I never fully appreciated until now.'

Ben tucked the gun into his waistband, in that old familiar place behind his right hip where he was convinced he had a Browning-shaped hollow from all the years of carrying one concealed. He untucked his shirt and let it hang loose to hide the pistol's butt. He said to Brooke, 'Finish the story.'

'There's not much more to tell. They all jumped aboard the van and slammed the doors and took off down the street, leaving me standing there alone. The couple of witnesses were long gone. I wanted to call for help, but my phone was in pieces. I ran down to the bottom of the lane and told the staff at the restaurant what had just happened. Or tried to. I was in such a state of shock that I probably wasn't making much sense. One of the waiters called the police for me. When they finally turned up, I led them back here and described things pretty much the way I just did to you.'

'What about the van's registration number?'

'Got it, memorised it, told it to the police. It was a local plate, with a DL for Delhi. Took four days for them to come back to me and tell me it was a stolen vehicle. I'd already guessed as much.'

'Okay,' Ben said. 'Anything else?'

'That's all of it,' she replied with a deep sigh. 'Every last detail I can remember. Which basically adds up to zero. We have nothing.'

Ben shook his head. 'We don't have nothing.'

Chapter 13

The street kids had done their duty and the Jaguar was still in one piece. Brooke paid them off with more rupees, then turned to Ben. 'You want to get something to eat? We're in the right place for it. Or we could have lunch at the house.'

'Later,' he said, getting into the car. 'I'm not hungry.'

'Me neither.'

'And we're not going back to the house. Not just yet.'

'Fine with me,' she said. 'What did you have in mind?'

'This Mr Prajapati of yours. The best private investigator in Delhi.'

'He's not mine,' Brooke replied, a touch irritably as she got in the passenger seat. 'I told you, Amal hired him to look for Kabir, then I hired him to look for Amal.'

'With sensational results on both counts. When was the last report you got from the guy?'

'Days ago. Don't ask me how many. I've more or less given up waiting for him to call.'

'Then I think it's time we had an update,' Ben said.

'Want me to call him?'

'I was thinking we could drop by his office and say hello. You know where it is?'

'I've only been there, like, eight times. I think I can remember the way.'

'Then let's pay Mr Prajapati a visit.'

The offices of the P. P. Detective Agency were on the second floor of a dirty building on a busy pedestrianised precinct in Janakpuri District Center, between a shop advertising LAPTOP AND DESKTOP REPAIRING and a boutique selling cheap knockoffs of designer-name jeans.

'Classy location,' Ben said. 'If this guy's the top private eye in the city, imagine the worst.'

'He did come highly recommended,' Brooke said. 'He spent thirty years with the Delhi police.'

'What better recommendation is there?'

She led the way inside the building. 'I always take the stairs. The lift makes creaking sounds like it's going to stick. And it smells as if someone's been keeping chickens in there.'

'Good idea.' Ben thought the whole building and the street outside smelled pretty bad too, but maybe he just hadn't been in the city long enough to get used to the ambient aroma that hit the olfactory sense like a mixture of pollution, sewage, sweat, cooking fumes, decaying vegetation, tropical flowers and incense that had been mulched up together in a giant cauldron and stewed for a couple of thousand years.

One thing he was getting used to, and fast, was Brooke's company. The tension between them had melted away and being with her felt more natural and comfortable with every passing minute they spent together. He had to keep reminding himself not to touch her as they walked.

On the second floor a placard outside the offices read proudly, *The Prateek Prajapati Detective Agency specialises in cases relating to anonymous letters and suspicious telephone calls, pre-matrimonial investigations, divorce and adultery, kidnapping and missing persons, extortion, financial crimes and cheatings. Fully licensed and qualified.*

'A man of many and varied talents,' Ben commented. Brooke knocked, walked in, and he followed her through the door. The small reception area was full of artificial plants, with a desk in one corner behind which sat a small, middle-aged Indian woman in a bright blue sari. Opposite the desk was a cramped waiting area with a couple of plastic chairs. A pair of internal doors led off from the reception area, one marked BATHROOM and the other plain. The receptionist frowned at them over the top of a Dell monitor as they approached the desk. The plastic monster plant next to her needed dusting. If there was any air conditioning in the building it didn't seem to be working.

Brooke rested her hands on the desk and gave the woman a polite smile. 'Brooke Ray, to see Mr Prajapati? It's concerning the case of my husband, Amal.'

The receptionist checked her screen, spent a moment tapping and scrolling, frowned a bit more and said, 'You do not appear to have an appointment. Mr Prajapati is very busy. If you do not have an appointment he cannot see you right now.'

Ben said, 'Oh, I think he'll see us.' Before the woman could react or hit the intercom button on the phone in front of her, he stepped towards the unmarked door and pushed straight through without knocking.

Delhi's top private detective was lounging on a sofa with his feet up and a sports magazine in his hands. He was a large, jowly man in his late fifties, with jet-black thinning hair and a bushy moustache that were obviously dyed. Dark rings around his eyes gave him a panda-like appearance and his mound of a belly strained at his shirt buttons. At Ben's sudden entrance he launched the magazine up into the air and almost fell off the sofa in alarm.

Brooke stepped into the office behind Ben and stood with

her hands on her hips. 'It's good to see you so hard at work finding my husband, Mr Prajapati.'

Jumping to his feet, Prajapati straightened his rumpled shirt and crooked tie and smoothed his hair and began to bluster indignantly about the need to make an appointment, and how he was just taking a short break in a hectic day. Ben eyed the remains of a large takeout lunch on the desk. Pretty obvious how the busy super-sleuth had spent the last hour or so.

Brooke said, 'I've been hoping you might call to keep me updated on how your enquiries are progressing. Perhaps you lost my number? Anyhow, I just happened to be in the neighbourhood, so I thought I'd stop by.'

Prajapati shot a deeply suspicious glare at Ben, pointed a thick finger his way and said, 'Who is this person?'

'I'm your new assistant,' Ben said. 'Come to work with you on the Ray kidnap case. It's a real honour for me.'

'I have no need for an assistant.'

'Then I'll just have to manage on my own,' Ben said. 'Shame.'

Brooke said, 'This is Mr Hope. He's travelled to India to assist me, doing what it seems nobody else here is willing or able to do. That is, to find my husband and bring him home safely.'

More collected now, Prajapati walked over to the desk and perched on its corner with one leg dangling, like a link of sausage. He laced his fingers together over his belly and looked at Ben with flat cop eyes. 'You are wasting your time, my friend.' To Brooke he said, 'Mrs Ray, please let me remind you that locating your husband is, under the circumstances, a very difficult business.'

'I'm aware of that. That's why I hired you, on the understanding that you were the best person for the job. Are you saying you've made no progress at all? And have you heard anything from the police inspector in charge of the investigation? Because I haven't. All this waiting for the phone to ring starts giving you the strangest idea that nothing's actually happening.'

'In fact I was intending to call you today,' Prajapati replied gravely. 'Mrs Ray, you need to prepare yourself for bad news. Please, take a seat.' He motioned at the pair of fabric director's chairs the other side of the desk.

Brooke didn't sit down. Her face turned pale and her jaw tightened. 'You've heard something. You're going to tell me that Amal's been found dead. Is that what you're going to tell me?'

Prajapati shook his head, and his jowls wobbled. 'No, Mrs Ray. It isn't. Your husband has not been found. But in such a case as this, where no ransom demand has been made and the motivation for the crime is obviously something other than financial, a revenge attack perhaps, the chances of a happy outcome are very slight. Very slight indeed. That is why I say you should prepare yourself. The call I had been intending to give you, which now you are here in person is no longer necessary, was to inform you that after much consideration I am resigning from this case. Because in my professional opinion it is almost one hundred per cent certain that your husband is no longer alive, and at this stage we are looking for a corpse.'

Chapter 14

But Prajapati was wrong. Because Amal Ray was still very much alive. For the moment, at any rate – though for how much longer, he was too petrified to contemplate.

Amal could still see the last look on Brooke's face as they ripped him away from her. Could still hear the echo of his own voice yelling, *Run, Brooke, run!* Then the van door slamming shut, and the start of the nightmare journey into the unknown. He remembered the van stopping. Sounds, footsteps, voices. Then a sudden flood of harsh light making him blink as the back door was wrenched open. A glimpse of brickwork in the background: had he been taken to a garage or a warehouse of some kind? Then the terrifying sight of one of his kidnappers, the one in charge, his face masked like a terrorist's, coming up to him with a hypodermic needle in one gloved hand and an evil glint lighting up his eyes.

After that, there was a gaping hole in Amal's memory. Whatever sedative they'd pumped into him could have rendered him unconscious for minutes, hours, he had no idea. The next thing he'd known was awakening in this place, head aching, feeling nauseous and utterly afraid.

And he'd been here ever since. Long enough to have examined every square inch of his strange new environment a hundred times over.

His prison was thirty feet square, a figure he'd paced out accurately over and over, back and forth and round and round like a zoo animal in a caged enclosure. It was lit by a single naked bulb in the middle of the ceiling that burned around the clock, so that it was impossible to tell night from daytime hours and hard to keep track of the days passing. His captors had taken away his watch, along with his wallet and shoes. Why the shoes, he'd wondered at first. Maybe to make it harder for him to run away, in the unlikely event that he managed to escape this place. Or maybe to prevent him from hanging himself with his laces.

Not that there was anywhere to hang himself from. The ceiling was more than six feet above his head, and the three silver duct pipes that ran across it from end to end were too far up to reach. The ducts looked industrial, making him wonder about the kind of building he was in, and what might be above the ceiling or beyond the four walls that surrounded him. The walls felt like solid concrete, and no matter where he tapped and thumped he could produce no hollow sounds. They could have been a mile thick.

The absence of any windows and the feeling of total insulation from the outside world had led him to conclude early on that he was below ground. Deeper down than a basement. More like a cellar, or some kind of underground bunker. The flight of metal steps that led steeply upwards to the only entrance tended to confirm that impression.

But the cellar wasn't some dank, stinking hole full of rats and filth. Amal understood that his captors had gone to certain lengths to make his stay here reasonably comfortable. The walls had been painted white to reflect more light, obviously in a hurry, judging by the crude job that had been made of it, and obviously not long ago, judging by the smell of fresh paint. The bed they'd provided for him was narrow and basic, like an old-fashioned hospital bed with a creaky iron frame, but the mattress and pillow were new. He had a plastic chair to sit on, and a small table, which, likewise, he understood were luxuries not necessarily afforded to most people in his predicament.

The same was also true of his toilet arrangements. His kidnappers could have just given him a bucket. Instead, they'd provided him with his own little separate bathroom, albeit a makeshift affair set up in the corner opposite his bed and consisting of two plywood sheets for walls and one for a ceiling, with a doorway sawn out. Inside the bathroom was a chemical toilet, a plastic basin on a stand and a water pipe that was cemented into the wall and protruded a couple of feet with a tap attached to its end. He wouldn't have drunk the water, but it seemed okay to wash with. He had a toothbrush and toothpaste and spare rolls of toilet paper. They'd even left him some pieces of cheap soap and a couple of towels.

All the comforts a man could wish for, apart from the basic freedom to walk out of here.

The cellar door was the one feature that kept reminding him of what this place truly was, a prison cell. It was solid timber, not ply. No visible hinges, no interior handle, no keyhole, no peephole or window. Only a small trapdoor hatch near its base, about eight inches square, which looked to Amal like a cat flap, except it opened only outwards. It was too small for him to poke his head out of, on the rare occasions when it wasn't bolted shut, which was when his unseen captors brought him his meals and drinks.

His diet consisted mainly of tinned beans and stewed meat, warmed up and served on disposable paper plates with a plastic fork and spoon to eat with. Each meal came with a litre bottle of water, more than enough to keep him hydrated with a little left over for brushing his teeth. All of which seemed like an excess of consideration on the part of his kidnappers, who seemed oddly prepared to go the extra mile for his wellbeing. They'd even provided him with a fresh T-shirt and jogging bottoms the right size, enabling him to change out of the stale clothes he'd been wearing the night of the kidnap. They were evidently intent on keeping their prisoner adequately nourished, reasonably healthy and clean. For which he was thankful, under the circumstances. But why?

It was the coffee that perplexed him the most. It was served in paper cups along with his food and water. Instant decaf, lots of milk, lots of sugar. Exactly how he drank it at home.

How on earth could they possibly know that?

Amal couldn't shut those bewildering questions out of his head. He'd sit for hours by the hatch, waiting for it to open so he could scream through the hole, 'WHO ARE YOU PEOPLE? WHAT DO YOU WANT FROM ME?'

But he never got the chance, because the trapdoor only ever seemed to open when he was sleeping. He'd awaken, look up the steps and there would be his next meal waiting for him by the locked hatch. He'd shuffle up the steps to collect it, then shuffle back down to his living quarters, slump in his chair at the table to go through the motions of refuelling his body, then carry the empty plate and cup back up to the hatch when he'd finished. Next time he awoke, they would be gone.

With no chance of escape and nothing else to do, Amal had had no choice but to settle into the mind-numbing routine of eat, sleep, pace his cell, wear himself out fretting, and then fall into his rumpled bed to try to lose himself once more in sleep. His mind felt so scrambled and befuddled that he feared he was losing his grip on reality. In the more lucid intervals between spells of anguish and dread, he had plenty to think about. And although he had no idea who was keeping him prisoner like this, from the moment he'd been kidnapped he'd had a strong feeling that he knew why this was happening to him.

It was all about the secret Kabir had told him. What else could it be? By its very nature, it was the kind of thing that could get people into terrible trouble. That much had already proved true for Kabir himself.

It was on the third day of his incarceration, as far as he could tell, that Amal's suspicions had been confirmed. And from that moment, his nightmare had truly begun.

Chapter 15

Brooke was visibly upset after the visit to Prajapati. As they drove away she was angrily saying, 'What's he talking about? A revenge attack? Revenge for what? What has Amal ever done to anyone? He's the gentlest person I've ever known. This summer we found a baby bird injured in the garden. It must have fallen from a nest and been mauled by a cat. Amal had to put it out of its misery. He was inconsolable for two whole days afterwards. *That's* the kind of man he is. So what's this idiot saying about a revenge attack?'

Ben replied, 'Maybe he thinks the brothers were into something.'

She looked at him sharply. 'Into what?'

'Something illegal, presumably. Something that would entail running with a bad crowd. And invite certain risks and reprisals, even if they were only peripherally involved.'

'Crime? Are you serious?'

'There is the matter of the gun,' Ben said. 'I mean, who keeps a nine-millimetre pistol handy by their bedside unless they reckon they have good reason to need it?' He shifted in the driver's seat and felt the hard lump of the Browning trapped against the small of his back.

Brooke turned in her seat to stare at him, incredulous. 'You actually think that?'

He shrugged. 'It had crossed my mind.'

'Then you've got your head up your arse just like Prajapati, and I'm the only one who can see things properly. Jesus Christ!'

'I said it crossed my mind. I didn't say it stayed there very long. Got to consider every possibility, Brooke. Even if it's just trying it on for size to tell what doesn't fit.'

Brooke threw herself back in her seat and closed her eyes. Ben fished in a pocket for his pack of Gauloises, tapped one out and lit it, rolled down his window to let the smoke out and went on driving in silence.

After a pause Brooke said in a softer tone, 'I'm sorry I lashed out at you just then. It was wrong.'

'It's okay.'

'It's not your fault. It's that idiot and the things he said. He made me so angry.'

'Maybe I should have shot him. We could go back, if you like.'

Brooke gave just a flicker of a smile, and fell silent for another long pause. Then she said, 'The thing is, though, the reason he touched such a nerve is because I must think, deep down, that he's right.' It was just like her to analyse everything psychologically, even at times like this.

Ben replied, 'You can persuade yourself rationally that Amal's dead. But do you feel it? Do you believe it in your heart?'

'I'm so tired I don't know what to believe. What do you think?'

'I think Prajapati seemed very sure of himself, considering he seems to have damn all proof to support his opinion.'

'But what if it's true? How do we know it isn't?'

'We have no reason to suppose it is.'

Her lips tightened. 'You don't have to humour me, Ben.

94

I'm not a child. Let's say Amal's not going to make it out of this. Or he's dead already, like Prajapati says. What then?'

'The usual things. You'd bury him, mourn him, and move on. Like everyone does.'

'I don't mean that. I mean, *what then?*'

'Then we'd move on to the next phase. The hunt would switch gears and become about finding the people who did it. But it's too early to start talking this way.'

'And if they could be found? You'll take them down?'

Ben looked at her and saw the seriousness in her eyes. She wanted them dead, no mistake. He nodded slowly. 'You said it yourself, Brooke. Whatever it takes to make this right.'

'You'd do that for me?'

'And for Amal,' Ben said. 'He's my friend too.'

She reached out and touched his hand where it rested on the wheel. Her fingers lingered for a moment, then she drew her hand quickly away. 'What about Kabir?'

'If you're right that the two cases are connected, then it means the same bad guys are behind both crimes. In which case, we get the people who took Amal, we're also getting the ones who got Kabir. Two birds with one stone.'

'And if I'm wrong, and the two aren't connected at all?'

'Then all we can do is take it step by step. It's a process of elimination. Forget about Prajapati. Even if he hadn't just taken himself out of the equation, he's of no use to us. Which takes us to the next name on the list, Samarth. At this point, I'd like to be introduced.'

'Why now?'

Ben replied, 'Because he's the only one of the three brothers still available to talk to. Because I'm a visitor in his home and it's the polite thing to do. And because he might actually know something that could lead us to the next level.'

They passed a busy street-side kebab stall and the aromas

of chargrilled lamb and chicken with hot chilli peppers and spicy okra wafted through the car's open window. Brooke asked, 'Not hungry yet?'

'I want to keep moving.'

'Same here.' She reached for her handbag, took out her purse and riffled around until she found a business card. Black with gold edging and script, expensive and glossy. 'Here it is. Ray Enterprises, Connaught Place. That's the main business district, where all the big corporate offices are.' She copied the postal code into the on-board sat nav and peered at the screen for directions. 'You need to get turned around here.'

'Let's do it.' Ben dropped a gear and the Jaguar's engine growled happily as he cut across the lanes of chaotic traffic to head back in the opposite direction.

That was when he spotted the car in the rear-view mirror. A dusty white Toyota sedan had peeled suddenly out from the traffic flow and pulled a sharp U-turn in his wake. In any other country Ben had travelled in, it would have been the kind of manoeuvre that elicited a symphony of honking horns from angry motorists. Evidently not in India, where nobody seemed to care much what you did on the road, but it caught Ben's eye nonetheless. Not exactly subtle.

Someone was following them.

Chapter 16

Ben kept it to himself, because he didn't want to alarm Brooke. Not until he was sure he was right. Then she'd find out soon enough, depending on what happened next.

He took the next right turn, veering sharply into the junction at the last moment. A motor rickshaw driver and a couple of pedestrians had to move fast to get out of his path. Brooke glanced at the sat nav and said, 'What are you doing? This is the wrong way.'

'Sorry, my mistake,' he replied. In the mirror he saw the white Toyota follow them into the junction. Hanging back, keeping its distance, allowing a few other vehicles to filter in between itself and the Jaguar. It had passed the first test. Or failed it, depending on one's point of view. One more, and Ben would be sure. He said, 'Let me pull in here and get turned around again.'

He clicked on his indicator, steered nearer the kerb and slowed. A battered taxi sedan, two tuk-tuks and a motorcycle buzzed past. The white Toyota didn't. It had slowed too, and hovered at the kerbside forty metres behind the Jaguar as though anticipating their next move. Ben waited for a gap in the traffic, then threw the Jag around with a squeal of tyres and accelerated back towards the junction.

Right on cue, the Toyota U-turned and followed.

Brooke still had no idea what was going on, and Ben had decided to say nothing yet. Connaught Place and the Ray Enterprises HQ were twenty minutes away, which he hoped was enough of a distance to provide him with a chance to lose their tail. He left her alone with her thoughts as he followed the sat nav west across the city, cutting and diving into gaps, braking hard now and then to avoid facilitating the suicide of various scooterists and pedestrians, and all the while watching the white Toyota in his mirror. He'd already memorised its Delhi registration number. The glare of the sunlight made it hard to see through its windscreen, but he thought he could see the shapes of two guys inside.

He wondered who they could be. Goons working for Prajapati? Possible, though unlikely.

A traffic light up ahead was changing from green to amber. Ben saw his chance and put his foot down, and the Jaguar surged through just as the light turned red. Some way behind them, the driver of the Toyota had to make a quick decision. He raced through the red, almost collided with a truck, swerved to avoid a motorbike, and kept on the Jaguar's tail. Ben switched lanes a couple of times, took a couple more turns as directed by the sat nav. He was momentarily distracted by a bus that was trying to force its way up the wrong side of him. Then when he looked in the rear-view mirror again, expecting the Toyota still to be there, it was gone. He slowed a little to let traffic stream past and check that the Toyota wasn't just lurking further back. Definitely no longer there.

Maybe he'd imagined it, he thought. Then again, he was experienced enough to be pretty damn sure he hadn't. The stunt back there at the traffic lights had probably been the deciding factor, when the Toyota's driver had taken the bait and drawn too much attention to himself. It had been time to bail out.

But just because the Toyota had dropped out of the game didn't mean it was over. Vehicle surveillance, done properly, almost never involved a single tail. The Toyota had most likely passed the baton to another of the surveillance team. The new player could be another car, a van, bike, or even a helicopter if their resources stretched that far. Ben kept glancing around him for a likely suspect, but could see nothing. The view through the Jaguar's sunroof showed a clear sky above. If someone was still following them, they were being a damn sight more discreet about it than the Toyota. The question was, who might that someone be, and what was their intention?

'You're awfully pensive,' Brooke said.

'Focusing on driving. This traffic's terrible.'

'Welcome to Delhi. Better get used to it.'

Soon afterwards they reached the headquarters of Ray Enterprises. Connaught Place, and the impressive steel and glass tower itself, were a galaxy away from Prateek Prajapati's seedy neighbourhood. Just a few miles across the city, the slick, contemporary corporate architecture of the business centre rivalled anything London or New York had to offer. This was the world Brooke had married into. Switching off that thought the instant it flashed through his mind, Ben turned down a ramp to the building's underground car park. Nobody followed them inside. Something to worry about later, Ben decided.

They found a parking space, left the car and walked to a lift. Surveillance cameras watched from every angle. A sign said NO SMOKING WITHIN 15 FEET OF ANYWHERE, which struck Ben as a bit Draconian and tempted him to light another Gauloise just out of defiance. Eight security guys would probably appear and threaten to shoot him if he dared to.

The lift was spacious and modern, and nobody had been keeping chickens in it any time recently. The soft music wafting through its sound system sounded distinctly un-Indian to Ben's ears. He asked, 'What floor?'

Brooke replied, 'Top.'

'Silly question.' He pressed the button for the eighteenth floor. The doors hissed shut.

'Samarth has the whole floor to himself. I hope he's there,' she added fretfully. 'We should have called ahead.'

'If he's half the workaholic he's cracked up to be, he'll be there.'

The lift whooshed upwards. Ben watched the illuminated floor numbers on a panel above the doors tick off, all the way up to eighteen. Then Brooke said, 'Here we are,' and to the sound of a two-tone chime the sliding doors hissed open again to reveal the plush surroundings of the company CEO's personal domain. There wasn't a dusty plastic plant in sight, the air conditioning worked beautifully, and a secretary or PA a third of the age of Prajapati's receptionist and much more attractive in her manner greeted them warmly when Brooke walked up to the desk and introduced herself as Mr Ray's sister-in-law. The PA checked the computer, slim fingers skipping over the keyboard. She wore a ring on her thumb and a name tag marked 'Salena'.

'He has a two o'clock meeting, but I believe he's free for a few minutes. Please hold on while I check for you.' Salena picked up the phone, spoke briefly in Hindi, then motioned towards a door at the end of a passage and said, 'Please go through, Mrs Ray. He'll be very happy to see you.' Her dark eyes lingered on Ben, and she flashed him a coy smile.

'Pretty,' Brooke said in an undertone as they left the reception area.

'Is she? I hadn't noticed.'

'I'll bet you hadn't.'

Brooke was about to knock at the door when it opened, and Ben met Samarth Ray for the first time.

Chapter 17

Samarth was several years older and a couple of inches taller than Amal, the same height as Ben at just under six feet. The fraternal similarity was discernible, but you'd have had to look twice. Where Amal was somewhat slight of build and not the sportiest of people, Samarth had the athletic look of a guy who played squash and worked out in the gym four times a week. And while Amal played up to his writerly image by slouching about most of the time in jogging pants and T-shirts, his elder brother was immaculately tailored and carried himself as ramrod-straight as an army colonel. The light grey silk three-piece looked Italian, like his shoes, and the gold ingot on his wrist was Swiss. His thick hair was swept back from a high brow, greying just enough at the temples to add to the look of urbane polish. But for all the veneer of dynamism and success about the man, the signs of stress, fatigue and grief were only thinly hidden below the surface.

Samarth embraced Brooke with real tenderness and invited them into his office. Floor-to-ceiling windows on two sides offered a sweeping panorama of the city. The furnishings were as tasteful and expensive as those at the house.

'I apologise for dropping in on you out of the blue like this,' Brooke said.

Samarth touched her arm and replied graciously, 'It's always a joy to see you, my dear, even under these tragic circumstances.' His English was as polished as his appearance, with barely a trace of an accent.

'I'd like to introduce you to my friend Benedict Hope.'

'Just Ben,' Ben said as they shook hands. Samarth's grip was strong and dry. 'A pleasure to meet you, Mr Ray. Please may I offer my condolences at this difficult time.'

'You're very kind. Thank you. Now, to what do I owe this pleasure?'

'I came to tell you some news,' Brooke said. 'Both bad and good.'

Samarth replied sadly, 'Given the choice, it's always better to hear the bad news first. Can anything you have to tell me be worse than what's already happened?'

'I had a meeting with Prajapati this morning. There's been no progress in the investigation.'

'Unfortunately that comes as no great surprise to me,' Samarth said.

'And he's resigning from the case.'

'Again, not entirely unexpected. And not entirely negative news, from my perspective. I was never persuaded that he needed to be hired in the first place.'

Brooke said, 'We need all the help we can get, Samarth. And that's why I brought Ben to meet you.'

Samarth looked at Ben. 'Is this the good news?'

Brooke said, 'There's nobody more expert when it comes to finding people. He's come to India to offer us his services.'

Samarth gave Ben a sad smile. 'Your reputation precedes you, Mr Hope. You're the military man of whom my brother has spoken with such great admiration. A genuine hero, I gather.'

'Ex-military man,' Ben said. 'As for a hero, I don't know.

But I do know the world of kidnap and ransom. I'm here to do anything I can possibly do to help resolve this situation.'

'I'm touched by your kindness, Mr Hope. Please, won't you sit?' Samarth stepped across to a plush white leather armchair by the window, and slumped in it as though suddenly deflated by so much worry.

Ben perched on the edge of an armchair opposite. Brooke settled on a chair by Samarth's desk. Ben said, 'Mr Ray, I know you're a busy man, so I'll get straight to the point. It seems that Amal had reason to believe he knew why Kabir disappeared, and who might be responsible for the attack on him and his associates. We're working on a possible theory that Amal's own disappearance might be connected.'

Samarth looked blank for a moment, then frown lines etched his face. 'I don't understand. Connected in what way?'

Brooke said, 'Amal told me that Kabir confided a secret to him, just before he left for Rakhigarhi.'

'A secret? I'm sorry, again I don't understand what you mean. What kind of secret?'

'We think it concerned Kabir's work,' Ben said. 'Some discovery he'd made, something he'd found, that he was very excited by and shared with Amal. Something of great importance or value. We're speculating that it could be some archaeological find, but we don't know what. I was hoping that you might be able to shed light on the matter. It could provide us with a real insight into what's happened, not just to Kabir but to Amal as well.'

Samarth began tapping at the arm of his chair with a finger. 'Are you saying that you believe my brothers' disappearances to be the work of a single abductor?'

'Perhaps more than one, but working together. We can't be sure of that yet.'

Samarth placed his hands in front of him on his lap and laced his fingers together with a thoughtful, sombre expression. 'It strikes me that this theory you're working on is really little more than a hypothesis. Do you have any tangible evidence to support it?'

'Only what Amal told Brooke the night of the kidnap. That he'd found something.'

'That's it? He found something?'

'That's it,' Ben said. 'At this point I'm simply trying to build a picture.'

Brooke said, 'Samarth, did Kabir tell you what he told Amal? About his work, this thing he'd found?'

Samarth reflected for a moment, then slowly, gravely shook his head. 'No, I don't recall his mentioning anything of that nature. I'm afraid I have no idea what this *thing* could be.'

Brooke looked crestfallen. 'Are you sure? It might just have been in passing. Some small detail that might not have seemed important at the time.'

Samarth nodded. 'Quite sure. Whatever conversation my two brothers might have had, I wasn't party to it.' The weary sadness had drained out of his expression, replaced by something colder and harder. He pursed his lips, paused a moment longer, then said, 'Brooke, Mr Hope—'

'Please call me Ben,' Ben said.

'I understand your desire to seek answers to the many mysteries surrounding these terrible recent events. Who feels that pressing motivation more painfully than I?'

Ben sensed a 'but' coming.

Samarth went on, 'However, if you will allow me to speak frankly, I don't consider this to be a productive line of enquiry. Believe me, I wish it were. But as you admit yourselves, you have no evidence to back it up. It's just pure conjecture. Speculation. One might say, wishful thinking. Or, to use another expression, it seems to me you're clutching at straws.'

Brooke stared at her brother-in-law. 'Were you there, the night Amal was taken?'

Samarth levelly returned her gaze. 'You know that I wasn't. It's a foolish question.'

'No, you weren't. But if you had been, and you'd heard what Amal said, seen the look in his eyes, you wouldn't be so quick to dismiss it. He meant it, Samarth. He knew something. There's more to this than anyone reali—'

Samarth cut her off. 'As I've made clear more than once, Brooke, I was unhappy with the involvement of a private detective in our family affairs. Now that Mr Prajapati is no longer in the picture I'm just as unwilling to reopen the case up to another investigator, however decent his intentions, and however much I appreciate his travelling all the way to India to offer his services.'

Samarth turned to Ben. 'Naturally, I will be more than happy to reimburse any expenses you may have incurred, Mr Hope. Please submit your invoice to my secretary, and it will be taken care of immediately. Then it remains only for me to thank you for your concern, and to wish you a pleasant journey home.'

Brooke's cheeks had reddened and she looked perplexed. 'Samarth, your father was very keen to have Ben come to help us. He pulled a lot of strings to cut through the red tape and speed things along.'

Samarth replied, 'I'm well aware of the calls that my father made to his friends at the Foreign Office, Vivaan Banerjee and others. He still commands a huge deal of respect and influence. But as much as it pains me to say it, my father is old and sick and no longer the man he once was. His decisions aren't always the right ones. Just as I've had to assume control of running the business he founded, there are times when I must take charge of other matters, for the good of the family.'

'For the good of the family,' Brooke repeated, sounding dumbfounded.

'Indeed. The loss of two sons has been an unimaginably devastating blow to my parents. I now find myself facing the heart-breaking prospect of organising one brother's funeral, which has already been delayed too long, and preparing myself to organise the other. This is a time for what's left of our family to try to find solace and mourn our loved ones. It's not a time for raising false hopes in the pursuit of some unsubstantiated wishful theory that can only cause more pain and suffering. Surely you must see that?'

'I can't believe what I'm hearing. How can you just make these assumptions?'

Samarth heaved a sigh. He got up from his chair and approached Brooke with an outstretched hand of sympathy. 'My brother found a fine woman. I sincerely admire your strength and resolve, Brooke. I urge you to find within yourself the strength to accept the truth that is glaring us all in the face. My brothers aren't coming back. You know that, don't you? Deep down you believe it as much as I do.'

'I don't believe it,' she said. There was a crack in her voice and the muscles of her face were tight.

'Help her to understand, Mr Hope,' Samarth said. 'Explain to her that with no ransom demand, this is no ordinary kidnapping.'

'It's no ordinary kidnapping,' Ben said. 'That much is true.'

Samarth clasped Brooke's hand. She bowed her head and

didn't try to snatch it away. He said gently, 'Listen to reason, my dear girl. Accept what you already know in your heart. Go back to England. Your home is there, not in India.'

Brooke was too shocked and choked up with emotion to reply, so Ben spoke for her. 'I understand how you feel, Mr Ray. You believe you're acting in the best interests of your family, and I respect that. But I'm not just here for the family. I'm here for Brooke, because she asked me to come. And I intend to remain here, with her, until we come through this. One way or another. Because where I come from, we don't start digging the grave until the body is pronounced dead.'

Samarth let go of Brooke's hand, stood straight and fixed Ben with a look of the utmost pain. 'Have you ever lost a brother?'

'A sister,' Ben said. 'Long ago. She was taken by human traffickers in Morocco, as a child. Vanished without a trace. It didn't take the authorities long to call off the search.'

'That's a very sad story. You have my sympathies.'

Ben nodded. 'It was a bad time. Ruth's disappearance and its aftermath tore my family apart. So trust me, I know what you're going through right now. I've been there.'

'Then you, of all people, must understand the need for my family to mourn our loved ones in peace and privacy.'

'I do understand,' Ben said. 'And I'm sorry for your troubles. I hope there are no hard feelings.'

'None,' Samarth replied. Ben put out his hand, and Samarth took it, and they shook for the second and last time.

'Just one thing you ought to know before I go,' Ben said.

Samarth asked, 'What's that?'

Ben said, 'I found my sister.'

Chapter 18

Back in the car, Brooke said, 'So what does he think happened? It's just a coincidence, and they're dead, there's nothing more to be done, no hope, and leave it at that?' Her anger against Samarth seemed to have driven all her earlier doubts and uncertainty from her mind.

'Don't be too hard on the guy,' Ben said. 'He's going through a lot. He looks pretty knackered. Which, incidentally, you do too.'

'At least I'm not rolling over and giving up so easily. Give me a cigarette, will you?'

'You don't smoke.'

'Now seems like a very good time to start.'

Ben shrugged and lit a Gauloise for her, then one for himself. She drew too hard on it, and coughed out a great cloud of smoke.

'Take it easy.'

Brooke puffed another cloud and waved the cigarette agitatedly, making little smoke circles in the air. Apparently she wasn't ready to take it easy just yet. 'So it seems I'm not considered a family member. Well, that's fine. Can we go back to the house, please? I've got a lot of packing to do.'

He took his eyes off the chaotic traffic to shoot her a quizzical glance. 'You're not leaving, are you?'

'Just because Samarth, the new self-appointed head of the family, said so? Get real. I'm staying right here. But I damn well won't be an unwelcome guest in that house another day. Soon as I'm packed, I'm booking into a hotel.'

'Let me help you sort yourself out. We'll go there together.'

She shook her head. 'Thanks, but I need to be by myself for a while, okay? This is really hard for me. Anyhow, I want to say goodbye to Esha before I go, and that's something I'd like to do alone.'

'No problem. I have another lead to check out.'

She was too distracted to ask what. 'Hang onto the car if you need it. I'll take a cab.'

They returned to the house in silence. The checkpoint guys were all smiles again, but Brooke was so lost in her thoughts that she barely seemed to register them. Ben rolled up the long driveway of the Ray residence and halted in front of the house.

'You sure you're okay?' he asked her as she opened her door.

'I'm fine. I'll call you from the hotel.'

She looked so sad and pale and forlorn that his heart went out to her, and he almost got out of the car to take her in his arms and kiss her. Instead he just nodded and drove off. In the mirror he saw her small, tense figure disappear inside the big house.

The quiet, leafy street was still just as empty as Ben drove away, the only other vehicle in sight being a domestic-brand light commercial van with painted-over side and rear windows, parked on the opposite kerb a little way up the road. Belonging to a tradesman, like a garden services firm or a plumbing contractor, come to service the fancy neighbourhood. Ben passed it and drove on in the direction of the food district.

When he got there, he parked up and walked along the busy main drag, merging with the crowds of people and taking in the smells. Hunger had finally caught up with him, and he stopped at a BBQ grill stand where two guys in aprons were doing a brisk trade in seekh kebabs whose mouth-watering aroma carried for fifty yards up and down the street. He watched as they prepared the mix of lean ground chicken and lamb with an eclectic blend of finely powdered pepper, cardamom, mace, nutmeg, turmeric, mint, chilli, coriander and ginger, kneading it all up with their hands. The kebabs were speared on iron skewers and spent ten minutes sizzling and spitting over the coals before Ben took his late lunch back to the car, picking up a bottle of Maharaja beer from another stand to wash it down with.

As he ate, he thought about Brooke and all the old feelings that had resurfaced since seeing her again. Then he put those thoughts to the back of his mind and took out his smartphone. It was time for some good old-fashioned detective work, chasing leads the hard way.

When Brooke had said earlier that they had nothing to go on, he'd insisted that wasn't so. Privately, he had to admit to himself that it was truer than he'd wanted to let her think. But since the trail seemed to lead back to Kabir and his mysterious discovery, however frail and tenuous that connection might seem right now, that was where Ben had decided to go looking. If it took him nowhere, he might have a problem. But he'd cross that bridge when he came to it.

In between bites of his kebabs, he ran an internet search on Captain Jabbar Dada, the police chief in Rakhigarhi, and called his office number. After some haggling with the staffer who insisted that the great man was much too busy to be disturbed, Ben was put through. He'd already decided that a straightforward, more or less honest approach was his best option. He thanked the captain for speaking to him and introduced himself as a friend of the Ray family and a private missing persons specialist from Europe, come to India to help locate the whereabouts of Kabir Ray.

'I understand that you suspected the attack on Kabir and his associates to have been the work of dacoits, local bandits. Is your department still operating on that theory?'

Dada was gruff and brisk in his manner at first, but lit up at the mention of bandits and seemed all too happy to talk about what was obviously his passion in life. He described himself as an 'encounter specialist', whose primary law enforcement priority was the total eradication of his province's serious problem with dacoits, the roving and heavily-armed criminal gangs who caused untold mayhem and suffering in Haryana and elsewhere. The way Dada described it, he made it sound like a full-scale war was going on. Ben soon formed the impression that the captain probably enjoyed his work a little too much.

'They are scum,' Dada grated down the line. 'They breed like rats, live in holes like rats and must be exterminated like rats. Nowhere in India is more rife with them than my province.'

With a certain pomposity he described to Ben how he'd been personally appointed by the Director General of Police himself to lead a special task force, which had been instrumental in taking down some of the largest criminal gangs in India during a countrywide police sting called Operation Bawaria in 2005. Since that time, Dada's unit had expanded both in size and achievements with hundreds of dead dacoits to its credit. In the captain's proud opinion, which he was happy to share, his men were the best-armed SWAT team in the country. The unit even possessed its very own police patrol helicopter, which was unique in India and a testament

112

to the stature of its commander. But for all their successes, Dada admitted frankly that his region's bandit problem had been anything but eradicated.

'It's even worse now. The dacoits are robbing banks, attacking farms and villages, raping and murdering as they please. Last year our district Congress Committee president was assassinated. It took me eight months to track the dacoits who carried out the killing. One by one, we ran them to ground, cornered them like animals and finished them.'

Listening, Ben wondered if the guy had the heads stuffed and mounted on the wall above his desk.

'Until all the dacoits are slaughtered down to the last man, the wave of crime will just get worse,' Dada said. 'Sadly, we are still a long way from achieving that goal. Many more innocent victims, like your clients' relative, will continue to suffer.'

'Is there any actual evidence that bandits carried out the attack?' Ben asked.

'The evidence was all over the crime scene,' Dada replied. 'I was there, Mr Hope. And what I saw was no different from what I have seen many times before. When you have dead bodies shot to pieces, and blood spattered on the rocks, and hundreds of bullet casings everywhere, you know you are looking at the work of dacoits. These cutthroats will murder anyone for any reason. I understand that Kabir Ray was a wealthy young man. He was probably carrying cash, or wearing an expensive watch. Even a pair of nice shoes will get you killed. There is no need for any other explanation for what happened to him.'

'Even though you never found a body.'

'These bandits have a way of making people simply disappear,' Dada said. 'As do wild predators. This is India, Mr Hope. It is a very different place from your country.'

'So I gather,' Ben said, thinking it was time to wind this down. 'I appreciate your talking to me, Captain. Sorry if I interrupted your day. Happy hunting.'

Ben took another bite of kebab, then went on with his internet search. This time he keyed in 'Professor Kabir Ray', and was led to the website of the Institute of Archaeology, the academic wing of the Archaeological Survey of India. Its address was the Officers' Mess building, Red Fort, New Delhi, and it offered two-year diploma courses in related fields like structural conservation, heritage and environment, epigraphy and numismatics, excavation and exploration, and museum management. The Department of Mysterious Secrets That Can Get You Killed or Kidnapped was disappointingly absent from the faculty site, but it was a reasonable start nonetheless. Ben noted down a contact number, called it and asked to speak to the Institute Director. After a short wait he was put through to a Professor Imran Gupta.

Ben repeated the same introduction that he'd used with Dada. 'Hello, my name is Ben Hope. I'm a friend of the Ray family, a private missing persons investigator based in Europe. I'm trying to locate the whereabouts of Kabir Ray.'

At the mention of Kabir's name the director sounded genuinely upset. 'Everyone here is in such a state of shock. Nothing like this has ever happened before.'

'I understand,' Ben said. 'I was hoping you might spare me a few minutes of your time.'

There was a pause on the line, as Gupta momentarily got his hopes up. He said, 'May I ask whether you are pursuing specific lines of enquiry, or clues, or whatever they're called in your profession? I mean, should we be optimistic about the chances of seeing our dear friend again?'

'It's really too early to say, Professor Gupta. I'm just

collating all the information I can for the moment. To that end, I was wondering if it'd be possible for me to come to speak to you, as well as anyone else at the Institute who knows Kabir well?'

'Everyone knows Kabir. He is the most popular member of staff we have ever had here.' The director was happy to do anything he could to assist, and readily agreed to a meeting that afternoon. Three thirty was the earliest he could manage, which meant Ben had no choice but to kill some time. He unhurriedly finished his kebabs, which tasted so good he went back to the grill stand and bought a couple more. With those and two Maharaja beers inside him, he fed the address of the Archaeology Institute into the Jaguar's sat nav and set off for an exploratory reconnaissance of his route.

His destination was to the north, in the crowded and dilapidated old part of the city that had once been the walled fortress-capital of the Mughal Empire, Shahjahanabad, until the days of the British Raj. As he was driving, his mind wandered back to Brooke. He was half expecting her to call him at any time to say she was on her way to a hotel and to arrange for him to meet her there later.

But that train of thought came to an abrupt halt when he spotted an old friend in his rear-view mirror. He said, 'Hello.'

The white Toyota was back.

Chapter 19

This time his followers were being much more brazenly obvious about their intentions, making no attempt at all to shadow him covertly. The car sat right on Ben's tail for a mile and a half through the traffic, coming up close enough for him to be able to clearly make out the shapes of the two guys sitting up front. There were another two in the back. None of the four appeared to be the giant hulk from Brooke's account of Amal's kidnappers. And since nobody inside the Toyota was doing much smiling, it was hard to tell whether any of them was missing any front teeth.

But that didn't rule out the possibility that the same guys were back looking for more. The Jaguar was easily traceable back to the Ray family. Which potentially added a whole and interesting new dimension to the situation.

What to do about it? The way Ben saw it, he had three choices. One, he could simply wait to see what happened. Which might be nothing, but from the way they were acting his instinct told him they were building up to making a move. Two, he could pre-empt them by screeching to an unexpected halt in their path, getting out of the car and confronting them, gun in hand. Which might go a number of ways, including scaring them off, or else maybe provoking them into doing something rash like shooting him to death in the middle of the street. Not the best idea. Or three, he could put his foot down and give them the slip. The five-litre Jaguar was plenty fast enough to get away from just about anyone.

Which Ben was seriously considering as his top option. There were just a couple of problems, however. Firstly, then he'd never get to find out who these people were or what they wanted, at least not until they caught up with him again. Secondly, the road congestion up ahead was thickening so much that the whole notion of escape might be about to become unfeasible.

A few moments later, his fears on that score were proved right. There was suddenly nowhere to go as the traffic flow ground to a halt amid a chorus of honking horns. Peering beyond the ocean of brake lights ahead of him, Ben could see why. A heavily laden delivery tuk-tuk had overturned on a busy street corner and shed its load of fruit and vegetables all over the road. A large crowd had gathered to watch as dozens of motorists got out of their vehicles, yelling abuse at the bewildered driver, who was gamely trying to stop enterprising passersby from helping themselves to all the free merchandise that was suddenly up for grabs. It looked as if a fight was about to break out over a crate of melons. Some of the more civic-minded onlookers were getting together to heave the capsized tuk-tuk back upright again, so the obstruction could be cleared and the traffic could start moving once more.

Unable to go any further until that happened, Ben came to a halt behind a barricade of stopped cars and trucks. The traffic ground to a stop around him. He glanced to his left and saw a dented, dirt-filmed yellow Peugeot taxicab pull up on that side of him. Then glanced to his right and saw a Kawasaki sports bike roll to a halt on the other. The rider was hunched low over the handlebars, impatiently blipping the throttle. He was carrying a male pillion passenger, perched high up on the bike's narrow tail. Both rider and pillion were wearing full-face helmets with black visors closed over their faces.

Then Ben looked in the rear-view mirror and saw that the white Toyota had drawn up close behind him, sitting virtually bumper to bumper and boxing him in from behind. He could see all four men inside staring at him as though he owed them money. Then the driver turned to his front passenger and nodded. A meaningful kind of nod, not in response to a conversational question, but very clearly a signal saying 'Okay, let's do it.' The passenger nodded back. Saying, 'Here we go, then.'

Even before it happened, Ben sensed what was coming next. And he was right. The white Toyota's front doors opened, left and right simultaneously, and the two guys in front started getting out. Then the rear doors swung open as well, and the other two guys in the back stepped from the car.

Unless they'd run out of petrol and elected to abandon their vehicle in the middle of the road, or decided they had time to saunter over to the nearest café for a drink and a bite before the traffic jam cleared, they obviously had a particular purpose in mind, one that involved him. And judging from the way all four men began approaching the Jaguar, Ben was pretty sure what that might be.

Ben thought *fuck it*, killed his engine, opened the door and stepped out into the oppressive heat and smell of the street. All four guys stopped and stared at him. The driver was wearing a loose flowery shirt that hung over his belly. His right hand slipped under the hem and came out clutching a black pistol. His eyes were locked right on Ben and his expression was deadly serious. The gun came up in a two-handed hold. His front-seat passenger and the two guys from the back did the same. Four weapons pointing directly Ben's way. Not much room for doubt.

In the next instant the doors of the yellow Peugeot taxi flew open and three more men scrambled out. Just as armed, just as intently focused on Ben, and just as serious-looking.

Not good.

Kabir's Browning was still nestling in Ben's waistband. But seven on one wasn't his idea of favourable odds in a gunfight, least of all in broad daylight in the middle of the street. So he moved fast away from the Jaguar and made for the kerb. To reach it he had to get past the motorcycle that had pulled up on his right. As he bolted towards the pavement the bike rider blipped his throttle and dumped his clutch, and the machine lurched forwards in a deliberate attempt to block his way. The front wheel caught Ben's leg a glancing blow and made him stumble, but he managed to stay on his feet and kept going. People in the crowd were noticing and reacting in alarm at the sight of the guns. A cry went up, spreading fast. In less than two seconds the whole street was erupting into chaos of a whole new kind as the overturned tuk-tuk and its spilled cargo were completely forgotten.

The four men from the white Toyota and the three from the taxi raced after Ben. The guy in the flowery shirt yelled out, 'Stop!'

But Ben had no intention of stopping. He made it to the kerbside and ran.

Chapter 20

The crowd scattered in panic as Ben pushed his way through, yelling 'Get out of the way! Get down!' If his seven pursuers opened fire a lot of innocent bystanders were going to get caught up in it.

The motorcycle that had rammed Ben's leg revved hard and mounted the kerb, ploughing frightened pedestrians aside as the rider came after him. A woman in a green silk dress screamed and only just managed to yank her small infant to safety. The rider braked sharply to avoid her, its front forks plunging against their stops, then surged onwards with a howl from its twin exhausts and charged across the fast-clearing pavement to cut off Ben's escape. The passenger dismounted from the pillion and blocked Ben's way as he ran.

Ben saw the gun in his gloved hand, and ran straight into him without slowing down, shouldering the guy hard in the chest and knocking him flying. The guy's helmet hit the pavement with a loud crack. Ben ran on, pulling out Kabir's Browning as he went. The bike rider gunned his machine and came on again, roaring straight towards him. Ben ducked aside to let it pass, then grabbed the rider by the belt of his motorcycle jacket and felt his arm stretch as the rider was yanked off his seat. The riderless motorcycle hurtled into a parked truck at the kerbside, caved its whole side in with a tremendous crash and toppled over.

Ben let go of the dismounted rider, who was too stunned to give him any more trouble. The seven men from the cars were another matter. They were in hot pursuit and Ben had no time for anything except to run.

Then the guy in the loose flowery shirt pulled out a cop badge and yelled, 'POLICE! STOP!'

The sight of the badge sent multiple thoughts spinning through Ben's mind, all at once. This was India. The badge could be a fake. These guys might not be cops at all. But if the badge was real and they actually were cops, he wasn't going to do the search for Amal any favours by getting into a running gun battle with them. Plus, they could shoot him dead in the street and nobody would blink twice.

Ben stopped running. He let go of Kabir's pistol drop from his hand. The cops closed around him. The one with the flowery shirt and the badge said, 'I'm Detective Rajiv Lamba, New Delhi Police. You're under arrest.'

As he said it, a pair of marked police patrol cars arrived on the scene and uniformed officers jumped out, instantly deferential to Lamba and his plain clothes colleagues. Maybe they were real cops, after all.

Ben said, 'For what? Not shooting at a bunch of guys trying to jump me? You have a strange way of conducting your business, Detective.'

One of Lamba's guys picked the Browning off the pavement, unloaded it and bundled the separate weapon, magazine and unchambered loose round into a plastic bag while another one frisked Ben for more firearms and took his passport, wallet, phone, cigarettes and lighter. Ben asked him, 'What do you think I'm going to do, set fire to you?'

Lamba said, 'Come with us, Mr Hope.'

They walked him back towards the cars. The motorcyclist and pillion passenger were back on their feet and had taken off their helmets, standing at the kerbside near their wrecked bike and the van it had ploughed into, whose owner had appeared and was arguing loudly with one of the uniformed cops. The capsized tuk-tuk was still lying on its side in the middle of the road, but the fruit and vegetables scattered around it were no longer the focus of attention for the crowd of bystanders, which had doubled in size as everyone stared in fascination at the police detaining the foreigner, probably a mass murderer or American intelligence agent caught spying. There was a lot of animated discussion and pointing and snapping of selfies with the arrest scene in the background.

Lamba sent one of his men to wave the onlookers away. Another clambered into the Jaguar, while Ben was herded into the back of the unmarked white Toyota with a detective either side of him. Lamba got in the driver's door, started the car and used his concealed flashing blues and a few whoops of his siren to force a path through the stopped traffic as he U-turned back the way they'd come. The same three guys who had emerged from the yellow taxi got back in, and the taxi fell in behind the Toyota with a marked patrol car bringing up the rear.

Ben asked, 'Anyone care to tell me what this is about? I have an appointment to keep this afternoon. I'd be very upset if I missed it.'

Nobody spoke. The detective who'd relieved Ben of his cigarettes took out the pack and offered them around to his buddies. Ben glowered at him. The guy threw back a smirky grin, lit up and puffed smoke in Ben's face.

Lamba drove in silence, and twenty minutes later they were arriving at a shabby, low-slung building with a bilingual

POLICE STATION sign above the doorway in English and Hindi. Lamba drove around the back, down a side street full of litter, and pulled into a compound with mesh security fencing and a motley collection of police vehicles. Lamba parked beside them, joined by the yellow taxi and the marked patrol car. He turned to Ben in the back seat and said, 'Let's go.'

Ben didn't particularly want to go anywhere with these guys, but for the moment he let things roll. The seven plain-clothes detectives and a couple of uniforms escorted him inside the building, which was as dishevelled and grubby on the inside as it was on the outside. So far he hadn't been handcuffed or read any rights. Which was interesting, as it meant they weren't properly arresting him. Not yet, at any rate.

Once inside the station the uniforms and four of the detectives drifted off. Lamba and the remaining two walked Ben down a series of corridors to a nondescript interview room and sat him down at a plastic table with four plastic chairs around it. The tabletop was bare apart from a plain card folder containing some papers. There was a single barred window, so dusty and cobwebbed that it was opaque. The room smelled of mildew and, faintly, of vomit.

Lamba motioned to the other detectives. One was ghoulish and reedy with a few strands of grey hair left on top, the other portly with the same kind of dyed black moustache and panda eyes as Prateek Prajapati. Lamba said, 'These are my colleagues, Detective Savarkar and Detective Agarwal. We have a few queries we would like you to answer for us.'

'Me too,' Ben said. 'Such as, what am I doing here? And when do I get my phone call? If I'm to be questioned I want a lawyer present.'

'There's no need for that,' Lamba said with a smile. 'This

123

is not a formal interrogation. We're all friends here. Aren't we, boys?' Savarkar and Agarwal responded with nasty grins. Lamba lowered himself into a chair across the table from Ben, picked up the card folder and opened it to sift through the paperwork, which was a mixture of handwritten notes and badly-photocopied official documents.

Then the questions began.

Chapter 21

Detective Lamba kicked off the interview. 'You entered this country shortly after ten thirty this morning, without a proper travel visa.'

Ben shook his head in amazement. 'Is that what this is about? Wowee, you people are on the ball. I've only just got off the plane.'

'That's not what this is about,' Lamba said, leaning back in his chair with his fingers laced over his belly. The butt of his pistol stuck out of his belt, like some TV hard guy he probably had thought looked cool. He reached out and tapped one of the handwritten sheets in front of him. 'According to my information, you represent the interests of the Ray family. That's what we'd like to discuss with you.'

'Then your information is as screwed up as your arrest procedures,' Ben said. 'I represent nobody. I'm here in India for personal reasons that are my own business and no one else's. And if I'm not under arrest I can get up and walk out of here any time I want.'

Savarkar, the reedy ghoul, said in a thick accent, 'We only want to talk to you. Nothing more.'

Ben replied, 'Is that why you've been following me all day, for a chat? That's a lot of unnecessary manpower to expend, when all you had to do was walk up to me and say hello.'

Lamba said, 'We were hoping we might get you alone. Simpler that way. The opportunity arose. Here we are. Now please tell us what your involvement is with Amal and Kabir Ray.'

Ben said, 'I don't think I'm under any obligation to tell you anything. But seeing as I'm a generous kind of person, I don't mind divulging that members of the family asked for my help. You might be aware of the recent incidents that have affected them.'

'Which family members?'

'Specifically, Amal's wife, Kabir's sister-in-law. And Amal's father, Basu Ray.'

Savarkar scribbled a note on a pad. Lamba asked, 'How well do you know Basu Ray?'

'Never met the man. Or Kabir. And I only just met the eldest brother, Samarth, for the first time today. I really only know Amal and Brooke.'

'The Englishwoman. You spent the morning together.'

'She's an old friend,' Ben said. 'Do you have a law against friends spending time together?'

'That depends on what they're up to,' Lamba said. 'So tell me, what kind of help were you asked to provide to the family?'

'To assist with the missing persons enquiry, in a private capacity. Apparently, local law enforcement have been doing a less than spectacular job of locating the where-abouts of the brothers, and of tracking down those responsible for the kidnap and the attack on Kabir and his associates.'

'Rakhigarhi is a long way from Delhi,' Lamba said. 'What happens there is technically outside of our jurisdiction.'

'Very convenient. All the more reason for bringing in an outside consultant.'

'That's what you are, a consultant?'

'I have some experience of finding people who aren't easily found. It's what I used to do, among other things.'

'Among what other things?' Lamba asked.

'I'm sure you've already checked out my past record, or the parts of it that flunkies at the lower pay grades are allowed to see.'

'You served with the British Army. Retired several years ago, rank of major, operational details not disclosed.'

'And if my former overlords in Her Majesty's Ministry of Defence don't feel bound to share that information, far be it from me to betray their trust.'

'Very well,' Lamba said. He glanced again at his hand-written notes. 'And now you own a business in France. What is this "Le Val"?'

'No secrets there,' Ben said. 'It's what it says on the label, a training facility where we teach guys like you how to do their jobs properly. You ought to think about signing up for a course or two. Maybe get a season ticket. God knows you need it.'

Detective Agarwal didn't much appreciate the dig. 'We're doing our job,' he said sourly.

'Not with any great degree of success, obviously. Or else you might have found Amal and Kabir Ray by now.'

Savarkar said in his impenetrable accent, 'You think you can do better? Doesn't look like it to me.'

'I'm just getting started,' Ben replied evenly. 'Or was, until you butted in and disrupted my schedule. I'm supposed to be meeting someone right now and you're making me look unprofessional by not turning up. I'll have to offer my sincere apologies on behalf of Delhi's finest.'

Lamba smiled. 'So, as a professional, what's your opinion on the chances of finding Amal and Kabir Ray? Optimistic?'

'Not pessimistic. In my experience, when someone kidnaps someone, there's always a way to find out who did it and where they've taken them. They might not be alive any longer, but that's a different story.'

'Sounds like you're pretty confident you can easily solve this case,' Savarkar said. 'Maybe that's because you already know who did it.'

Ben turned to him with a cold look. 'That would be news to me, Detective. But I'd be interested to know how you came to that conclusion.'

'A lot of these ex-military types end up drifting into things they shouldn't,' Savarkar replied with a noncommittal gesture. 'We see it all the time.'

'Do I detect a subtle whiff of accusation in there somewhere, or I am being paranoid?'

'Let's cut the crap, okay?' Lamba said. 'We have a pretty good idea that the disappearances of the Ray brothers aren't a coincidence. And we think we know why. We think you do, too.'

'I'm with you on the first part,' Ben said. 'But as for the second part, if I'm correct in assuming that we're talking "criminal activity", I hate to be the one to break it to you, but you're pissing on the wrong fencepost.'

Savarkar scowled. 'What is that supposed to mean?'

Ben said, 'It means you're making a fallacious judgment, officers. Or maybe you're just plain stupid. Let me see if I'm understanding this correctly. You believe that these two individuals, both with perfectly clean records, one a respected archaeology professor and the other an aspiring playwright who happens to live in another country, are, or were, involved with some sort of criminal associates here in India, of whom they've now fallen foul. Drugs being the top possibility for what they were up to, seeing as narcotics are at the root of the vast majority of organised crime. All of which adds up to the Ray brothers as being regarded more as suspects than as victims of wrongdoing. Right so far?'

Lamba said nothing but the look in his eyes as he gazed thoughtfully at Ben was answer enough. The other two exchanged glances.

Ben said, 'So my appearance in the middle of all this now has led you to regard me as a potential suspect, too. But you don't have anything to really base it on, other than some vague supposition that a guy with my background is probably involved in a lot of dirty dealings, everything from gun running to mercenary contracts, maybe some muscle work on the side, the odd hit here and there. Hence this little fishing expedition of yours. Am I still on the right track?'

Agarwal growled, 'You're in a lot more trouble than you think you are. We could charge you for possession of an illegal firearm, for a start.'

Ben said, 'And I could get onto my friend Mr Banerjee at the Indian Foreign Office and complain about the unlawful harassment of a British citizen. You snatch me off the street at gunpoint, now you're holding me without charge, refusing me the right to make a phone call or seek legal counsel, and making all kinds of defamatory accusations. You're way out of your depth.'

'Oh, we know how well connected the Rays are,' Lamba said.

Ben replied, 'And you obviously know that their influence in the right places is the reason I'm in the country without having gone through the official hoops to get a visa. Now two of them disappear in two unexplained incidents that might appear disconnected but most certainly aren't, one involving death and bullets, the other a kidnapping without a ransom demand. Strange, I grant you. You're not the only ones baffled and intrigued by it. But how you people choose to interpret the facts is to build a picture that casts the Rays as some kind of organised crime empire, like the Indian mafia. I'm guessing this is part of some agenda against them going back years. Maybe old Basu made some enemies coming up, and this is a chance for certain parties to get their own back by dragging his family name and reputation through the mud, or maybe even getting them into real trouble. I really don't care. But according to this theory, let's suppose that the crooked Ray brothers were involved in some turf war against a rival outfit. Next thing, they're taken out of the picture. Whereupon I suddenly turn up, out of the blue, magicked into the country under the radar. That pricked your ears up enough to put together a surveillance team. You've probably watched me coming and going from their gated estate, seen me driving around in their car. And you've been foaming at the mouth to find out, what's this guy doing for them? What's his role in this?'

Lamba just shrugged and said nothing.

Ben went on, 'And like a bunch of impatient children who sneak downstairs early on Christmas morning, you just couldn't wait to find out what Santa brought you. So now your way to crack the case is to lean on me, hoping I might incriminate myself. Or if you get really lucky, I might outright break down and confess to my crimes in the hope that you'll go easy on me.'

Lamba was silent. Savarkar was staring out of the opaque window. Agarwal seemed to have taken a sudden and intense interest in his fingernails.

'Which tells me that you guys must be desperate,' Ben

said. 'Because not only is bringing me in like this on a wing and a prayer the worst tactical move in the world, if I really was guilty, it positively screams that you've obviously got not a shred of evidence to back up your little fantasy scenario. If you had, you'd have got yourselves a search warrant and been all over the Ray family residence like a plague of locusts hoping to find their stashes of heroin and cocaine, and maybe a few large bundles of illicit cash that you could "confiscate".'

All three detectives remained quiet.

Ben said, 'This is why Prajapati, the private investigator, dropped the case and backed off. Because you people told him to. He was one of you, for thirty years. Probably owed someone a favour, or else someone had some dirty on him. You didn't want him poking around and getting in the way of what might turn out to be a major drugs bust. Worse still, taking credit for it.'

'We should be careful, boys,' Lamba said to his colleagues. 'It seems we're dealing with a superior intellect here.'

'A real genius,' Agarwal snarled. 'He's got it all figured out.'

'Not all of it,' Ben said. 'Not yet. I don't have much of a clue what Kabir and Amal Ray had got themselves into, or who stands to gain by targeting them. But I'd bet the bank it wasn't drugs, or anything remotely like it.'

'You sound very sure about that,' Lamba said.

'If you knew Amal, you'd laugh at the idea of him as a drugs kingpin. This is a guy who cries over a dead baby sparrow, won't have a gun in the house and can't drink caffeinated coffee. As for his brother, I've checked out his academic profile and believe me, it's pretty dull stuff. In short, Detectives, you're wasting your time. And mine, which is in short supply right now seeing as I've got at least one missing person to track down. So if you're not going to charge me, I think we're done here.'

The detectives finally relented. They had nothing to hold Ben on, and no option but to let him go. Lamba ungraciously handed him back his passport, wallet, phone, car keys, Zippo and what was left of his cigarette pack. Ben said, 'I'd like that pistol back, too. This city's a dangerous place. You never know when a bunch of trigger-happy amateurs might try and accost you in the street.'

'Don't push your luck, Mr Hope. And remember, we're watching you.'

'Watch and learn,' Ben said. 'And try to stay out of my way next time.'

Chapter 22

As he drove fast away from the police station, Ben called Professor Gupta at the Archaeology Institute to apologise for the delay and ask if they could reset their meeting. Gupta was running late himself, and happy to see Ben now. Ben hustled across the city and this time managed to reach his destination without incident. No more white Toyotas, fake taxicabs or motorcyclists with black visors shadowed his route. Or none that he could see. You could never really tell for certain.

Once the citadel and stronghold of the Mughal emperors, the Red Fort was an impressive sight, encompassing a complex of buildings and gardens spread over 250 acres and encircled with a red stone wall more than two kilometres in length and a hundred feet high, dotted all around with towers and domes and ramparts that dominated the skyline and dwarfed everything around it, glowing blood red under the hot sun. As Ben had pretty much expected, the seventeenth-century landmark was a magnet for tourists even this late in the season, and the busy car park was thronging with crowds, tour guides and pamphlet vendors. There was also a noticeable security presence. Ben recalled that the Red Fort had been the target of a terror attack about eighteen years earlier.

He parked beside a couple of military security forces trucks, and threaded his way through the press of tourists. Professor Gupta had arranged to meet him in the Officers' Mess building within the complex, so he bought a little map and guidebook from a kiosk to orientate himself. The usual no smoking signs were everywhere, so he lit up a Gauloise too.

He followed the crowds through the main entrance, a monumental red stone gateway that his guidebook informed him was Lahori Gate, from whose ramparts the Prime Minister made an address every August on Indian Independence Day. Ben noticed that the windows of the high towers flanking the gateway had been walled up in modern times, presumably to prevent an embarrassingly public assassination by sniper attack.

Lahori Gate led through to a vaulted arcade, the Chhatta Chowk or covered bazaar, which must once have been a splendid architectural sight but was now, in true Delhi style, tightly crammed with shops and stalls peddling souvenirs to tourists. Ben was walking briskly through the bazaar when a voice said, 'Hey, excuse me.'

Ben turned, expecting to be accosted by some do-gooder objecting to his cigarette. Or maybe he was about to be arrested again.

But the two thirtyish Indian guys who had stopped him definitely didn't look like do-gooders, and they weren't cops either. One was about Ben's height and build, in an open-fronted purple shirt with a thick gold chain around his neck. Slicked hair, blunt features, mirror shades hiding his eyes, an air of masculine confidence about him. The other was shorter and plumper, with a T-shirt featuring a muscled-up Sylvester Stallone brandishing an M60 machine gun. Both of them had unlit cigarettes dangling from the corners of their mouths. The taller guy said, 'We need a light.'

Ben said, 'I can see that.'

The taller guy said, 'Do you have one?'

Ben said, 'Yes, I have.'

The taller guy said, 'Do you think we could get one from you?'

Ben said, 'I don't know. Maybe you could, but you'd have to ask me first.'

'Could we have a light, please?'

Ben said, 'Certainly.' He took out his Zippo, thumbed the wheel, held it out for the taller guy to suck in the flame, then held it a little lower for his Rambo fan friend to do the same.

The taller guy said, 'Thanks, buddy.'

Ben said, 'You're welcome.'

His good deed done for the day, he moved on, finding his way about the complex. Beyond the bazaar were innumerable gardens and fountains, which like many of the damaged, decaying internal architecture and crumbling walkways were not all in pristine condition. It was as though the place had never fully recovered from being used as a garrison by the occupying forces of the British Army back in the days of the Raj. There was litter everywhere, so Ben didn't feel too bad about flicking away the stub of his cigarette. He used his map to head for the southernmost of the various palaces within the complex, the Mumtaz Mahal. According to the guidebook it had once been used as an officers' mess, and now housed the Red Fort Archaeological Museum and the headquarters of the Institute.

The palace was a white stone pavilion, built on a humbler and less opulent scale than most of the complex's other buildings. It was cool inside, with only a small handful of tourists drawn to view the museum exhibits from the Mughal Empire. Ben wandered from one gallery to another, keeping an eye out for the man he'd come to see while glancing at the collections of paintings, porcelain and jade, textiles, astronomical artefacts and furniture, like a spectacular marble chair used by Bahadur Shah II, the last Mughal emperor, who had been forcibly overthrown by the British, tried for treason right here in his own Red Fort and then exiled to die in Rangoon in British Burma. Another gallery housed an impressive collection of nineteenth-century weaponry used in the disastrously failed rebellion of 1857 against British commercial interests in India, which had spelled the formal end of the Mughal era and consolidated Britain's iron hold over its 'jewel in the crown'.

The days of the Raj may have been long gone, but its memory still cast a long shadow. Despite having spent a significant part of his younger days enthusiastically fighting for Queen and country, an older and wiser Ben was far from proud of his nation's historical legacy of brutal conquest and aggressive domination over much of the world. It was an internal conflict that he still struggled to reconcile.

No sign yet of Professor Gupta. Ben started glancing at his watch and hoping he hadn't wasted his time coming here. Just then, a dapper little white-haired man of around seventy in a khaki suit and red bow tie appeared as if out of nowhere, and greeted him with a melancholic smile.

'Mr Hope, I presume? I am Imran Gupta.'

Ben apologised again for the delay, and thanked the professor for sparing the time to talk to him. Out of courtesy, he felt it was appropriate to comment on the museum's impressive collection of artefacts. Gupta seemed pleased, but replied sadly, 'Unfortunately, however, what you see here is but a small fraction of the surviving treasures from the Mughal era. Many of the most beautiful and valuable pieces from that time, such as the Koh-I-Noor diamond, the jade wine cup of Shah Jahan, and the magnificent crown of Bahadur Shah II, were looted by our beloved colonial rulers, along with anything else they could steal. Over a century and a half later, the British government still refuses to return these priceless examples of our national heritage to their rightful place.'

Ben's guilt trip was evidently not over yet. He said, 'I hope you get them back one day.'

Gupta gave a weary smile. 'Not in my lifetime, I'm sure. But you came to talk about far more pressing matters than our national squabbles over history. Why don't we step into my office? This way, please.'

He led Ben through a door marked PRIVATE and down a corridor to a minute office that Ben at first thought must be a cupboard. The cramped space was stacked from floor to ceiling with a weight of books and files that threatened to bring down the ancient shelving units and bury Gupta's tiny desk in an avalanche of paper. There was little room for anything else, except two simple chairs.

Gupta sat primly behind his desk in one of them, invited Ben to sit in the other, and offered him a cup of tea. Ben accepted, just to be polite. Gupta rang a little bell, and moments later a shrivelled old woman who might well have dated back to the Mughal era herself hobbled in bearing a pot and two dainty porcelain cups on a tray. She set it down on the desk and hobbled away without a word.

Gupta ceremoniously poured the tea, took a sip and then said, 'Now, Mr Hope, I am at your service. Like everyone else here, faculty and students alike, I was devastated by the appalling incident at Rakhigarhi. Manish and Sai were such gifted and bright young souls. What a heart-breaking and tragic waste of life. I pray that the perpetrators can be brought to justice.'

'Manish and Sai were Kabir's companions on the trip?'

'They were two of his graduate students, who were closely involved in his research projects.'

Ben wondered if Kabir's research projects had anything to do with the cryptic secret that he'd confided to Amal before the incident. Wanting to broach the subject as delicately as possible he said, 'Professor, perhaps you can enlighten me. I understand that the location of the attack is very out of the way, so much so that Kabir flew there by helicopter. But I'm not clear as to exactly what they were doing in that area.'

Gupta sipped more tea and replied, 'That's a good question. In fact, Mr Hope, the precise details of his trip's purpose were something that Kabir was keeping rather hush-hush between himself and his assistants.'

Ben was surprised. 'He didn't tell you? His boss?'

Gupta shook his head sadly. 'Kabir is . . . was . . . dear me, I never know whether to refer to him in the past or present tense. This is so awful.'

'Let's keep it positive until we know more,' Ben said.

'Very well. Thank you. As I was saying, Kabir is very much his own person. In any case I have never regarded myself as his superior, more as a kind of mentor. I know he would have fully informed me, when he felt the time was right. But I do have a good idea why he chose to visit that particular location. Its proximity to the major archaeological excavations at Rakhigarhi, only a few miles away, strongly suggests that his interest in the site was connected with his interest in the lost Indus Valley Civilisation. I can think of no other reason why he would have travelled out to such a remote and inaccessible spot.'

'The Indus Valley Civilisation?' Ben repeated. His abandoned theology studies had taught him some scraps of knowledge about ancient history, ancient peoples and cultures, but he'd never heard of this one.

'Kabir's passion,' Gupta replied. 'You might say, his obsession. He has devoted his entire career to the subject, and staked his professional reputation on his research findings. You would be surprised what a hotly-contested area of archaeology it has become. Even I am flabbergasted at how much debate and controversy the study of a long-lost Bronze Age civilisation can generate, several thousand years after the fact.'

Hotly-contested debate and controversy sounded like the stuff that secrets were made of. Ben had caught a trace of a scent here, and wanted to know more. 'Perhaps you could enlighten me a little?'

Gupta said, 'I can do better than that. Would you like to see Kabir's work for yourself?'

Chapter 23

Gupta led Ben from his office and down a narrow passage. He stopped at a door with a nameplate marked PROF. K. RAY. For a moment he seemed about to knock before entering, then caught himself, and his wiry shoulders sagged with grief. Sighing loudly he pulled a jangling ring of keys from his pocket, found the right one and unlocked the door. Ben followed him inside Kabir's office.

The room was about twice the size of Gupta's own, but the array of computer equipment it contained could have comfortably filled a space twice as big again. Wires trailed all over the floor and every inch of horizontal surface was covered with screens and monitors.

'Nothing has been touched since Kabir disappeared,' Gupta said. 'It remains exactly as he left it. Some men collect motor cars, others are greedy simply for money. Kabir's passion is for accumulating knowledge, and all of it is right here in this room. So is almost every single computer that the Institute possesses. Kabir commandeered them for his own use, as he had so much data to crunch.'

'So what was this Indus Valley Civilisation?' Ben asked.

'Everyone has heard of the legendary ancient cultures of China, Egypt and Mesopotamia,' Gupta said. 'And yet so few know of arguably the greatest and most widespread early civilisation of them all, which thrived across a vast area of what are now India, Pakistan and Afghanistan between three and five thousand years ago.'

'Forgive my ignorance,' Ben said.

'It's perfectly understandable,' Gupta explained patiently, 'considering how very little is known about the Indus Valley Civilisation. It is in fact one of archaeology's greatest mysteries, its very existence having completely eluded scholars until its chance discovery in the nineteenth century, when a deserter from the British Army, a man named Charles Masson, happened to stumble across some ancient ruins while wandering through the remote parts of the Northwest Frontier not controlled by the empire. At first he thought he had discovered the remains of a brick castle, but on further exploration realised he had found the remnants of a lost city that stretched for twenty-five miles, an incredible discovery. Even then, no excavations were attempted until many years later, in 1921. Only recently have archaeologists realised the sheer scale of the mysterious civilisation that once occupied the Indus Valley, stretching over an area of some one and a half million square miles from the great mountains in the north, to the alluvial plains of the Indus and Ganges rivers, to the tropical rainforest of the Malabar Coast.'

Gupta stepped over to one of the computers. 'You will have to excuse me, as I'm not as adept as my younger colleagues with modern technology.' He turned on a monitor, and its screen flashed into life with an image of a map of India and neighbouring Pakistan, as they had looked three thousand years before Christ. The inscriptions on the map were all in Hindi. Gupta reached for a mouse and began pointing the cursor arrow here and there over the screen as he went on excitedly, now quite taken with his subject.

'The first major finds were the lost cities of Harappa and Mohenjo-Daro, which after the post-war partition of India in 1947 fell into the territory of Pakistan. For many years it was believed that these two sites represented the most important centres of the Indus Valley Civilisation, or the IVC, for short. This of course was cause for much frustration for Indian archaeologists, given the unhappy state of tension that has long existed between our two countries. How unfortunate that politics should enter into the pursuit of knowledge.' He shook his head regretfully. 'However, as more and more sites were discovered and the true size of the culture began to emerge, that situation changed dramatically. Today, of 1022 IVC cities known, 406 are situated in Pakistan and the remaining 616 here in India, though fewer than a hundred have yet been fully excavated. You can imagine the enormity of such a project.'

Ben agreed that he could, although he was beginning to wonder where this was going. The professor, just like every academic he had ever come across, was in danger of nattering on all day without revealing anything of practical interest. Ben decided to give it a few more minutes before he pressed him on.

Gupta closed that window and opened up a menu of picture files, which he scrolled through before selecting a file marked RAKHIGARHI and clicking it. The screen flashed up an image of a barren, featureless rubble field that, to Ben's untrained eye, looked like the aftermath of a massive earthquake. Gupta explained that this was the excavation site at Rakhigarhi in the Hisar district of Haryana, some hundred and fifty miles from Delhi and about twenty miles south of the scene of the attack on Kabir and his associates.

'When the ruins were first discovered, they were thought to be a relatively minor find. But what began as a small-scale excavation project might now turn out to be far more signif-icant. Its sheer size has led some archaeologists to speculate that Rakhigarhi might even have been the capital city of the entire Indus Valley culture. If that's correct, well, it's just incredible.'

Gupta stood marvelling at the incredible rubble field, obviously able to see a lot there that Ben couldn't. Then he closed that image file and opened up another one that couldn't have been more different. It was a panoramic scene of an ancient city. Except this one, instead of being levelled to a ruin of broken rocks with barely a tower standing, was totally intact and appeared to be a thriving, bustling, indus-trious metropolis of many thousands of inhabitants. By pressing left and right arrow keys, the professor was able to pan the image across the screen to give a full 360-degree rotating view. The city seemed to stretch in all directions as far as the eye could see. 'Impressive, isn't it?' he said proudly.

'It looks as if it had been built yesterday,' Ben said, surprised.

'That's because it's not real. This is Kabir's computer simulation of what the IVC city at Rakhigarhi might have looked like some four thousand years ago, based on what's been uncovered there and similar finds elsewhere. You can clearly see the grid plan on which the Indus Valley architects designed the layout of the streets and buildings, much like a modern city, set out in blocks with distinct residential neighbourhoods, commercial centres, parks and recreation areas. They devised elaborate drainage and sewer systems employing underground pipes. Many houses had running water. Even the baked mud bricks from which their cities were built were manufactured according to a standard system of weights and measures, using a 1:2:4 ratio that is quite unlike any found in Mesopotamia or Egypt. The same remarkable degree of sophistication is reflected in the quality and craftsmanship of the countless items of pottery and art objects and even children's toys that have been recovered from these sites. This was definitely no primitive culture, as you can see.'

As he gazed at the screen, Ben was trying hard to imagine what was here that Kabir could have cryptically confided to Amal. The trace of a scent that he had picked up on earlier on seemed to be fading fast. Maybe he'd wasted his time coming here after all.

He said, 'You said there was a lot of controversy and hotly-contested debate around this Indus Valley Civilisation research. It seems that an awful lot is known about it. Where's the mystery?'

Gupta turned away from the computer screen to look at Ben. 'Indeed we know a good deal, and are learning more all the time. But that is only a tantalising fragment that has captured the imaginations of every specialist in the world. Kabir being one of them. He has for some years now been one of the leading lights in the quest to discover the secrets of this lost culture. And believe me, there are many secrets, which remain incredibly resistant to our understanding to this day.'

Ben wanted to fish for all the secrets he could get. He said, 'Give me an example.'

While Ben and Gupta were continuing their discussion inside Kabir's office at the Archaeology Institute, a separate conversation was going on elsewhere. Separate, but very closely related. It was a three-way merged phone call between two groups of men, each inside a separate vehicle in a different part of the city, and a third party who was the overall boss of the operation and calling from a base elsewhere.

One vehicle was a black Mahindra four-wheel-drive, India's answer to a Jeep Cherokee or a Honda CR-V. It was parked not far away from a silver Jaguar that its occupants had been following that morning, doing a better job than the inept cops who'd temporarily interrupted things earlier that day. Four men inside, one of them being the leader of the crew, phone in hand. He reported, 'He's still in there.'

The other vehicle was a rusty, dirty Tata Motors light commercial truck with side and rear windows painted over except for a few deliberate scratches that allowed a view out. Like the Mahindra, there were four men inside, and the driver was on the phone as his three passengers watched the driveway entrance across the quiet, leafy street within the upmarket neighbourhood where their target lived. The driver of the van waited until his crew leader in the black Mahindra had finished speaking. He was much more afraid of him than he was of the third party. After a deferential pause he said, 'No movement here either. She's still in the house.'

The third party listened to both reports in turn, then replied, 'Stay on both of them and let me know if anything changes.'

The crew leader in the black Mahindra asked, 'So when do we move on the guy?'

The third party replied, 'When the time is right. Not a moment before.'

The crew leader in the black Mahindra asked, 'When's that?'

The third party said, 'When I tell you. Then you can do whatever you want to him. String him up by the ankles and make Bihari kebabs out of him. What do I care? As long as he's out of the way.'

The crew leader smiled and said, 'That's what we like to

hear. Because we're not patient people. And all this waiting around shit, that's not what we do.'

The third party said, 'It's what you're getting paid for. Until I give the word, you do exactly as I say, understood? No mistakes this time. When Hope leaves, you follow him. Do not allow him to see you. I want to know where he goes next.'

'And the woman?'

'She's part of the deal too, as agreed,' the third party said. 'But same terms apply. Only when the time is right.'

'Better be soon.'

'Relax, Takshak,' the third party said. 'You won't be waiting around much longer.'

Chapter 24

Gupta thought about Ben's question for a moment, then replied, 'What makes the Indus Valley people so mysterious? All right, consider this. Here is a magnificent and, for its time, incredibly advanced society that flourished and spread at a phenomenal pace for a thousand years or more to become greater in scope than the mighty kingdoms of Egypt and China. Yet, by around 1700 BC, it was falling into sudden and catastrophic decline. Why?'

Ben said, 'You're the professor. You tell me.'

Gupta explained, 'The answer is one that's been eluding archaeologists and historians ever since the Indus Valley Civilisation was discovered. They weren't overthrown or invaded by a rival neighbour, as so many other cultures in history were. Rather, their decline appears to have been an internal one, occurring over a remarkably compressed period of time.'

'Meaning it happened quickly.'

'And radically. Later examples of their arts and crafts show a dramatic lowering of sophistication and quality of workmanship. Their houses during this declining period were less carefully built and have survived less well than earlier ones. Even their traditional standards of weights and measures seem to have been abandoned, so that builders resorted to using whatever rough materials were at hand. The examples of complex street planning that had been the culture's hallmark become less and less common as it moves into its later phase.'

Ben asked, 'And is this what Kabir was investigating?'

Gupta said, 'It's what everyone's investigating. Every specialist in ancient archaeology wants to know what happened to these people. It's as if they simply didn't care any more, as if all their drive and energy had drained away and they were no longer prepared to make the effort. Like a kind of collective apathy or depression that was contagious throughout the whole culture, and from which they never recovered. Eventually, predictably, they simply died out. And while many archaeologists have offered speculative reasons why, nobody knows for sure how such a long-established and widespread society could have simply disappeared, its very existence known to us only by chance.'

'Okay,' Ben conceded. 'So that's a mystery.' He asked himself what relevance it could have to a modern-day kidnapper or killer, however. Answer: none in the slightest that he could see.

Gupta nodded. 'Certainly a mystery, though by no means the most baffling. Even when the Indus Valley Civilisation was at its peak, it was an enigma. They don't seem to have temples or deities the way every other ancient culture does. There are no statues honouring the gods, no monuments of worship, nothing that teaches us about their religious traditions. Likewise, nothing about their architecture reveals a sense of social hierarchy in the way we would expect, with palaces for the ruling elite, bigger, better homes for the wealthier members of the society and smaller, humbler dwellings for the poorer citizens. Their social structure seems to have been strangely egalitarian, apparently able to organise itself without formal rulers or a class system. How did they govern themselves? What were their laws, their beliefs, their values, their traditions? We simply don't know.'

Gupta shook his head in amazement, and went on. 'Nor has any IVC excavation to date revealed evidence of forts, castles or military installations, which again is extremely unusual, virtually unique in fact. While experts have been able to devote entire careers to studying the weaponry, armour, military organisation and battle tactics of historical civilisations all throughout the ancient world, we are yet to find as much as a bronze spear or sword among the excavations of IVC ruins. Were they a completely peaceful society, depending on no army to defend their territory? If so, how did such a spread-out and apparently defenceless civilisation manage to maintain the integrity of its borders for so long, in an age where marauding invaders were continually chasing conquest after conquest all across Asia? Once again, one person's guess is as good as another. And on it goes. Almost everything about these people remains a puzzle, and will remain so until we decipher their language. Because that, Mr Hope, is the biggest mystery of all.'

Ben was on more familiar ground now, as he cast his mind back to his theology studies and all the ancient languages that scholars had been able to translate and understand for centuries, like Persian cuneiform, Babylonian script and ancient Egyptian hieroglyphs. He said, 'That strikes me as pretty weird. What's so different about their language that it can't be understood?'

Gupta smiled. 'If there's a Rosetta Stone waiting to be discovered that could give us the key to understanding the Indus script, we haven't found it yet. It's the last of the ancient languages to be understood. And so far, incredibly, it defeats all attempts to decipher it. The archaeologist who cracked the code would instantly become a superstar within the profession. And that was what Kabir was trying to do. In fact it was the main focus of his work.'

Gupta turned and swept an arm around the piles of equipment that filled the room. 'This is why he needed all this computer power, to build a modelling system that would help him to unravel the secrets of the Indus script. Four hundred different symbols generates a bewildering number of possible combinations, all of which needed to be analysed and cross-referenced in order to tease out their meaning. Let me show you.'

He walked over to another desk, turned on another computer and within a couple of moments Ben found himself looking at a screen showing a sequence of strange symbol markings, arranged in a row of eight. They were nothing like Egyptian hieroglyphics, or any other language script Ben had ever seen, not that he was any kind of expert. One symbol crudely resembled a flower, or a child's drawing of one. Another looked like a crooked wagon wheel with six radial spokes, and another brought back a childhood memory of the brass tongs that his mother had used to put logs on the fire, in the rambling old Hope family home in the Cambridgeshire countryside, a million lifetimes ago.

Gupta said, 'These are just a small sample of the Indus script glyphs. So far we have identified over four hundred different symbols, which appear on the large number of clay tablets, seals, pots and other objects excavated from IVC sites. Many of them are totally obscure, like these. Others represent animals, such as elephants, bulls, rhinos, and some creature that looks like a unicorn. Generally speaking, the symbols bear little or no resemblance to any used by other ancient cultures. Scholars can't even fully agree on whether the writing flows from left to right, like English and all the other European writing systems derived from Latin and Greek, or whether it's meant to be read from right to left like Hebrew, Arabic or Urdu.'

Gupta went on, 'That's not the only puzzle. The very way the symbols are arranged remains a mystery. While most types of writing feature blocks of text, sometimes long ones conveying a lot of information, everything from legal contracts to epic poems, the Indus symbols never appear in a single line longer than fourteen characters long, the average being more like five. These abbreviated lines have led some scholars to believe that the Indus symbols don't constitute a linguistic script at all, that is to say, they're not really a language but instead just a kind of symbol graffiti. Kabir was firmly opposed to this idea, maintaining that the Indus script was not only a real, proper language, but a fully developed and highly sophisticated one that we just hadn't yet learned to understand.' Gupta affectionately patted the computer monitor, as though he was rewarding a child or a well-trained dog. 'Thanks to the computer model that he developed with his graduate students, he was very close to proving his theory right. In fact, he believed he was just a few steps away from cracking the code entirely. That caused a lot of controversy, even furious anger, in some quarters.'

Ben, who was listening to all this and remembering why he'd never been able to appreciate the joys of palaeography, or the study of ancient writing, suddenly felt his ears prick up. 'Anger?'

'Oh, you would be amazed how these matters that appear so dull and lacking in relevance to the modern world can cause tempers to flare in our closed little academic community. A lot of people become very worked up, and exchanges between rival debaters can get quite abusive. It might seem strange, but it's really quite easy to understand why. As I said before, whoever finally managed to decipher the Indus script would become one of the most famous and celebrated archaeologists of all time. A superstar, a veritable hero. They would be like the future astronomer who discovers intelligent life in another solar system, or the physicist who finds a way to deliver cheap nuclear fusion power to the electrical grid, or the engineer who creates a car that runs on water. To us, it would be no less revolutionary. But in so doing, they would potentially kindle a lot of ill feeling among their peers.'

Ben said, 'Out of jealousy, because they didn't discover it first?'

'That would be the motivation for some. For others, it would be that they were deeply embarrassed and humiliated, having committed themselves publicly to the opinion that the Indus script wasn't a genuine language, only to be proved completely wrong. Even worse, all the peer-reviewed articles and doctoral theses and research papers on which they'd built their academic reputation would become obsolete overnight and their contribution to our discipline would be consigned to the dustbin. In short, for there to be a winner, there must also be a loser. In this case, a good many losers.'

Ben was sniffing the scent again, and this time it seemed to be getting stronger. Because the more powerful the negative emotions someone's work could stir up, no matter how petty and trivial the whole thing might seem to outsiders, the higher the possibility of that negativity, anger and resentment tipping over into physical actions. The idea of squabbling scholars hiring gunmen to take out their academic rivals seemed crazy. But this was a crazy world.

He asked Gupta, 'And what kind of ill feeling did Kabir spark off with his computer model?'

Gupta replied, 'He mentioned to me that, not long after

he published some of his initial findings, a few months ago, he received some very unpleasant anonymous emails.'

Ben asked, 'Did he show you these emails?'

Gupta shook his head. 'No, I believe he deleted them as soon as he received them.'

'Maybe he described their content to you?'

'He only said that his research had rattled some cages, so to speak, and that there were some nasty, spiteful little minds out there. Those were his words. "Nasty, spiteful little minds." I don't think that he took it terribly seriously. The hacking was a much more troubling matter.'

Ben's ears pricked up a little more. 'Hacking?'

Gupta nodded. 'It happened twice. First, around the time of the anonymous emails. Then again more recently, perhaps five weeks ago.'

Five weeks ago was just a couple of weeks before Kabir and his associates were attacked. Ben said, 'Tell me more about it.'

Chapter 25

Gupta said, 'It seems that some unknown individual, presumably motivated by the kind of professional ill-will that I described earlier, attempted to infiltrate the computer model, with the intention of infecting Kabir's data files with some malicious virus. I gather that there are different kinds, some designed to provide access to the files from outside—'

Ben said, 'Spyware. Or rootkits.'

'—and others that can cause havoc, delete entire programs and render the whole system inoperable. It seems this was one of those. Someone apparently wanted to ruin his Indus script research. Fortunately, after the first incident Kabir had taken the precaution of backing everything up on another server, protected by . . . what are those things called? Walls of fire.'

'Firewalls.'

'Yes, of course. As I told you, I'm hopelessly ignorant when it comes to all this high technology. The young ones are so much more knowledgeable.'

Ben didn't consider himself too much of an expert either. He belonged to a generation that had managed just fine growing up without computers, and as adults neither entirely trusted nor liked them. But he still had to live in the modern world, and he had some basic understanding of how these things worked. He asked, 'Did Kabir have any idea who tried to hack into his research? If he could have found out their IP address, from there he could have managed to trace where the attack was coming from, and taken the appropriate action.'

Gupta looked blank. 'No, no, I don't think so. I really couldn't say.' Then his face turned a shade paler as it dawned on him what Ben was thinking. 'But surely you're not suggesting that someone within the archaeology community could have . . . I mean, academic rivalry is one thing, but—'

'I have it from a reliable source that Kabir was holding onto a secret. Most likely, from what I can tell based on limited information, it was connected to his archaeology work. I'm guessing that his helpers, Manish and Sai, must have been in on the secret too, but to my knowledge Kabir told only one other person outside his immediate circle of trusted associates. That person is now in a great deal of trouble. Is that a coincidence?'

Gupta swallowed hard. 'A secret of what kind?'

'Specifically, to do with a discovery he'd made. He was very excited about it. Said it was something hugely important. That's all the detail I have. Before, I thought perhaps it was something physical he'd found, or dug up, since that's what field archaeologists do. Now we're having this conversation I'm wondering if it was something else. Not physical, but information-based. Had he cracked the Indus script code?'

'I'm certain that he would have told me if he had,' Gupta said. 'I can't believe he would have kept something that important from me. We talked about it so many times. I was his mentor right from the start of the project, even though I couldn't keep pace with his methodology.'

'You said Kabir was his own person. Independent-minded.

You also said he was keeping quiet about why he travelled to the Rakhigarhi area. So he didn't always keep you abreast of everything he did.'

'That's true,' Gupta admitted.

'At least, not right away,' Ben said. 'Maybe he was planning on telling you later. Maybe he needed to confirm something, before he could be totally sure.'

'I don't see what that would have been. But it's possible.'

'Isn't it also possible that someone else found out first, before Kabir got around to telling you? Maybe the same person who'd sent him the antagonistic emails? Perhaps the same someone who'd already tried twice to hack into his computer model, not just to access the information but to infect it with some kind of malware that would mess up the whole system. Someone obviously paying very close attention to his every move. What if that person was so intent on destroying Kabir's research that they'd resort to the ultimate extreme?'

Gupta stared at Ben in disbelief. 'Do you really think this could be so?'

Ben replied, 'You'd need to ask the engineer who really did invent a car that runs on water. Except you couldn't ask him, because he's dead. Someone murdered him. Guess why.'

Gupta turned a shade paler. 'Dear me. Oh dear me. I had never realised—'

Ben said, 'People hurt and kill one another for the slightest of reasons, Professor. Take it from me. And if someone was trying to threaten Kabir's work, that's a lead I'd very much like to investigate further. If we knew who had sent the emails or tried to hack his computers, it would be an important first step.'

Gupta began chewing his lip and wringing his hands in agitation. 'I really have no idea. I don't suppose that Kabir found out. If he did, he never mentioned it. But Haani might. Yes, now that is an idea. You should speak with him.'

Ben asked, 'Who's Haani?'

'Haani Bhandarkar.' Gupta spelled it, and Ben wrote the name in his pad while Gupta explained, 'Another of Kabir's graduate students who worked as his assistant, along with Manish and Sai. Haani helped him set up the cyber-security measures against further hacking attacks. He had also accompanied Kabir on several archaeology field trips in the past, and would have gone with them that day if he had not sprained his ankle in a kabaddi match a week before.'

Ben knew that kabaddi was one of India's most popular sports, a rough-and-tumble team contest that was a more violent version of the tag games schoolkids used to play at break-time. Like rugby, but without a ball. 'Lucky for him. Where can I find Haani? Here at the Institute?'

Gupta shook his head and replied, 'I haven't seen him since . . . since the incident. He was as profoundly shocked by what happened as the rest of us. Even more so.' He thought for a moment, then added, 'I might have his home address in my office. Strictly speaking, I shouldn't divulge personal information, but under the circumstances . . .'

'I would appreciate that very much, Professor.'

Gupta locked up Kabir's office and led the way back down the corridor to his own. Ben stood by the desk and waited and watched as the professor spent several minutes rooting through drawers crammed with paperwork, gave up and then switched his search to a battered filing cabinet in the corner.

'Here it is,' he said eventually, pulling out a file, which he laid on the desk and flipped through until he found a dog-eared sheet of paper that was Haani Bhandarkar's enrolment form as a student at the Institute. Clipped to the top left corner of the sheet was a passport-sized photo of a young Indian guy. He was a good-looking kid. Probably popular with the girls. His raven-black hair was longish and unkempt and he had a devil-may-care, F-you kind of look in his eyes. Attitude. The date of birth on the form made him twenty-two years old. Below that were filled out an address in Delhi, a mobile number and an email contact. Ben copied them down in his notebook. Gupta started giving him directions to get there, but Ben cut him off and said, 'I'll find it.'

He thanked the professor for his help, and left. He checked his phone as he retraced his steps back towards the car, and saw that Brooke hadn't called him, meaning she must still be at the house, packing her stuff and saying her goodbyes to Esha. Which gave Ben some more time to kill before he had to meet her at the hotel; and now he had a good use to put it to. He worked his way through the tourist throng, got back to the car, jumped in, stabbed Haani Bhandarkar's address into the sat nav, and took off in a hurry.

In too much of a hurry to notice the black Mahindra SUV leaving the Red Fort car park at the same time he did, and slipping into the traffic several cars behind him.

The same black Mahindra SUV that had arrived just after he had, with four men inside. Of whom the pair in the front seats were the same two who had stopped Ben in the Chhatta Chowk bazaar earlier and asked him for a light.

The guy with the Rambo tee was driving, with the taller man in the open-necked purple shirt next to him. Though the taller one wasn't the biggest man in the SUV, by a margin of several inches. The back-seat passenger behind him was a hulking monster of a man, closer to seven feet than six, so wide that he took up most of the rear bench and so heavy that he made the suspension of the vehicle creak and list when he got in. As usual, the hulk was sitting in silence. It wasn't his job to talk.

Squeezed up next to the hulk, his back-seat companion with the swarthy complexion and the bulging eyes was just as quiet, because he was too preoccupied with his missing upper front tooth and bruised lip to say much. He spent a lot of time thinking about the bitch who'd punched him in the mouth. And about what he'd have loved to do to her by way of revenge.

The guy behind the wheel glanced at the taller man in the front passenger seat and said, 'What are you thinking, Takshak?'

'I'm thinking the man we're working for is full of shit, for a start,' the one called Takshak replied. 'Fuck him. I don't trust him, never have. And I'm done obeying orders like a dog. It's going to be time to start doing this our way. Just like we planned all along. We're taking over.'

'Then what do we do? You want to hit this Hope guy now?'

The one called Takshak replied, 'We will. And the Ray bitch, too. But it has to be done right. We have other priorities, remember. So for the moment, we just follow him and see where he leads us. Like the boss said.'

'I thought you just said the boss was full of shit.'

'He is. But we might have some more loose ends of our own to tie up before we can put our plan into action. Which means we need to follow this guy for the moment. Careful, though. Stay right back. Don't let him spot us. He's a smart one.'

The driver looked worried. 'And now we let him see our faces. I don't know if that was a good idea.'

'I wanted to get the measure of him,' Takshak said. 'Up close and personal. See what kind of man I'm up against.'

'So now you got the measure of him, what do you think?'

'I think if he's really a friend of the Rays, they've got more interesting friends than I thought.'

'He looks like a soldier. Ex-British Army kind of guy.'

'Maybe,' Takshak said.

'They've got some serious black ops ninja kinds of hard cases. You think he's one of those? Looked that way to me.'

'Maybe,' Takshak said again.

'The kind of guys who can fuck you up in a heartbeat. Slash your throat wide open, shove their arm down deep inside right up to the elbow and rip your guts out in their bare fist before you even see them coming. Right?'

'Wrong,' Takshak said. 'That's the kind of guy I am.'

Chapter 26

After days with no direct human contact whatsoever, trapped in a hostile captive environment with zero hope of escape and total uncertainty as to what might lie in store, even the strongest mind starts to fall apart like an unravelling jumper. Amal had been married to a hostage psychology expert long enough to have picked up some scattered bits of knowledge about what it felt like to undergo one of the worst mental tortures a person can be subjected to. But when Brooke talked about her work with victims suffering from post-abduction trauma it was just an impartial glimpse of another world, one that Amal considered totally separate from his own. Why would he, in a million years, ever imagine for the slightest moment that he would one day end up living the nightmare for real himself?

And yet, here he was.

Nobody had hurt him, and he was being reasonably well looked after. But from early on in his incarceration he'd become terrified that that could change at any moment. His cell door would burst open and two or three or four masked men with guns were going to come trampling down those steps and grab him, hold him down and start pressing information out of him. He remembered how easily they'd physically overpowered him the night of the kidnap. They were tough, brutal men. They'd use harsh methods to make him talk. No possible way he could withstand them.

You promised, Amal kept telling himself. *You gave your word to Kabir that you wouldn't give away his secret.*

Yeah, I know I did, would come the reply from inside his head. *But Kabir's probably dead. I'm not going to help him by keeping his secret. I'm only going to end up dead, too.*

To which he'd counter-reply to himself, *A promise is a promise. Even if Kabir really is dead. Even if they kill you, too. Don't die a coward.*

Then: *Who am I kidding? I'm just a softy, a nerd, a writer. I'm not a hero. Not like some people I know. Not like . . .* Searching for an example . . . *Not like Ben Hope. He wouldn't let these bastards break him. But what chance do I have of holding out? And what's the point?*

Then: *Fine. Then spill the beans and let yourself be remembered as a weakling who blabbed his guts out because he was too afraid.*

Torture. Mutilation. Waterboarding. Beatings with a rubber hose. Electrocution. A whole chamber of horrors kept crowding his thoughts. It wasn't easy, being brave and resolute.

It was on the third day – as best he could tell, given how hard it was to keep track of time – that the interrogation had begun. But it was nothing like Amal had imagined. It was almost worse. The door stayed shut. Nobody came down the steps to hurt him.

Instead, the voice began to talk to him.

It came from hidden speakers overhead, mesh-covered holes in the ceiling that he hadn't noticed until the first time he heard it. It invaded every square inch of space inside the cellar, enveloping him, filling his ears, impossible to shut out, deep and reverberating and infinitely malevolent. So calm and yet so menacing. Its tones were distorted through some kind of electronic masking device that twisted and scrambled the sound frequencies to a sinister effect that made his flesh crawl with horror. Like a demon's voice talking to him. Amal would soon come to live in constant dread of hearing it again. And he did, day after day.

There was no predicting when the next session of questioning would begin. It could come at any time. But the questions themselves were always the same ones, over and over. And here they came again now, booming at him from the walls, threatening and terrible, making him want to fall to his knees and pound his face and rip out his hair.

The spine-chilling voice began with the same opening line as always.

ARE YOU READY TO TELL ME WHAT YOU KNOW, AMAL?

'I know nothing!' he yelled back at the walls. The same answer he always yelled back, until he was hoarse with repeating it. 'How many times do I have to tell you? Why can't you let me go? Please! Just let me go!'

THE TRUTH WILL SET YOU FREE, AMAL. TELL ME WHAT YOU KNOW, AND THIS WILL ALL BE OVER.

Then the crux. The question at the heart of all the others. The reason why these faceless people were holding him prisoner in this hellhole.

WHAT DID YOUR BROTHER FIND?

Amal screamed, 'For the millionth time, damn you, I don't know what Kabir found! I swear to you he didn't tell me a single thing about it!'

DON'T LIE TO ME. OR YOU WILL NEVER LEAVE THIS PLACE. DO YOU UNDERSTAND? NEVER.

'Why can't you believe me? All he told me was that he'd found something, but he didn't say what. If I knew, I'd tell you. But I can't! He's just an archaeologist, for God's sake! A teacher! What could he have found that matters so much to you anyway?'

WHERE IS IT?

'I don't know what you're talking about!'

WHERE IS IT?

'I don't *knooooowww!!!*' Amal bellowed back at the walls. 'If I don't even know *what* the hell it is, then how can I possibly know *where* the hell it is?'

How long could he go on lying to them? How much worse was he making things for himself by holding back the truth? Even more frightening was the thought that if he continued giving them nothing, they might start believing him. Then they would have no further reason for keeping him alive. That door at the top of the steps would suddenly swing open, his captors would come down inside the basement – perhaps one of them would be the owner of the awful demon voice, Amal would never know – and they'd put a gun to his head and murder him.

The voice was silent for a few moments, as though the monstrous creature it belonged to was contemplating another approach. Then it spoke again.

WE HAVE YOUR WIFE, AMAL.

The words hit Amal like a tremor that swept his legs out from under him. He fell to his knees. Stared up at the ceiling. The pair of square mesh-covered holes stared back at him like two eyes in a huge blank face, inscrutable, merciless. He tried to open his mouth to say something, but all that came out was a gasp.

DID YOU THINK WE'D JUST HAVE LET HER GO? SHE'S RIGHT HERE.

'Prove it!' Amal shouted. His voice was cracked with desperation. 'Let me speak to her!'

SHE CAN HEAR YOU. BUT SHE CAN'T TALK.

'Don't you hurt her! You can't!'

NO? I THINK I CAN. I CAN DO ANYTHING I WANT.

'Please! I'm begging you not to harm her!'

THAT DEPENDS ON YOU. ARE YOU READY TO START TELLING ME THE TRUTH?

Amal was drenched with cold sweat. His hands were shaking uncontrollably and his heart was fluttering. He bowed his head and closed his eyes and tried to breathe steadily. He couldn't. He felt as if he was about to throw up. The conversation he'd had that night with Kabir now came flooding through his mind again, replaying like a flashback. He heard his own voice, filled with the amazement that had been his reaction when Kabir had let him in on his secret.

'Are you serious, Kabir? Buried treasure? It's like something out of Robert Louis Stevenson. X marks the spot, and all that stuff. You're not winding me up?'

And Kabir's voice on the other end of the line, long distance from Delhi to London, a little crackly and faraway, but the excitement in his tone coming through as sharp and clear as if they'd been in the same room together talking face to face. *'I'm totally serious, Bro. This is huge. Massive. Monumental. It's everything I ever dreamed of. The culmination of years and years of work.'*

'And you actually found it?'

'As good as, near enough. It's just sitting there waiting for us to dig it up and bring it home. Might need more than a single helicopter load, though.'

'Bloody hell, that's incredible. It's awesome. How much value are we talking about? Millions?'

Kabir had laughed. 'Hey, why not? Millions, billions, zillions. Dollars, not rupees. All the money in the world.'

'It's a bad line, Kabir. You're breaking up.'

'Hold on. Let me step out onto the balcony. That better?'

'Much better.'

'What was I saying?'

'About all these millions and billions you're about to get hold of.'

Kabir had replied, 'It's not really about the money, though. We're talking about human knowledge, you know? Cracking a mystery whose secrets have been hidden away for thousands of years. We had no idea, Amal. I mean, we just didn't have a clue about these people and what might be lying buried under our feet. And now we will. Can you believe that? It's so fucking exciting, I can't wait to get there.'

'When do you leave for Rakhigarhi?'

'Four days from now. All packed and ready to roll.'

'I'm blown away. This is amazing, Kabir.'

'But you have to promise to keep quiet for now, okay? Not a word to anyone. There are people who'd kill to know what I know. Seriously.'

At the time, Amal had thought his brother was joking. It wasn't until soon afterwards, when Kabir had disappeared, that those words would come back to haunt him.

'Whatever you say. But keep me posted, won't you?'

'Of course I will. Talk soon, Amal.'

'Take care, Kabir. Call me when you get home again.'

The flashback ended. Amal opened his eyes and found himself back in his nightmare, kneeling there on the floor with his world in pieces. They had Brooke. Nothing else could possibly matter any more.

The game was over. Time to start telling them the truth.

Utterly spent and defeated, he slowly raised his head to look up at the ceiling. The speaker holes continued gazing down at him, as though waiting for him to speak.

His voice was just a croak. 'Kabir found treasure. Lots

166

of it. Ancient. Priceless. Worth millions, billions, who knows?'

I'M LISTENING, AMAL.

'If I tell you everything I know, you'll let her go? You promise?'

TRUST ME, AMAL. NOW TALK.

Chapter 27

The neighbourhood where Haani Bhandarkar lived was a far cry from the living standards of the Ray family. Ben hacked northwards across Delhi to find himself in a teeming residential area that rivalled pretty much any of the war-torn and desperately deprived urban communities he'd encountered on his military travels and since. He passed endless slum colonies that consisted of makeshift shanty dwellings made of cardboard and tin, straw and mud. Drove through streets where huddled shapes of beggars and homeless people, many of them pitifully disabled and malnourished, lined every step and doorway, sharing space with the rotting litter that lay piled knee-high against the buildings and the human effluent that ran thick down the gutters, mixed with that of goats and mules and rats.

Even for someone who'd been to the places Ben had been and seen the things he'd seen, the depth and scale of the poverty were breathtaking. The inevitable consequence of cramming more than 37,000 people into every square kilometre of a sprawling slum hellhole with no facilities, no clean water and, for those fit and able enough to scrape it together, an average monthly income that equated to about eighty euros.

Haani's apartment building was far enough from the

worst of the slum to be habitable, but that was about it. It was one of several haphazardly-constructed multi-storey blocks crammed like factory farms, with jutting balconies everywhere covered in washing and garbage and a criss-crossed confusion of electrical wires overhanging the fume-choked tumult of the street below. One of the buildings had listed at an angle and was leaning up against its neighbour like a drunk. People were still living in it.

Ben left the car, with no idea whether it would still be there when he returned. After checking the address one last time he entered the apartment building. It was still upright, for the moment at least.

Haani lived on the top floor. Ben wouldn't have used the lift, even if there had been one. Forget air conditioning. The heat seemed to get worse as he made his way up the creaking stairwell. He could smell cooking and damp and decay. He could hear babies crying, angry people arguing, televisions blaring, the loud music of radios and boom boxes blending together into a welter of meaningless sound. There was a dead dog on the first-floor landing. On the third floor a wizened old woman in a headscarf peeped out of her door as Ben passed by, and quickly shut it again.

It was a little quieter on the top floor. Five identical doors were spaced out in a row along a narrow landing, each one crudely marked with a hand-painted number in white paint. Ben checked his notebook for the apartment number. Haani's door was the one at the far end. He paused for a moment to think about what he was going to say, then knocked twice.

His knuckles made a hollow sound on the door. It was a rudimentary item, not well made. Two sheets of cheap, low-grade plywood nailed together either side of a framework of cheap, low-grade lumber, and filled mostly with air,

169

along with probably some sawdust. It was as flimsy and fragile as it was a poor sound insulator. When there was no response to his knock, Ben pressed one ear to the door and covered the other ear with his hand to block out the ambient noise of the apartment building. He could have detected a mouse scampering about inside the room, but he could hear nothing.

He rapped on the door again, loud enough to be authoritative without being menacing, still pressing his ear to the door. Still heard nothing. Nobody home. He thought, *damn it*, stepped away from the door and pondered what to do next. Maybe it had been a mistake not to call before turning up here. He took out his phone and dialled the mobile number he'd copied from Haani's student enrolment form. He put the phone to his ear and heard it ringing.

Inside the apartment. Just the other side of the flimsy door. The amplified resonant buzz that a mobile phone set on vibrate mode makes when lying on a tabletop. So either Haani had gone out and left his phone at home, or he was there behind the door and not answering.

Ben took a step back towards the door and heard another sound from inside. Not the scampering of a mouse, but something not dissimilar. It was the sound of someone stepping quickly, lightly, furtively across the room to turn off their phone in case the person outside the door could hear it ringing. As if there could have been any doubt.

The ringing stopped. Ben turned off his own phone, slipped it back into his pocket, moved closer to the door and called out, 'Haani Bhandarkar? Is that you in there?'

No reply.

'My name's Hope, Ben Hope. I'm a friend of Kabir.' Which latter statement wasn't strictly true, except in the broadest sense, intended to reassure. But it didn't seem to

170

make Haani want to open the door. Ben could sense his presence in there, visualise him standing stock still just a few steps away, frozen by uncertainty as to whether to open up or not. His anxiety was so palpably crackling with nervous energy that it felt to Ben like an electrical static field penetrating the flimsy wood of the door. What was he so afraid of?

'I'm working for Kabir's family,' Ben said through the door, making his voice sound relaxed and amiable. 'I've come here from the Institute, where I was speaking to Professor Gupta. He told me about the Indus Valley script research, and the computer hacking, and how you helped Kabir with the antivirus protection and firewalls. That's what I'd like to talk to you about. It'd be a lot easier if you let me in.'

Still no response from the other side. Ben was losing patience. It wouldn't take much force to open the door. It could be secured with deadlocks and bolts and all the hardware in the world, but a lock could only be as strong as the wood it was screwed to.

Ben said a little more firmly, 'Haani, it's really important that I speak with you. This isn't just about Kabir, it's about his brother Amal too. Ignoring me isn't going to make me go away. Please, open up.'

There was no answer from inside the apartment.

'Haani, I can hear you breathing in there,' Ben said. 'Last chance. I'll count to three and then I'm coming in, okay?'

Haani didn't reply.

Ben counted 'One.'

No response.

Ben counted 'Two.'

Silence from inside.

Ben counted 'Three.' And took a step back from the door,

171

and kicked it in with the sole of his boot planted just below the handle, putting all his weight behind the impact. The door gave way with a splintering crack and flew open, banging hard against the inside wall. Ben stepped quickly into the room. The tiny apartment was dark, with the blind drawn over the single window, and smelled of curry and human sweat. Furnishings were minimal, though clearly not for stylistic reasons. There was a kitchen area crammed into one corner, sink piled with dirty dishes, a small table with a single wooden stool pulled up to it. Just one inner door leading off the main room.

But no Haani.

For a second, Ben thought the guy must have clambered out of the window, maybe hopped over to the neighbouring balcony and managed to make his escape. He stepped over to it and yanked the cord to roll up the blind, and saw that was impossible. No balcony. The window was barred on the outside. Great idea, if the building should ever happen to go up in flames, which seemed a distinct possibility judging by the state of the electrical wires hanging like ghost ship rigging over the street.

But that didn't answer the question of where Haani was, except that he must still be inside the apartment. There were two interior doors. One was closed, the other open enough for Ben to see that it led into a rudimentary bathroom not much larger than a cupboard, with a stained toilet bowl, cracked mirror and grimy shower cubicle, and that it was empty. He turned towards the one that was closed.

Before he could open it, the door burst open to reveal a tiny, rumpled bedroom. And suddenly there was Haani Bhandarkar. He looked like his passport-sized photo. A good-looking kid. Probably popular with the girls. Longish, unkempt raven-black hair. That was where the similarity

172

ended, because in the photo Haani hadn't been plastered with sweat and looking as though he was about to faint with pure terror.

And in the photo, he hadn't been holding a nine-millimetre Browning handgun almost identical to the one the police detectives had confiscated earlier that day. This one was pointed at Ben's face.

Chapter 28

Ben had long ago lost count of the number of times he'd had a gun pointed at him. All kinds of people had threatened him that way. Some of them had been experienced combatants, some bumbling amateurs. Some had been supremely confident in their abilities, others had been scared shitless. Ben had so far survived such encounters, but he was well aware that the day might come when he wouldn't. And in his experience a very frightened assailant was just as dangerous and likely to shoot you as someone calm and unemotional. Perhaps even more dangerous, because they weren't in control of their reflexes. Haani's right index finger was inside the trigger guard and Ben could see the nail and the flesh around it turning white as it stacked up pressure on the trigger.

But Haani was no professional, and where amateurs invariably fell down in these circumstances was from having only seen actors pointing guns in movies. As he came bursting out of the bedroom with the pistol aimed in Ben's face he was making the classic mistake of holding it out at full stretch, too close to his opponent.

Which for Ben made it a simple, more or less risk-free matter of twisting the weapon right out of Haani's grip. If he'd wanted to be nasty he could have trapped Haani's right

174

index finger inside the loop of the trigger guard and used the leverage to snap it like a twig. But Ben wasn't interested in hurting the guy, only in saving his own skin.

So less than a second later, the gun was in Ben's right hand, retracted close to his torso where it couldn't be snatched and now pointing in the opposite direction, with nobody having been shot and lying bleeding on the floor. A happy outcome for both of them. With his left hand Ben motioned towards a worn armchair by the window. He said, 'Let's start over, okay? Sit down, calm yourself and talk to me.'

Haani was panting as though he'd done a hundred-metre sprint. His face was ashen with fear and the raven-black hair was stuck to his damp forehead. His eyes gleamed as they flicked up and down, at Ben, then at the gun, then back up at Ben. 'You're going to kill me. You're one of them.'

'Haani, if I had any intention of killing you, you'd have been dead before you got up this morning. Now sit.'

Haani gulped hard and very slowly backed away three steps until the backs of his legs touched against the chair, still not taking his eyes off Ben or the gun. He lowered himself into the chair, sitting rigidly upright, blinking and sweating. 'Okay, if you're not going to kill me, then what do you want?'

Ben stepped over to the kitchen area, grabbed the wooden stool and carried it over so he could sit opposite the window. There was really no need to keep the gun pointed at Haani as though he was any kind of a threat. Ben thumbed on the safety catch and cradled the weapon in his lap with his finger outside the trigger guard. Now that the situation had calmed, he was able to give the pistol another glance or two. It really did bear a striking resemblance to the one that had belonged to Kabir, which Brooke had borrowed from his bedside drawer and given to Ben, and which was currently in the possession of the New Delhi police. The piece he was holding now was similarly old and scuffed, but well maintained and smelling of fresh oil. Ben popped the magazine out from the hollow of the pistol grip. Fully loaded, thirteen rounds, nine-millimetre full metal jackets, the cartridges manufactured by the Indian government's Ordnance Factory Board. Not available to civilians.

The exact same model of pistol as Kabir's, in the exact same condition as Kabir's, loaded with the exact same military ammo as Kabir's.

An interesting coincidence.

Ben replied to Haani, 'I already told you what I want. Information. Nothing more, nothing less. Apparently, you didn't believe me.'

'About Kabir's computers?'

'More precisely, about who might have tried to hack into them.'

Haani said, 'And you really spoke to Professor Gupta?'

'Unless the man with whom I had a pleasant and informative conversation earlier today was an impostor.'

Haani pursed his lips and said after a beat, 'So you're not one of the bad guys?'

'Is that who you were expecting to show up at your door?'

'They murdered my friends.'

'And now you thought they were coming after you.'

Haani nodded.

'Hence the gun.'

'A guy has to protect himself,' Haani said.

'Is that why you gave one to Kabir? For self-protection?'

Haani blanched a little, like a child caught out in a lie. 'How did you know it was mine?'

'Not one, but two Browning nine-mils. That's a lot of hardware for an archaeology student.'

'They were a matched pair. My father's. He was a sergeant in the army.'

'Does your father know you're running around with loaded guns?'

'He's dead. Died two years ago of a heart attack.'

'That's a shame,' Ben said. 'Just like it's a shame that Kabir didn't take the threat seriously enough to carry it with him that day. Or things might have gone differently for the three of them.'

'Tell me about it.'

'So are you ready to trust me now?' Ben asked.

But Haani still wasn't sure. 'You could be tricking me. How do I know you didn't hurt Professor Gupta, beat the information out of him or something, and now you're going to hurt me too?'

Ben said, 'You want to call him and ask how he is? He's worried about you. Says he hasn't seen you around lately.'

'What else did he tell you?'

'That you couldn't go on the helicopter trip because you sprained your ankle in a kabaddi match. I'd have thought a young guy who plays rough sports like that could have handled himself a little better just now. If I really had been a bad guy, you wouldn't have stood a chance.'

Seeing that Haani still wasn't fully convinced, Ben popped the gun's magazine, quickly shelled out its contents, then jacked out the extra one in the chamber and slipped all fourteen rounds of loose ammunition into his pocket for safekeeping. Then he replaced the magazine and tossed the unloaded weapon over to Haani. 'There you go. Now I'm not armed any more. You can have the ammo back when we're finished talking.'

177

'This could be another trick,' Haani said. 'A bad guy would be carrying a gun of his own. Or a knife.'

'Give me a break, Haani. You want to frisk me for concealed weapons, then go ahead. I won't stop you.'

Haani seemed to think about it, then relented. 'That's okay.' He toyed with the empty gun, looking more reassured. 'So maybe you're not a bad guy. Then who are you?'

Ben said, 'I'm the bloke who's been called in to find the men who killed your friends. Who maybe killed Kabir too, and almost certainly abducted his brother Amal.'

'I don't know him. He lives in Britain, right? That's the connection. You're British. Are you a cop?'

'Half Irish,' Ben said. 'And no, I'm not a cop. I used to be a soldier, like your father. And the connection is Amal's wife. She's the one who called me in.'

'Kabir said his brother had married this seriously hot British chick.'

'She's an old friend of mine,' Ben said. 'From before she knew him.' He wondered why he'd felt the need to add that part.

'Oh.' Haani paused, reflecting. Then asked, 'What do you mean by "maybe killed Kabir"? You think he might still be alive?'

'I don't know,' Ben said. 'That's one of the things I'd like to find out. Along with the whereabouts of Amal and the identity of the people who did these things.'

'What are you going to do when you find them?'

'I'm going to teach them the error of their ways,' Ben said. 'But first I need your help. Because you seem to have some answers to the questions I need to ask.'

Haani nodded. Fully on board now.

Ben said, 'Okay, first and most obvious question. Who are the bad guys here?'

Haani replied, 'I told you. The same murdering bastards who killed Sai and Manish, and probably Kabir too. You want names or something? How am I supposed to know that?'

Ben said, 'Okay. Next question. Who hacked Kabir's computers at the Institute?'

Haani seemed momentarily puzzled by Ben's line of questioning. Then he recovered and said with a note of pride, '*Tried* to hack. We stopped them, thanks to the shitload of security software I uploaded to the system for him.'

'Did you manage to trace the source?'

'Nah, man. I spent ages trying, but they covered their tracks pretty well. It could have been anybody from a rival archaeologist here in Delhi to some snotty-nosed teenager in Tokyo or Seoul working off a laptop in his bedroom.'

Ben had been hoping for a more positive answer. He was disappointed, but it wasn't the end of the world. 'What about the anonymous emails Kabir received before that?'

'What about them?' Haani replied, looking mystified by the questions he was being asked.

'Didn't you see them?' Ben said.

'No, he deleted them as soon as they came in,' Haani replied. The same thing Imran Gupta had said. Which, again, was not the answer Ben had been hoping for. And this time it *was* a step closer to the end of the world. The threatening anonymous emails were an important potential key to understanding who was attacking Kabir's work, and Haani Bhandarkar was the only person left who might have been able to shed light on them.

'Even if you didn't see them,' Ben said, 'you might have some idea who sent them. Even just a suspicion. Kabir must have said something.'

Haani shook his head. 'None. I knew he got a bunch of

weird emails, but he never said much, and I can't tell you any more than that.'

Perplexed, Ben asked, 'So if you didn't know what threats had been made against Kabir, why did you feel it was necessary to lend him a gun for self-protection?'

'Because of what he found,' Haani replied with a frown. 'Why else?'

'I know what he found,' Ben said, irritably because he was getting confused by Haani's strange answers. 'The key to decoding the Indus Valley script. That's what this whole thing is about. Kabir was on the verge of going public with these big important revelations that were set to make him famous and piss a lot of people off, and someone was desperate to block him. First the anonymous emails, meant to intimidate him. Then when those didn't work, the two hacking attempts intended to scrub all his data. Then when that didn't work either, the enemy switched to a more radical approach. It became full-on war, against Kabir and anyone else who knew about his research.'

Haani was staring at Ben with a growing look of bewilderment on his face. 'Oh man, is that what you think this is about? Because if you do, you're totally way, way, *way* off the track. You have no clue. That's not what this is about at all. Not even close.'

Ben stared back at him, even more bewildered. 'It's not?'

Haani shook his head emphatically. 'Kabir was still months away from decoding the Indus Valley script. He might never have even got to the end of that project, it was so complex and difficult. What he found was something totally different. Something much, much bigger. *That's* why I gave him the gun.'

Chapter 29

Ben sat and listened as Haani Bhandarkar now told him the story of how he'd been there when a chance discovery had turned into the luckiest, and at the same time the unluckiest, find of Kabir Ray's life.

'It was a few months ago, back in late April. The first and only time I ever went with him to the Rakhigarhi area. Manish and Sai were there too, all our gear packed into Kabir's helicopter for the trip. See, Kabir was one of those archaeologists who believed that the Rakhigarhi site was the most important IVC city that had ever been found. Which meant that its ruins must be buried under a huge area of land, so he was into the idea of making lots of small exploratory digs across a wide area all around the main site, to test how far the city's boundaries might have spread.'

Ben said, 'Okay. Go on.'

'We were in the middle of this rocky wilderness miles to the north of the primary dig when we stumbled on a cavern. They're everywhere. It was dark, stank like hell of rats and dead things. Just the kind of nasty place Kabir loved checking out. So in we went, hunting for the usual bits of ancient stuff that anyone else would think were just garbage. And that's where we found it. Or should I say, found him.'

'Found who?'

181

'Well, there wasn't much left of the poor guy,' Haani said, and his gaze took on a faraway look as though he was revisualising the grisly discovery. 'He was all curled up deep inside the cavern, as if he'd crawled in there to die. Just a skeleton, covered in a few tattered bits of clothing. There was a bullet hole in his skull big enough to poke your thumb through. At first we all thought, shit, someone's been murdered, we'd better call the cops. But then we realised the police wouldn't be much bothered about him, because he'd been lying there long enough to become an archaeological relic himself. Just another forgotten corpse from long ago. But there were four clues to suggest who he was, where he'd come from and what he was doing there. The first was a leather Sam Browne belt wrapped around his body. It was mostly rotted away and eaten by the rats, but there was enough left to tell that it was the kind that the British Army used to issue to their troops, back in the days of the Raj. It even had some big old cartridges left in the ammunition pouches, the type they made for the single-shot rifles they had then.'

'Martini-Henrys,' Ben said. 'The gun that helped carve out the wonderful empire for us.'

'And on his belt he was still wearing an empty bayonet scabbard for the same kind of rifle. There were lots of former British soldiers roaming colonial India in those days. Some had ended their military service, others had just gone AWOL. Like Charles Masson, the army deserter who discovered the ruins of Harappa.'

'Gupta told me about him,' Ben said, to save unnecessary explanation.

'Whoever shot our guy, bandits or hostile tribesmen, probably took his gun and bayonet, but they didn't take everything. The other three clues told us exactly where he'd been and what he'd been doing since he quit the army. He'd

182

been carrying them wrapped up inside a metal waterproof box. The robbers had broken it open, probably thinking there was money inside, but when they saw it was just a bunch of books they left them alone.'

'Books? Is that what this is about?'

'Not the books, what was in them. They were a set of three leather-bound journals, like diaries. The leather was all mouldy on the outside, and rodents and mildew had ruined a few pages and the handwriting was faded, but the rest was pretty well preserved. The guy had written his name on the inside cover of each of the three volumes.'

So this was about the dead man himself, as much as anything else. Ben said, 'Okay, who was he?'

'He was called Marmaduke Trafford. Definitely an Englishman, with a name like that. He'd been keeping the journal for years, highly detailed and painstaking, with dates and maps and drawings. Like a travelogue of all the uncharted corners and wild frontiers of India that he'd visited between 1829 and 1840, when he made his last entry.'

'Fine, but what was the huge discovery?'

'We didn't realise about it, until after we took the journals back to our camp down the hillside and looked at them more closely. We spent half that night reading Trafford's accounts of the places he'd explored, learning local languages and customs, getting into scrapes with hostile tribespeople, man-eating tigers, poisonous snakes. Really cool stuff. He was something of an amateur archaeologist, too, collecting artefacts and hunting for ancient lost cities. He might have been inspired by Charles Masson, who was already famous by then for his discoveries. It was pretty amazing. But then, we came to the really awesome part. Halfway through the second of the three journals, in an entry dated 1839, he talked about how he'd found this piece of clay tablet covered in weird script, like nothing he'd ever seen before. He knew it was really old, but couldn't figure out what the writing meant. He copied some of the characters into his journal.'

'Indus script?'

'You got it. I mean, nothing else looks like it. It's uniquely different from any of the other known ancient languages.'

'I've already heard that lecture,' Ben said.

'Listen, okay? Not long afterwards, travelling through Haryana, Trafford had a bad fall in the mountains and was injured. He'd have died if he hadn't been rescued by members of a remote outer Himalayan mountain tribe, who took him back to their village and nurtured him back to health.'

'This is all in the journals?'

'In so much detail that when you read it, it's like you're there yourself, living it with him. He spent the winter there, recuperating, making friends among the tribe and learning to communicate with them, finding out about their history and such. According to Trafford they had this whole legend about a past civilisation they called "the Old Ones", which has got to be a reference to the Indus Valley people.'

'Does it? That sounds like you're making a big leap of logic.'

Haani shook his head. 'I might have been, except for one piece of evidence that clinches it totally beyond doubt. Think about why Trafford had to spend a whole winter learning their language. After years of travelling around India, meeting so many different tribes, you'd have thought he would have been familiar enough with them all to have been able to pick up a dialectic variation quite easily. But this tribe spoke a language different from any he'd come across before. It didn't just sound different, it used a whole totally

184

different form of written alphabet. See where I'm heading with this?'

'You're telling me that the tribe spoke the old Indus language.'

'Something derived from it, at any rate. Trafford might never have made the connection, if he hadn't shown them the weird clay tablet he'd found, and realised they could understand the writing on it pretty well. Maybe this tribe were descended from the last remnants of the culture, and had retained the language. Of course, that got Kabir seriously excited, because if Trafford had learned the meanings of the undeciphered ancient Indus symbols and written them in his journals it could have given us the key to unlock the whole thing. His work would have been complete.'

'And did it?'

'If he figured out the translations for the symbols, he never wrote them down. Or if he did, they were lost. Which was a huge blow to Kabir. He'd have been heartbroken, except for one major compensation.'

'Which was?'

Haani's eyes were full of anticipation, as though he was coming to the best part of his story and savouring it. 'Well, you see, one of the old legends they told Trafford was kind of special. It was the tale of a lost treasure.'

Chapter 30

Ben said, 'Now this is beginning to sound as if you're telling me something.'

Haani explained. 'According to their folklore, the treasure was associated with these same ancient people they called the Old Ones. It wasn't clear what shape it took, only that it had been lost aeons ago. Naturally, Trafford was eager to know more about it. With their help he was able to draw a rough map of the treasure's supposed location, way down the mountain in a huge rocky valley. Some adventurous villagers had tried and failed to find it through the centuries. It had become part of their tribal myth and legend, like the Holy Grail is to Christian tradition. Trafford decided that if anyone could find it, he could. As soon as the winter snows cleared, he set off on his journey. Turned out to be his last.'

Ben said, 'I'm presuming that he never found what he was looking for.'

'If he did, he never got the chance to record it for posterity. More likely he was killed while he was still hunting for it. But he got close.'

Ben thought for a moment. 'How far north of Rakhigarhi did you find Trafford's remains?'

'Twenty-two miles, give or take.'

'About two miles from the location Kabir was scouting when the attack took place.'

Haani nodded.

'Which suggests that Kabir was searching for the same treasure.'

Haani nodded again. 'You bet that's what he was looking for. Trafford's journals changed everything. Kabir became so fired up about them, he even put his Indus script project on ice to put everything he had into this instead. And I mean everything. He was in the process of arranging his own private excavations. It was going to cost him a hundred million rupees.'

Ben let out a deep breath. So this was what the whole thing was about. This was Kabir's big secret. Not some obscure academic quest to decipher some ancient coded language that only a handful of fuddy-duddy scholars cared about. It was a genuine, bona fide, down to earth, meat and potatoes, good old-fashioned treasure hunt.

Suddenly, everything made so much more sense. As though mechanical components of a dismantled machine that hadn't wanted to fit together before suddenly clicked neatly into place.

He asked, 'What kind of treasure are we talking about here? Gold and jewels?'

Haani shrugged. 'Who can say? Maybe. I mean, gold and jewels is the obvious assumption that most laypeople would make. But the fact is nobody knows what might have been hiding there under the ground for the last three to five thousand years, waiting to be unearthed. Or even whether it exists at all. But if it does exist, it's going to be massively significant. This was a highly advanced culture in its day. Their levels of engineering and craftsmanship were like nothing else of their time. For them to have considered something to be a valuable treasure, it must be mind-blowing. It could be worth an unimaginable amount of money.'

Ben said, 'And you, Sai, Manish and Kabir were the only ones who knew about it?'

'As far as we knew, nobody else had any inkling what we'd discovered. How could they? The journals were the only source of the information. Trafford's remote mountain tribe are history now, erased and forgotten. In theory we were totally safe. But it was freaking me out nonetheless. Because this wasn't just about archaeology any more. When wealth and riches come into the equation, there's a million people out there who'd cut your throat to get a piece of the action.'

'You shared these concerns with Kabir?'

'Of course I did, but he wouldn't take me seriously. I virtually had to force him to borrow the gun, just in case. He took it in the end, partly out of gratitude to me that I was looking out for him, and also because he was kind of fascinated by it as an object, being a normal kind of guy, but I don't think he ever believed there was any threat. I guess that's why he left it at home that day. But I was right all along. It happened exactly as I said. Somehow these bastards found out. And I'm scared they must know about me, too.'

'Where are the journals now?'

'Under lock at key at Kabir's place, as far as I know.'

'Meaning whoever got him now has the key?'

'There's no actual key. It's a combination code. Only he knew it.'

'No copies?'

'Kabir scanned a few pages, including the treasure map, into his smartphone. He had that with him the day of the attack.'

Ben said, 'And we can presume that the attackers took it from him. So even if the original journals are locked up, the enemy now have the map, or the nearest thing to it. And they also know that hardly anyone else is in on the secret, or else they'd have had more competition.'

'They, they, they,' Haani said. 'This is driving me nuts. Who are *they*? How did they know? This wasn't information stored on a computer, potentially hackable like the Indus script program. We were really careful about not telling anyone. Not even Professor Gupta.'

'Kabir told his brother Amal,' Ben said.

Haani's eyes opened wide with surprise. 'He what?'

'Maybe not everything, but enough.'

Haani sighed and shook his head. 'So that's why Amal was kidnapped. So he'd lead them to it.'

'Which still doesn't explain how someone else knew. Amal wouldn't have blabbed. He was so protective of Kabir's secret that he wouldn't even tell his wife.'

They both fell silent for a few moments, thinking hard. 'None of it makes sense,' Haani said. 'Like, why go to so much trouble? If the bad guys knew Kabir was on the trail of a big find, the smart thing to have done would be to hold back and wait for him to dig it up, and then make their move. Instead, they jumped in and killed people, and now they have to kidnap some other guy in the hope that he'll help them finish the job of finding it. Who would do that?'

'Someone not too bright,' Ben said. 'Which tells us that the trigger pullers who carried out the attack weren't the brains behind the operation. Trigger pullers are seldom the brains behind anything. Therefore, it's likely that the attack was premature, not part of the plan. Whoever hired them to do the job might not have foreseen that they were the kind of violent cretins who'd go in like Flynn and not be able to resist opening fire on three innocent people just for the hell of it.'

'Kind of naïve,' Haani said bitterly. 'What kind of people did he think they'd be? Assuming that the brains is a he. I'm not sexist. I just don't believe a woman could be that much of a fucked-up murdering bastard.'

'Very naïve,' Ben agreed. 'And that tells us something more about the boss man. Since, I agree, he probably is a he. This isn't a seasoned crook. He doesn't normally move in those kinds of circles. He lives in a whole different world, one where violence isn't a habitual thing. If he's resorted to hiring a bunch of gung-ho crazies to do his dirty work, it can only be because he had no other recourse. But after the first phase of the plan went horribly wrong, he was forced to go ahead with the next phase and let himself get dragged in deeper.'

'We're still missing how the hell he could have known to kidnap Kabir's brother,' Haani said glumly. Then he raised a finger in the air, as though a fresh thought had come to him, and added with a sly look, 'Unless.'

Ben looked at him. 'Unless what?'

'Unless the whole thing's a setup and Kabir's brother wasn't really kidnapped at all. Maybe he faked it, because he knew more than we're assuming he knew, and he wanted the treasure for himself.'

'You're in the wrong job, Haani. Ever considered a career with the New Delhi police?'

'What's that supposed to mean?'

'It means I've heard some pretty preposterous theories about the Ray brothers today, but that one beats them all. Trust me, Amal didn't fake his own kidnap. It happened.'

The question was, what had happened next? Ben had his thoughts about that. And it wasn't looking good.

Chapter 31

Now that there was a clear motive that not only explained Amal's kidnapping but linked it beyond a shadow of a doubt to the attack on Kabir and the others, it was a much simpler matter than before to predict the bad guys' strategy. It also painted a worse picture, if that was possible, than the one Ben had already had in mind.

What made it so much worse was the treasure element in the equation. Whoever had Amal would have laid pressure on him to reveal facts that he might not even know: first, its location; second, its nature; third, its quantity and value. Squeezing out those details would entail frightening the hell out of him, threatening him with all kinds of horrors, probably hurting him physically to some degree – though not too much, not venturing deep into the realms of harsh torture, because torture could be badly counterproductive if things went too far and the weaker subjects closed down; and even the most moronic thug would realise that Amal was not a physically resilient person. But however they went about it, assuming that he knew what they wanted to find out, sooner rather than later he would crack.

And it had been nine days now since the abduction. Ben thought it unlikely that Amal would have lasted more than a couple of days of rough treatment before the truth came out. He might have lasted only a matter of hours, or even just minutes. When the dam broke, it could go two different ways. He would either spill out everything he knew, which could be extremely bad news for him as it then rendered him obsolete. Or else he could persuade them that he genuinely knew nothing, which was an equally grim prospect, because then he was literally worthless to his captors. It was a no-win situation for the kidnap victim, whether the treasure existed or not.

By that logic, Amal had already been dead for days. A virtual one hundred per cent chance that his corpse was here in Delhi somewhere with its throat cut or its face shot off, buried in a shallow grave or dumped in a sewer or left to rot in some dingy slum or disused industrial space and never to be found.

Not good at all.

Ben pushed deeper into his thoughts, like an underwater swimmer churning through a pitch-black river. He tried to put himself into the minds of the kidnappers. To think like them. To plan the next step, from their perspective. What would they do? It depended on the outcome of the interrogation. If they'd managed to extract the desired information from their captive, their logical next move would be to go and start searching for the loot.

And if they hadn't learned anything from Amal? What would they do then?

Ben spent a few moments working out the answer to that question, and realised that maybe the kidnappers' next move didn't necessarily depend as much on the outcome of the interrogation as he'd first assumed. Because greed was the motivating factor here. And greed made people irrational, and impulsive, and desperate for short-term gain. Say that after twelve hours, or eighteen, or twenty-four, of tough questioning, the villains twigged that their hapless captive really didn't know anything at all. Fine, bad break, but it wouldn't lessen their overwhelming resolve to enrich themselves with whatever fortunes lay buried under the rocks and dirt twenty miles north of Rakhigarhi. It didn't take away from what they already knew. Inevitably, their next move would be to think, 'Fuck it', as Ben had done many times himself, and head for the hills to try their luck whether Amal had come through for them or not. Who cared if they were just a bunch of amateurs armed with nothing more than shovels? Who cared if they didn't stand a snowball's chance in hell of finding some three-thousand-year-old buried treasure in the middle of a vast rocky wilderness with nary a marker to go by? They'd still go for it anyway, because that was the kind of men they were.

In short, if the bad guys hadn't already made a bee line for Rakhigarhi, they soon would. And once they got there, hunting for the treasure wouldn't be a quick in-out operation. It would take days, weeks. Or forever, possibly, since the chances of it even existing had to be fairly slim, and the probability of a gang of untrained thugs actually hitting the spot considerably slimmer still. If Ben wanted to find them, that was where he needed to go too.

And that train of realisations now led him to consider a fresh possibility. What if he'd been too quick to assume that Amal was dead? Say Amal had indeed come through for them, and could help find the spot to start digging: wouldn't they perhaps take him with them, as a kind of hostage-cum-guide-cum-forced-labourer? That would make sense. Even if Amal hadn't come through for them and was useless as far as information was concerned, they might keep him alive simply as an extra pair of hands who could dig until he dropped. That made sense, too. Kind of.

Ben wasn't wildly optimistic, but he was willing to recalculate his previous near hundred per cent estimate of the probability of Amal being dead already to something south of ninety per cent, eighty-five at best. His chances of having survived this far really depended on how clever and forward-thinking the kidnappers were. Which, based on their track record up until now, was hardly reassuring. Maybe eighty-seven and a half per cent was a more realistic baseline.

As for Kabir's chances of still being alive, that was anyone's guess.

Ben had been sitting lost in his thoughts for some time. Haani broke the silence by asking, 'What are you thinking?'

Ben replied, 'Do you know the exact location where Kabir and the others were searching?'

Haani replied, 'I don't remember the exact coordinates, but I've seen the map and I know the lie of the land out there. I have a pretty good idea where to go.'

'Then you can take me there,' Ben said.

Haani stared at him. 'You can't be serious. Take you there when? Right now?'

Ben replied, 'Tonight. I have some things to attend to and some sleep to catch up on. I'll meet you here this evening. Be ready to leave immediately.'

'How are we getting there?'

'By car, as straight and fast and far as we can. Once the road runs out and we hit harder terrain, we may have to improvise alternative transport.'

'You're not giving me much choice, are you?'

'You wanted to go treasure hunting. You missed out last time around. Now you're getting a second chance. And bring the gun, too. If I'm right, we stand a good chance of meeting up with the bad guys there.'

Haani thought about that, and seemed to be gradually

warming to the idea. 'You and me against the bad guys. A chance to get back at those murdering cowards.' He rose from his chair, suddenly all fired up with fierce enthusiasm. 'I have more guns, if they're any use to us.'

'They can't hurt,' Ben said. 'Not us, at any rate.'

'Come and see.'

Ben followed him into the tiny bedroom, which smelled of unwashed sheets, stale socks and rising damp. A poster-sized photo of Haani playing kabaddi was tacked to the wall by the bed. His team wore green tops and white shorts, and the opposition were in red tops with yellow shorts. It looked like a critical moment in the match, and as if everyone was yelling at the top of their lungs. Haani was at the heart of the melee. The lens had caught him in mid-leap as he went to tag one of the enemy team, a look of intense determination on his face. The real-life Haani was wearing the same kind of expression as he skirted around the edge of the rumpled bed, crouched down by a cheap bedside cupboard unit and opened it to reveal a battered cubic metal safe, eighteen inches high, wide and deep, with a rotary combination on its front. 'This is where I keep my stash,' he explained.

'You're a regular armourer,' Ben said.

'My father left me his whole collection when he died. My mother wanted to sell them, but they were illegal, so finding a buyer was risky. And we couldn't just throw them away. What if street kids found them and used them to commit crimes and hurt someone? In any case, they meant a lot to my father. So I kept them.'

Ben watched as Haani turned the combination dials. It was a four-digit number that also happened to be a date, 1-9-7-2. He guessed it was probably the birth year of Haani's father or mother. For Ben it marked the Battle of Mirbat, one of the SAS's most legendary historic engagements when just a handful of troopers had resisted a large army of Communist insurgents in Oman, during another of those wars Britain was never officially involved in. Haani turned a handle and the safe door swung open with a creak. Inside nestled two more handguns, wrapped in oily cloths. Haani lifted them out and laid them on the bed and peeled away the cloths for Ben to see.

'May I?' Ben picked each up and inspected it in turn. The smaller of the two was a little .32 automatic made by the Indian arms company Ashani. A relatively piffling calibre, okay as a last-resort measure if your opponent was someone with thin skin and a delicate bone structure, standing three feet away and wearing nothing heavier than a light cotton T-shirt. The larger gun was more useful. Something of a relic from British colonial days, a big old Webley service revolver that looked as if it had seen action in both world wars and done a lot of police duty in-between. Battered and worn, nearly all the finish gone. But a gun was a gun, as long as it was still mechanically sound, and this one was. The old warhorse fired a slow, heavy .455 calibre bullet that had earned it a well-deserved reputation as a manstopper, back in the day. It would function just fine in trench mud and desert sand and was rugged enough to be used as a club if you had nothing else.

Ben asked, 'What about ammunition?'

Haani pointed at the safe. 'Box of fifty for the Ashani, about twice that many for the revolver. Plus a whole load of those military surplus nine-millimetre rounds for the Browning.'

'Forget the .32,' Ben said. 'Lock everything up again for now, and have the Browning and the Webley packed and ready for when I come back later.'

'What if the bad guys turn up in the meantime?' Haani asked, suddenly worried. 'I can't close myself in here, because you smashed my door in.'

Ben took out his wallet and peeled off a sheaf of cash. 'I'm sorry about the door. This should cover the damages, and then some.'

'It'll take a week to get anyone in to fix it.'

'Then go buy some nails and a hammer, and board yourself up.'

'Great.'

Ben said, 'As it happens, I don't think the bad guys will show up here. Why would they? They've already got what they want. But if it makes you feel better, you don't have to stay in the apartment. Go for a walk. Blend into the crowds. Sit in a café. Take a scenic tour of the slums, admire the architecture. I'll meet you outside the leaning apartment block at nine o'clock.'

Just then, Ben's phone buzzed in his pocket.

Brooke was calling.

Chapter 32

She said, 'Okay, I'm here at the hotel now.'

'You were a long time at the house.'

'I was saying goodbye to Esha. She was very sweet. Gave me a big hug, apologised for her husband's behaviour and said she'd miss me. What have you been doing?'

'Just keeping busy.'

'You sound tired.'

'I'm fine.'

'Something's on your mind.'

'When I get there. Where's your hotel?'

'It's the Leela Palace, on Africa Avenue, close to the embassies.'

'I'm on my way,' Ben said, and ended the call. He said to Haani, 'Don't disappear on me, now, okay? I'll be back in a few hours.'

'Nine o'clock,' Haani said. 'Don't you worry about me.'

Ben left the apartment and trotted back down the stairs, past the blare of music and babies crying and people still arguing, and the old woman still peeking furtively from her doorway, and the dead dog still inert on the landing. He stepped outside into the choking fumes and heat, walked past the subsiding block that was still leaning at the same precarious angle, found the Jaguar miraculously unmolested where he'd left it, jumped in and reset his sat nav for the Leela Palace hotel.

And if his head hadn't been full of what Haani had just been telling him and the prospect of meeting up again with Brooke, he might have noticed the black car parked across the street and the four men inside, all watching him as he got into the Jag and drove off.

The stink of the slums was still lingering in his nostrils by the time he'd cut back southwards across the city to Brooke's hotel, which might as well have been on a different planet and made the Ray residence look like a modest suburban bungalow. Here was five-star luxury on a scale that very few residents of the sprawling urban mess could ever imagine, let alone experience. The hotel stood in lavish grounds that loomed majestically above the city and was, as far as Ben could tell, an actual palace. Or perhaps a luxury fortress might have been a better description. His way was blocked by security guys who wanted to see ID before they let him in. They were suspicious of his bag, and insisted on rummaging around inside to check for bombs and explosives. Content that he wasn't a terrorist, they waved him through.

The lobby was the size of an airport, with enormous smooth gleaming white stone columns rising up past galleried balconies to the decorative ceiling far overhead, and glittering crystal chandeliers, and marble-topped gilt rococo-style tables and tasteful couches draped with silk cushions. Ben made himself comfortable on one of the couches and called Brooke's phone to say he'd arrived. Three minutes later she emerged from a lift and hurried across the vastness of the lobby to meet him, breaking into a happy smile. She looked more refreshed than earlier, and had changed into a green dress that brought out her eyes and hugged her figure, drawing looks from men as she walked. The outfit was probably expensive, but Brooke could have looked good in dungarees and a donkey jacket.

Ben stood up as she reached him. She laid a warm hand on his, and rose on tiptoe to kiss his cheek. Green shoes, matching the dress. 'Hi.'

'Nice little place you found for yourself,' he said, motioning at the sumptuous décor all around.

'Samarth's paying for it. He doesn't know it yet, but I'm charging the bill to Ray Enterprises.'

'That'll hurt.'

'The price of not having me in his house. I could have been really hard on him and taken a top-floor suite. Those come with their own dedicated butler. But I compromised and went for what they call a Royal Premiere room instead.'

'You always were the thrifty one,' Ben said. He was just making conversation, and his voice sounded tight and strained like a person with unpleasant news to break and stalling like crazy. Which was exactly what he was.

She took a step back and scrutinised him with concern. 'You really do look exhausted. You haven't stopped since you got off the plane. Which I appreciate more than I can say. But you need to rest.'

He nodded. 'A nap sounds good, if I could borrow the sofa in your Royal Premiere room for an hour or two.'

'It does actually come with a bed.'

'But first we need to talk. Is there a bar in this place?'

'I think there are several, as well as five or six different restaurants.'

'Let's get a drink.'

She frowned. 'I was right. There is something on your mind. What's up? What happened?'

'Let's get a drink,' he repeated.

They found their way to the library bar on the lobby level, which lived up to its name with handsome bookcases filled with an impressive collection of leather-bound classics. The décor was richly old world, all reds and browns, and had the ambiance of a London private members' club. Acres of burnished wood panelling that gleamed subtly in the subdued light, parquet flooring as smooth as ice and magnificent wall hangings and art and sculptures giving the Eastern touch. You could almost forget the starving cripples and the rats and the disease-ridden filth of uptown. The library bar offered more than five hundred varieties of wine and champagne, 172 different single malt whiskies and a selection of the finest cigars. They passed on the cigars, but Ben took advantage of the hotel's urbane smoking policy to fire up a Gauloise without having to shoot warning looks at anyone who tried to stop him. Brooke ordered a glass of chilled white wine for herself, a scotch for him. Single malt, naturally, double, no ice, no water. She knew his tastes and didn't have to ask. Like the room, the bar tab was going to Ray Enterprises.

The drinks came quickly. Ben snatched his glass off the gleaming counter and swallowed half of it down at a gulp. Brooke noticed, and gave him the frown again. 'I get the feeling that you're building up to telling me something. Something not good.'

He said, 'Come and sit down.'

Her body posture stiffened up and she stood there rigidly still, staring at him. 'It's bad news. I can tell. You found him and he's dead, and you're trying to break it to me gently. I know you, Ben. I can see it in your eyes.'

'Come and sit down,' he said again.

He gently took her elbow and led her across the luxurious room to a corner table. Time seemed to stand still here, as though nothing had ever changed. The pair of them could have been back in the colonial era. An officer and a gentleman escorting his elegant lady friend to her table for some civilised refreshments after an invigorating game of croquet in the hotel gardens.

Except time didn't stand still, and things did change, and not always for the better, and the real world wasn't so civilised, and never had been. Ben sat facing the entrance with his back to the wall, and took another drink of whisky. Two old habits. One that made him feel a little more secure, while the other one just pretended.

But you needed all the sense of security you could get at a time like this, when you were just about to tell the woman you secretly loved that there was an eighty-seven and a half per cent chance that she'd just become a widow, and that her husband's corpse was lying somewhere in the city with its throat cut or its face shot off, buried in a shallow grave or dumped in a sewer or left to rot in some dingy slum or disused industrial space and never to be found.

Brooke wasn't touching her wine. Her face was as white and hard as the marble tabletop. Biting her lip. Eyes dry, back straight, hands neatly folded in her lap. Composed and ready to hear the worst.

He said, 'I didn't find him.'

'But he's dead.'

'I didn't say that.'

'You haven't said anything yet. Talk to me, Ben, for God's sake.'

And so he did.

Chapter 33

Ben laid out everything that had happened during their time apart. His encounter with the police, his conversation with Imran Gupta, the things he'd learned from Haani Bhandarkar and the decision to travel to Rakhigarhi that night. He was frank with her, and left nothing out. Brooke took in every word with concentration and remained silent the whole time he was talking. Her eyes were fixed downwards on the tabletop. Her face registered a whole range of suppressed emotions, a flicker of a cheek muscle here, a tightening of her jaw there. Now and then she reached for her wine glass and took a small sip. There were no more tears. Just a calm acceptance of the facts, as they stood.

'That's it,' he said when he'd finished. 'Now you know everything I know.'

'So, basically, in short, he might be alive,' she said after a beat. Her voice was husky.

'There's a chance, Brooke. A real chance.'

'But a considerably more real chance of the other. The stakes have gone up. It's worse than we thought. You said so yourself.'

'I'm sorry if I upset you. I felt you needed to know the truth.'

'I appreciate your honesty, Ben. You were always honest with me, no matter what.'

He said nothing to that, sensing the reference to the troubles of their past.

Brooke went on, 'And the truth is that the odds are bad. And that I should be getting ready for the worst outcome. Just like Samarth said.'

'Maybe, or maybe not. There's only one way to find out, by seeing what's what in Rakhigarhi. Could be tonight, could be tomorrow. Soon. I promise. Then we'll know, for better or for worse.'

She took another sip of wine, set down her glass and twirled it thoughtfully on the tabletop. 'And where exactly will I be while this is happening?'

'You'll be here at the hotel, where I can be certain you're safe. This has got to be the most secure location in Delhi.'

She looked up from the table and fixed him with an emerald green look that went through him like a laser. 'Ben Hope, if you think you or wild horses can keep me from coming with you to Rakhigarhi, you're either more naïve than I've given you credit for, or you just don't know me. I will not be squeezed out of this.'

'Brooke—'

'I'm coming with you,' she insisted. 'That's absolutely and utterly final. No argument. End of discussion.'

'I'd almost managed to forget how stubborn you can be.'

She snorted. 'That's a good one, coming from you. Give me one good reason why I should stay behind.'

'This is dangerous.'

'You know I can handle myself. I've been in tight situations before.'

'And I work alone.'

'Except you're taking this Haani along for the ride. So why not me?'

'He's been there before. He knows the terrain.'

'And he's a guy.'

'Don't start that.'

'No place for a woman, right? Scared I'll slow you down? Get in your way?'

He looked at her. 'You want honesty?'

'Always.'

He said, probably a little more sharply than he intended to, 'The honest truth is that I care more about what happens to you than anything else in the world. More than what might happen to me. In fact by comparison I don't give a shit what happens to me. I worry that if you're there, I won't be able to focus on what I need to do because I'll be too distracted by the absolute bloody terror of you getting hurt. Because I couldn't live with myself if that happened. Because you matter so damn much to me, and you always have, and you always will. *That's* why I want you to stay behind.'

His words seemed to snatch her breath away for a few moments. She opened her mouth to reply, then closed it again. She blinked a few times. Then flushed scarlet and looked back down at the table, and shifted around in her chair.

He said, 'I'm sorry. That didn't come out the way I meant.' As he watched her, he saw a tear well up in the corner of one eye, then the other. She wiped them quickly away.

'Yes, it did. I'm sorry too. Let's go upstairs. You need to rest. It's going to be a long night.'

Ben was feeling rueful as they headed up to Brooke's room. He was glad of the fact that the lift was full of other hotel guests, giving him an excuse to stay quiet. Brooke seemed ill at ease, too, and he sensed it wasn't just the strain of what she was going through with Amal. The lift glided open on the seventh floor, which was no less richly decked out than the rest of the place, and they walked in silence to her door.

The Royal Premiere room might have been the thrifty option but its sheer unabashed luxury still made the London Dorchester look like a cheap bed and breakfast. In the city with the biggest poverty problems on earth and four million souls living trapped in the most subhuman conditions imaginable. Ben wouldn't have been able to get the disparity out of his head, if he hadn't been so dog tired. Besides, he had enough to feel guilty about right now. He made straight for the plush sofa and was about to throw himself down on it when Brooke touched his arm and smiled and said, 'You really don't have to sleep on the sofa.'

The first words she'd said to him since they'd left the bar. They also happened to have been the very same words she'd spoken to him on the memorable evening he'd visited her place in Richmond, years ago, when they first got together. He didn't know if she remembered it, but he certainly hadn't forgotten.

He had raised no objections on that occasion, and for different reasons was in no mood to protest now. He crossed the broad expanse of Persian rug towards a four-poster bigger than a Cadillac Fleetwood, kicked off his boots and collapsed face-down on the cool, silky bedspread, closed his eyes and felt his muscles relax. Not even the self-blame and regret for opening his mouth too big earlier, let alone the worries about what lay in store at the end of the road to Rakhigarhi, could stop the rising tide of sleep from swallowing him up.

He drifted off within seconds.

Chapter 34

When he awoke, he was instantly aware of Brooke's presence close by. He propped himself on an elbow and twisted his head upwards to look at her. She was sitting on the edge of the bed, one foot dangling towards the floor, the other tucked under her, leaning on one hand with her body canted diagonally across his legs but not touching him. She'd removed the green shoes. Her toes were as cute as he remembered them. She was gazing pensively at him, with her head cocked to one side so that a cascade of auburn curls hung low across one shoulder and rested along the curve of her arm. He realised that she'd gently draped a blanket over him as he slept. The drapes were drawn and a dimmed bedside lamp cast a soft glow.

'Hello,' he said. 'What time is it?' He looked at his watch, bleary-eyed.

'Nearly eight o'clock,' she replied softly, still gazing at him the same way.

'Have you been sitting there all this time?'

'I like watching you sleep. You looked so restful. Like a little boy. Not a care in the world.'

'That's me all over,' he said.

'And I was thinking about a lot of things while I watched you, and I wanted to say I'm sorry.'

He sat up straighter on the bed and leaned his back against the satin headboard. She shifted her body away from his legs to give him space.

'It's me who should be sorry,' he replied after a pause. 'What I said earlier, it was crossing the line. It was a stupid thing to come out with.'

She shook her head, and the auburn curls danced against her arm and shoulder. 'Actually, no. It was a lovely thing to say, Ben. You just caught me a little off balance, that's all. But I wasn't talking about that. It's other things I'm sorry about.'

'What other things?' he asked, still too half-asleep to grasp her meaning.

'About us,' she replied quietly. 'About what happened between us. The way it all went so wrong, after being so happy together.'

'Yes, we were. And we both know what went wrong. It was my fault. I let you down.'

She shook her head again. Her eyes were full of pain and shining from the glow of the lamp. 'That's how I used to think. I blamed you so, so much. It took me a long time to understand what really happened, and why I was wrong.'

'I walked out on our wedding,' he said. 'I deserted you, and I paid the price. I've been paying it ever since. No less than I deserved.'

'You were going off to help a friend in need,' she said. 'Roberta was in trouble. She knew that you were the only person in the world who could get her out of it, and so she came to you. Just the same way that I came to you, because I know you're the only person who could help me now.'

'I'm glad you did.'

'When you dropped everything to go off with her on the eve of our wedding, it felt like you were dropping me, first

208

and foremost. Going off with the old flame who'd come back into your life out of the blue. That's how it seemed. I've never felt so rejected. It broke my heart.'

He wished she'd stop. It was too painful to hear. 'You think I don't know that?' he whispered.

'But if I hadn't let my emotions rule my mind, I'd have realised that's just who you are. That's what you do. When people need you, you go to them. You make things right. No matter what the situation. No matter what the risk. That's why you're Ben Hope.'

Ben said nothing.

'And now I needed you the same way. Now *I* was the old flame, popping up out of nowhere and disrupting your life with my cry for help, except I didn't even have the courage to come to you directly, and I sent Phoebe to do it for me. But you still dropped everything without hesitation to come to help me and Amal, just like you did for Roberta.'

Ben just listened.

'I'm ashamed that I treated you the way I did back then. My heart was broken, and so I had to break yours in return, just out of anger and hurt pride. I let my stupid ego destroy everything we had together, and I know that now, and I don't know where to begin to ask for your forgiveness.'

Ben said, 'There's nothing to forgive, Brooke.'

But there was a lot to be sorry about. Like a lifetime of happiness together that had been snatched away forever. Like a thousand unhappy memories that still felt like a knife in the guts and that the passing of time could do nothing to heal. Like the pain that he was feeling right now, being here with her and reliving the bitter emotions all over again.

'If I could take it all back—' she breathed, then stopped herself from saying more.

'You shouldn't talk that way. You're happy with Amal.'

She said nothing. There was a lot going on behind those green eyes.

'Aren't you?'

She said, 'And now what? What if—?'

'Don't talk like that either.'

She tried to smile, the eyes filling up with tears now. 'How do you want me to talk?'

'Maybe it's best not to talk at all,' he said. 'Shush now.'

She leaned towards him, and held him so tightly that it was as though she was clinging to him out of desperation. He felt the muscle tension in her arms, and knew from the soft heaving tremors in her body that she was crying. 'I'm so glad you're here,' she murmured in his ear. Her voice sounded snuffly and hoarse. 'I've missed being with you. So much.'

'Me too,' he replied. Something was stinging his eyes and hurting his throat. He swallowed. Damn it all. He nuzzled his face into her shoulder and squeezed her tighter.

She whispered, 'Take me with you. Please don't leave me alone here. I don't think I could bear it.'

'I won't leave you alone, Brooke.'

Chapter 35

That was how it was decided that Brooke would join Ben and Haani in driving to Rakhigarhi that night. After Ben had quickly showered and changed and munched most of the sandwiches they ordered up from room service, it was time to head down to the car and set off across the city to collect their travelling companion. The weather had turned, the evening sky heavy and sultry and threatening a downpour of rain. Brooke unpacked a lightweight raincoat from one of her expensive Burberry suitcases, and crammed it into her handbag along with an extendable travel umbrella.

'Good to see you brought your survival gear,' Ben said. 'We might need it.'

'Don't mock. These things are very practical.'

'I don't know how the SAS copes without them.'

They rode the lift down to the lobby and made their way out to the car park. The black night sky was shrouded with even blacker clouds and the air was moist. As they clambered into the Jaguar, Brooke asked for the dozenth time, 'Are you sure we can trust this Haani?'

'He's okay,' Ben replied. 'And he's seen the map. He's the only person left who was closely involved from the beginning. Nobody else can guide us better than he can to where Kabir believed X marks the spot.'

'Unless we drove over to the house instead and got the map for ourselves. Then we'd be independent.'

'By breaking into Kabir's safe? Only he had the combination.'

'You've broken into safes before.'

'With explosives and power tools,' he said. 'Not exactly discreet. Having your brother-in-law call the police and get us arrested for attempted burglary might set back our plans somewhat.'

Ben was getting adept at carving fast through the chaos of the Delhi traffic, which was even denser and wilder at night. He retraced the same route he'd taken earlier, in reverse, heading northwards. Brooke had never seen the worst parts of the city, and was shocked at the sight of the slum districts. 'I knew it was bad, but this is dreadful. Those poor people. Folks in the West just have no idea what poverty really is, do they?'

'I don't know about that,' Ben said. 'Life can be pretty tough when you can only take two overseas holidays a year, drive a downmarket brand of new car and have to settle for an older generation iPad.'

Right on schedule, they reached Haani's street and Ben parked in the same place he had earlier. He and Brooke stepped out of the Jaguar and looked around them. The neighbourhood was still bustling, though the street vendors were gone, replaced by other tradespeople of a more nocturnal variety, like the prostitutes and drug dealers who had come out to play. Though if the skies opened up the way they were threatening to, the street would soon empty as everyone ran to shelter from the deluge. Brooke had her handbag on her shoulder and was keeping her umbrella handy, with her thumb on the spring release catch like a flick knife ready to be deployed.

Ben looked at his watch. Nine o' clock precisely. Dead on time for their rendezvous, but he could see no sign of Haani at the appointed meeting place. 'He said he'd wait for me outside the leaning apartment building.'

Brooke said dryly, 'Obviously he must have changed his mind. Maybe we'll have to get the map for ourselves after all.'

'Or else he decided to wait indoors. It's going to chuck it down any minute now.'

'Not much of a Boy Scout, your Haani.'

Ben looked up at the windows of Haani's building, to see if he could tell which was his apartment and whether anyone was at home. That was when he noticed that there were no lights on in his building at all. Every single window on every floor was dark, as though the residents had all collectively decided to go to bed early, defying the noise from the street and the bright illumination of the tightly-clustered neighbouring blocks. Ben said, 'We'd better go up and check. And he'd better not have let us down.'

Ben returned to the car to grab his bag, inside which he always carried a small, bright flashlight. He switched it on, slung the bag over his shoulder, and they entered the dark building with the strong white torch beam probing and sweeping ahead of them. The creaky staircase looked even grimier and more dismal than it had during the daytime. The earlier noises of music and arguing and crying babies had all gone quiet, and a strange kind of anticipatory hush hung over the building. Reaching the first-floor landing, Ben saw that the dead dog had been removed. In its place stood a group of residents gathered outside their apartment doors, one of them holding a dim electric lantern, everyone talking agitatedly in low voices the way people do in the darkness.

Brooke stopped and spoke to them in Hindi. The old

213

man with the lantern replied at length, seeming to believe she was someone in authority and then looking disappointed when she wasn't. Brooke translated for Ben, 'There was a power outage earlier this evening. The lights flickered, went dim, and then died. They're waiting for someone to come and do something about it.'

'Good luck with that,' Ben said.

'He says they all think someone on the top floor tripped the power. Some kind of party going on up there, apparently. All kinds of noise and carrying on.'

'Whatever,' Ben said. 'Let's go and find Haani, and get out of here.'

He led the way up and up the dark stairs until they reached the top floor, then tracked along the pitch blackness of the narrow landing and past the row of doors to Haani's at the far end. Whoever had been partying up here earlier on and making all the noise, it was all over now. The top floor felt deserted and oddly desolate.

Ben flashed the light on Haani's door and saw that it was hanging ajar by a couple of inches. Which, in itself, was no great surprise, considering the damage it had received earlier. But he was getting a bad feeling, and it wasn't just the eerie darkness and silence of the building.

Brooke was right behind him, standing very close by. He whispered over his shoulder, 'Wait here.' He sensed her reluctance, but she said nothing. He pushed the door softly open. And stepped inside the darkness of the apartment, probing the way ahead with the torch beam.

And his bad feeling got worse.

Ben's first sense impression inside the room was a smell, or a combination of smells. Like something that had got burnt while cooking, mixed up with the acrid scent of melted electrical insulation. The latter possibly to be expected, in a

214

building with dodgy wiring that had just suffered a blackout. But another smell was mixed in too. One Ben knew well. The smell of death and blood.

He remained very silent and still. The pool of white light scanned slowly around the inside of the room, picking out features and objects. The blind covering the inside of the barred window. The two interior doors, both closed. The chair he had pulled away from the table earlier to sit on, still in place. The armchair Haani had sat in while they talked. The tiny kitchen area with the piled dishes in the sink.

But no Haani.

Slowly and cautiously, Ben moved across to the bedroom door, pushed it open and swept the light around the bedroom. The rumpled bed, the kabaddi posters on the wall.

Still no Haani.

Ben retreated to the living room. There was one interior door left to try. Haani's tiny, rudimentary bathroom. He stepped over to it, quietly turned the handle and nudged the door and shone his light through the gap. And his bad feeling suddenly grew worse still. As bad as it could get. So did the smell of death.

And now it was clear to Ben what kind of party had been going on up here on the top floor before the lights went out.

Chapter 36

Haani was in the shower. But he hadn't gone there to get cleaned up before the journey that night. He was stripped to his underwear and hanging by his tethered wrists from the shower curtain rail. His knees had buckled under him, so that all his weight hung from the rail and threatened to rip it down from its mountings on the mouldy bathroom wall. The floor pan of the shower cubicle was a mess of blood and urine.

Haani had been eviscerated with a large, sharp blade. His intestines were hanging out. The bare end of an electrical wire torn from the bathroom light fixture lay at his feet. His killers had amused themselves by treating him to some shock therapy before they'd put the knife in. Haani's chest, arms and legs were covered in ugly blackened burns and blisters. That pretty much explained the power cut, Ben thought. And the burnt cooking smell, which now turned out to be sizzled human flesh.

It had probably been lights out for Haani himself soon afterwards, but only after a good deal of suffering. His face was a mass of blood and swellings and his teeth were all smashed and splintered. Whoever had gone to work on him had done a thorough job, no mistake about that. But they hadn't tortured him for the pure entertainment of it. They'd intended to make him talk. Which meant the bad guys had known Haani knew something, and had paid him a visit in order to extract it from the poor guy.

So his paranoia had been justified after all. Except, like Kabir before him, he obviously hadn't had his weapon close to hand when he most needed it. Wherever Haani might have left the Browning before he was caught unawares, it was gone now.

Ben heard a sudden movement behind him and turned quickly, swivelling the torch beam towards its source to see a figure inside the apartment. Brooke, looking anxious and tense. She blinked in the light, and he lowered the beam from her face. 'Stay back,' he told her. 'I don't want you in here.'

'Let me see,' she said tersely.

'Not a good idea.'

'Let me *see*, Ben.'

Stubborn to the last. He relented and flashed the light back on Haani in the shower, just long enough for her to get a good glimpse. Brooke wasn't the kind of woman to start screaming or having fainting fits. She'd been in nasty situations and seen nasty sights before, and let out only a muted gasp. 'Jesus Christ. Who did this?'

Then, as though the reply to her own question had flashed through her mind half a second later and she realised the implications, she gave an involuntary shudder of horror and fear. Because the answer was: beyond any doubt, the people responsible for this were the same people responsible for taking Amal. And were therefore perfectly capable of doing the same thing to him. And maybe already had done. Maybe the grisly sight of Haani's body was an exact duplicate of what Amal might have looked like, sometime in the last few days.

Brooke turned away and walked quickly out of the room. Ben closed the bathroom door, came after her and found her in the darkness of the living area leaning against Haani's armchair, breathing hard. He asked, 'You okay?' Wishing she hadn't seen that. Wishing she'd stayed in her comfortable safe haven at the hotel.

'We should call the police,' she said quietly.

'Someone else's job,' Ben replied. 'We're out of here.'

'We can't leave him like this.'

'It doesn't make any difference to him. He's dead.'

Privately, Ben felt bad for Haani. He partly blamed himself, since he'd been the one who'd compromised the guy's safety by rendering his door incapable of locking. The killers could have easily smashed it in themselves nonetheless, but maybe Haani would have been alerted to the sound and been able to get to his gun in time to save himself.

On top of his remorse Ben was confused, too. What did these people want? They already had the map, and the location, and Amal, if he was still alive. And why had they targeted Haani now, at this particular moment, in between Ben's visits to him? The timing was uncomfortable. It felt too close to be coincidental.

Whatever the case, danger was closing in. That wasn't good. And worse, Brooke was exposed to it. But there was nothing he could do about that now. And other things that he could do to make a bad situation better.

He carried his bag into Haani's bedroom, walked around the side of the bed and crouched down in the narrow space between the bed and the wall. He shone the torch on the little bedside cupboard and opened it to reveal the hidden gun safe. With his free hand he punched the combination number onto the button panel on its front. 1-9-7-2. The year of the Battle of Mirbat. A lot of battles had been fought since then, big and small. And another one was about to begin.

The safe door swung open. Ben reached inside and took out the two handguns and laid them on the bed like before. Haani had wrapped them back up in their oily cloths. He'd also taken the precaution of loading them both in readiness for the journey. Ben stuck the big revolver in his belt and dropped the smaller .32 automatic into his bag. Then reached back inside the safe and pulled out the boxes of ammo. There were seven in all, heavy oblong blocks still in the manufacturers' original packaging, which in the case of the antique .455 Webley made the two cartons of cartridges for it collectors' items. Fifty rounds in one, fifty minus six in the other. He dumped them in his bag too, together with the single box of ammo for the automatic. He hesitated over grabbing the boxes of 9mm military surplus stuff too, because he had nothing to fire them with. Then he took them anyway. As Rudyard Kipling had once said, a man can never have too much red wine, too many books or too much ammunition. The wine and reading would have to wait until later.

Good to go. Ben stood up and slung his load over his shoulder, now somewhat heavier than before, and hurried back out of the bedroom to where Brooke was waiting anxiously and clutching her handbag. He took her hand and said, 'Come on, let's hit the road.'

'Where are we going?'

'Anywhere but here,' he said. 'Before any more unwanted visitors show up.'

But it was too late for that.

Because they were already here.

Chapter 37

Ben and Brooke made their way back along the landing, passed the four closed doors, reached the top of the stairs and started heading downwards, Ben leading the way in the darkness with his torch, Brooke following close behind. The building was still very quiet. The only sound was the creak of their footsteps on the stairs. Then, as he reached the fourth one down, Ben heard something else, coming from behind and above them on the landing they'd just left.

He turned in the direction of the sound. The door next to Haani's was opening. A dazzling light emerged from behind it, bobbing at chest level. A powerful torch beam. Ben paused mid-step and shone his own back, and could see the figures of two large men behind the light as they stepped out onto the landing and approached the top of the stairs.

Under different circumstances Ben's first thought might have been that these were residents coming out of their apartment, equipped with a torch to see what was going on and perhaps politely enquire about the status of the power cut repair. But such domesticated and mundane assumptions were furthest from his mind at this moment. He was trained to recognise threats – and he knew instantly that this was one.

In the next instant, the threat doubled. The bright glare from the landing illuminated the descending stairway enough to show another pair of large, dark figures of men slowly and purposefully climbing the stairs towards them, shoulder to shoulder, very deliberately blocking the way. Two had just become four, and Ben and Brooke were sandwiched between them.

The trap was simple and neat, and well thought out. The bad guys could have sprung their ambush while their intended targets were still inside Haani's apartment, but they had probably reasoned that the presence of so many doors, potential obstacles and improvised weapons could easily complicate matters. Whereas holding back and waiting for the targets to come out and position themselves on the stairs put the attackers at a significant strategic advantage. Take the high ground, block the only escape route, and pin the enemy down into a narrow space offering no cover and very hard to defend.

Ten out of ten for forward planning, Ben thought. Now what?

Nobody had spoken yet. The two men on the landing walked slowly towards the top step, the one with the torch still shining it down the stairwell. The beam was very white and strong, much brighter than Ben's compact flashlight. Maybe a six-cell Maglite or similar, equipped with LEDs. As useful as a blunt impact weapon as it was to light up a dark space. Its dazzle was filling the whole stairwell, so that Ben could see the two men coming up the stairs in his peripheral vision without having to shine his torch on them. He kept it pointed upwards at the two men on the edge of the landing. They were the immediate threat. And advancing, whereas the two below seemed to have stopped and were hovering in position.

Which told Ben that they were the B team, their job for the moment being simply to block the escape route, while staying safely out of range.

But out of range of what? Logic dictated that at least one of the four was packing a firearm, the one they'd taken from Haani. Ben's guess that the gun was being carried by one of the two on the upper landing, the A team, but he couldn't be sure of that. Either way, so far it didn't look as though opening fire was their plan. Not yet. Whatever their intention was, Ben knew he was about to find out. Behind the glare he could make out the smiles of anticipation on the men's faces.

In a blur of thoughts, calculating strategy like the world's fastest chess computer, Ben evaluated his options. He doubted whether the attackers knew he was armed. That gave him an excellent element of surprise, but such tactical advantages were easily wasted. If he opened fire on the two guys on the higher ground, he couldn't be sure that the pair on the lower ground wouldn't start shooting before he could turn the gun on them next. He was fast. Very fast, in his own modest opinion. But not that fast. And he couldn't risk it with Brooke standing right next to him in the open. His only option was to let the bad guys make their opening gambit, reveal their tactical plan, then respond accordingly.

The move came soon enough, as the man not holding the torch took something from his pocket. Handling it carefully. A weapon, but neither a gun nor a knife. A fat plastic syringe. Filled with some kind of clear liquid that looked briny and viscous in the torchlight. Then the guy with the torch used his free hand to reach into his own pocket and take out an identical syringe. Each one held between forefingers and middle fingers, like a couple of fat cigars. Thumbs on plungers. Nozzles aimed in a parallel trajectory down the stairwell.

Ben's mind stepped up into overdrive. For about an eighth of a second after seeing the syringes he was thinking *needles, sedatives, abduction.* Thinking that the bad guys had come to add him and Brooke to their collection of captives. Another fraction of a second later he realised he was wrong. You can't administer kidnap drugs without a needle. Syringes that big would be fitted with one the size of a lance. Long and thick enough to gleam and glitter in the light. But that wasn't happening. Because the syringes had no needles attached at all.

Now one of them spoke. It was the one with the torch, and he said in English, 'Poke your nose in where it's not wanted, fuckhead, and you'll lose it.'

That was when Ben understood what was in the syringes. Acid, one of India's most popular cheap and effective means of inflicting sadistic, irreversible harm on people. Most likely nitric or sulphuric, highly concentrated, just a squirt capable of burning through skin and flesh and bone in an instant and producing the most grotesque and horrific injuries. One dose for him, one for Brooke. It was why the two guys on the stairs below them weren't coming any closer, not wanting to get splashed with the stuff.

It also helped Ben understand the whole strategy here. Just like with Haani, the bad guys wanted to find out what he and Brooke knew, but they didn't have electrical voltages to play around with any more. The chemical option was an effective alternative. Blinded, disfigured, incapacitated and utterly helpless victims writhing in agony are easy to make blab their secrets before you spill their guts all over the floor. Probably more fun that way too, from a psychotic killer's point of view. But much less fun for the victim.

And Ben had no intention whatsoever of letting that happen.

And so he moved. Fast. Very fast.

Chapter 38

It all happened in the next two seconds.

At the same instant that the muscles in the attackers' hands were contracting to compress the syringe plungers into their tubes between fingers and thumbs to launch their payload of corrosive liquid through the air, Ben was letting his torch fall from his grip and grabbing Brooke and whirling her bodily around and behind him and simultaneously reaching inside the opening of her handbag and ripping out the extendable travel umbrella and thrusting it outwards and upwards and activating the release catch. In the blinding light beam he saw the twin jets of acid leave the nozzles of the syringes, arcing through the air under pressure, expanding into fine scintillating sprays of droplets, glittering like diamonds in the strong light as they headed straight for their targets.

But in the same instant the spring-loaded mechanism of the umbrella was doing its work, and he felt the kickback as it leapt forwards on its metal shaft and the canopy expanded with a rustling crackle, like an ultrafast time lapse replay of a flower opening its petals. The twin sprays both hit at the same time and spattered harmlessly against the shield of the umbrella. Powerful acid that could burn almost instantly through skin, flesh and bone was almost totally ineffective against a thin membrane of waterproof fabric.

By contrast a lead-alloy flat-nosed bullet weighing about 16 grams and launched from a six-inch pistol barrel at around 700 feet per second had no problem penetrating the flimsy cloth. Even as the last tiny droplets of acid were bouncing off the umbrella canopy Ben was yanking the Webley service revolver from his belt and firing blind through his shield in the general direction of their attackers, yanking the heavy trigger four times as hard and fast as he could work his index finger and feeling the recoil of the weapon hammer backwards into his palm. BLAM; BLAM; BLAM; BLAM. The blast filled the stairwell. The torchlight vanished into sudden total blackness as one of his bullets smashed its lens, but Ben knew the other three shots had hit their mark.

Now he had to worry about the two guys below him opening fire, because they could get lucky even in zero light conditions. As the bigger and heavier of the two guys on the landing crumpled and started toppling over the edge of the top step Ben caught his arm and whirled him around and sent him crashing down past Brooke and straight towards the two others on the stairs. Like playing with giant skittles in the dark. He heard a muffled grunt and the smack of the impact as the dead man's weight, assisted by gravity, cannoned into his still-living comrades and flattened them both, followed by the second dead guy an instant later. An avalanche of bodies tumbled and bounced down towards the landing below.

Ben had a rule about getting angry in combat. It generally wasn't a good idea to let personal emotions seize the moment. But now he was ready to break that rule, because the idea of Brooke getting hurt by acid didn't make him merely angry, it unleashed a torrent of lethal violence from inside him. He went bounding blindly down the stairs after them, trampling whatever dead flesh was underfoot. He snatched up his fallen flashlight and saw one of the two surviving guys lying sprawled out on his back head-first diagonally across the stairwell, trying to struggle up to his feet and clawing a gun from his jacket. Haani's Browning. Ben shot him in the face at close range and blood hit the walls and his head slammed back against the stairs. The last guy had managed to slither down to the level footing of the landing below and was staggering upright with a small snubby .38 revolver in his fist, which he was bringing up to point at Ben. The guy's aim was so wild that he was liable to miss, but just as likely to hit Brooke by mistake, which he probably intended to do anyway after neutralising Ben. Which Ben found hard to accept, so he used the sixth and last round in his Webley to plant one squarely between the guy's eyes. The guy's pistol hit the floor unfired. The guy himself crashed across the landing like a sack of mail immediately afterwards.

Then there was silence in the stairwell, except for the high-pitched whine in Ben's ear's. Tinnitus was always the price of victory in close-quarter gunfights. He raced back up the stairs to check on Brooke.

'Are you okay?'

'I'm okay. I think.'

Her eyes were wide with shock, but she was unhurt. His relief flushed the anger from his system as fast as it had flared up. He flashed his torch on the umbrella, which was lying on the stairs, crushed flat by one of the falling bodies and still gleaming with wet acid. 'You're right. Those things are very practical.'

She shook her head in amazement. 'I can't believe how

fast you moved. What am I saying? Of course I can. You're still the same old Ben I knew.'

They'd made a lot of noise and it wouldn't be long before the building's residents called the police. Ben wanted to be long gone by the time they turned up.

'But the question is, who are these idiots?' he said.

He walked back down the stairs and stepped over a body to crouch down beside another, the corpse of the guy who'd been holding the torch. The six-cell Maglite was lying beside him with a bullet hole through its lens. Ben shone his own light over the guy's body and saw that the other bullet had gone through his heart. He frisked the corpse for any kind of ID, and wasn't surprised not to find any. Then shone the light in the guy's face and asked Brooke, 'Look familiar to you?'

There was a reason why Ben had singled him out. Because of what he'd noticed about the guy's face, in the moments before the fight. As Brooke came down the stairs, treading carefully to avoid stepping on dead body parts, she saw it too. The bullet wound that had blown out his chest cavity wasn't his only recent injury. Not many days had passed since the guy had suffered a nasty blow to the mouth that had bruised up his lips and knocked out a front tooth.

Brooke looked up at Ben with a gasp. 'It's him. The man I punched. One of the kidnappers.'

'Shame the silly bastard forced us to kill him,' Ben said. 'He might have been useful.'

'What would you have done with him afterwards?'

'Don't ask.'

'It wouldn't be as bad as what I'd have done to him,' she said. And Ben could believe it. He gathered up the fallen guns, then quickly searched the other bodies. None of the dead men was carrying anything like a wallet, but he found two phones which he tossed in his bag along with the weapons. 'For future reference,' he said. 'As in, right now it's time we got the hell out of here.'

'I agree.'

The loud gunshots must have resonated all through the building, because the landings and stairways all the way down to the ground floor were deserted and empty, and not a single face dared to peep out from behind a door to see what was going on. Ben and Brooke made it out into the street unchallenged. If anyone had called the cops, they were still a long way off, and that suited Ben fine. The car was just a short distance away. 'Walk, don't run,' he said to Brooke. 'Don't act like you just shot four men.'

'You're the one who shot them,' she said.

'Think I overreacted?'

'They were lucky.'

Chapter 39

Ben and Brooke were halfway to the car when the skies finally opened and the rain came sheeting down, bouncing hard off the pavements and almost instantly burbling in rivulets through the gutter. In which case it was okay to run the rest of the way, since that was what everyone else was doing as they fled for cover, prostitutes and drug dealers included. They jumped into the Jaguar and took off, heading in no particular direction.

Ben cut randomly through the streets of northern Delhi at an even but brisk pace for twelve minutes, long enough to put plenty of distance between themselves and the crime scene. In any Western city they would have left a CCTV trail a blind man could follow. If there was anything good about the chronic backwardness of India's capital, it was that the tentacles of Big Brother electronic surveillance had yet to start encroaching on its citizens.

He found a quiet street flanked by dark buildings that looked too derelict to be habitable, though he was sure they were filled with twenty people to a room like every other possible living space in Delhi. Signs and awnings hung all over the street. By day the place was probably heaving with traffic and bustling crowds and all the usual stalls and music and colour and noise, but now it was still and empty as a ghost town, slicked by the torrential rain. He pulled up at the kerbside and killed the engine, lights and wipers. Water cascaded down the windows, blurring the outside world. It was like being in a car wash.

'We still have to get to Rakhigarhi,' Brooke said. 'But not without the map. We'll have to try getting it from the house, Ben. It's got to be worth the risk. Or else we do without the map altogether.'

Ben said nothing. His first priority was organising the small arsenal of weapons he'd collected. He reached behind him for his bag and spent a few moments reloading the Webley revolver, which he then passed to Brooke. The pipsqueak .32 automatic and their newly-acquired .38 snubby would each fit her hand better, but he wanted to be sure she'd knock down what she fired at, instead of just tickling it. Nothing like a big-bore hand cannon for that job. 'You know how to work this thing?'

'It's not rocket science. Point and squeeze. I've seen what it can do. Do you think I'll need it, or is that a silly question?'

'I sincerely hope not. But I'll feel better.'

Then Ben inspected Haani's Browning. Still fully loaded, thirteen in the mag, one in the chamber. Plus enough spare ammo to start a small war. He stuck the Browning in his belt. It felt comfortable and familiar there. Back in business.

'What about Rakhigarhi?' she asked.

'First let's see what we've got,' he said.

He reached into his bag for the two phones they'd taken from the dead attackers. One was a Xiaomi, the other a Samsung, both of the cheap pay-as-you-go variety, likely bought for cash, no names, no contracts, zero traceability. Not the best start, but you had to work with what you had. He gave the Samsung to Brooke, and they sat in silence as they started scrolling through the menus in search of information.

The only sound was the drum of rain on the car roof and the light tick-tick of Brooke's fingernails on phone keys.

'Doesn't look as if it's been used much,' Brooke said after a few moments. 'Message inbox and outbox are both empty. So's the contact list.'

'Same with this one,' Ben said. He checked the call record and found nothing there either, either incoming or outgoing. Either the phone was virgin new and completely unused, or the deceased former owner had been in the habit of routinely erasing everything for the sake of operational security. The deleted items could probably be retrieved from the device's backup memory, but Ben was damned if he knew how.

So far, not so good.

Then Brooke said, 'Wait, here we go. I have numbers.' She held the phone up to show him. Ben peered at the tiny lit-up screen in the darkness. She said, 'Actually, just the one number. From another mobile. It comes up in the sent menu seven times and in the call inbox nine times.'

'So, someone he's in regular contact with.'

Brooke shrugged. 'Doesn't have to mean anything. It could be his mother.'

'Then again, it could be the boss of the whole kidnap and murder operation.'

'What should we do?'

'We can't trace it,' Ben said. 'So there's only one thing we can do. Call it.' He took out his own phone. 'From this one, so they don't recognise the number.'

'And say what?'

'What's a really common surname in India?' he asked.

Brooke replied, 'The most common is Singh. There are about thirty-six million of them. Followed by Kumar. Just over thirty million of those, if I remember rightly.'

Ben looked at her. 'Why would you even know that?'

She shrugged. 'I married an Indian guy. I wanted to learn about the culture.'

'Fair enough. Then ask to talk to Mr Singh. With a bit of luck they'll say, "Sorry, wrong number, this is Mr Such-and-such."'

Brooke looked doubtful. 'I don't know. Would that work?'

'It's worked for me,' Ben said. 'Just the one time, about eight years ago.'

'Long shot,' she said.

'Nothing to lose.' He gave her the phone.

She flinched. 'What, you want *me* to do it?'

'Better coming from a woman,' he said. 'A man is more likely to open up to you. It's a guy thing.'

'Why?'

'You're the psychologist,' he said. 'You tell me.'

Brooke took a deep breath, then started dialling the number into Ben's phone. She suddenly paused. 'What if his name actually is Singh?'

'Then we'll know something about him,' Ben said. 'It's called gathering intelligence.'

'One out of thirty-six million people with the same surname. That'll really narrow it down.'

'Just do it,' he said.

Brooke keyed in the rest of the number, then thumbed the call key and flicked back her hair and tentatively held the phone to her ear. She closed her eyes, waiting. Her chest rose and fell as she breathed nervously. Ben heard the faint beeps of the dial tone muted against her skin. Then the sound of a voice answering the call. A man's voice.

Brooke tensed as she went to speak, then closed her mouth and said nothing. The man's voice went on talking, and Ben realised that the call had gone to voicemail. He said, 'Hang up, we'll try again later.'

But Brooke didn't hang up. She was clenching the phone tightly against her ear. Her whole body rigid as she listened to the answerphone message. She was staring at the rain-washed windscreen as if she'd seen a cobra coming at her through the glass.

Ben said, 'What?'

She shushed him. When the message had finished playing, she ended the call before the beep and then hit redial to listen to it again.

Ben could tell something was up. 'What?' he repeated.

She shushed him again, more impatiently. She listened to the message to the end a second time, then did the same thing and redialled the number to play it back a third time.

'Listen,' she said, holding the phone out to him. Her voice was strangled and urgent.

'Just tell me,' Ben said.

'Oh, Ben, please will you shut up and *listen*,' she hissed at him.

So Ben took his phone back from her, and put it to his own ear, and listened.

The answerphone message said:

'*Hello, you have reached the voicemail of Prem Sharma. I'm sorry I can't get to the phone right now, but if you would like to leave your name and number after the beep I'll get back to you as soon as possible.*'

Chapter 40

Ben ended the call and laid the phone on the dash. He said, 'Well, that's very interesting.'

Brooke was staring at him in the darkness. The rain was drumming harder than ever on the car roof and cascading down the windows.

She said, 'But what on earth does it mean?'

'It means that the bad guy with the broken tooth who kidnapped your husband made seven phone calls to the guy who works for the Ray family. And received nine from the same person. Which amounts to quite a correspondence. And tells us that your friend Prem Sharma isn't quite who he appears to be.'

'What are we going to do?'

Ben fired up the car. The engine roared, the headlamps stabbed rainy searchlight beams deep into the night and the wipers slapped a torrent of water clear of the glass. He replied, 'Slight change of plan. Rakhigarhi will have to wait. We're going to go back to the house and pay a visit to Prem.'

'I'll shoot him,' Brooke said.

'First he needs to tell us how he's mixed up in this, and what's going on. Then you can shoot him.'

'Right between the eyes. If any harm has come to Amal. And even if it hasn't. I swear, Ben, I will.'

'One step at a time,' he said. 'Remember?'

Neither of them spoke again for a while, as Ben sliced diagonally south-east back across the city towards the Ray residence. The rain was falling even harder now, cannoning off the windscreen like hail, the wipers working full tilt. Brooke rummaged in the glove box, found a small cable with a jack plug on one end and a USB connector on the other and used it to hook Ben's phone up to the car's audio system so they could both hear. Then she tried calling Prem's number again, but it was still engaged. She sat back in the passenger seat, seething with rage.

The revelation of Prem's involvement in the situation was a weird, baffling twist that Ben couldn't figure out at all, so rather than burn his brain out trying to understand, he kept his mind blank and focused on driving them there as fast as he could through the downpour. Brooke's presence next to him felt like a volcano ready to erupt. He knew her thoughts were boiling, but the fact that she stayed silent made it clear that she had no more of a clue what this was about than he did.

Meanwhile, the character of the city morphed radically in front of their eyes as they left the poverty and the squalor far behind them and neared the suburban havens where the other half lived. The closer they got to the Ray residence, the more Ben could feel Brooke tensing up in anticipation. She had her ethnic embroidered handbag on her lap with the loaded revolver in it, and a determined set to her jaw. To face an angry Brooke was a daunting prospect, as Ben knew from personal experience. He wouldn't have wanted to be in Prem's shoes for anything, once they reached the house.

But they didn't get as far as the house.

Three blocks before the security checkpoint, a small

two-seater Audi roadster Ben had seen before darted out of the junction fifty metres ahead, gave a momentary rear-end wobble as its wheels lost traction on the rain-slicked road and accelerated smartly away from them, its tail-lights receding fast into the night. Moving at an urgent pace.

'That's Prem's car,' Brooke said, pointing after it.

'Going off in an awful hurry,' Ben said. 'Maybe that's why he's not answering his phone. Something on his mind?'

'Only one way to find out,' she said.

'You bet. Hold onto your hat.'

The Audi was definitely in a hurry, and it had a head start on them. But Ben had no intention of letting Prem get away. He put his foot down hard and the eight-speed automatic gearbox dropped a few notches and the supercharged engine rocketed the car like a spurred horse, pressing them back in their seats. Fifty-five, sixty, sixty-five. The shrinking tail-lights of the Audi started growing larger, but then the difference levelled out and the Audi matched their pace. Ben needed to keep Prem in his sights without drawing attention to himself, which wasn't such an easy thing on the quiet, near-empty roads of a wealthy suburb at night. A couple of junctions later, they were heading into thicker traffic and Ben became less worried about Prem noticing the Jaguar's headlights in the mirror.

Then, without warning, the Audi darted into a sharp turn; then another, then up a slipway that took them onto the city's inner ring road. Ben followed and watched as Prem forced himself into the three lanes of cars and trucks and motorbikes that were ploughing doggedly through the pelting rain, a slow-moving, meandering, two-way river of light, red in one direction, white in the other. But Prem wasn't slowing down for anything. Foot to the floor, he carved a weaving slalom through the sluggish traffic as though it was standing still.

Ben had no choice but to keep up with him. Trees and barriers and light posts zipped past in a blur. The Audi's tail-lights were just smudges of red through a veil of rainwater spray thrown up in its wake. Eighty-five, ninety, ninety-five. Twice, then three times, then four times, the Audi came within a hair-raising inch of colliding with another vehicle as it went screaming by them. The Jaguar was just getting warmed up, but how long this could go on without the police jumping on their tail or Prem causing a massive pile-up, Ben couldn't say.

'He's crazy,' Brooke said. She was clutching the grab handle above her window and braced in her seat.

'Or scared half to death,' Ben said. 'But of what?'

'You think he's spotted us?'

'I don't think so. Whatever's got him rattled up like this, it's not what's behind him. He's way too preoccupied to even know we're here.'

'Let's see.' With her free hand she tried his phone again, turning up the car stereo volume to be heard over the engine noise. Like before, the engaged tone came loud and clear through the speakers. 'I can't believe he's talking on the phone while driving like that. He'll kill himself.'

'He might not be. Could just be trying to get through to someone.'

'How do you know that?'

'Just a feeling,' Ben said. 'He's clearly in a hell of a panic.'

Moments later, they got a phone call that proved Ben's feeling right. It came from the Xiaomi, one of the phones that they'd taken from the dead men at Haani's apartment building. Brooke quickly unplugged Ben's phone from the car audio system and connected the Xiaomi in its place, then hit reply. She glanced at Ben, as if to ask, 'What do I say?' Ben took a hand off the wheel and put his finger to his lips. *Say nothing.*

Brooke stayed quiet as the call connected. The caller hesitated and said nothing either, obviously taken aback by the strange silence on the line. In the background they could hear the ambient noise of the inside of a vehicle moving at speed and the slap of wipers working full pelt. No great mystery where the call was coming from.

Ben half expected the caller to hang up. But then the person on the other end broke the silence, and there was no question that the voice they could hear on the other end of the line, amplified in crisp, rich, deep tones and filling the Jaguar's cockpit, was Prem's. But not the calm, confident Prem who'd picked Ben up from the airport and shown him around the Ray residence. This Prem was babbling as fast as he could get the words out and sounded agitated to the point of wildness.

'Hello? Hello? Sanjay, is that you? I've been trying to get through to you, man. And Vijay, and Dhruv, and Ramesh. Where the fuck is everybody? I've got to talk to someone. Takshak called me earlier and now he won't pick up my calls. What's happening?'

Brooke glanced at Ben. Ben put his finger back to his lips. *Don't answer him.*

Prem waited a beat for a reply, then said, 'Hello? Sanjay? Speak to me. Hello?'

Ben took the finger from his lips and drew it across his throat in a slicing motion, like a knife blade. *Cut him off.*

Brooke shut down the call and turned to him. Up ahead, Prem was driving more crazily and erratically than ever. She said, 'You were right. He's in total panic, trying to get through to these people.'

'And Sanjay, Vijay, Dhruv and Ramesh are members of the crew,' Ben said. 'Or were. Four names, four dead men we left behind at Haani's building tonight.'

'Plus a fifth. Takshak. Strange name.'

'Because it's not a real name,' Ben said, recalling it from the dim and distant past of his student days. 'Takshak was one of the Nagaraja in Hindu mythology. The most venomous and feared of the snake gods.'

'Only you would remember something like that at a time like this.'

'It sounds like the snake guy is the leader of the gang. And it sounds like Prem's having some trouble with him.'

'But why's he even involved with them? What the hell's going on?'

Ben replied, 'I reckon we'll find out soon enough.'

Chapter 41

Signs for an exit flashed past in a rainy blur. The Audi's brake lights flickered on, off, on again. Prem veered across two lanes of furiously honking traffic, swerved to avoid a truck bearing down on him and then left the ring road, heading erratically west at the same dangerous speed.

Ben hit the indicator, sliced the Jaguar smoothly through a gap and followed. Less than a minute later, the Audi's brake lights were flaring again as Prem sped headlong towards a big intersection with traffic lights burning like beacons through the wet night. For a second it actually appeared as though Prem was going to stop for the lights.

Brooke said, 'Take him here. Grab him out of his car.'

'No, I want to see where he's going.'

Even as Ben said it, Prem changed his mind and went roaring through the red lights, straight out into the ocean of traffic that was rushing perpendicular to the junction. Cars skidded and spun out of control. There were multiple crunches and ricochets. A motorcyclist veered out of the path of a truck and was side slammed by a tuk-tuk.

Ben gritted his teeth and surged right after Prem into the heart of the chaos. Lights and horns and screeching tyres coming at them from all directions. He estimated he had about a five per cent chance of coming through it without a collision taking him out of the chase. Brooke was cringing in her seat, eyes shut. Ben sawed at the steering wheel and pumped the brake and gas like a church organist playing a wild toccata and fugue, and he somehow managed to steer a course through the carnage and out the other side. Part luck, part skill, no time to work out which to feel grateful for. He got clear and put his foot down hard and the Jag surged onwards in pursuit of the disappearing Audi.

'Now I really am going to shoot him,' Brooke said. 'Before he goes and kills somebody.'

It was another six cross-city miles before the insanity of the chase came to an end. The rain was slackening. The traffic was thinning, forcing Ben to hang further and further back so as not to let Prem spot him following. The Audi had led them through a sprawl of urban housing developments and now entered an industrial zone with a roughly equal amount of construction and decay going on. Crumbling warehouses were in the midst of being torn down and replaced with new ones. To the west, whole areas looked like the rubble fields of battlegrounds in Syria, Iraq or the Lebanon. To the east, giant cranes stood tall against the misty horizon, and concrete blocks were piled like skyscrapers. Some construction projects looked as if they had been abandoned, towers of scaffolding red with rust and others collapsed. To Ben's shock, people were living among the rubble, little makeshift encampments scattered here and there that made the slums of north Delhi look like a holiday resort. Some homeless folks were crowded around a smoky fire burning in a brazier made from an old oil drum. Scrawny dogs prowled through the destruction of the landscape like post-apocalyptic scavengers in search of human bones to gnaw.

Finally forced to slow down just a little, Prem threaded

his way through the industrial wasteland, his headlights bobbing and bouncing as the car pattered over potholes and strewn debris. By then Ben had killed his own lights and was following slowly at a safe distance, catching just occasional glimpses of the Audi's tail-lights ahead and hoping he wouldn't lose track of it in the maze of unfinished avenues and building site access roads that seemed to stretch out for miles. Prem eventually jammed to a halt outside a dark, looming structure that was part shrouded in scaffolding and looked as though it might be a half-built factory or warehouse complex. Or a block of flats. Or a future hospital, or the early stages of a shopping mall. Or maybe it had already been any one of those things and was in the process of being taken down. From where Ben had stopped in the shadows of another derelict shell of a building a hundred yards away, it was hard to tell. But whatever it was, Prem seemed to have a particular, and extremely pressing, reason for being here.

The Audi's headlamps turned off. The building fell into darkness, but there was still just enough light for Ben and Brooke, watching from their unseen vantage point, to make out Prem's silhouetted figure clambering out of his car and hurrying towards a doorless entrance of the building, just a gaping, black concrete arch. He lit up a torch as he went, making a pool of light that bounced and bobbed in front of him and illuminated his outline more clearly. His body language was that of someone burdened with massive acute stress. He was bent over, shoulders hunched up, holding a phone to his ear with his free hand. The distance was too great to hear whether he was talking, or still trying to get through to this Takshak.

Ben said to Brooke, 'Stay here. I'm going in after him.'

'You must be kidding. I'm coming too.'

They got out of the car and very softly shut the doors,

then trotted across the dark waste ground to the building, splashing through puddles of dirty rainwater. Prem had disappeared inside, and Ben decided it was safe to turn on his own torch. Up close, the site was more obviously a building project in the making, but one in which little progress had been made in a long time. Not entirely unusual in its own right. There could be all kinds of reasons why an unfinished construction job could stall. Planning problems, labour problems, companies going out of business. The crews would just abandon it until further notice, leaving the project looking exactly the way this one did. The wire fence around the building was rickety and half collapsed in places, and a hole had been cut through the mesh that looked like the work of vagrants or squatters using the place for their own purposes. That impression was confirmed by the rubbish and signs of fires having been lit here and there. Hardly unusual either, in a city so crammed with desperately poor people who would huddle into any living space they could find.

The question was, what was Prem doing in a place like this?

He must have slipped through the hole in the wire. Ben reached it ahead of Brooke, and held the gap open wider so she could step through more easily. While he waited for her, he shone his torch up and down, side to side. The wire was mostly red with rust. Ben's torch beam passed over the face of a rectangular tin construction company sign attached to the fence, hanging lopsided and swaying in the soft breeze. It was as rusted as the wire, the company name partially obscured but still legible.

Then he did a double-take and shone the beam on it again.

He nudged Brooke's arm. 'Look.'

She stopped, followed the line of the pointing torch beam and saw it, too.

The rusted lettering on the sign said:

RAY ENTERPRISES CONSTRUCTION DIVISION
PRIVATE PROPERTY – KEEP OUT

Chapter 42

Brooke stood there staring at it for a long moment, then turned to Ben with all kinds of questions in her eyes.

'Come on.' He shone the torch away from the sign and towards the hole in the wire. She stepped through, and he went in after her and led the way into the pitch darkness of the building.

The interior smelled of damp earth and urine and garbage and stale ash from fires. The ceiling loomed above them and the walls were bare concrete with yawning holes where the architects had planned doors and windows to be. The slab floor was caked in dust and construction dirt. From the general state of neglect the place was in, it was clear that no construction crew had been near the site for at least a year, or two, or maybe five. That was for sure. But there had been plenty of coming and going nonetheless, judging by the quantity of footprints in the dirt. The tracks led into the heart of the empty building, all following the same route, like a path made by animals to a waterhole.

Ben paused and put his finger to a couple of the freshest prints. They were still moist from the rainwater puddles outside. Made just moments ago. He studied the impression of the shoe. Quality footwear, leather soled, no tread pattern.

A decent pair of brogues. Just exactly like the expensive handmade items that Prem wore.

'He came this way,' Ben said softly. 'He can't be far ahead of us.'

'What's he doing here?' she hissed.

'The innocent explanation? This is his employer's building. He's come to check things out, make sure it's okay.'

'You believe that?'

'Not in a thousand years.'

'Then what's he doing here?' she repeated.

He said nothing. They moved on, following Prem's tracks. They were just one set out of many on the little pedestrian highway that cut deeper into the building. The tracks led past an empty lift shaft, from which a breeze of cooler, fresher air from outside was wafting. A little way further on, the tracks veered left and reached a concrete stairway, one flight leading upwards and the other leading down.

The tracks went downwards.

They followed. Ben cupped a hand over the end of the torch, turning his fingers blood red and muting the beam to give them just enough light to see by but no more. The steps were bare concrete, and steep. He counted seventy-two of them before they touched down to the floor below. They were in a narrow, curving corridor leading onwards into darkness. The air down here was stifling and stale. Some kind of basement, maybe intended for storage, or offices.

Ben stopped. He could hear something. The muffled rumble of a diesel generator, not too far away. Then around the next corner, they saw a glow of light that grew brighter as they moved on down the corridor. The walls were bare, solid concrete. No doors to the left or right. Only one way forward, only one way back. Not a safe place to enter. He wished that he'd done more to persuade Brooke to stay in the car, but it was too late to worry about that now. He killed his torch, slipped it in his pocket and eased the Browning from his belt. Round in the chamber, hammer back, safety off, index finger straight along the side of the trigger guard, low ready position, two-hand grip. Eyes fixed on the light coming from the curve of the corridor ahead. Waiting for the slightest sign of impending threat. Calm and ready.

The footprints had petered out by now as the rainwater dried off Prem's soles, but Ben no longer needed tracks to guide him. A door came up on the left, open a crack with light shining from inside. He motioned for Brooke to hold back, then padded cautiously towards the door and spent a full thirty seconds listening hard. Nothing. But that didn't mean Prem wasn't lurking inside, perhaps aware that he was being followed and prepared to do something about it. Ben took his left hand from the gun and nudged the door softly open.

Prem wasn't there. The room was lit but empty, though it had been used not too long ago. There was a cheap table inside, and four cheap chairs. Empty drinks containers and fast food packaging were littered about the rough concrete floor. Ben picked up a bottle of Coke off the table and shook it. Still fizzy. He put it down and glanced about him. Taking in the signs. There were two cardboard boxes sitting in the corner. One contained a roll of duct tape and a coil of paracord and a collection of disposable paper plates and plastic cups. The other was full of tinned food, beans and stewed beef and soup. There was a bag of sugar, a carton of long-life milk, a half-finished jar of decaffeinated instant coffee, a dirty metal teaspoon.

Ben examined each in turn, then went over to a couple of plastic garbage sacks that lay on the floor nearby, tied at the mouth. He gave each one a nudge with his foot to feel what was inside. Dismembered body parts felt heavier than garbage. This was just garbage. Still, good to check.

Brooke whispered, 'What *is* this place?'

Ben said nothing. He'd seen places like it before, many times. He turned back towards the door and peered out into the corridor.

No Prem. No nobody.

They moved on. The next door they came to was on the opposite side. It was quite unlike the first. Heavier, more secure, and fitted with thick bolts to lock it shut from outside. At the foot of the door someone had fashioned a crude hatch that hinged upwards and outwards, like a one-way-only cat flap, except it was held securely closed with a hasp and strong padlock. As Ben got closer to the door he could see the big, heavy bolts were drawn back and a thin crack of light was visible from within. He paused again, listened, like before. Then reached for the door handle and swung it softly, gently open.

What he saw beyond the doorway confirmed what he already knew. Before him, a short flight of steps led down to a sub-basement, maybe thirty feet square, brightly lit. The walls had been painted white, in a slapdash effort. The furniture was minimal and functional. Near the centre of the room stood a single chair left over from the same set as the ones in the first room, along with a similar cheap table on which rested a plastic cup and an empty paper plate. A basic metal-framed bed occupied the left-hand wall. A partitioned-off plywood corner section had been knocked up over to the right, forming a little space that Ben didn't need to look inside to identify as a crude, makeshift bathroom. All highly temporary, thrown together in a hurry, intended purely to meet the most basic living needs of its occupant. Which fitted the typical pattern Ben had seen a hundred times before, back in the day when he used to do this for a living.

It was a kidnap room. A holding cell.

And there was someone inside it.

Chapter 43

Prem was at the far end of the room, thirty feet from the bottom of the steps. He was wearing designer blue jeans and a tan leather flight jacket, which was probably as casual as it got for a well-to-do young guy of fashionable tastes. But he obviously had much more on his mind right now as he paced up and down the breadth of the room, talking on the phone with such intense focus that he was completely oblivious of the fact that he had company. He was clasping the phone tightly to his ear in one hand, the other pressed downwards to the top of his head with clawed fingers buried in his thick black hair, as though he had a migraine. Or was going crazy with stress. That was certainly the impression conveyed by his tone of voice, strained to breaking point. Whatever the phone call was about, it wasn't making him happy.

He was saying, 'What the fuck are you people doing? This wasn't part of the plan. Why are you doing this? I can't—'

A pause as the voice on the other end of the line interrupted him to reply. Prem stopped pacing and screwed his eyes shut with frustration, listening hard. Then he started shaking his head furiously. 'No, no, no. No fucking way, man. That's not the deal. That isn't what you're getting paid for. Listen to me—'

Ben had come halfway down the steps in total silence. He said softly, 'Prem.'

He might as well have let off a shotgun blast in the confines of the room. Prem wheeled around and froze rigid and helpless, like a lamped rabbit caught out in the open with nowhere to bolt to. His eyes boggled in Ben's direction, then towards Brooke, who was still at the top of the steps and watching him in cold rage and disbelief. The phone dropped out of Prem's hand and bounced off the concrete floor. His mouth opened to speak, but no words came out.

Ben reached the bottom step and walked slowly towards him. 'Imagine our surprise, finding you here like this. Where's Amal?'

Prem turned fish belly blue-white. 'He's not here.'

'But he was here. Wasn't he, Prem?'

Prem began to bluster, then must have realised there was no point. He just nodded, once, a slight rise and fall of his chin. His shoulders drooped in total defeat. He let out a heavy sigh and stared at the floor.

Brooke suddenly burst back to life. She came racing down the steps, as though she wanted to throw herself at Prem and rip his eyes out with her fingernails. Ben gently put out an arm to hold her back. He said to Prem, 'Who were you talking to just now? Takshak? I know it's not Dhruv, Vijay, Sanjay or Ramesh. Because they won't be doing a lot of talking to anyone any more, as of earlier this evening. But you are. You're going to tell us everything, Prem. About your involvement in this, about who took Amal, about him being brought here and about where he is now. So let's have it.'

Prem just stood there, so rigid he was quivering. His eyes were darting left and right as though he was desperately trying to decide which way to go. Considering his options.

He had only two. He could confess to whatever was the ugly truth, abandon himself to his fate and pray for leniency. Or he could attempt to force a way out of this.

A second later, Prem made his choice. Not the wisest one. But perhaps the most reckless gamble seemed like the only option he could pick. He darted a slender hand inside his tan leather flight jacket and came out holding a pistol.

But Ben had seen that move coming before Prem had even made his mind up. The gun was still in motion between its concealed holster and its aiming point when Prem's wrist was intercepted, blocked, trapped and twisted and his fingers opened involuntarily and lost their grip on the weapon. Which was now suddenly in Ben's hand. Prem let out a primal yell of terror and loathing and fury, all rolled into one. He jumped back half a step, then lashed out at Ben with the toecap of one of his expensive handmade brogues. Ben sidestepped the kick and hit Prem a savage blow across the side of the head with the frame of his own gun. Prem went instantly limp and slumped to the floor like a puppet with its strings cut. He lay very still at Ben's feet, oozing blood from a gashed scalp.

Brooke stared down at the inert form on the floor, then looked wide-eyed at Ben. 'Jesus. You killed him.'

Prem's gun was in keeping with his stylish, top-priced wardrobe: a Colt Delta Elite 10mm auto, stainless steel, brand new and shiny, in a class of its own next to Haani Bhandarkar's worn old clunkers. Fully loaded, but too immaculate to have ever been fired since it left the factory in Hartford, Connecticut. Ben flipped on the safety and stuck it in his belt next to the Browning, then stooped to pick Prem's phone off the floor. Whoever Prem had been talking with had hung up. For later, Ben thought, and slipped the phone in his pocket.

He replied to Brooke, 'No, I didn't kill him. But when he wakes up he'll wish I had.'

He stepped away from Prem, walked over to the makeshift plywood construction on the right side of the room, and opened the flimsy door. A bathroom, as he'd guessed. Rigged up with a chemical toilet and a basin for washing in, with a plank shelf for some basic toiletries, toothbrush and toothpaste. Not exactly the Leela Palace, but it was considerably more luxury than a lot of kidnap victims got to enjoy, in Ben's experience. Brooke peered in the bathroom doorway and seemed to reach the same conclusion. 'This place is weird,' she said.

'Very weird,' he agreed.

Ben walked over to the bed and pulled back the sheet. It was crisp and clean, and free of any bloodstains that could indicate rough treatment of the prisoner. Meanwhile, Brooke had spotted a pile of clothing on the floor. She rushed over to sift through them, and picked up a rumpled T-shirt with a philosophy quote across the front that said, *'Don't walk in front of me, I may not follow; Don't walk behind me, I may not lead; Just walk beside me and be my friend.'*

'It's Amal's,' Brooke said. 'His Albert Camus shirt. I bought it for him. He was wearing it the night he was taken.' She dropped the T-shirt back on the floor and examined a light blazer jacket. 'This is his, too. And these are his jeans and underwear. What's he wearing?'

'If they gave him clean sheets, maybe they gave him a fresh change of clothes, too.'

'Kidnappers don't do that,' she said. 'Do they?'

'Not in my experience.'

Ben turned to the cheap table and picked up the plastic cup. It still had half an inch of light brown dregs in it. He sniffed. Coffee. Or what passed for coffee among the unenlightened.

He took a small sip. Weak decaf, polluted by long-life milk and sugary sludge at the bottom. Revolting. And cold. But not that cold.

He said, 'How does Amal take his decaf?'

'Not too strong, lots of milk, lots of sugar.'

Ben put down the cup. 'Still slightly lukewarm. Meaning he was here not long ago. Prem wasn't lying about that part. Someone snatched him and took him away. And in a hurry. They left a load of provisions behind upstairs. I suppose they'll pick up more en route.'

'En route to where?'

'If I'm right, out of the city. Heading roughly east, about a hundred and fifty kilometres.'

'Wake that bastard up and make him tell us. Torture him if you have to.'

'I don't think he knows the full picture, Brooke. He seemed pretty shocked that Amal was gone. That's what this whole Takshak thing is about. Looks like someone turned the tables. Prem rushed over here the way he did because he was hoping to stop them. But he was too late.'

'You mean someone *else* has kidnapped him now?'

'Or someone cut our boy Prem out of the loop.'

'Who?'

'I have no idea,' Ben said. But he was lying.

'What are we going to do?'

'You wait here.'

'Where are you going?'

'I'll be right back,' Ben said. 'If he wakes up and tries to misbehave, knock him over the head again.'

'Gladly.'

Ben ran back up the steps and headed up the corridor to the room they'd passed on their way. Now he knew for sure what the room had been used for, while Amal was still being kept prisoner in the sub-basement. Even kidnappers need a place to rest, unwind, eat and drink.

The room was still empty, as expected. He went over to the box in the corner and grabbed the roll of duct tape and a length of paracord. Tools of the kidnapper's trade. Two could play at that game.

Prem hadn't woken up by the time Ben returned to the holding cell. He flipped him over onto his belly and bound his wrists behind his back with the cord, then wound a length of tape around them to make the bond so strong a gorilla couldn't have broken free. Next, he flipped the unconscious body back over face-up, tore two more strips of tape from the roll and pressed one over his mouth, the other over his closed eyes.

Brooke said, 'What about his ankles? He can still walk, when he wakes up.'

'That's the idea. Then I won't have to carry him back up all those stairs.'

'Where are we taking him? Not back to the hotel, surely?'

'No,' Ben replied, 'we're taking him home to the house. It's time for a conference with the family, or what's left of it.'

Brooke stared at him with eyes full of confusion. She wasn't stupid. Far from it. She was one of the two smartest women Ben had ever known, the other being Roberta Ryder. But the implications of what was unravelling here in front of them went so deep and were so troubling that even a mind as sharp and incisive as hers was balking at the inevitable conclusions to be drawn. 'I think I'm understanding what you're saying. I'm just not sure that I want to.'

'Whoever took Amal knew him pretty well,' Ben said. 'That's for sure. How else would they have been familiar with small personal details, right down to how he takes his coffee?' He pointed upwards. 'And those hidden speakers in the ceiling are telling us the same thing, just in a different way. They can only have been put there for one purpose, which was to enable the kidnappers to talk to their prisoner incognito. Or interrogate him, more to the point. They probably used some device to disguise their voice, for the same reason. But why go to such lengths to set all that up, when they could just walk into the room and question him face to face?'

'Because he'd recognise them,' Brooke said grimly. Getting it now.

Ben nodded. 'And a mask wouldn't do it. It's not enough just to hide your face. Not when your prisoner is someone who's known you all their life. Literally.'

Brooke's face tightened. She pursed her lips. The inevitable conclusion had focused to a pinpoint in her mind and there was no longer any dodging it. 'Samarth.'

'It's more than just supposition, Brooke. This is his building. Prem works for him. If that doesn't constitute hard evidence of involvement in this thing, you'd better explain it to me.'

Brooke shook her head in bewilderment. 'I'm dreaming. This isn't happening. Are we saying that Samarth—? But why would he do that? His own brother?'

'Both of his brothers,' Ben said. 'Let's not forget about Kabir. Not to mention that three other innocent men have died over this.'

'I don't get it. He was worried about Amal recognising him. Which sort of suggests he didn't intend him any harm. Dead men don't talk, do they? And he's providing coffee, and a decent bed, and private toilet facilities, and even a bloody toothbrush and toothpaste, but meanwhile he's running around killing people, including his other brother? There's no logical pattern to it.'

'I know,' Ben said. 'It doesn't make sense to me either.'

At that moment Prem made a loud groan from behind the tape over his mouth. A second later he started violently as he woke up to find himself bound, gagged and blind. He thrashed and writhed on the floor, wriggling his legs like a man running on the spot. Brooke stepped back to avoid getting kicked. Ben reached down, grabbed him by the collar of his jacket and hauled him roughly to his feet. 'Come on, matey boy, time to go home.'

Brooke said, 'Shit. I just remembered I gave Esha back my remote for the driveway gates.'

'No problem.' Ben held the struggling, moaning, groaning Prem steady with one hand and patted him down with the other until he found the guy's own remote in his jeans pocket, along with a ring of house keys and another little blipper for deactivating the alarm.

'Each gate remote uses a different access code,' Brooke said. 'We'll have to beat the number out of him.'

Ben looked at her. 'I understand your desire to slap him around, but I already know the code.'

'Pity,' she said.

They bundled their prisoner out of the kidnap holding cell and shoved and dragged and prodded and frogmarched him all the way back up the corridor, up the stairs, through the empty shell of the building and outside into the night.

Prem's Audi still had the keys in it. Brooke asked, 'What about his car? If the police find it, they might start poking around. Is that what we want?'

'I doubt it'll stay in place long enough for the police to find,' Ben said. He hauled and shoved Prem across the rubble-strewn waste ground to the Jaguar. Opened up the rear hatch, backed Prem up until the backs of his legs were pressed against the lower sill, then tipped him into the large boot space and folded him up and slammed the lid. Brooke got in the passenger seat. Ben took the wheel. He reset the sat nav destination to the Ray residence.

'Ready?'

'I'm ready.'

Ben fired up the engine, slammed the Jag into drive and took off. A crazy night was about to get crazier.

Chapter 44

On the way to the house, Ben reached in his pocket for the phone Prem had been talking on, and gave it to Brooke to check over. The other phones they'd taken that night had been of the cheap and cheerful prepaid variety, untraceable and disposable. By contrast, Prem had been using his personal iPhone to converse with his criminal associates. Brooke scrolled through the call records and quickly found the numbers Prem had either been in contact with or dialled without getting through to.

'It's Takshak we're interested in,' Ben said. 'The last person to call him, except us.'

'I'll try the number.' Brooke plugged the iPhone into the car audio system the way she'd done earlier, found the number and then hit redial. The tones sounded deep and rich through the Jaguar's speakers. And went on, and on, until the generic voice message kicked in to say that the person they were calling was not available.

'He's turned off his phone,' she said. 'And probably junked or destroyed it by now.'

'As any self-respecting real criminal would,' Ben said. 'Unlike our boy here. He's more than a little out of his depth dealing with these people, even as an intermediary.'

'That doesn't tell us much about who they are. Apart

from the fact that they have Amal. Jesus. This keeps getting worse.'

Ben said, 'As we both know, most kidnap victims don't get a bed with a real mattress, and their own private bathroom. They don't generally get a say in how their coffee gets made, either.'

'So?'

'So if they've taken measures to treat him okay, it means he's worth something to them. Which means they aim to keep him alive, healthy and in good condition. That's something to bear in mind.'

'And if he suddenly turns out to be less use to them?'

'It won't matter by then. Because we'll be closing in. Or we'll already have him.'

'You hope.'

'There's always hope,' he said.

'And you're my best,' she replied after a beat. 'You always were.'

Ben said nothing.

Before too long they were approaching the wealthy suburb where the Rays lived. Prem must have sensed they were getting close to home, which meant his moment of reckoning was drawing near. He was becoming restless in the back, and they could hear the thumps and muffled groans of protest coming from under the flimsy rear parcel shelf. 'This is why I hate hatchbacks,' Ben said. 'Give me a proper boot any day.'

'We can't get through the security checkpoint with him making all that racket back there,' Brooke said.

'You're absolutely right.' Ben checked his mirror, pulled over to the kerb and stepped out of the car. He waited for a passing car to come hissing by on the wet road, then walked round to the rear, opened the hatch, and tapped Prem on the skull a couple more times with the butt of his own Delta Elite to send him back to sleep for a while.

'That's more like it,' he said as he got back in and they set off again.

The checkpoint guards were full of all the usual smiles and charm towards Brooke. They were all so used to Ben's face now that they barely registered his presence at the wheel. Just another lackey working for the Rays, no doubt. Or maybe a bit of rough for the rich and beautiful Mrs Ray. Lots there for them to speculate and fantasise about. But definitely not a person of suspicion. As for the third occupant of the car, he attracted even less notice. The guards waved them through.

Minutes later, they were pulling up outside the closed gates of the Ray residence driveway. Ben took out Prem's remote, pointed it through the windscreen and keyed in the number sequence 4-1-9-8. Tuesday Fletcher's favourite IMR smokeless powder formulation. The gates automatically unlocked and began to whirr open to let them pass. Ben crunched slowly up the driveway towards the house.

'How do we do this?' Brooke asked anxiously.

'The simplest plans are the best. Let me scout the place first. One minute, to check the terrain and make sure we're good to go. All being well, we get inside, then you lead the way to Samarth and Esha's apartment. Then you get behind me, then we make our entrance. I need to know about domestic staff. Is there anyone else we're liable to bump into in there?'

'There's the cook, Inu, but she only comes in for a few hours a day. Chandni does the cleaning, usually mornings or afternoons. And there are a couple of groundskeepers. Nobody lives in.'

'All the better,' Ben said. 'In case we create a disturbance.'

'What kind of disturbance? You think Samarth is armed in there?'

'There's a lot we apparently don't know about Samarth. Therefore, for the sake of precaution, we should apply the golden rule.'

'What's the golden rule?'

'Speed, surprise and violence of action. The more of all three, the better.'

Ben put the stick in neutral and killed the engine and lights before they rounded the last bend in the driveway, and let the car coast silently up to the house. A few windows were lit up in the ground-floor west wing at the far side of the property, but the place was mostly in darkness as though winding down for the evening. That was good. All the signs seemed to suggest that nobody was expecting company.

Ben halted the car thirty yards from the entrance and slipped out first. He stalked as quietly as a ghost across to the garage block, let himself in and checked the cars. On the way over, he'd been considering the possibility that Samarth might be working late at the office that night. But his concern was proved unfounded when he saw Samarth's silver Bentley Arnage parked in its space next to Esha Ray's little yellow Fiat. The bonnet was cool. That was good, too. It meant Samarth had been back home long enough to shower, change out of his office clothes, and get nice and relaxed. Maybe a glass or two of something to soothe away the stresses of the day. Ben wanted the guy as chilled out and blissfully unsuspecting as possible. Especially if there was a home defence weapon in the equation.

He slipped back to the Jaguar. Brooke had got out and was waiting for him. Ben quietly opened the rear hatch. Prem was still completely out for the count inside, which meant he'd have to be bodily carried. Ben leaned down,

263

pressed a shoulder into Prem's side and flipped him up and over in a fireman's lift. Prem wasn't anywhere near as heavy as a fully-kitted-out SAS trooper injured in battle.

They cautiously approached the entrance. No security lights blazed into life, no hidden cameras or motion sensors gave them away as they approached the front entrance. Ben passed the ring of house keys to Brooke, holding them tight so they wouldn't jangle. She used the blipper to deactivate the burglar alarm, then found the right key and let them inside.

So far, so according to plan. Ben whispered, 'Lead on.'

Brooke whispered back, 'What if he's got a whole gang in there with him?'

Ben smiled. 'It wouldn't be enough.'

The Ray residence had seemed big during the day, but at night it appeared to go on forever as Brooke led the way left and right through endless shadowy hallways and corridors, Ben following with Prem's dead weight dangling like an army kit bag full of laundry over his shoulder. He had to be careful not to let the guy's dangling feet knock over a lamp or ornament, crashing it to the floor and signalling the presence of intruders. Though, technically speaking, they'd let themselves in using a key and without breaking anything, and two out of three of them either lived in the house or had done until recently, with the third having been invited as a guest – and so Ben wasn't sure if the term 'intruders' truly applied. But he was just as sure that Samarth wouldn't see it that way.

At last, Brooke halted at the interior door of the west wing apartment where Samarth and Esha lived. She turned to Ben and pointed, then stepped back as if to say, 'Over to you.'

As quietly as a comatose body can be dumped on a solid

marble floor in a large, high-ceilinged hallway with naturally reverberating acoustics, Ben let Prem's weight down from his shoulder. He stepped close to the door, listening. No voices from inside. Just the soft tinkle of pleasant piano music in the background. More modern than classical, from the post-Romantic period. Ben was a jazz person by taste, but he recognised the piece. Claude Debussy, *Clair de Lune* from his *Suite bergamasque*. If Samarth was in there with a whole gathering of hired thugs around him, they were enjoying a quiet evening of refined cultural pursuits together. Which seemed an unlikely scenario, but there was only one way to find out.

He took a step away from the door. Glanced at Brooke. She nodded, her eyes gleaming anxiously in the darkness. He nodded back. Reached down and grabbed a handful of Prem's jacket collar. Then took a breath, drew the Browning from his belt, thought *fuck it* and rocked back on his heel and gathered his strength and kicked the door in.

Chapter 45

Speed, surprise and violence of action. The more of all three, the better.

The door frame was a far more solid and chunky affair than the one Ben had destroyed at Haani's place earlier that day. But it couldn't put up enough resistance to prevent itself from crashing open with a noise like a grenade bursting. Splinters flew. Soft amber light from inside the room spilled into the hallway. Ben jerked the unconscious Prem as upright as his floppy legs would support him, and sent the guy sprawling headlong through the open doorway. If a dozen armed thugs had been behind the door ready to open fire on whatever came through it, Prem would have been riddled with bullets before he smacked face-first into the Persian rug.

They weren't, and Prem's smackdown was unimpeded. Because Samarth Ray was all alone inside the large, comfortable living room of his apartment. In the moments before the door crashed open, he had been reclining at his leisure in a deep buttoned-leather armchair with an open hardcover book in his lap and a tall iced drink on a pretty antique table at his elbow. He'd changed out of his business suit and was wearing casual chinos and a silk Paisley-pattern shirt with an elegant cravat. The criminal mastermind basking in peace and quiet after a hard day's kidnapping, murder and extortion.

As Ben had anticipated, the sudden appearance of his uninvited guests came as a complete surprise to Samarth. And if the guy was in any way armed, he made no attempt to reach for his weapon. After a second's shocked pause he shot bolt upright from the leather armchair, sending his book tumbling to the floor, his face mottling purple and veins of anger standing out on his high forehead. He stared at Prem sprawled out bound and gagged on the Persian rug. Then at Ben in the smashed doorway. Then at Brooke, standing at Ben's shoulder. Samarth yelled, 'What is the meaning of this outrage?'

Brooke forced her way past Ben and strode into the room, virtually trampling Prem. She yelled back, 'You utter bastard! You piece of shit! What have you done?'

Clair de Lune kept tinkling in the background, as if the pianist was too lost in the music to sense the disruption in the room. Ben remained in the doorway. He slipped the Browning back under his belt. He didn't think he was going to need it, but he was ready.

Samarth's bewildered gaze scanned from Brooke to Ben, then back to Brooke. But like any seasoned boardroom combatant he was a man used to surprises and confrontation, and he seemed to recover his wits quickly and held his ground.

'I have no idea what you're talking about, or what you think you're up to, bursting into my house like this. And what have you done to Prem? I'm calling the police!'

There was an old-fashioned dial telephone on a leather-topped writing bureau in the corner of the room. Samarth started towards it, reaching for the receiver.

Ben stepped into the room. He said, 'Samarth.'

Samarth stopped and turned to face him, the hand reaching for the phone hovering in mid-air.

Ben said, 'Sit down and stop messing around.' The voice of command. The same tone he'd learned and perfected, back in the day, issuing orders that weren't always entirely welcome, to men with supremely-developed skills, unbridled confidence and alpha-male egos to match. It had never failed Ben in those days, and it worked now. Samarth returned to his chair and sat down.

Ben took another step into the room and said, 'The indignant law-abiding citizen act won't work for you, and you know it. The last thing you want is for the police to turn up here. Plus, if you try to pick up that phone again I'll break your arm. Then if you try to grab it with the other hand, I'll break that arm too. You see how this goes?'

Samarth sat there simmering with anger. He didn't try to get up or reach for the phone.

'Sensible man,' Ben said.

'And you're a man of violence.'

'Where the occasion necessitates it.'

'You believe this is one of those occasions?'

'That's up to you,' Ben said. 'Personally I'd prefer us to conduct ourselves in a civilised manner.'

'I see. So you rough up my employee for reasons I'm yet to understand, then you barge uninvited into my home and threaten me with bodily injury if I try to call for help, and now you want to be civilised.'

'The alternative would be markedly more unpleasant for you than for me,' Ben said.

'You leave me little choice, then. May I ask to what I owe this unexpected visit?'

'We're here to continue our conversation from earlier,' Ben said. 'In the light of recent developments.' He walked

268

up to Prem's slumped form, snatched him up off the floor and deposited him on a Chesterfield settee that matched the armchair Samarth was sitting in. He yanked away the tape and cord binding Prem's wrists.

Samarth asked, 'What developments?'

'As if you didn't bloody well know,' Brooke seethed at him.

Ben ripped away the tape covering Prem's mouth. Then the tape covering his eyes. He did it fast, which was the less painful way, but still painful. Cruel to be kind. A bucket of cold water wouldn't have woken Prem up any more quickly than having half his eyebrows and eyelashes stripped away. He sat up with a yelp, and rubbed his face, and looked around him blinking frantically as consciousness came back and he realised where he was. He didn't seem too pleased about that, either.

Ben said, 'I'd like Prem to take part in the discussion, since he's involved. But first I'm going to ask you one simple question, and I'd appreciate a quick and truthful answer. Where's Amal?'

'That's right, Samarth,' Brooke said tersely, folding her arms. The handbag hung heavily from her shoulder. She hadn't forgotten what was in it. 'Where is he?'

Samarth stared at them both. 'Is this some kind of sick joke? My brother was kidnapped. If I had the remotest idea where he had been held prisoner, don't you think I would have used that information to get him back? If indeed he's still alive, which I doubt. I think I've already made my feelings clear on that score.'

'If he's dead,' Ben replied, 'he hasn't been that way long. No more than an hour or so.'

'How can you be so sure?'

'Because nobody else would drink such bad coffee,' Ben

said. 'He was alive this evening, and he was definitely alive when we came to see you at your office earlier. I'm pretty certain he's alive now. But then I think you know that. I think you knew it all along.'

Samarth grimaced. 'What are you trying to imply? That I had something to do with it?'

'We're not trying to imply it, Samarth,' Brooke said. 'We're outright stating it as fact. You paid a bunch of thugs to kidnap your own brother, and you've been keeping him prisoner in the basement of one of your own construction projects. Your loyal manservant here has been managing the whole operation on your behalf.'

Samarth exploded. 'What? This is insane! It's pure madness! You're delusional!'

'Sounds like a denial,' Ben said. 'What a surprise.'

'Say it again,' Brooke said. 'Let me hear you shout your innocence. That's all it's going to take to make me blow your brains out.' She reached into her handbag and took out the Webley revolver and pointed it in Samarth's face. 'I repeat. Your brother. My husband. Where is he?'

Samarth held his arms out wide. 'Why in God's name would I have my own brother kidnapped? Prem? What are they talking about?'

Prem didn't reply. He was fully conscious now, sitting grimly like the accused waiting for a judge to pass the death sentence.

Ben said, 'Because the first attempt failed, obviously. Your hired guns messed up the job of snatching Kabir. As a result of which, he went MIA, presumed dead as far as anyone was concerned. So then you opted for Plan B, because you suspected that Amal knew something about all this.'

'About all *what*?' Samarth screamed.

'About the lost Indus Valley treasure,' Ben answered.

'What's the matter, Samarth? Business not going so well? Stocks down? Made some duff investments? Maybe that's why the Ray Enterprises construction project we saw tonight has stalled, among other things. And why you made your wife sell her expensive car. The money troubles are obviously pretty bad.'

'I didn't make her sell her car.'

'Shut *up*,' Brooke snarled. She prodded him hard with the muzzle of the revolver.

Ben continued, 'Bad enough to make you justify that it's okay to get both your younger brothers hurt, maybe even killed, so that you could somehow get your mitts on the loot. What made you hate them so much? Is it resentment against the fact that neither of them wanted to come on board the family business, and left you to run it alone? Or are you really just a ruthless crook who was happy to take the money and put Amal and Kabir in the ground? And what if there is no money? What if this whole treasure thing is bullshit? What if it was all for nothing?'

'Prem, say something!' Samarth implored. 'Tell them this is all wild fabrication. Tell them neither I nor you had anything to do with this.'

Prem was silent.

Brooke said, 'Prem was there tonight. That's where we found him. In the basement. In the building. *Your* building. With *your* fucking name on it. Right where you were holding Amal, until you moved him. Apparently Prem didn't know that was happening. He's been on the phone to your rent-a-thugs trying to find out more. You've obviously been holding out on him. Maybe because you knew that Ben's here now, and that we're gradually sniffing out the truth, and you were crapping your pants that we'd find him and the whole thing would come out. You couldn't trust Prem, in case we got to him first. So where have you moved Amal?'

Samarth stared at Prem. 'Is what she's saying true? You knew where Amal was being held? You were in touch with the kidnappers? I don't believe it. I don't understand.'

Prem didn't speak.

Samarth asked him, 'Why would you not have told me any of this?'

Ben was looking at Samarth. Here was a guy who lived in the fast lane, wheeling and dealing and negotiating all day long. Shrewd, and sharp, and able to think on his feet like a master tactician. He could easily be stalling and bluffing like crazy while working out all kinds of ways to wriggle out of this situation, claiming innocence and acting as though he was just as shocked as Brooke had been by these revelations. But the acting part was key. Because if Samarth was putting on this compelling show of absolute sincerity, it would blow the greatest Oscar-winning performance of all time clear into the weeds. He should have gone into the movie business and become the most celebrated star of his generation, with scripts flooding in and leading directors banging on his door.

And for that reason it was dawning on Ben that Samarth might not actually be acting at all. He might, conceivably, be actually telling the truth. While Prem wasn't telling anything at all.

And Prem was the second reason why Samarth's protestations of innocence sounded so uncomfortably plausible. Because if Samarth had been guilty as charged, Prem's very presence in the room would have constituted a massive risk for him. All Prem would have had to say was 'Yes, he made me do it. I was only obeying my boss's orders. How could I refuse such a powerful man?' Knowing he was already in deep. Knowing that his only hope was to plea bargain his way to some kind of better deal. That would have been it. Cut and dried. Not a jury in the world would have failed to convict the obvious bad guy.

And yet, Prem still hadn't said a word.

Therefore maybe things weren't that cut and dried after all.

Samarth said, 'Prem, as your employer I order you to explain yourself, right this instant. Do you hear me?'

Prem said nothing.

'Brooke, give me that gun,' Samarth said. 'If he doesn't want to talk, there are ways to make him.'

She shook her head. 'You must be nuts if you think I'd let you have this.'

'You still don't believe me? You think I hurt my brothers? My own flesh and blood? You think I would be capable of such a thing?'

Brooke made no reply. Prem still wasn't talking. Ben was watching the dynamic unfold. Scrutinising Samarth. Reading his expression. Certain now that there was much more to this than either he or Brooke had realised. That he was getting it completely wrong and had stormed into the home of an innocent man with guns and threats and accusations.

A big mistake.

Then another door opened, and everything changed.

273

Chapter 46

Everyone turned to look as a woman walked into the room. Ben had never seen her before. She was tall and elegant and attractive, closer in age to Prem than to Samarth, somewhere between mid and late thirties with just a few streaks of grey in her raven-black hair. She wore large loop earrings and a bright green top, with a saffron-coloured sari that flowed over one shoulder all the way to her feet. Which were bare, with rings on her toes. The long sari swished as she walked. There was something dignified, almost regal, about her. Though for all the poise and bearing with which she carried herself, there was a stiffness to her movements as though all the tension and sorrow in the world were locked inside her body, wanting to come bursting out.

But what Ben noticed more than anything else was that her eyes were red and smudged from crying.

Brooke's hard expression instantly softened. 'Esha!'

Prem was staring at her. His mouth was hanging open and there was something aghast in his expression. Ben wasn't yet sure why the sight of the lady of the house would make him react that way.

Samarth frowned at his wife and blurted out, 'How long have you been standing there?' Without waiting for her to

274

reply, he went on, 'Have you been hearing what these lunatics are saying about us? And since when did I force you to sell that car? You told me it was too big and powerful for you to drive. Is everyone lying to me? Or am I going insane?'

Esha Ray walked a few more steps into the room, and stopped, and gazed at her husband, then at Prem. Prem went on staring at her with the same expression. Eyes wide, as though imploring. Every muscle of his face drawn and tight. She held his look, and tears streamed down her cheeks. She said, 'It's no use, Prem. It's over. They know.'

Prem struggled to his feet, all in a flustered panic as if to prevent her from doing something terrible and irreversible. 'No! They don't know anything! Don't tell them!'

Which to Ben's ears was the closest thing to an admission of guilt that he'd heard so far that night.

'We have to do something,' Esha Ray said. 'For Amal. Before it's too late. Before they . . .' She pressed her hands to her face. Her fingers were long and slender, the nails varnished the same colour as her sari. Her shoulders gave a heave as she began sobbing again.

Samarth made no move to embrace or comfort his wife. He was boggling incredulously at her. 'What are you talking about, woman? What do or don't we know? Before what's too late?'

Ben was interested in knowing the answer to that, too. For several long seconds there was total silence in the room, apart from the sound of Esha weeping. Prem's fists were clenched tight and his face was cadaverous. Then through her tears, Esha Ray said, 'I'm sorry. I'm so, so sorry. None of this was ever meant to happen.'

Ben looked at Brooke and saw the same baffled expression he could see on Samarth's face, and must have been on his own. All five of them in the room were standing frozen, as though the moment had stunned them all into inertia. Ben broke the spell by taking four long steps towards Esha Ray. He reached for her hand. It was wet with tears. Gently, he led her towards the nearest armchair and helped her to sit. She was crying so hard that she couldn't speak.

Ben said, 'I think it's time for Prem to explain to us what this is about.'

All eyes were on Prem, except Esha's. He was breathing hard, fists still balled at his sides. His head sank until his chin touched his chest.

'No,' he said. 'It wasn't meant to happen this way. None of it was. And here we are. It's all gone to shit. What does it matter now?' He gave a bitter laugh.

Ben watched him for a moment, then turned to watch Esha, then back at Prem. The two of them looked like a couple of rueful children caught in the act of doing something bad and now having to face the music. Except they weren't children. Ben was beginning to understand. So, judging from the look in her eyes, was Brooke.

'How long has it been going on?' he said.

Samarth still hadn't got it. Which, Ben thought, seemed to fit the picture. Evidently, some things were just taken for granted. Such as a wife's undying love and devotion, and the durability of a neglected marriage.

Samarth said, 'How long has *what* been going on? Well? Isn't anyone going to explain?'

'You're so blind, Samarth,' Brooke said. 'They've been having an affair.'

Samarth gaped at his wife, still weeping where she sat. Then across at his loyal employee. His face darkened. 'It's impossible. I can't believe it.'

'You'd have found out soon enough,' Ben said. 'When the star-crossed lovers ran away together and left you in the

276

lurch. That is, if their plan had worked out. Didn't quite happen that way, did it, Prem?'

'What were we supposed to do?' Prem muttered. 'We wanted to set up a home together, as far away from here as possible, but with what?' He thrust an accusing finger in Samarth's direction. 'He wouldn't have given her a penny. That tight-arsed bastard would rather see her starve than let her be happy.'

'And you were going to make her happy,' Ben said. 'With a scheme to filch a few rupees to start your cosy new life together. Or maybe a few hundred million. Or so you hoped. It must have seemed like serendipity when you overheard Kabir talking on the phone to his brother in London. Listening at doors is very bad, Prem. Or were you actually tapping the line? Because I can't think how else you could have found out.'

Samarth slumped in a chair, looking as though he'd been gut-punched. He barely glanced at his wife. No 'Please, Esha, I love you'; no 'Darling, where did I go wrong? I thought we were so happy together.' Not even a 'Who are you calling a tight-arsed bastard?' He started fumbling to loosen his silk necktie and muttered, 'I think I'm having a heart attack. You had better call me an ambulance.'

Brooke snapped at him, 'Sit still and shut up.'

'I just happened to be nearby,' Prem confessed. There was no point in hiding anything now. 'The door was open a crack. It was the mention of money that got me listening. They were talking millions, billions.'

'I suppose you pictured heaps of iron casks filled with gold and diamonds, just sitting waiting to be loaded onto trucks and brought home, easy as pie,' Ben said. 'Like something out of a movie. I'll bet you were so excited, you didn't stop once to ask yourself what Kabir had actually discovered, or how close he was to getting it out of the ground.'

'All I heard was money talk,' Prem said. 'It sounded like a done deal, but I didn't get to listen in on the whole conversation. I think they had a bad line. Kabir moved away from the door and went out on his balcony to get a better reception.'

'So you just let your imagination get the better of you. Whose idea was hiring Takshak and his gang? Yours? Hers?'

'Esha didn't know about the plan at first,' Prem said. 'I only told her later, after I'd made the first contact with them.'

'Through a guy who knew a guy who knew a guy,' Ben said.

'A man who used to work for the company, and was sacked for stealing. I'd heard he was in with some bad people. I was scared to approach him.'

'Hence the gun?'

Prem nodded. 'I bought it in a pawnshop. I don't know if it's legal, or if it even works. I just wanted it for show, in case there was any trouble. Next thing, I was in a car, and next thing after that I was having my first meeting with Takshak.'

'Not his real name,' Ben said.

'It's the only one I have for him. I don't know anything about him.'

'So you explained what the job was, and Takshak named his price.'

'Two million rupees.'

'Which you didn't have. This is the real reason Esha had to sell her Porsche.'

Prem nodded miserably. 'We sold it for four million and gave him half up front, in cash.'

'How many in the gang?'

'Ten, a dozen, I'm not sure.'

Ben did a quick calculation. Two million rupees might

have sounded like a fortune but it converted to only about twenty grand sterling. Divided between a dozen guys, not exactly pay dirt. Every country in the world was filled with small-time crooks willing to do just about anything for pocket change, but Prem had found himself a real bunch of beauties.

Ben said, 'Okay, keep talking.'

'Everything happened so fast. We only had a couple of days before Kabir was due to fly out there. We thought we had everything planned. Takshak and the men were to camp out in the general area, then look out for the helicopter incoming. It's all rocks and empty desert there, you can see for miles. Then they were supposed to drive their trucks to the landing spot, do the job and get out of there. It was supposed to look like a bandit raid. You have to believe me that—'

'That nobody was supposed to get hurt?' Ben cut in. 'I believe that's what you told Takshak. But I can't believe you could have been stupid enough to trust it wouldn't happen. You were swimming with sharks, Prem. What did you expect?'

'I never dealt with people like that before. Especially Takshak. The guy's insane. I had to humour him all the time. I had no idea they'd actually shoot anyone. Afterwards they tried to say they'd seen the sun glint off something. Thought it was a gun. Then everything went to shit.'

'Kabir wasn't armed. He left his pistol here at the house.'

'I know that,' Prem protested. 'I didn't believe their story. I threatened them, demanded the money back, but they just laughed at me. Two dead men, and they make a joke about it. Those filthy pigs.'

Ben said, 'Hold on. *Two* dead men?'

Chapter 47

Prem suddenly fell silent, as though the air had been sucked out of him. Or, more correctly, Ben guessed, as though he'd realised that he'd said too much.

Esha was still crying in the background. Ben ignored her and kept his eyes fixed on Prem as he repeated the question. 'You said there were two dead men. Kabir and his associates Manish and Sai left Delhi for Rakhigarhi that day. None of them came back. By our count, that makes three, not two. Unless you know something we don't.'

Prem said nothing.

'Prem? You were doing well until now. Don't screw it up.'

Prem breathed in, breathed out, and replied, 'Okay, it's true. There is something else. The fact is, Kabir got away.'

Ben glanced at Brooke and caught the look of astonishment on her face. But it was Samarth who reacted first, starting out of his chair. 'What? Kabir is alive?'

Prem gave another sigh and replied, 'I didn't say that. There was a lot of shooting. Takshak thought they might have winged him. He fell down a slope. A steep one. They went down there after him and searched all over, but they couldn't find him.'

Samarth slumped back in the chair. It had been a fleeting moment of hope and now it was dashed. 'They shot him.'

Prem nodded. 'It's been over three weeks. If nobody's seen him since, he must be dead by now. Maybe from the bullet, maybe from the fall. I'm so sorry.'

Ben said, 'You sound it.'

Brooke was still clutching the Webley revolver. It was dangling loosely at her side, but she looked ready to bring it up to aim and plug Prem through the forehead with it. 'Jesus Christ. And you never thought to tell anyone about this? Don't you think that information might have been useful to the police at the time?'

'I couldn't run the risk of incriminating myself,' Prem protested. 'I mean, they'd have wondered how I knew and started asking all kinds of difficult questions.' He shrugged. 'Anyway, would the police have done anything differently, even if they'd known? This is India.'

'Where life is cheap and people are animals,' Ben said. 'Just about the first thing you told me when I got here. And you'd know, wouldn't you?'

Brooke shook her head slowly in disgust. 'You're an even bigger piece of shit than I thought, Prem. There's only one reason I'm not blowing your bloody brains out right now.'

'I said I was sorry. I meant it. You think we weren't devastated by what happened? You have no idea. Both of us. But what were we supposed to do? It was way past the point of no return. We were in too deep.'

'So you went to Plan B,' Ben said. 'Which was to go back to Takshak and his gang with a new job, pay them the rest of the four million rupees to snatch Amal and ask them very nicely not to mess it up this time.'

Prem opened his mouth to answer, but it was Esha Ray who spoke for him. 'Don't blame him for that. Blame me. Hate me all you want. I know I deserve it.'

Brooke turned to look at her. 'You?'

'Kidnapping Amal was my idea,' Esha Ray said. 'And I wish I was dead. I'll never forgive myself. Never.'

'Samarth's empty building? That was your idea too?'

Esha said, 'We did everything we could to make it comfortable for Amal. He's family. We love him dearly, Brooke. I know you can't believe me.'

Brooke just stared at her.

'We even bought the right kind of coffee for him. Prem's idea, since he'd been preparing it for him here at the house. A comfortable bed, decent food, clean clothes. And this time, the men understood that nobody was to lay a finger on him. He was not harmed in any way, I promise. All we wanted was for him to tell us what Kabir told him.'

'So you interrogated my husband through those hidden speakers in the ceiling.'

'That was me,' Prem admitted, shamefaced. 'I used a device to alter my voice.'

'And did he tell you what he knew?' Ben asked.

'Not at first. He denied knowing anything at all. Which I knew was impossible, based on what I'd heard of their conversation. It kind of threw us that he wouldn't talk, because we had no way to pressure him, except to let Takshak's guys into his cell to use force against him. And there was no way we were going down that road again. But then we came up with another idea.'

'You threatened him,' Brooke said. 'At the very least. You scared the wits out of him. Or worse. Tell me you didn't make him suffer somehow. Because he'd never have told you, otherwise. He wouldn't even tell me, out of loyalty to Kabir.'

'We leveraged him,' Prem said. 'What does it matter now?'

'That's a good word,' Ben said. '"Leveraged". But what does it mean?'

'We told him—' Prem sighed.

'Yes?'

'We told him we had his wife.'

'And threatened to hurt her if he didn't cooperate,' Ben said.

'We didn't make that threat,' Prem insisted. 'Not specifically.'

'But you made it implicitly. You let him believe it. You made him think that his kidnappers were going to start cutting bits off Brooke if he didn't talk. Or maybe douse her with acid, since that's obviously a favourite method of your little cronies. You forced him to confront the worst, darkest fears he could possibly imagine. In other words, you tortured him.'

A tear welled up out of Brooke's eye and rolled down her cheek. Then another, from the other eye. She wiped them away with the back of the hand holding the gun. Prem couldn't look at her. He said again, 'I'm sorry. If it's any consolation, we only had to use that threat just the one time. He broke right away.'

'And he told you everything.'

'As much as he knows. Which turned out to be not much more than we already knew. The two of us decided we'd have to let him go.'

'But by then it was too late,' Ben said. 'Because Takshak's people were getting tired of playing nursemaid, waiting for you pair of amateurs to get results when they thought there was quick and easy money at stake. Did you really think men like that were going to do all the work of digging up the loot for you and then content themselves with the smallest share? They've been looking to double-deal you from the beginning. And the moment you got Amal to start talking, you sealed his fate. They saw their chance to turn the tables on you and snatch him for themselves, right out from under your nose. For all they knew, he could lead them right to the money. X marks the spot. And their methods to force him to talk won't be as gentle as yours. You want to see the kind of treatment they dish out to people, I can give you an apartment address in north Delhi where you can go and view it for yourself. A man you probably never even heard of, Haani Bhandarkar, died there tonight thanks to you.'

Brooke had gone white. The tears were dry now. She said, 'You started this whole thing and now it's out of control. And whether Amal helps them find the damn treasure or not, they'll kill him.'

Chapter 48

Brooke turned to face Esha Ray. 'I thought you were my friend. My confidante. Someone I could really talk to. Someone I could trust. How could you have done this to us?'

'They're my brothers too,' Esha said in a cracked voice.

'Or were,' Ben said. 'Thanks to your actions, we might have to refer to them in the past tense from now on.'

Esha screwed her eyes tight shut and hung her head. Prem seemed to have run out of words to say. All that remained was a hue of sorrow and regret so deep, so painful, that it left little room for anger.

Though not for everyone present. Samarth glowered at the two of them. His eyes were rimmed with red, like a man who hadn't slept for a week, and the fingers clenching the arms of his chair were as bloodless as a corpse's. He said, 'I hate you both. I would wish you dead, but instead I hope that you live to the age of a hundred and spend every moment of the rest of your days thinking about the lives that you destroyed.'

'What'll happen to us?' Esha whispered.

'The police will come and take you away,' Ben said. 'You'll go to jail for a long, long time. When they eventually let you out, you'll both be very old and grey and so feeble you can hardly walk. What you call love will have withered away to nothing but bitter memories, and even if you have a few years left, you'll both be too ashamed to want to set eyes on each other again. That's what's going to happen. And the worst part is, you did it to yourselves. This is all on you.'

'Absolutely,' Samarth said, pale and trembling. Fists clenched. Teeth bared. A man hungry for retribution. The crueller and more drawn-out the better. 'Call the police. I want to watch as they're dragged away in chains.'

'They'll get what's coming to them,' Ben said. 'But not yet.'

Samarth looked confused. 'Why not yet?'

'Because the last thing we want right now is a certain Detective Lamba and his goon squad swarming all over this house, poking into our affairs, asking a lot of questions, calling their brethren in Rakhigarhi and unbalancing a very delicate situation. Third World cops love nothing better than a good old shootout with armed bandits. Bad news for hostages.'

'India is no longer part of the Third World.'

'Go tell that to the police,' Ben said.

'But we need them. They're the only hope for getting my brother out of the hands of these murderers.'

Ben shook his head. 'Believe me, Samarth. We don't. And they're not. Bringing the police in on this would be the same as shooting Amal yourself. That's why I'm afraid I can't allow you to make any calls to anyone.'

'I don't take orders from you!' Samarth stood up and started marching towards the bureau where the old-fashioned dial telephone rested. Ben got there first. The hand moving towards the phone was snatched out of the air, while at the same instant the wire was ripped from the wall. Ben hated to damage a nice old instrument. But it was about to become a collateral casualty of war. With the hand that wasn't still clutching Samarth's wrist he snatched the phone and smashed it to the floor.

'Remember what I said about necessity and violence,' Ben said. 'They don't have to go together, but it's up to you. The part about the broken arms still applies, too.'

'Listen to him, Samarth,' Brooke said. 'He's right. The police are certain to mess this up. We've seen it happen before. We have to think of Amal.'

Samarth stopped struggling. Ben let him go. 'Give me your mobile.'

'I-I left it at the office.'

Ben snapped his fingers. 'Give.'

Samarth hesitated, rubbing his sore wrist. Then took a sleek phone from his pocket, sheathed in a black leather wallet bearing a silver Apple logo. He handed it over. Ben yanked the phone out of its wallet and snapped it in half and dropped it on the floor with the remains of the dial phone. He said, 'Samarth, as of this moment, you're under house arrest.'

'What?'

'It's a trust thing,' Ben said. 'You've just proved that you don't warrant any. So, you will remain right here in this apartment. No contact with the outside world. You'll go nowhere, see nobody, talk to nobody. Except your guard, who will be watching every move you make.'

'And who is that? Some hired thug of your own? Another arm-breaker just like you? Why, you're no different from the mindless criminal trash who have my brother.'

'This is your guard,' Ben said. He pointed at Brooke.

'*Her?*'

'She'll make sure you don't get up to mischief while I'm gone. Try not to give her a reason to shoot you.'

'Me?' Brooke said.

Ben could hear the hurt in her voice. 'This is how it has to be, Brooke. I'm sorry.'

Except Ben wasn't sorry at all. This was exactly where he needed Brooke to be. Safely tucked away at base in the heart of the most privileged and protected neighbourhood in India. As far away from trouble as she could be. Trouble was where he was heading, like steel to a magnet. It was his element.

'I wanted to come with you,' Brooke said.

'But you can't. I do this alone. My way. The only way.'

Brooke absorbed his words and her expression turned from dismay to reluctance to acceptance. She nodded slowly. 'But how can I guard him all on my own? Sooner or later I'll need to sleep or use the bathroom.'

'Lock him in a cupboard. Tie him to the radiator. Improvise. You'll think of something. If he gives you any trouble, bang him over the head.'

'And for how long do you intend to keep me a prisoner in my own home?' Samarth demanded.

'For as long as it takes. Maybe a couple of days. Maybe more.'

'This is intolerable!'

'Take it easy, Samarth. Remember what we said about conducting ourselves in a civilised manner.'

Samarth seemed about to protest, then relented. 'Very well. I will give you no trouble.'

'Good.'

'But the domestic staff will be here in the morning. They're going to wonder what on earth is happening.'

'Not if you call them first thing and give them the rest of the week off. A special bonus for all their service.'

Brooke motioned towards Prem and Esha, who were

watching with haunted looks on their faces. 'What about those two?'

'Only one thing for them,' Ben replied. 'The same treatment they dished out to Amal.' He turned back to Samarth. 'This is a big house. I'm guessing it would have some kind of secure basement?'

Samarth was quick to come up with his answer. He pointed at the floor. 'Not as such. But there is a wine cellar right beneath where we stand. My father had it built many years ago, before this wing of the house was constructed over the top of it. It's sunk ten feet below the ground. For optimum humidity and temperature control. The wines are extremely valuable, so naturally they have to be shielded from theft. The walls are thick stone and the sole access is a strong steel door, locked at all times. Impossible to break into, or to escape from.'

Samarth was actually smiling, as though his only comfort in this personally humiliating moment was knowing that the culprits would be spending the next few days stuck in a hole beneath his feet.

'You think it's okay to keep them together?' Brooke asked.

Ben shrugged. 'It's the last time they're going to see each other. Where's the harm?'

'You can't lock us up down there,' Prem complained. 'It's not human.'

'Oh, it's not human,' Ben said.

'It's dark and cold. There's nowhere to sleep except a bare earth floor. There's no running water.'

'But plenty of wine,' Ben said. 'If it was me, I'd take the opportunity to drink myself to death rather than spend the next several decades in an Indian prison. You think about that.'

Chapter 49

Then there was a lot of work to do. Samarth showed the way to the wine cellar, the access to which was down a couple of worn stone steps off a back kitchen in the west wing. He hadn't been joking about the security. Old Basu Ray must have loved his wines, that was for sure.

Samarth refused to speak to, even look at, his wife as Ben introduced her and Prem to their new temporary abode. Esha was crying so bitterly and Prem looked so ghastly that Ben almost felt sorry for them. Maybe it would be better just to shoot them. Or maybe not. He slammed the heavy iron door shut, threw the bolt and clicked the massive padlock, and left to attend to the next item on the agenda. Namely, to leave Samarth under Brooke's supervision downstairs while he paid a visit to Kabir's apartment on the second floor.

The middle brother's quarters weren't what Ben would have expected of a young, wealthy, single guy who drove a red Ferrari and flew a helicopter. Kabir seemed to have lived like a student, and in place of designer décor and flashy boys' toys had filled his apartment with collections of old artefacts from every century of Indian civilisation since the time of the Buddha. Barely an inch of wall space was left uncovered by historical prints and hangings. It was clear that his archaeology work had been his overriding interest in life.

Just as it had turned out to be the indirect cause of his violent death.

Ben was looking for a combination safe, probably not a big one. There was no sign of it in the living area. He cut through to the bedroom, which was where Brooke had said Kabir had stashed his pistol by the bedside, like Haani. And just like Haani, it turned out that Kabir had kept his precious things locked up near to him while he slept. The safe was similar in type to Haani's, but shiny and expensive and probably ten times harder to break into. With no combination number, Ben could have been there for days trying to liberate its contents. Nor did he have a crowbar, which could have speeded things up considerably. But he did have a 10mm Colt Delta Elite. Only a millimetre bigger in bullet diameter than the time-honoured Browning Hi-Power, but it packed a lot more punch and could handle chamber pressures up to 37,500 pounds per square inch, not too far behind a .44 Magnum.

It was a good thing that the house had no close neighbours. The gunshot was as loud as a quarry blasting charge. But the reward for Ben's jangled eardrums was an open safe door. Inside he found two gold watches, a stack of money, and a collection of three old leather-bound journals that looked as though they'd spent the better part of two centuries rotting in a remote hill cave next to the cadaver of their former owner. Ben slipped off the elastic holding the three books together, carefully opened the cover of the top one and saw the faded name inscription.

Marmaduke Trafford.

This was it, no question. Haani's description of the journals' poor condition had been pretty accurate. Ben flipped through the rat-chewed, mildewy pages. Among Trafford's faded yet neat cursive handwriting were many sketches of the things he'd seen on his extensive travels through nineteenth-century India. Ancient ruins. Fearsome tribesmen. Unusual flora and wildlife. The guy had been a true naturalist, a category of science now lost in history. And a keen linguist, judging by the pages and pages devoted to the Indus script-based language used by the remote mountain community who had saved his life and with whom he'd spent a winter, living as one of them. He'd also been a pretty capable amateur cartographer, and it was the maps Ben was most interested in.

One map in particular. It showed the winding course of a river, and a variety of other topographical details like hills and valleys and escarpments, marked with old-fashioned geographical coordinates calculated with stars and compass. Folded between the pages was a much newer sheet of paper, a printout of a scan Kabir had made of the map with modern GPS location data superimposed over the originals. Ben would have other landmarks to orientate himself by, as well. Like whatever would be left of Kabir's helicopter nearby, if the police hadn't taken it away. And the presence of a band of armed bandits camped out in the vicinity, with their hostage in tow.

If indeed their hostage was still alive. Amal's continued survival was hanging by a very thin thread. The longer Ben was delayed in reaching Rakhigarhi, the worse those bad odds were going to get.

He wrapped the journals back together with the elastic and replaced them in the safe, deciding he needed to take only the map printout with him. He refolded the paper and slipped it in his pocket, then left Kabir's apartment and hurried back downstairs and went outside. The rains had left the night feeling cool and fresh, as though the downpour had washed all the soot and dust out of the air.

Now that he had the map he needed transport. Something solid and robust that would eat up the miles between here and Rakhigarhi quickly and efficiently. Roomy enough on the inside to use as a mobile base camp, if needed. Tough enough on the outside to withstand a little punishment, should the situation require. The Ray family fleet offered him a selection to choose from. The Jag ticked most of the right boxes, as did Samarth's Bentley. Kabir's Ferrari ticked only one of them, namely the speed element, and was woefully inadequate for the rest. While Esha's Fiat ticked none at all.

But only one of the vehicles in the Ray family fleet was perfect for the job. Because none of the others had a twelve-cylinder twin-turbo engine making more than six hundred horsepower, wrapped inside an armoured shell capable of withstanding everything from small arms fire to grenade and bomb blasts to chemical weapons attacks. The ex-Presidential Mercedes-Benz Maybach S-Class Pullman limousine. A little ostentatious for Ben's liking. But otherwise the nearest thing he was going to find to a hardened rapid assault vehicle without breaking into the nearest military facility.

The fleet keys were all hung up on a fancy row of hooks above an antique stand in the front entrance hall. He snatched the one with the Mercedes-Benz star emblem on its leather fob. Map. Guns. Wheels. He was good to go. He had just one more thing to do before he got on his way.

Brooke was still in Samarth's apartment living room. She was sitting quietly on the Chesterfield settee Prem had been on before, gazing into the middle distance while Samarth paced up and down by the window at the far end of the large room, muttering to himself, hands clasped impatiently behind his back, deeply preoccupied with his own troubles.

Ben lingered silently in the doorway for a moment, watching her. She was still and composed, back straight, hands resting on her knees. The soft amber light of the room accentuated the perfect curves of her brow and cheekbones, chin and neck. Lines he knew so well that he could have drawn them on paper. She looked beautiful, even though the emotional strain of all that had happened that night was clearly visible on her face. Ben was suddenly able to imagine what she'd look like ten or fifteen years from now. Or twenty, as the silver threads began to creep into the auburn of her hair. Years that they could have shared together, ageing gracefully and happily as a couple. The pain stabbed his heart.

She seemed to sense his presence there, and turned her head to look at him with a brief, sad smile. He stepped into the room and walked over to where she sat. Samarth kept on pacing and muttering in the background, oblivious.

Ben laid down his heavy bag and settled beside Brooke on the Chesterfield. The soft rich leather creaked and sank under his weight, so that they pressed together as close as lovers, thighs touching.

'Time I was on my way,' Ben said to her. 'You going to be okay?'

'Not as okay as I would have been, if you'd let me come with you.'

'It's better this way. Trust me.'

'You could have used some help. We don't even know how many of Takshak's gang you're up against.'

'You're helping plenty enough by keeping an eye on our prisoner here. And we do have a pretty good idea. Prem said about a dozen, call it thirteen with Takshak. Minus the rear guard he left behind to tidy up loose ends while the rest of them headed out of town. That's four guys who won't be rejoining him.'

'Makes nine,' Brooke said with a frown. 'Against one.'

He smiled. 'See? Only nine. Out of which at least one will be tied up with guarding their hostage. That whittles it down to eight, maximum, all worn out from shovelling rocks if they've started digging by now, which you can be sure they will have. They'll probably be working shifts, four of them sleeping while the other four will be too hard at it to see me coming. Their hands will be so blistered from all the heavy labour that they'll hardly be able to pick up a weapon, even if they get the chance. Which they won't.'

'You're only saying this to reassure me.'

'Walk in the park,' he said. 'Nothing easier. Two of us going in would be a waste of resources.'

She was still frowning. 'It's not working. I'm worried about you.'

'Don't be. Sit tight and I'll be back before you know it. With your husband.'

Brooke reached out and touched Ben's arm. She said softly, 'He's not the only one I care about, Ben Hope. You know that, don't you? I mean, I—' She drew in a deep breath and it caught in her throat like a tiny shudder.

Ben said nothing.

'Don't make me say it,' she said.

'It's better if you don't say it,' he replied. 'Same goes for me.'

She nodded. Her green eyes gazed into his for the longest time. Her hand was still touching his arm.

'You be safe, Ben,' she said.

'As houses,' he replied.

She looked as if she wanted to cry, but was gamely bottling it all up until after he was gone. He hesitated for a moment, then raised his hand to her face and stroked her cheek with his finger. It felt as soft as velvet. He kissed the top of her head.

Then, without another word, he stood up and left.

Back outside in the rain-washed coolness, he paused again to light a Gauloise. Closed his eyes, and saw her face there. Then he opened his eyes, took a deep breath of his own and walked to the limo and got inside and took off into the night.

Chapter 50

Ben's route west out of Delhi was India's National Highway 9, as flat and straight and wide and bland and featureless as any modern motorway in the world. Most of the night-time traffic consisted of lumbering freight trucks and monster tankers, interspersed here and there with late-hours delivery tuk-tuks puttering along so slowly by the feeble beams of their candle-glow lights that Ben passed them as though they were standing still. The Maybach wafted down the highway at 150 kilometres an hour, all five tons of it gliding as smoothly as a hovercraft riding a cushion of air while Ben lounged in the cream leather driver's seat and guided the huge car with a toe on the gas and two fingers on the wheel.

The limo had all the toys that a VIP traveller could possibly expect to enjoy within their air-conditioned, bulletproof bubble of serenity. The on-board navigation system was like something from the flight deck of a Boeing, while an inbuilt jammer served the purpose of protecting the occupants from RCIED, or radio-controlled improvised explosive device, attack. Just the thing when cruising the mean streets of Delhi. The Maybach was even wired to play internet radio, and after minimal fiddling with the controls Ben found a station that played uninterrupted jazz, no chit-chat, no adverts.

Music heaven. To the mellow guitar sounds of Pat Martino he let the comfort of the car envelop him like a soft blanket, shoved his whirling thoughts to the back of his mind, lit another cigarette and watched the road zip by.

He drove hard for two and a half hours and then pulled in at a truck stop to refuel and grab something to eat. About a hundred large trucks filled a floodlit waste ground off the highway. Many of them were ancient workhorses with serious mileages and worn tyres, personalised with colourful paint schemes and ornamentation and all kinds of cargo haphazardly lashed to their roofs and flatbeds. Some goats and a couple of cows lounged in the dirt nearby. You could probably do what you wanted to the goats, but this being India they'd hack you to death you if you laid a finger on the cows. The night air was full of the tang of diesel and hot engines and the more aromatic scents coming from a tin-roofed grill shack around which a crowd of hungry truckers were gathered. After refuelling the limo and getting a few strange looks, Ben wandered over to the shack, where three leathery guys who looked like they'd been working for a week without rest were busily preparing handmade breads, dals and meats cooked in stone wood-fired ovens and sizzled over glowing charcoal beds. He bought Tandoori chicken wrapped in a flatbread and took it back to eat in the car.

He parked the limo on the beaten-earth waste ground behind the truck stop, surrounded by broken-down huts and mountains of junk and rusty oil drums and derelict vehicles. Swapping the driver's cab for the relative vastness of the Pullman compartment he spent a few moments playing with the touch-sensitive switches on a control panel while his chicken dinner was still too hot to eat. The first switch activated the privacy blinds, shutting out the world. Another made one of the back seats elongate into a plush

298

bed better than anything on a first-class flight. He flipped more switches, and other hidden compartments popped open to reveal various toys and gadgets essential to the convenience and security of a Presidential passenger. There was a stowable desk complete with mini-laptop, fountain pen and paper; there was a gas mask fitted with an oxygen cylinder, in case those nasty terrorist assassins managed to breach the car's chemical warfare defences; and there was a satellite phone, presumably for making emergency calls when out of mobile range. The sat phone was made by Thuraya, based in UAE. Ben had once trained bodyguards for the company chief executive. He tossed the phone in his bag along with the rest of his stuff. Some gadgets were possibly worth holding onto, where he was headed.

The last switch Ben flipped was the one he'd really been hoping to find. It whirred open a console between the seats, which housed a mini-bar complete with cut-crystal tumblers and a bottle of eighteen-year-old Macallan. 'Now we're talking,' he murmured aloud.

He sat on the soft bed and ate his Tandoori chicken, marinated in yogurt and spices and seasoned with cayenne, and as tender and delicious as anything the best restaurants of Delhi might have served up. Then he poured himself a generous measure of scotch, lit another cigarette and leaned back and smoked and savoured his drink and thought about what lay ahead of him. Tomorrow would be a long day. Perhaps a difficult one. He'd played that part down for Brooke's sake. The reality might be rather more challenging than he'd let on.

After a nightcap or two he turned off the lights, lay back on the bed, closed his eyes and slept.

But not for long. Ninety minutes later Ben was back on the road again. Somewhere near the Haryana city of Hansi he left the NH9, still a long way south of his destination. He then cut back on himself, heading north-east as far as the city of Jind, then westwards again towards Mirchpur, which his smartphone told him was one of the Indus Valley sites overshadowed by the main site at Rakhigarhi. It was a sign that he was getting close; at which point he fished the map printout from his pocket and entered Kabir's GPS coordinates into the Boeing flight deck sat nav system. The nineteenth-century explorer might have had to make do with his compass, but the wonders of technology would lead Ben to within a few metres of the exact spot he needed to be.

From Mirchpur his route led him north-westwards towards the Rakhigarhi area, from where he bent his course due north, heading into remote countryside further and further from any kind of main road. The Maybach took the rough surface in its stride, only the smallest hint of vibration feeding back through the controls as the landscape ahead grew ever wilder. After spending so much time in the crowded, bustling environment of Delhi he had the distinct feeling of leaving civilisation far behind.

The blood-hued glow of dawn found him carving a winding and solitary path deeper into a rocky, hilly landscape that had been harshly arid for thousands of years. Only a smattering of hardy vegetation survived here, now and then a stand of withered-looking trees. The topography reminded Ben of the parts of Afghanistan and Pakistan that he'd known, back in the day. For the next solid hour he kept following Kabir's GPS directions, the road growing rougher and rougher until it was a rubble-strewn track with deep ruts that swallowed up his wheels and raised jagged boulders that scraped and thumped against the armoured underside of the Maybach. It had definitely not been intended for off-road duty. Still, Ben figured that if the thing could withstand landmines, a few rocks couldn't hurt. As long as the wheels kept turning and finding traction, that was good enough for him. The first farm or village he came to, he might consider trading it for a rusty Mitsubishi 4x4 or ratty truck more suited to the rough going.

But no farms or villages came into view, mile after lurching, bouncing, grinding mile. He went on pushing the car mercilessly over the terrain like an injured tortoise. The orange sun climbed in the sky, and even cocooned inside the air-conditioned cabin Ben could sense it was going to be a hot day. According to the sat nav he was close now, only half an hour from his destination. The track was leading him onto a broad, sweeping plateau with barely any vegetation, where the ground sloped downwards to form a deep rocky V that seemed to stretch onwards forever.

Ben ploughed on. The valley grew deeper and narrower until it was virtually a canyon. Rough-edged boulders that had tumbled down the slopes on either side overlaid ancient rocks smoothed to the sheen of marble by what he guessed had, once upon a time, been the course of a deep, fast-flowing river. The bottom of the river bed was his road now, forcing him to stick to its route. He could neither scramble up the banks to higher ground nor turn the long car around. The only way was straight on, if the ancient river's twists and bends could ever be called straight.

Twenty minutes later, Ben came to a spot where a long section of sloped river bank to his left had fallen away to create a sheer drop down into a lower valley, obviously the result of a major landslip, some indeterminate period of time in the past. Ben guessed that only something as powerful as an immense earthquake could have caused damage like that. It could have happened a hundred centuries ago, or last year. He was no geologist.

Then, running his eye up the slope of the still-intact bank to his right, he spotted an incongruous object catching the sunlight about three hundred yards ahead. And he knew he was in the right place.

Chapter 51

It was Kabir's abandoned helicopter. A Bell Ranger, its bright red fuselage dulled by dust. Or what remained of its fuselage. The aircraft was perched near the edge of the bank overlooking the river bed, the key landmark Ben had been hoping to find. Its landing spot was almost exactly bang-on the coordinates Kabir had added to the map. But if he and his associates had found anything up here before they were attacked, there was certainly no sign of it now.

Ben stopped the car in the river bed below the stationary chopper, turned off the engine and got out into the sand-dry heat. There was dead silence except for the whisper of the wind. Nothing moving but the wave of the odd bush and shrub. The white sun in the pale sky above him, bleached rocks and nothingness all around him.

He scrambled up the slope, dislodging larger stones and making little slides of smaller ones. Reaching the aircraft he could see why Samarth had made little effort to have its remains salvaged, because after three weeks of locals stripping it for spare parts or scrap metal to sell, not much was left but a bare carcass. The main and tail rotors were missing, probably now doing wind-turbine duty on some remote farm in these hills, while the seats graced somebody's living room. Ben wondered what possible rustic kind of use a fuselage panel could have. A roof for a pig pen, maybe.

Standing next to the chopper on the top of the bank he slowly turned in a circle and got his bearings. The winding river bed was heading roughly south–north. A hundred yards further along its twisty course, a big clump of dry-looking thorn bushes was partially blocking the way ahead. To the east, the intact river bank flattened out into a broad, feature-less plain dotted here and there with trees and rocks. North-west, across the other side of the river bed where the demolished section of the opposite bank had once been, the sheer drop opened up a barren vista that extended for miles.

The only direction that offered limited visibility was due west, where the intact part of the opposite bank formed a flat-topped rise blocking his view. But generally he was able to reconnoitre most of the terrain for a good distance around. And he could see nothing moving, not a living soul anywhere. If he'd been expecting to spot a contingent of Takshak's men organised into a treasure hunt party, busily digging away with picks and shovels while guarding their prisoner tethered up nearby, he'd have been bitterly disap-pointed. But that would have been too easy.

Once more he took out Kabir's printout of Trafford's map, and spent a few moments studying it. Even accounting for the landslip that might have demolished the opposite river bank since the map had been drawn, something wasn't quite right. While the coordinates seemed to correspond and the line of the river looked about the same as the sketch on the map, some of the other topographical detail appeared to clash. Like the range of hills over to the south-west, which didn't feature on the map at all. Ben wondered whether Kabir had noticed the anomaly, too.

But there was little to be learned by standing there gazing

at the landscape. Ben scrambled back down the slope and began exploring the area on foot, starting in smaller circles around the car and gradually expanding his search for clues, tracks, anything of interest.

It wasn't long before he found the first spent cartridge case lying on the ground, tarnished and dusty. Then the second, and the third, and more, until he'd picked up over twenty and was satisfied they were all the same type of military surplus 7.62 NATO rifle round that had been used by Takshak's gang in the attack against Kabir, Manish and Sai. Some of the cases were flattened as though they'd been driven over or crushed under a heavy boot. Ben could tell from the scatter patterns of the ejected cartridges which way the shooters had been firing, diagonally across the river bed with the slope and the parked chopper behind them. He guessed they must have made their approach down the slope, either on foot or in off-road vehicles. Kabir and his guys must have ventured some way from the chopper by then, making them a medium-range target for the trigger-happy morons who'd opened fire on them.

Ben began walking along the imaginary trajectory of the gunfire, eyes scanning the ground for more evidence. Forty yards, fifty, sixty. Then he stopped and bent down to pick up something small and shiny among the rocks of the river bed. He held it up to examine it more closely.

A piece of glass from a shattered wristwatch dial. It had dried blood on it. Which could have belonged to any of the three victims, either the two who'd died here or the third who'd managed to escape the scene.

Prem had reported second-hand from the gunmen that Kabir had fallen down a slope while making his break for it. The angles and distances told Ben that the slope in question had to be the fallen-away left river bank. A fit man, even injured, could have made it from here to the edge at a run.

He walked over and looked down the steep valley that the landslip or earthquake had created. It was quite a drop, almost a precipice, its edge crumbly and precarious. A man would have had to be desperate to throw himself off it. Though anything was better than getting shot to pieces.

Ben wasn't here to solve the mystery of what had happened to Kabir, but curiosity was getting the better of him. He walked along the edge, peering down. Then he stopped, noticing something else on the ground. It was a small flat rock, smoothed by millennia of river current. Imprinted on its surface was a russet-brown handprint. The colour of blood after baking in the heat for about three weeks.

No question, this was where Kabir had gone over. The sheerness of the incline made it impossible to see the foot of the slope. Ben tried to scramble down the incline, but after a few yards he was in danger of losing his footing on the loose rocks and tumbling all the way to the hidden bottom, which could be a long drop. He needed a rope, preferably an abseil harness too, and had neither. But if he skirted along the edge of the drop to where the river bank was still intact and made his way to the top of the rise there, he should be able to find a good vantage point from which he could observe the foot of the slope.

The police had claimed to have searched the area, but that didn't necessarily mean much. Ben was prepared to believe that their efforts to find Kabir's body had been desultory at best. Which could very well mean that it was still down there. Only one way to find out.

He reached the base of the bank and clambered up the steep rise on all fours, making little landslides as he went. It was about a forty-foot scramble to the top, and as he'd guessed, the summit of the rise gave him a pretty good view westwards and north-westwards, spanning the hills beyond the ancient river bed and the deep valley that the earthquake had carved out below. He could see all the way to the bottom, some two hundred feet down, where huge chunks of rock had piled up into mounds now thinly grown over by thorn bushes. A few trees had grown up at the foot of the valley, making it hard to observe with the naked eye.

He wiped his hands on his trousers and delved inside his bag for the compact binoculars that accompanied him everywhere on his travels. He raised them up, twiddled the knurled focus ring for a sharp picture, and slowly scanned the thicket of trees at the bottom of the slope. He was half expecting to spot the rumpled shape of a corpse down there, not looking too pretty after three weeks in the sun.

No sign of anything. If Kabir was down there, Ben couldn't see him.

But then something else caught his eye. Something he'd have missed if he hadn't climbed up to the top of the rise.

Two hundred yards to the west, a column of black smoke was rising.

Chapter 52

The source of the smoke was hidden from view by the undulations of the terrain, which rose and fell like waves. But as the old saying went, there was no smoke without fire. And whatever was burning down there, Ben wanted to investigate. He put the binoculars away, shouldered his bag and started making his way towards it, jumping and clambering over rocks, scrubby brittle vegetation tearing at his trouser legs.

The wind was blowing gently westwards, or else he'd have smelled the acrid stink that reached his nose as he got closer. The smell of burning rubber and diesel was one of the battlefield scents forever imprinted on his memory. He wondered what he was about to find down there.

Some three hundred yards from the remnants of Kabir's Bell Ranger, Ben jogged up the last of the blind rises blocking his view, and finally was able to see where the smoke was coming from. The wreck of the old Mahindra four-wheel-drive truck looked as though it had been blazing for a long time, and still had a while to go before its tyres burned away completely. Its windows were shattered and the interior was just a melted-out shell. Its blackened, heat-blistered bodywork was punched through with so many bullet holes that it looked like a colander.

So did the body of the man who was lying nearby.

The guy had been dead for about as long as the truck had been burning. He was sprawled out flat on his back with his left arm carbonised by the flames. He didn't smell too good, either. Ben crouched beside the corpse and looked him over. He was Indian, lean, stringy, twenty-something with a shock of wild black hair and a long black beard, all dusty and caked in blood that had leaked from his mouth after he'd been lungshot. It was hard to tell whether that had been the bullet that killed him. He'd taken at least half a magazine full in the belly and chest. His tattered, bloody clothing was a bastardised mixture of obsolete military surplus stuff and he wore a green canvas ammunition bandolier crossways over one shoulder, bandit style. The bottle-necked rounds in the bandolier matched up to the old Russian-made AKM military rifle that lay in the dirt a few inches from his clawed, outstretched right hand. He'd probably been rattling off bullets even as he fell dead.

The guy had not died alone. Ben found eight more corpses scattered among the rocks and bushes, in a ten-metre radius of the burning truck. All similarly bearded and scruffy and lean, armed with ex-Soviet hardware, and kitted out in guerrilla-style military surplus outfits that had obviously seen a lot of countryside. They'd all suffered a similar fate, too, pretty much shot to bits. The ground all around them was littered with spent brass. Two of them were wearing utility belts with live hand grenades still attached. This had been quite a skirmish. But against whom had they been fighting, and over what?

Ben discovered the first part of the answer when he came across a further three bodies lying among a cluster of bullet-scarred rocks forty yards away. All three had met the same violent death. And all three had also been packing

309

the same kind of gun, different from the ones they'd been shot with. These were old decommissioned SLRs, short for self-loading rifle. The official military appellation had been L2-A1, the squad automatic weapon version of the L1-A1 that had seen decades of service with the Indian and British armies. A squad automatic weapon was, in essence, a lightweight machine gun. Serious pieces of kit that had been released by the thousand onto the black market when the Indian military had modernised their stock.

But what most interested Ben about the guns was that they fired the same 7.62 NATO round that had been used against Kabir and his friends.

Examining the corpses one by one, he soon found more of interest. The first was still wearing the same Rambo T-shirt he'd had on when he and his buddy had approached Ben for a light at the Chhatta Chowk bazaar back in Delhi. A favourite garment, no doubt, though it was past its best now. Stallone's head was a big hole where a rifle bullet had blown out its wearer's chest cavity.

The second body, Ben didn't recognise. While the third was that of a particularly stumpy fellow, squat and wide. *Built like a fireplug, or a fire hydrant, one of those things.* Brooke's words, when she'd described Amal's kidnappers to him the day he'd arrived in Delhi. *And very hairy, like an animal.* The hairiness in question was now all matted and slicked down with blood from multiple high-velocity gunshot wounds and a grenade blast that had severed his right leg below the knee and blown a crater in the ground. Otherwise, Brooke's description fitted the guy perfectly.

Which meant these three belonged to Takshak's gang.

Ben thought back to the encounter at the bazaar. He visualised the taller man in the open-necked purple shirt who had been with Rambo that day and done all the talking.

He remembered the mirror shades, the blunt features, the air of masculine confidence. The guy had been about Ben's own height, and of similar build. Which matched Brooke's description of the leader of the kidnap gang the night Amal had been snatched. Ben hadn't put it together until this moment. Now he was wondering: *had the guy in the purple shirt been Takshak?*

Then Ben ran back through the series of events since. Soon after the bazaar incident, Takshak had turned the tables on Prem and snatched Amal for himself. Up until that moment Prem must have instructed the gang to tail Ben and keep tabs on him, considering him a threat to the operation. Or, possibly, to find the appropriate moment to take him out of the picture entirely. If that was the case, Rambo had missed his chance now. Ben wondered if he'd been part of the original kidnap team along with his hirsute fireplug comrade, and maybe the other guy too.

But none of those speculations could solve the riddle of what had happened here. Ben sat on a rock, lit a cigarette and thought about it. The eight dead men on the other side looked fairly hardcore, like guys who lived rough in the hills and had been doing so for most of their adult lives. They'd probably never set foot in the big city. Real bandits, Ben guessed. As opposed to Takshak's crew, who were more of the urban guns-for-hire, loan shark, wide boy, bone-breaker and drug dealer set. If his guess was right, it looked as though shortly after arriving here, Takshak's gang had drawn the notice of some local dacoits, who'd probably decided their territory was being invaded by some rival group and put up a fight.

From the imbalance of casualties, three to eight, Ben had the impression that Takshak's crew had come out decisively on top. Whereupon, the victorious survivors hadn't hung around for long, and had evidently been in such a hurry to get away that they'd left behind a small arsenal of weaponry along with their dead. Maybe more dacoits had been incoming. Or maybe Takshak's gang had managed to beat off a force of superior numbers, and then made their escape before they came back.

Ben didn't really care, either way. Three dead men among Takshak's crew meant three fewer he'd have to deal with himself. He salvaged the best of the SLR squad weapons they'd been using, along with four full spare magazines, which he dumped in his bag. Then he walked back across the killing ground to revisit the eight dead dacoits and unclipped the hand grenades from their belts to stuff them in his bag, too. With enough munitions to start a small war, all he had to do now was track down the rest of the gang.

And kill every last one of them.

And find Amal. And bring him home.

To Brooke.

Then, as Ben was strapping up his bag, he heard a sound that made him turn and peer upwards at the sky with his hand shading his eyes.

Chapter 53

It was the unmistakable thud of helicopter rotors in the far distance. Scanning the horizon he caught the tiny glimmer of the incoming chopper as it reflected the morning sun. Still a very long way off, just a speck against the sky, but he had no doubt it was heading this way. The black smoke still rising from the burning truck could probably be seen for miles across the hills and rocky plateaus stretching to infinity westwards.

Ben had no desire to make the unexpected visitors' acquaintance until he knew who they were, and probably not then either. Easy enough to hide himself, but the huge black limo was another matter.

He started running back towards the car. Three hundred yards across rough terrain with little time to waste. The sprint took him a minute and five seconds exactly, which was one second longer than the average time for a fit young police or military trainee. But that was on a running track, not leaping and scrambling over rough ground and rocky slopes carrying a rifle and a heavy pack. Ben reached the limo only slightly out of breath. He glanced up again at the sky. The chopper was closer now. Too much closer, and the big black Maybach would soon be unmissable from the air.

He set down his weapon and bag. Got behind the wheel of the car and fired up the engine, slammed it into gear and hit the gas. The Maybach's tyres scrabbled for grip on the loose rocks of the river bed. He didn't have far to drive. Just a hundred yards upriver was the thick clump of thorn bushes partially blocking the way, which he'd have had to negotiate if he'd gone on in that direction. The car lurched and bounced and scraped its way towards the bushes. He steered towards the densest part of the thicket, meeting resistance at first, then giving it a little more gas to push the nose of the car deeper into the tangled mass. Once he'd forced an initial gap, the bushes parted with a lot of squealing and raking of sharp thorns against metal to engulf the front wings and the whole length of the bonnet. He yanked the gearstick into neutral, killed the engine and quickly opened his door and jumped out as the car went on rolling deeper into the bushes under its own momentum. Five tons of armoured limousine was swallowed up among the thorns as though it had never been there.

Satisfied it was well enough hidden, Ben turned and sprinted back the hundred yards to where he'd left his rifle and bag. The chopper was a fast-growing black and yellow blob against the western sky, like a giant wasp. The screech of its turbine and the thud of its blades were becoming loud. Definitely heading right this way, and losing altitude as though it were coming in to land. There was a slender chance that he might already have been spotted by an eagle-eyed pilot or co-pilot, but he was willing to gamble.

He snatched up his things and ran hard for the bank. Hoping that the angle of its slope would hide him from view he scrambled back up to the top of the rise and headed quickly towards a cleft between two huge, craggy grey rocks that were leaning together to form an inverted V shape, like a cavern. More of the same thick, tangled kind of thorn bushes had grown up across its mouth. He stepped over the thorns and pressed himself into the cleft and crouched down to hide. His cavern was deep enough to conceal him, but shallow enough to see out, with a clear view of the incoming helicopter.

He'd been right. The chopper was heading towards the burning truck. It was steadily dropping. Coming down to land, two hundred yards from Ben's hidden observation point. With relief, he decided that he hadn't been spotted. He laid down his rifle, pulled the binoculars back out of his bag and lay flat on his belly with his elbows planted in the dirt like the legs of a rifle bipod and the binocs pressed to his eyes.

And watched.

As the helicopter came closer he was able to make out the HARYANA POLICE markings on the fuselage. Which, he noted, was painted in the same colour scheme as UK police helicopters. He recognised it as an older model of light-utility Eurocopter, probably a hand-me-down from the British in the spirit of post-colonial international relations, and a somewhat snarky, condescending message to the effect of 'You can't even get your own police helicopters unless we give them to you.' Not that Indian law enforcement had many. In fact Ben had talked to the police chief whose unit boasted ownership of the only patrol chopper in the entire country.

That could mean only one thing. Captain Jabbar Dada and his special bandit-hunting task force were about to arrive on the scene.

The downdraught from the landing aircraft whipped at the smoke and fanned the flames of the burning truck. Its skids touched the rocky ground, flexed, rocked and then settled as the pilot found a solid place to put down. Ben could see him through the Perspex screen of the cockpit. A swarthy, stocky man in khaki clothes and sunglasses with a headset and mike, flipping switches to power down the rotors. Movement behind him as the helicopter's passengers started getting out of their seats. The side hatch swung open, and out swung a pair of short, thick stumpy legs clad in combat trousers and black army boots. The legs dangled in space for a moment, and then the rest of the body they were attached to wriggled out and jumped to the ground.

Ben had no doubt at all that he was looking at Captain Dada, the celebrated bandit hunter himself. All five foot two or three of him, clad in a diminutive olive-green fatigue uniform that looked more military than law enforcement. Even at this distance, it was obvious that Takshak's hairy fireplug associate would have towered over the great man. Small in stature, but big on pride. That was obvious, too, confirming the impression Ben had got of him on the phone. Dada carried himself as though the earth should shake at the approach of his footsteps. *Look out, world, here I come.*

Dada strutted away from the helicopter like an olive-green pigeon. One hand was clamped to his head to stop the wind from the slowing rotors from blowing off his red beret. The other clasped an INSAS light machine gun that was absurdly bigger than he was. It made him look like a child carrying a regular-sized assault rifle, which was something Ben had seen plenty of in various developing countries around the world. Half a dozen of Dada's men emerged from the chopper in his wake, all wearing the same khaki paramilitary garb and red beret as their captain, minus the gold braid insignia that denoted his rank. Each man was toting his own INSAS Indian Army-issue automatic weapon, though nobody's was as big as Dada's. Ben wondered if the captain was wearing a Rambo T-shirt under his uniform, too. He smiled to himself and went on watching them.

The bandit hunter approached the burning truck and stood for a moment thoughtfully scratching his bushy black moustache while his men gathered at his sides. Ben had a pretty good idea of what had brought them out here. The wily old fox had obviously been watching the area for dacoit activity in the weeks following the incident with Kabir and his associates, no doubt eager to satisfy his monthly quota of slaughtered bandits. They must have been making a dawn patrol flight when they'd spotted the smoke rising in the distance and rushed over to investigate.

Dada turned away from the flames and went over to examine the bodies of the dead dacoits. Even from so far away Ben could read his disappointment that someone else had got the chance to gun down eight of them instead of him. Ben suspected that he'd mark it up to his own credit anyway.

It was clear that they intended to stick around for a while. Maybe they were planning a picnic, Ben thought.

Dada turned to his men and started issuing orders and pointing this way and that. One of them got on the radio while another ran back to the chopper to fetch something and the rest were designated to drag the bodies of the dead bandits closer to the burning truck and pile them in a heap. The reason why became apparent when the errand runner came back from the chopper clutching a camera with a long lens. Dada waved everyone away while he posed proudly in front of the flaming wreckage to have his picture taken with one foot placed on the pile of corpses, brandishing his machine gun as though he had personally slain the lot of them. Just another morning's work for Captain Dada.

Ben shook his head and went on watching.

But Ben wasn't the only one observing the scene from a distance.

Chapter 54

Takshak much preferred his scary-sounding moniker to his real name. He hadn't gone by Ravinder Khan for a long time, not since it had been preceded by 'Sergeant'. Six years with the Indian regular army, then four with the elite Ghatak Commandos, before he'd had enough of busting his balls and risking his life for crappy pay, and quit to start employing his talents in a more lucrative fashion. If he was gonna die with a gun in his hand, it would be for something he believed in. Which more or less boiled down to himself, a pocketful of cash, and enough booze and hookers to keep him sated for the immediate future.

But Takshak hadn't given up ten years of his life without picking up a few tricks. Like all proficient rifle marksmen, of which he'd been one of the more adept in his unit, he possessed the ability to lie for hours in position, utterly still, waiting for the perfect window of opportunity to make his killer shot against a target at a respectably long range.

He was somewhat closer than that to the target he was watching right now, perched high on a rocky hillside behind his scoped rifle. It was a fine weapon, fitted with a Schmidt and Bender 12x50 that had cost him more than the gun itself. He kept his rig immaculately clean and oiled and would often spend whole evenings lovingly polishing it. Another prized piece of kit was his Bushnell compact laser rangefinder system, which was effective out to extreme distances and was pinpointing his current range from target at exactly 823 metres, a pretty easy shot for a guy like him.

In actual fact, the target he was observing was really two targets, even several, between which he was panning back and forth with tiny, incremental movements of his rifle muzzle. He was acutely focused on the presence of the police chopper and its occupants, whose appearance on the scene hadn't totally surprised him as he'd been expecting some kind of heat ever since the pitched battle his men had fought against those stupid interfering dacoits during the night. Now the bastard cops were probably going to hang around half the day, delaying Takshak's operation still further by forcing him and his gang to lie low until the coast was clear. As tempted as Takshak was to pick the policemen off one by one, which would have given him much satisfaction and taken little effort at this distance, the last thing he needed was the whole area teeming with a whole horde of the pigfuckers for days or weeks afterwards.

Much less expected had been the arrival of the Brit, this guy Hope who'd been running around Delhi the last couple of days causing serious problems. He was supposed to have been eliminated, though that hadn't worked out so well for the four men tasked with the job. And now here he was again. The cops had no idea Hope was holed up in the rocks just a couple hundred yards away, watching their every move. But Takshak, scouting for the return of more dacoits or the arrival of the police, had been observing the Brit with a certain detached curiosity from the moment he rolled up in that ridiculous stretch limo and started exploring the scene.

What was he doing here? How had the clever bastard figured out where to come? He must have rumbled Prem Sharma, Takshak thought. Another idiot.

Takshak had had all these questions in his mind as he watched the Brit's antics, though he doubted he'd ever get the chance to ask him. It didn't really matter anyhow, seeing as the prick would soon be dead anyway.

It was as Hope had finished checking out the bodies and returned to the burning truck that Takshak had got him perfectly framed in his crosshairs and been about to let off his shot. Then the fucking asshole cops had shown up and Hope was on the run again, too fast-moving a target for a reliable hit at this range.

A missed opportunity. But Takshak wasn't worried. Another would come, and soon enough.

As expected, it looked as if the sisterfucker police weren't going away any time soon. Takshak knew that they'd likely find the bodies of his own three guys, but he wasn't worried about that either. He also knew all about the special anti-dacoit task force in these parts. The filthy sons of whores were probably hoping that if they hung around long enough they might get to kill a few bandits for themselves. Best thing to do was leave them alone, and they'd soon get bored and return to base.

Takshak picked up his rifle and slipped away to pick a path back down the rocky hillside to rejoin his men. Their base camp was a cave at the base of the hill. There were caves all over this godforsaken dump of a wilderness. This one had been discovered by chance not long after they'd arrived and started scouting around in search of the place to start digging. Its opening was a fissure just wide enough to squeeze their vehicles through, but which opened up to offer plenty of room for the whole gang to stay hidden in relative comfort. And their honoured guest, too. Though his comfort wasn't high on their list of priorities.

The delay created by the police presence was just another setback in a whole series of frustrations. After all the big talk of treasure and riches he'd heard back in Delhi, Takshak had been full of confidence at the prospect of an easy score. Since then his confidence had been shaken somewhat by a day and a half of fruitless searching this barren wasteland, and it seemed the alluring promise of X marks the spot had been too good to be true. But he was no quitter, never had been, never would be. Nobody, not those asshole dacoits, not the law, and least of all that Ben Hope character, was going to deter him from getting his job done.

Takshak reached the bottom of the hill, glanced about him to make sure nobody was in sight, then entered the dark fissure of the cave entrance. The sunlight penetrated only a few paces into its interior. From outside, nobody could have guessed what it was being used for.

The glow of paraffin lamps shone dully off the three off-road trucks parked inside, and the faces of his men as they looked up to greet their leader's return. All fifteen of them. Which wasn't too shabby a number, considering that Takshak had started out with twelve and lost four in Delhi, then another three here, thanks to the dacoits. He still had five good men from his original gang: there was big Samunder, so massive and tall he kept cracking his head on the roof of the cave; and there was Hashim, who'd been a contract killer for the Delhi mob; and Jitender, and Kuldeep, and Gulshan. His loyal inner circle, supplemented by ten new guys he'd been able to hire using Prem Sharma's four million rupees. They were just the kind of personnel he needed. Neeraj had murdered a cop in Uttarakhand. Sardar had been arrested for his part in a gang rape and was on the lam after jumping bail. Jarnail . . . now he came to think of it, Takshak couldn't remember what Jarnail had done. Strangled some kid or something. All routine stuff.

Of course, Takshak had no intention of allowing the ten hirelings to take a share of the treasure. They were here strictly as labourers. Once their work was done, the hole out of which they'd dug up the loot would double as their mass grave. They just didn't know it yet.

The four million rupees had also allowed Takshak to invest in a new Jeep for himself, plus four decent off-road trucks, recently retired from the military, in which he'd planned to cart away his prize once unearthed. One truck was now up in smoke, but he figured that was just the cost of doing business. As was the loss of three men. Shit happens.

A figure approached him in the gloom of the cave, holding a lantern. It was Hashim, the former hitman. Takshak considered him his second in command. Hashim wasn't a big guy, but he was harder than wood and as dangerous as a leopard. The only man in the crew who'd killed more people than its leader, if anyone was counting.

Takshak sensed that Hashim wanted to talk, so he led him to a corner of the cave where they wouldn't be overheard if they kept their voices low. Hashim said, 'So what's happening?'

Takshak replied, 'We have company. Fucking cops are hanging around the place like flies on dog shit.'

Hashim spat. 'It's all the fault of those dacoit fucks. They should never have come looking for trouble. The cops will have marked this area now.'

'It was marked before we got here. We knew that, right? It was a risk worth taking.'

'Yeah, but it's worse now. They'll mount a regular patrol to scout for more of those morons. What are we gonna do, with them all over us?'

'We wait.'

'We can't sit here forever,' Hashim said.

Takshak replied, 'We won't have to. They'll scratch around for a while and then fuck off back to base, and we can get on.'

Hashim frowned, not convinced. 'Yeah, and say we find it and we've got it half dug out of the fucking ground when they decide to drop by again? How you planning on keeping something that big out of sight?'

'So what if they do?'

'So they'll try to grab it for themselves. And we'll have a serious fucking fight on our hands. Dacoits is one thing. Cops is another.'

'So we'll teach them the same lesson we taught the dacoits. You don't mess with us.'

Hashim shrugged. 'We're with you, Takshak. Whatever it takes. Just bad luck those *benchods* had to turn up right here, right now.'

'Benchod' being a popular insult in several northern Indian languages, referring to the exercise of unwholesome inclinations of an incestuous nature between siblings of opposite gender.

Takshak glanced back at where the rest of the men were sitting. Nobody was listening to their conversation. Gulshan had lit up a ganja joint the size of a parsnip and was passing it around while telling a dirty joke that had them all entranced.

Takshak lowered his voice still further and said, 'They're not the only ones. The Brit is here.'

'Seriously?'

'No kidding. I just saw him. I was about to off the bastard when the cops landed.'

'What's he doing here? Come to rescue his little buddy?'

'He must have got Sharma to talk,' Takshak said. 'Which means he's gonna be after the treasure, too. Seems like everyone wants a piece of it.'

'That's not good. He's dangerous.'

'So are we,' Takshak reminded him.

Hashim frowned. 'Where is he now?'

'Out there somewhere. Relax. He'll never find us here.'

'But maybe we should go and find him.'

'Not while the fucking cops are here, remember?'

'Shit. This is getting complicated.'

'No, it's simple,' Takshak said. 'We'll post a lookout on the hillside to watch that chopper and keep an eye out for Hope. The moment the cops fuck off, it'll be time to deal with that piece of shit. Then once he's been taken care of, we can finish what we came here to do.'

'Sounds good to me. I'll send Gulshan.'

'No. He smokes too much of that shit. Probably fall asleep.'

'Who, then? Not Samunder, surely. You might as well put an elephant up there, for all to see.'

'Kuldeep has a sharp eye, and he's quick and careful. Give him a pair of binoculars and a radio and tell him to stay in contact. And tell him not to get himself seen, or I'll shoot him myself.'

Hashim nodded and said, 'Okay. I'll go tell him.' But he didn't move. Takshak sensed he had more to add. He asked, 'What?'

Hashim hesitated a moment longer, then said, 'It's the hostage.'

'What about the hostage?'

'He's in a bad way. I think he's gonna die on us.'

Chapter 55

Takshak walked with Hashim to the far back of the cave, where Takshak's personal Jeep was parked in the shadows. There was a length of steel chain padlocked to the Jeep's rear bumper. The chain ran for a couple of yards along the hard-packed earth floor to where its end was attached to one bracelet of a pair of steel handcuffs. The other bracelet was fastened tightly around the ankle of the huddled shape on the ground. He was covered in a thin blanket. All that was visible of him were the bare soles of his feet, striped with cuts from forced marching over rocky ground.

He wasn't moving.

Hashim said, 'I checked on him a couple of times while you were out earlier. He hasn't moved for hours. Hardly seems to be breathing.'

Takshak stepped closer and gave the inert body a nudge with the toe of his combat boot.

No response. Takshak kicked him harshly in the ribs. Said, 'Hey, asshole, your boyfriend's here looking for you. But don't get too excited. We got plans for him, just like we got for you.'

Amal gave a soft groan, stirred and slowly, slowly, raised his head to squint up at Takshak's lantern-lit face through his good eye. The other eye was so badly bruised that it had swollen shut. His lips were split open and his cheeks were puffed out and discoloured and covered in dried blood. He seemed to focus for a brief moment and his broken lips moved as though he was trying to speak. Then his good eye rolled over white, he fell limply back into unconsciousness and lay still as a corpse.

'Doesn't look so terrible to me,' Takshak said.

Hashim looked worried. 'I don't know. We beat him up pretty bad yesterday.'

'We've been beating him up pretty bad ever since we took him back from those two morons. What's new?'

'I think we went a little overboard,' Hashim said. 'Reckon he's got concussion. People can die from that. And if he dies . . .' He shrugged. 'That's all I'm saying. Think I'd give a shit, if it wasn't for the money?'

'I'm beginning to think he's not gonna be of much use to us anyway. If those two nicey-nicey amateurs hadn't pussy-footed around so much, they might have figured out he knew nothing and saved us a load of trouble.'

Hashim still looked worried. 'You might be right. Maybe he doesn't know anything. Then again, he could still be holding out on us.'

'Then what am I supposed to do, lay into him harder? You just said he was nearly dead already.'

'Maybe we should have found another way to persuade him. Like grab his bitch and bring her along for the ride, too. We'd soon have found out if he knew anything.'

'It's too late for that now,' Takshak said. 'Anyhow, his bitch was with Hope. We couldn't get to her without going through him. Tried that, remember?'

'Yeah,' Hashim agreed wistfully. 'Shame. Could've had some fun.'

'It is what it is,' Takshak said. 'We wait for the cops to

leave, then we take care of the Brit.' He pointed at Amal. 'Then it's his choice. Last chance. He doesn't deliver the goods, he gets a bullet in the head. Which he's gonna get later anyhow. Either way, I'm not leaving this place until *I* get what's coming to *me*.'

'What if he's too fucked up to deliver the goods, even if he could?'

Takshak kicked Amal again. 'I think he's a tougher little bastard than he looks. He'll be okay.'

Forty minutes later Kuldeep, the lookout, reported over the radio that the cops were finally getting ready to depart. Takshak asked, 'Any sign of anyone else down there?'

'Nothing's moving,' Kuldeep replied. 'I can't see a soul.'

'Roger. Stay out of sight until I give the word.'

Soon afterwards, the sound of the helicopter taking off could be faintly heard from inside the cave. Takshak grabbed his rifle, and he and Hashim ventured cautiously outside and scrambled part way up the hill to watch the police flying away. The sun was fully up and bearing intensely down on the barren hills and valleys. It was going to be a long, hot day. And an eventful one, Takshak hoped.

The truck had more or less burned itself out by now, giving off just a wisp of smoke that was dispersed by the wind blast of the climbing chopper. The aircraft rose to fifteen hundred feet and banked around westwards to return to base. Takshak watched it through his rifle scope. Once he was satisfied that it wasn't a ruse and they were really leaving, he clambered a little further up the hill, to a flat rock from which he could scan the spot where he'd seen the Brit go into hiding earlier. Just as Kuldeep had said, there was nothing moving. But that didn't mean Hope wasn't there.

Takshak rejoined Hashim and they scrambled together back down the hill. Takshak radioed Kuldeep and said, 'Okay, get your ass back here pronto.' Five minutes later, a breathless Kuldeep returned from his post. By then, Takshak had unpacked a fresh box of ammo from his Jeep and was in the process of pressing rounds into three spare magazines. Hashim came over and said, 'All right, so what's the plan? You want me to send three or four of the boys out there to search for the Brit?'

Takshak shook his head. 'They won't find him. But I will. And I'll deal with him. Alone.'

Takshak was taking no chances. He stuck his spare mags into the pouches on his tactical vest, then thrust a fully-loaded pistol in his Kydex belt holster. He donned his mirrored aviator Ray Bans and strode out, rifle in hand, to search and destroy his prey.

The only problem was, his prey seemed to have well and truly vanished. After several long minutes observing Hope's earlier hiding place from the hillside, Takshak was forced to conclude that he was no longer there. Swearing under his breath he made his way back down, and trekked across the arid plateau towards the river bed. The march took him several minutes. Now and then he glanced up at the sky behind him, in case the cops were doubling back. But mostly he was concerned that Hope was watching him from some new hiding place. 'You think you're so clever,' he muttered. 'I'll show you who's clever.'

Takshak reached the dry river bank and slithered down its rocky slope. No sign of the Brit. He walked the hundred yards to where he'd watched his enemy hide his car. It was still there. Some kind of crazy government limo, the kind of thing that was all armoured up against dumbass ideological assassination attempts. But no Brit.

It was as if the bastard had flown off in the chopper with the police, Takshak thought. For a moment he played with the idea that maybe he had, because maybe he was one of them. But nah, that didn't make sense.

Takshak spent the next two hours traipsing all over the barren wasteland in search of his enemy. Zero. Zilch. Nothing. A total waste of time. Fuming, dusty and covered in sweat, he gave up and returned to base camp.

'Well?' Hashim asked. 'Did you deal with him? I didn't hear any shots.'

'Fuck him. Let's get on with what we came here to do.'

'Whatever you say, boss. Where do we start?'

'Back at square one,' Takshak said. 'And that benchod hostage had better come good for us.'

And so, the day's work began. They reversed the trucks out into the hot sun and everyone clambered aboard except Takshak, who was riding in his personal open Jeep, and the semi-conscious and bleeding hostage, dumped in the load space and still chained to the back bumper in case he tried to escape. The three-vehicle convoy bumped and lurched over the difficult terrain, past the spot where the dacoits had attacked them. Takshak didn't so much as glance at the bodies of his three men, now all mottled and bloated as they began to decompose in the heat. Then they hit the steep rise up towards the river bed where Takshak had patrolled on foot earlier. The trucks struggled and slithered and pattered all over the loose ground as their diesel engines snorted and rasped and their suspension creaked and their four-wheel-drive transmissions strained to haul themselves up the slope and everyone inside clung onto whatever support they could find.

At last, all three vehicles had made it back to the killing ground where Kabir Ray and his associates had been shot that day. Square one. Ground zero. Still the closest thing they'd found to X marks the spot.

Takshak jumped down from his Jeep and marched around to the back to interrogate the hostage. Hashim and a few of the others gathered around, clutching their weapons. The shovels and picks were still in the trucks.

'This is it,' Takshak snarled in Amal's face. 'Last chance. Where is it? You don't start talking, my son, you'll wish you had.'

Amal's good eye blinked. He tried to speak, but all that came out of his torn lips was a croak.

Takshak pulled a face. 'What'd he say?'

Big Samunder said in his sub-octave bass voice, 'I think he said, "Go fuck yourself", boss.'

Takshak stared at Amal for a second. Then he flung open the Jeep's tailgate, grabbed Amal by the throat and dragged him violently out of the load space and threw him to the stony ground. The chain rattled. Amal hit the ground with a cry of pain. But then he did something that amazed them all. He staggered to his bare feet and stood there swaying defiantly.

'See, I told you he was a tougher little bastard than he looks,' Takshak said with a smile.

Slowly, painfully, turning around in small shuffling steps, Amal looked about him with his one usable eye. His gaze rested on the rocks of the river bank below where the remains of Kabir's helicopter stood. Then he raised a grimy finger and pointed in that direction. He croaked again, paused to spit up a gout of blood and then said more coherently, 'Over there. That's where you need to start digging.'

'Let's find out, shall we?' Takshak sneered. 'You heard him, boys. Get to work.'

Chapter 56

Which they proceeded to do, relentlessly, for the next several hours, sweating under the searing glare of the sun. All that could be heard was the steady scrape and clang of steel against rock and the occasional grunt of effort as they toiled, while Takshak and Hashim leaned against the back of the Jeep and smoked cigars and the hostage slept on the end of his chain. It was back-breaking labour, virtually impossible without a mechanical digger. Big Samunder was the nearest thing they had to one of those, hefting up rocks that nobody else could lift with his massive hands and flinging them away with a roar. By early afternoon, the efforts of fourteen men pushing themselves to the brink of exhaustion had produced nothing better than a dry stony crater measuring eight feet deep by twelve feet wide. Like a large grave intended for several occupants.

Jarnail, the kid killer, stopped digging to wipe the sweat from his eyes. His hair was dripping with it. He leaned on his shovel and groaned, 'This is fucked up, Takshak. There's nothing here but rocks.'

Takshak blew smoke and said, 'I'm paying you money to dig, so dig.'

'Screw you. I've had it with digging.'

Takshak said, 'Really? Give me your shovel, then.' He flung away his stogie and stepped away from the Jeep, holding out a hand.

With a grin of triumph for having upstaged the boss, Jarnail handed the shovel over. It was a quality tool, with a long hardwood shaft and stainless steel blade, bought specially for the purpose from a hardware store back in Delhi. Takshak paused a moment to roll up his sleeves and rub spit between his palms. Then he grasped the shaft with both hands, hefted it like an axe and buried the edge of the blade deep in Jarnail's frontal cranium.

Jarnail was clinically dead before his body had made it all the way to the ground. The idiot grin had never left his face, and now it was frozen there like a rictus.

Takshak turned to the rest of the crew. 'Is anyone else tired of digging? Because if you are, now's the time to step forward and be relieved of your duties.'

Everyone was suddenly as fresh as a daisy and perfectly happy to go on all day long. Takshak threw down the bloody shovel, returned to the Jeep and lit another cigar. The hostage went on sleeping.

Another three hours later, the utterly spent work party had excavated a hole the size of a house foundation. Their hair was white with dust, their clothes black with sweat, and the shafts of their picks and shovels were wet from burst blisters. They were earning their money, that was for sure. Nobody dared complain directly to the boss. Anyone who even thought about it only had to glance over at the body of Jarnail, still grinning at them through a mask of blood, and they'd quickly decide to shut up. But some of the guys were giving imploring looks to Hashim, as if to say, 'Please, do something to make it stop.'

Just as Hashim was plucking up the resolve to say

something, Takshak held up his hand and yelled, 'Enough! Everyone, step away from the hole!'

There were groans of both relief and pain as the twelve stiff, aching workers climbed out of the crater. Sardar and Neeraj staggered no more than a couple of steps before they collapsed with fatigue. Kuldeep leaned hard on his pickaxe, panting as though he'd run a marathon. Even Samunder looked ready to drop.

Takshak strode over to the hole, stood at its edge with his hands on his hips and looked down. What he could see that wasn't stones and boulders was a kind of sandy loam that they'd hit about six feet down. And a curled-up dead scorpion that Samunder had chopped with his shovel. And part of the exposed root ball of a prickly shrub growing nearby. No gold, no diamonds, no rubies or emeralds. Not so much as a clay cup.

Takshak went on staring at the empty hole. Everyone was watching him. They could see the strange light that had come into his eyes. Nobody spoke. Then Takshak turned away from the hole and went striding back towards the back of the Jeep, where the hostage was either fast asleep or comatose. Takshak drew out his pistol and pointed it at Amal's head. Amal didn't move.

'I warned him. This was his last chance. Now he dies.'

Hashim could see that his boss was serious. 'Whoa, wait. Boss, please.'

Takshak kept the gun pointed at Amal's head. 'He's just messing with us. I'm sick of it.'

'Don't do it.'

'No? Watch me put a bullet in his face.'

'We can't kill him yet. Just in case.'

'Just in case of what?'

'We can't go away empty-handed.'

'We got the map,' Takshak said.

'The map's no good, remember?' Hashim reminded him. 'The geography's all wrong. You're the one who spotted it.'

'So there's a mistake on the fucking map, so what? Or maybe those fucking hills sprouted up since it was made. The archaeology asshole must've figured out this was the right place. He wouldn't have come here otherwise.'

'Yeah, maybe. And maybe he'd have led us to it, but we shot him. Which is why we need his brother.'

'Assuming that the asshole told his brother.'

'But we can't assume that he didn't. You said that too, remember? If we blow this guy's brains out now, we're totally screwed. Trust me, boss. Don't do it.'

Takshak lowered the gun and let out a long breath. 'I want this bastard dead so bad, it hurts.'

'He will be. But this is not the time.'

Takshak nodded slowly. He turned to his men. 'All right. Pack it up for today. Back to base for some rest and we'll start over in the morning.'

'I really, really wish we had brought the bitch along with us,' Hashim muttered.

Thoroughly exhausted and demoralised, they heaved themselves back into the vehicles and returned to camp. Sixteen men had set out, only fifteen were returning. Their one consolation was that there had been no sign of the police coming back to hamper their efforts, so with no reason to keep the trucks hidden any longer, it was decided to leave them parked outside in order to make more space. Crates of beer and tinned meat and vegetables were unpacked, lanterns were lit, and for the next few hours the men sat around and ate, drank, smoked, rested their weary muscles and tried to relax. Samunder gathered up some twigs and enough handfuls of some kind of desiccated animal dung

335

to light a small campfire whose glow flickered at the centre of the cave. The smoke drifted up to the naturally domed ceiling and escaped through a fissure that acted like a chimney.

But the atmosphere in the cave was tense. Nobody could openly mention what had happened to Jarnail, out of fear of the same happening to them. That didn't stop the private mutterings that passed between the more disgruntled and resentful crew members. Such as the whispered conversation held by Neeraj and Sardar in a dark corner while the others were eating.

'We're working for a crazy ass nutjob psycho. You do realise that, don't you?' Neeraj said.

'The thought had occurred to me, yeah,' Sardar agreed.

'And we're not gonna find anything out here. It's all bullshit. And you know what else I think? Even if we do, he's not gonna cut us in for a penny. He's gonna leave us out here to rot like Jarnail.'

'I get you, man. But what can we do about it?'

'I say we cut our losses before it's too late. Knock'm on the head and get the fuck out of this—' Neeraj broke off as he noticed Hashim lurking nearby. 'Can't talk here,' he whispered. 'I'm going for a piss. Count to thirty, slowly, then come and meet me behind the trucks. Make it look natural. I'll tell you my plan.'

When Neeraj had left the cave, Sardar ticked off thirty seconds inside his head, then as nonchalantly as possible meandered out after him, casually picking up another can of beer on his way, joking to the guys, 'This stuff goes through you, doesn't it?' Bad liars always explain too much.

It was dark outside. The moon was just a pale sliver behind the clouds, and there was no wind. As evening had fallen, so had the temperature. Sardar shivered and peered about him in the darkness, eager to resume the mutinous plans he and Neeraj had started hatching.

He whispered, 'Neeraj? Where'd you go, man?' But there was no sound. No sign.

'Neeraj?'

As Sardar hunted about in the darkness, he realised that something weird was up. He could have sworn that they'd parked all three of their remaining trucks outside the cave entrance earlier. But there seemed to be only two. He blinked and looked again. It was odd. Maybe he'd drunk too much beer.

He was still trying to figure it out when his foot snagged something heavy on the ground and he almost tripped, dropping his can. He swore under his breath, and crouched down to grope among the shadows where it had fallen.

That was when he realised what he'd tripped over.

Neeraj was lying sprawled on his back. His flies were undone. His open eyes glistened sightlessly in the soft moonlight. His head was at a strange angle to his body.

And there was something else, too. A small white rectangle lying across Neeraj's chest. Sardar picked it up. It was a piece of paper. A page from a notebook, folded in half.

Sardar forgot all about his beer, along with his terror of Takshak and any idea of mutiny. He ran back into the cave, clutching the piece of paper and yelling at the top of his lungs, 'Neeraj is dead! Neeraj is dead!'

Everyone sprang to their feet in alarm. Takshak instantly appeared from the shadows, holding up a lantern. 'What happened?'

'I don't know,' Sardar blabbered. 'He went for a piss and now he's dead, just like that!'

'What the fuck are you talking about?' Takshak demanded impatiently. He snapped his fingers. 'Kuldeep, Jitender, go

337

out there and see what's up.' The two men instantly snatched up their weapons and hurried out of the cave mouth into the darkness.

'I think his neck is broken,' Sardar said urgently. 'And I found this.' He held up the folded piece of paper to show them. 'Think it's a note.'

'From who?' Takshak said, snatching it off him with a frown.

Hashim came close, so that he could look at it. 'What's it say?'

It was a page torn from a notebook. Takshak held the lantern up to see better. Just four words were handwritten in the centre of the page, in bold capital letters marked with a felt-tip pen. They said:

COMING TO GET YOU

Takshak laughed nervously. 'What the fuck does that mean?'

He looked at Hashim. Hashim looked at him. They both looked at Sardar. Then all three of them turned to look out of the cave entrance.

Then the night sky outside suddenly lit up like daylight as a violent, stunningly loud explosion shook the ground under their feet and ripped the trucks apart.

Chapter 57

Earlier that day Ben could have offered some professional advice to Takshak. Namely, *don't give away your shooting position by letting the sun glint off your nice, shiny weapon.*

Part of the advanced tactical riflemanship course at Le Val was showing students the best ways to camouflage their equipment against the natural propensity for smooth, reflective metal surfaces to catch the light, to which end the sniper rifles in Ben and Jeff's armoury had all been treated to a military desert camo matt paint finish, stippled and roughened to make them blend chameleon-like into a multi-terrain background. Failure to take precautions like that could all too easily lead an otherwise perfectly chosen vantage point to be as obvious to the enemy as if you planted a giant day-glo flag saying 'Here I am!' in letters five feet high while letting off a crateful of magnesium flares.

And it was precisely that – the starry twinkle of sunlight on studiously polished, well-oiled blued steel – which had alerted Ben to the fact that he hadn't been the only hidden observer watching the police helicopter land that morning.

It had happened just after Captain Dada had finished having his trophy photo taken with the dead dacoits. Ben had been shaking his head in cynical amusement at the guy when the sparkly glitter had caught his eye and he'd canted his binoculars a few degrees sideways and upwards to trace its source. It was coming from high up on a hillside, more or less due west and a good six hundred yards beyond where the cops were going about their business.

For a large, cumbersome weapon, a scoped bolt-action sniper rifle looks relatively small when pointing right at you, especially from eight hundred yards away. Ben's compact binoculars offered only modest magnification even on maximum zoom but he made out the shape instantly. And behind it, the shape of a man in dark paramilitary clothing, hunkered down among the crags a hundred feet up the hillside, looking over the plateau that stretched between him and Ben's own hiding place.

Ben thought, *Hm.* And went on watching, now far more interested in the distant sniper than he was in the police.

In the end, the rifleman had given up and left some time before the cops had, as though he'd got bored with observing. As he'd slipped down the hillside, thinking himself unnoticed, Ben had crept away from his own hiding place and begun skirting around the edge of the plateau, ducking from rock to rock, bush to bush, head down, leaving no trail, well out of view of the cops but never losing sight of his quarry. Right from first visual contact, Ben was certain this was the same man he'd last seen wearing a purple shirt. The leader of the gang. Takshak himself.

The guy was quite good, all things considered. He moved with far more poise and circumspection than some common criminal, like the coarse-grained thugs Ben and Brooke had briefly encountered on the stairs at Haani's place. Clearly a trained man, Ben thought. Almost certainly ex-military. Ben figured him for what was termed in army-speak a DM, or designated marksman. Highly skilled with the queen of all small arms, the rifle. But that level of weapons training focused mainly on the art and science of long-range shooting itself, without delving into the whole complex world of advanced fieldcraft and tactics that distinguished a mere marksman from a true sniper. The real deal was a totally different animal. A stealth operator who could reach out and put the finger of death on you from a mile away, any time, anywhere. They would strike out of thin air and then disappear like a ghost. Never seen. Never captured. Ready to return and crucify the next victim in their scope crosshairs just when it was least expected. One of the most dreaded pieces on the chessboard of war.

Ben had been one of those men. Evidently, Takshak had not. And Takshak had just made a fatal mistake in letting himself be spotted.

Ben never let him go after that. When Takshak had returned to his cave, glancing cautiously left and right as though to make sure nobody was watching, he'd had no idea his every movement was being monitored. Just as it was when he'd re-emerged from the cave a little while later to watch the police helicopter leaving.

Ben could so easily have taken out the lookout that the gang had posted on the hillside. He'd have done it so quickly and quietly that the guy wouldn't have known what was happening until he woke up in hell. But the sentry was bound to be in radio contact, and sooner or later he was bound to be recalled to base. If he went incommunicado or failed to return, it would only serve to alert the rest. In a situation like this, everything was about timing.

Likewise, when Takshak himself had set out on foot to hunt for Ben, it would have been easy to ensure that he didn't come back. He'd never know it, but as he'd been checking out the Maybach concealed in the bushes, Ben was standing just ten yards from him, as still and silent as empty

341

air. The sole reason Takshak had survived his unwitting close encounter was because of what would have happened if his men suddenly found themselves without a commander. Panic, disorientation and chaos were all highly desirable effects to wreak on the enemy, but not when there was a precious hostage involved. It took only one nervous, over-reactive trigger finger for things to turn out very badly for the prisoner.

Instead, Ben wanted them to feel completely safe and comfortable. For the moment, until the time was right. And so, when the gang had piled into their vehicles and left the cave to begin their day's work, he'd scouted along in their wake and watched from a bushy ledge high up in the rocks just eighty yards away. The three medium utility trucks looked like the kind of thing that military logistics corps would sell off to the civilian market after a hard service life. Their olive paint was scuffed and worn, and their open load spaces had skeletal metal framework where the canvas roofs would have been. Ben counted four men in the back of each truck, plus a driver. The convoy was moving in single file behind a battered open-top Jeep, at whose wheel Ben recognised the man he'd identified as Takshak, the leader.

Sixteen men in all. A larger number than he'd anticipated. Then Ben spied a seventeenth. He was different from the others, not least in the manner in which he was travelling. He'd been bundled into the back of the Jeep and was grimly hanging onto its roll cage to keep from being too badly jostled about.

Even from far away, Ben knew him instantly. It was his first glimpse of Amal. He looked as if he'd been knocked around quite a bit. He was barefoot and his shirt was torn and bloodied down the front. But he was alive.

The relief flooded through Ben's system like an intravenous

triple shot of cask-strength scotch. *Just hold on a little longer, Amal. I'm coming for you soon.*

Ben had been expecting to have to follow the vehicles on foot, which concerned him in case he lost them. He needn't have worried, because they didn't travel far. As he sat watching, they stopped in almost the very same spot where Kabir and his friends had been attacked, in the dry river valley just a few hundred feet from the abandoned helicopter. Everybody got out. It was the first time Ben had been able to get a good look at the enemy forces all massed together.

Takshak was the only gang member armed with a pistol, in military officer fashion, while the rest of his crew carried rifles like the lower-rank infantrymen they were. Ben guessed they'd soon be exchanging their weaponry for the collection of pickaxes and shovels that lay in the backs of the trucks. He went on watching, hidden, immobile, physically relaxed but mentally on constant high alert for the slightest sign that he'd need to intervene.

His own rifle lay ready to hand, for that purpose. The old SLR warhorse had been much respected for its medium-range combat accuracy back in the day, and would be more than adequate at eighty yards. He'd use it if he had to, though the last thing he needed right now was a pitched battle with sixteen armed criminals and an unprotected hostage in the middle.

The first anxious moment had happened almost as soon as they arrived. Takshak walked around to the rear of his Jeep to speak to Amal. It didn't look like a friendly conversation. Ben couldn't make out the words Takshak was yelling in Amal's face, but he cou ld guess. The reason Amal was still alive was because Takshak thought he needed his help to find Kabir's treasure.

Whatever Amal had said in reply, Takshak didn't like it.

When he'd grabbed his prisoner by the throat and flung him violently to the ground, Ben had thought, 'Shit, here we go,' and snatched up his rifle.

But then Amal had done something that had surprised Ben even more than it seemed to surprise his captors. He got up again, a little wobbly but standing his ground, and pointed at the rocks near Kabir's helicopter. Ben lowered his gun and picked up the binoculars again to resume his observation. He could see Amal was okay. And relatively safe for the moment, because he was staying in control by pointing out the spot to start digging, as though he knew exactly where the loot was buried. Clever, too, thinking on his feet like that, capitalising on the greed of his captors to buy him more time. Not to mention, he showed considerably more mental and physical toughness than Ben had ever given him credit for. Ben had to smile out of admiration.

Maybe, just maybe, Brooke had married the right guy, after all.

The crisis over, Ben had settled in for the long haul and gone on watching as the work party got organised and began to dig. From the way the group interacted, some of them seemed to know each other better than others, which suggested that several were new guys, hirelings brought on board for this particular job. It seemed unlikely that Takshak would be willing to divide up his loot so many ways. He wouldn't be planning for them all to return to Delhi, that was for certain.

By a process of elimination, Ben was able to identify the core members of the gang. The only other man apart from its leader not allocated a shovel or pickaxe was obviously Takshak's second in command. He looked like a serious kind of character, not someone to tangle with casually. Possibly ex-military like his boss, Ben thought. The others didn't have that look. Especially not the big guy, because no regular army quartermaster on earth would be able to provide boots or a uniform to fit a giant of his stature, still less a parachute strong enough to break his fall from an aircraft. When Brooke had described one of Amal's kidnappers as being seven feet tall, Ben had thought she was letting her imagination get the better of her. But she'd been right on the money. The guy was a monster, so huge that Ben found himself wondering how many bullets it would take to bring him down, when the time came.

Hours came and went. The men dug. Takshak and his Number Two went on doing little except smoking and chatting. Amal was lying still in the back of the Jeep. Now and then, Ben laid down the binocs and stretched his muscles. Nothing was happening.

Not until the second dramatic event of the day's dig. One of the hirelings had seemed to have an issue. Words had ensued. Then Takshak had calmly relieved the guy of his shovel, paused a beat and then chopped his skull open with it.

Under normal circumstances Ben would have appreciated the sight of the enemy killing one another. It made his own task that bit easier. Something to be encouraged. But it didn't comfort him to witness the fact that Amal was in the hands of an obvious psychopath. He could tell from the body language of the other crew members that several of them were having exactly the same thought, not for Amal's sake but their own.

In the next moment, Takshak had whipped out his sidearm and pointed it at Amal's head. Ben's rifle was instantly on target. Eighty yards. Finger on trigger. If Takshak hadn't lowered the pistol when he had, Ben would have spattered his brains all over the rocks. He'd have had no choice, even though it would have ruined the plan taking shape in his head.

Then the imminent danger had passed by, and Ben had known they wouldn't kill Amal. Not until tomorrow, when the next fruitless dig caused Takshak to lose control altogether. He'd watched as the weary work party tossed their shovels and picks into the three trucks and climbed in with them. Takshak led the convoy back the way it had come, with Amal chained up once again in the back of his Jeep.

From Ben's hidden OP he had a view of the whole vista stretching between the dig site and the enemy's base camp. The convoy threw up a plume of dust in its wake as it bounced and lurched back across the rocky basin and scrambled up the slope to the mouth of the cave. Takshak's Jeep drove straight through the dark fissure and disappeared, while the trucks parked haphazardly outside and the men disembarked and dragged their tired feet in after him. They left their tools in the trucks but carried their weapons inside.

Then, nothing. Stillness and silence returned to the landscape, just the low whistle of the wind rustling the dry vegetation. Ben had let some time pass, thinking through his plan and making a few preparations. One preparation in particular, which had come into his mind earlier as he'd lain there watching the men dig.

When that was done, he'd left his OP and scouted closer to the enemy camp. The terrain undulated away from the cave entrance in a series of rocky dips and rises studded here and there with dense clumps of the same kind of thorn bushes as he'd hidden the car in. He'd found a good spot due east of the cave to set up a temporary camp of his own, made himself as comfortable on the hard ground as he was going to get, and waited. He was good at waiting.

Evening had begun to fall. The sun inching lower in the

west, turning from golden yellow to shimmering arterial red. Ben had narrowed his eyes against its last rays, and watched as it slipped into the band of darkening clouds on the far, far distant horizon, way beyond the mountains, over the border into Pakistan. The red orb flattened out like a squashed egg and then sank from sight, and the shadow drew over the empty land as though someone had closed a curtain, and the light faded away.

Ben had gone on waiting. The night enveloped him and grew colder. He caught the whiff of campfire smoke drifting up out of the fissure that served as a chimney outlet from the cave. Working by feel alone, he carried out a final inspection of his weapons and the grenades he'd taken from the dead dacoits. Then checked the faint green glow of his watch dial. Thinking back through the plan, step by step, contemplating distances and speed and synchronisation and a whole host of complicated factors that had to be balanced if things were going to work out right.

Events had been set in motion now. There was no going back. The clock was ticking. Timing would be everything, like always. Strike too early, strike too late, you fail. You lose. And the wrong people die.

Another hour had passed. He had become just another shadow in the night, as rooted and immobile and patient as the hills and valleys. He was in his element here in this dark, savage place. He was ready. Waiting for the right moment.

And then, at last, the right moment had come.

Chapter 58

Ben gathered up his bag and rifle, and slipped away from the cover of the bushes to stalk as close as he dared to the cave entrance. The ground sloped gently upwards to its foot. He pressed himself into the shadowy crevices of the rocks a few feet away, and watched, and listened. He could see the flicker of firelight and the glow of paraffin lanterns emanating from within. Heard the low mutter of voices.

All fifteen remaining members of Takshak's crew were right inside the cave. Trapped with no backdoor means of escape. But that was also the problem from Ben's point of view, because Amal was trapped in there with them. And there was no way one man could storm an enclosed space like that, against those kinds of odds, without getting the hostage killed – if not himself along with him. Which was precisely why Ben's plan called for a diversion. This would only work if he could get the enemy *out* of their hidey-hole, into the open air where he needed them to be.

He moved silently away from the entrance and looked up the faintly moonlit hillside. The trickle of campfire smoke was still rising gently from the natural fissure that was serving the gang as a chimney. Careful not to dislodge any rocks he clambered up the slope towards it, and flattened himself on the ground to peer down through the crack. The smoke

348

stung his eyes and throat, but he could see right inside the cave. The fissure was easily wide enough for a man his size to scramble through. He estimated it would be about an eight-foot drop to the cave floor. Getting in would be easier than getting out. The law of gravity could be as much your enemy as your friend, at times.

Ben made his way back down to ground level and skirted wide around the cave entrance towards the three trucks. They were parked in an untidy row, all facing down the slope to make it easier to set off for tomorrow's excursion.

He crept up to the nearest. Its sides were chest high, so he had to pull himself up to peer right down into the load bed. It was full of dusty picks and shovels, along with a few other tools, a coil of rope and bits of the kind of assorted junk people carry around in utility trucks. He had no use for the tools, but the rope was handy. He took it and lowered himself down and looped the coil around his body like a mountaineer. Then stepped along the length of the truck and peered inside its cab through the open driver's side window. It was too dark to see properly. Not daring to use his torch he reached an arm through the window and ran his hand down the steering column until his fingers brushed the dangling ignition keys. They would make his job a little easier.

He unlatched the truck door, very slowly so as not to let it creak. Then hauled himself up behind the wheel and laid his bag and rifle in the passenger footwell. Next he slipped the gears into neutral and softly released the handbrake, and the truck began to roll down the slope away from the cave entrance. Its knobbly tyres crunched softly on grit and dirt and its suspension gave out a few low creaks and groans as it picked up speed and the heavy body pitched from side to side on the uneven terrain. All kinds of subtle noises that

Ben was worried could be heard from inside the cave. He kept his eye on the mirror, watching the entrance.

Nobody came out. There were no shouts of alarm. No gunfire splitting the silence of the night. So far, so good.

He let the truck roll another fifteen yards, to where it was swallowed up by the shadow of a big rock. He braked gently to a halt. Slipped the gearbox into first and tugged the handbrake tight, taking care not to let the ratchet mechanism make any sound. He got back out of the truck, taking his bag with him but leaving the rifle behind. He'd return to it later. With a Browning and a Colt nestling in his waistband and a whole collection of other hardware in his bag, he didn't feel too badly unarmed as he stalked back up the slope towards the other two trucks. He crouched in the shadows next to them.

Phase one of the plan was complete.

He checked his watch once more. There was no practical way to verify that his timing was right. He was a little more dependent on intuition and luck than he'd have liked, but it wouldn't be the first such situation he'd been in, and he was still alive.

In the darkness he opened up his bag and took out the grenades he'd scavenged from the bodies of the dead dacoits earlier that day. There were seven of them, generic devices manufactured by the Indian Ordnance Board but pretty much identical to any made anywhere, with the classic pine-apple shell made of brittle cast iron and packed with enough TNT explosive to rip a powerful destructive swathe some twenty-seven metres in diameter, killing or maiming any enemy within the circle. The combined effect of seven of them would be enough to get anyone's attention, that was for sure.

Ben piled six of the grenades in a little mound under the

truck, keeping the seventh one by as the detonator. He'd only have to pull that one pin, because its blast would instantly set off the others. The standard fuse delay time was four seconds, just long enough for him to get the hell out of there and scramble under cover. Few things could make you run faster than the imminent prospect of a shrapnel shower hot on your heels.

He hesitated, nervous about kicking things off prematurely. But if the timing of this whole plan was wrong, then it was wrong, and it couldn't be helped. *Fuck it*, he thought, and grasped the pin of the seventh grenade and went to yank it out.

And then stopped. Because the shape of a man's figure had appeared in the mouth of the cave entrance. Coming this way.

Ben shrank back into the shadows and watched him. The guy walked over to the trucks and stopped, just a body's length away from where Ben was crouching. The toe of his boot maybe eleven inches from the mound of grenades. Ben heard the zip of his flies being yanked open, followed a moment later by the splash and patter of his urine against the truck tyre. Men, like dogs, seemed inclined to piss on tyres. A male territorial thing, Ben had always thought. Some primal remnant of human evolutionary psychology. Or maybe they were just dirty bastards.

The guy was too busy to notice the dark shape that rose up out of the shadows behind him. Not that he'd have been able to do anything about it, if he had.

Ben grabbed him from behind and cupped a palm over his mouth and jammed him hard against the side of the truck to stop him from crying out or struggling. Then twisted his head up and sideways, and felt the resistance in there, and twisted harder and felt it give, and heard the muted *crunch* as the guy's neck broke. Brain death wouldn't be quite instant, but near enough as dammit. He kept a grip on the guy until he felt the tension go out of him, then let the body slump to the ground. Now he could get on with his business.

Or maybe he couldn't just yet. Because almost exactly thirty seconds after the guy had stepped out of the cave, another figure emerged.

Ben gritted his teeth and thought, *Oh, for Pete's sake*. Watched as the second guy walked from the cave. He seemed to be searching for the first guy. Ben heard him softly call out, 'Neeraj?'

Ben's initial intention was that second guy would quickly meet the same fate as his friend. Maybe, he mused, all thirteen of the others would take turns stepping outside for a toilet break, at convenient intervals, allowing themselves to be disposed of one by one until there were none left and Ben could just walk in there and get Amal. An interesting possibility, but unlikely.

Then a new idea came to him. Because his plan was all about creating a diversion. And the best diversions were the ones that spooked the enemy to the maximum.

Ben reached into his jacket pocket and pulled out his notebook and pen. He silently ripped a page free, wrote his brief note and folded it in two and placed it on the dead man's chest before retreating back into the shadows. In retrospect the words *coming to get you* were ambiguous, depending on whether they were addressed to Amal, in which case they carried a promise of help – or to Takshak and his crew, which offered the threat of much darker things to come. But they were true either way. Ben watched the second guy hunt about in the dark, still looking for his friend. For a moment it looked like he might walk right by without noticing the body on the ground. But then the second guy stumbled right into it. Moments later, he was running back to the cave, clutching Ben's note and roaring and braying at the top of his voice.

Perfect.

This was it. Ben counted off as many more seconds as he dared to wait, picturing the scenario taking place inside the cave. Then he pulled the pin on the seventh grenade, tossed it under the truck, saw it roll and come to a rest next to the mound of its six companions.

And he bounded away from the trucks and ran like hell for the safety of the rocks.

Four seconds to showtime.

Chapter 59

Several things happened in those four seconds. First, Ben could hear a lot of commotion going on from inside the cave, just as he'd intended. Then, right on cue, more figures appeared in its dimly-lit mouth. Two of them hurried outside with weapons in their hands. They paused for a fraction of a second at the cave entrance, peering out into the darkness with a mixture of anxiety and anger in their body language. Then they split up and charged out into the night. One of them skirted around the side of the trucks while the other ran down the narrow aisle between them, obviously in the hope that he might find the prowler lurking there.

He found something else, though he'd never know what.

The explosion of the grenades happened in a ripple effect as the initial detonation set off a chain reaction lasting maybe a quarter of a second longer than a single bomb blast. But the difference was academic. The erupting fireball lit up the night, blinding white at its core and spreading out into a fiery orange halo. The massive combined pressure wave lifted both trucks off their wheels and sent them spinning in opposite directions like children's toys. The unfortunate guy caught between them had stepped right into the heart of the blast. If a forensic team had later tried to examine what was left of him, they'd have found nothing but fine paste mixed up with pulverised bone fragments, and maybe a boot with a foot still in it two hundred yards away. Meanwhile his friend hadn't been quite so close to the epicentre of the explosion, but not so far away as to escape the deadly shrapnel wave that simultaneously blew him off his feet and sliced him into pieces, dashing what was left of him against the base of the hillside.

The blast was over as suddenly as it had gone off. It was followed by a long moment of stunned silence. TNT high explosive makes for a sooty, smoky detonation. Its aftermath blotted the dim moonlight to total blackness. It took several seconds for the smoke to dissipate. One of the shattered trucks had turned a triple somersault in the air and was lying belly-up several yards away, burning brightly, one wheel spinning. The other had been blasted clean in two, little remaining but a twisted chassis and a few bodywork panels crumpled like tin foil. Smaller patches of fire were burning all over the place. The thorn bushes behind which Ben had been hiding earlier were ablaze.

Then after the silence came the inevitable mayhem as the smoky darkness suddenly came alive with running shapes of men bursting out of the cave entrance, yellow-white muzzle flash spurting from their guns as they fired in all directions against the invisible enemy that had launched the attack on them.

But by then the invisible enemy was already on the move, making his way up the hillside. Crackling gunfire filled the air. Yelling and chaos all around. The essence of a perfect diversion. Phase two of Ben's plan was complete.

Now for the hard part. He reached the fissure at the top of the cave and crouched low beside it. A wisp of campfire smoke was still trickling up out of the crack. The men down below were all far too busy milling around the scene of devastation, shooting at shadows and yelling their heads off in fury to have noticed him. He unslung the rope coil from around his body and quickly secured one end to a jutting rock. Then fed the loose end down through the smoky hole and scrambled in after it.

The fissure offered all kinds of handholds and footholds for him to climb down. He had to scrape and wriggle his way through about ten feet of rock before he'd reach the inside. For a moment he felt a jolt of fear as he thought he'd get stuck; then he gave a twist and was free again. He felt his legs dangle in mid-air as they emerged from the cave ceiling. This was the moment of maximum exposure and greatest vulnerability, but it lasted only a second as he let go and dropped the last eight feet to the cave floor like a parachutist. His boots crunched down into the middle of the dying campfire, scattering sticks of blackened wood and snuffing out the last of the flames. He let his knees flex and his body roll over to break the fall, and came back up on his feet with the Colt Delta Elite drawn and ready. Saw the shape of the man he'd caught unawares with his surprise entry. Saw the gleam of frightened eyes catching the lantern light as the guy spun around to face him, just ten paces away. Saw the glitter of the man's weapon swivelling his way.

Ben fired twice. Double tap, centre of mass, pure instinct with no conscious aim. Saw the shape of the man crumple up and fall, heard the thud of his weapon hitting the floor and his muted grunt as he died.

Ben kept the gun pointed long enough to make sure the guy wasn't getting up again. He wasn't. There was still enough wild firing going on outside to have disguised the sound of the shots from within the cave, but they'd sounded pretty damn loud up close. Ben's ears rang as he glanced around him. The cave walls were rough and craggy in places, smoothed in others as though by the passage of a thousand years' worth of fast-flowing water. To his front was the sliver of the entrance, some ten feet high and just wide enough to squeeze a truck through. To his back was the shape of Takshak's Jeep, reversed into the deep shadows at the rear of the cave.

The guy he'd shot must have been left behind to guard the prisoner. Which had to mean the prisoner was still alive. Or so Ben could only hope. He hurried over to the Jeep. Whispered hoarsely, 'Amal?' There was no reply. He could make out the dull glint of the chain lying like a snake across the ground. He picked it up and tugged on it. One end was attached to the Jeep's rear bumper. The other end to a dark, slumped shape that had crawled into a recess at the very back of the cave and wasn't moving.

Ben whispered again, 'Amal?'

Still no response. Ben's heart froze in terror that he was too late. He ducked into the recess and reached out to the silent huddled shape on the ground. He dreaded the touch of cold, stiff, dead flesh.

Then the relief spilled through him all over again as he heard the groan and felt the stirring as Amal woke up and raised his head from the ground. He appeared frightened at first, unable to recognise Ben's face in the darkness. Ben took the torch from his bag and shone it over himself.

'Ben? BEN!?'

'You're okay,' Ben said. 'You're safe now.'

Chapter 60

Though that statement was far from true. Takshak's men would soon return, and when that happened the cave wouldn't be a good place to be. Ben ran the torch beam over Amal's face. Up close, he looked worse. The splits in his lips needed stitching and his bad eye was puffed up to the size of a pomegranate, which were bad enough. But the fresh bruising all over his face was plenty enough evidence of a more recent beating. The bastards had been laying into him that evening.

'How are we doing?' Ben asked him.

'Arm's broken,' Amal croaked, and his one open eye rolled sideways to glance at his right arm. Speaking made the cuts reopen and ooze blood from his lips. 'Takshak did it. As punishment for what happened today.'

Ben swallowed back the hot surge of anger. No time for sentiment. Outside the shooting was still going on, but beginning to quieten down and become more sporadic as it gradually dawned on the defenders that nobody was shooting back.

'I thought no one was ever coming for me.'

'Then you thought wrong.'

'Brooke—?' Like Amal was almost too afraid to ask.

'She's the one who sent me, Amal. She's fine. You're going

to see her again soon. But first we have to get out of here, and fast. Can you walk?'

'Got no shoes.'

Ben said, 'Turn your face away and cover your ear.'

Amal stared at him, then understood and did what he'd been told, clamping his usable hand to the side of his head. Ben held the torch between his teeth and pulled the chain taut from Amal's ankle. A pair of bolt croppers would have been useful. He'd just have to do it the noisy way. Taking out the Colt he pressed its muzzle against the chain links. Too close to Amal's foot, the gases from the blast would cut and sear his flesh. Too far away and Amal would be trailing a length of chain until Ben managed to get the cuff off. Ben compromised on six inches.

He pressed the trigger and the loud gunshot kicked up dust and stone chips from the cave floor. The broken chain fell loose like a shot snake. A nine-millimetre might not have been effective against tempered steel, but its big brother did the job just fine. Ben made the weapon safe and thrust it in his waistband. He quickly took off his belt, refastened the buckle and looped it around Amal's neck. Amal gritted his teeth as Ben gently lifted the limp broken arm and inserted it through the improvised leather sling. One glance close-up at the rock-lacerated soles of Amal's bare feet was enough to tell him there was no way he could walk.

Ben darted over to the dead body on the cave floor. It took him a few moments to rip off the dead guy's boots. Two sizes too large for Amal, but they'd do fine. Amal winced as Ben jammed the boots onto his feet. Then Ben gripped his good arm and helped him to stand. Amal was unsteady and weak, his face contorted with pain. 'How are we getting out of here?' he gasped.

That was a good question, to which there'd never been

an easy answer. Ben had begun the rescue knowing that his exfiltration plan left a lot to be desired. In an ideal world, if Amal had been in a fit state to do so, they'd have made their exit the way Ben had come in, get away unseen and make it to the truck that Ben had purposely separated off from the others to use as an escape vehicle. But this was anything but an ideal world, and getting a weakened, half-blind man with a broken arm back up through a narrow crevice in the roof eight feet off the ground with just a thin rope to shinny up was not an option. And as slender and light as Amal was, Ben couldn't make the climb for both of them.

So he threw that part of his strategy out of the window without a second's hesitation, along with any hope of getting out of here undetected. Plan B was going to be just a little bit less subtle.

'We're going to drive straight out the front door,' he replied.

'You're crazy.'

'And you're going to have to hold on tight. Think you can manage?'

'You just watch me.'

'It's going to hurt.'

'Better than being dead,' Amal replied, and Ben couldn't argue with that. He helped Amal into the passenger seat. The Jeep was a dedicated off-roader, with a utilitarian instrument panel, a full roll cage and oversized tyres as knobbly as a tractor's. At some point in its life it had been fitted with five-point harness safety belts, like a rally car. He strapped Amal as tightly to the seat as he could, then piled in behind the wheel.

The firing outside had stopped. Any moment now, Takshak's crew were going to come running back into the cave, and there was little doubt in Ben's mind that they'd still have plenty of rounds left in their guns. This rescue mission could come to a bad end as quickly as it had begun.

But not if Ben could help it. He twisted the ignition and the Jeep's engine rasped into life, loud and echoey in the confines of the cave. He flipped on the lights, slammed the transmission into gear and stamped the accelerator to the floor. The big knobbled tyres bit down hard and the Jeep went surging towards the cave mouth, lighting it up brightly in its headlamps.

Not a moment too late. A pair of Takshak's men suddenly appeared in the entrance and froze blinking in the dazzling light, momentarily too confused to raise their weapons and shoot. Ben had no intention of giving them that opportunity. He kept his foot down and piled right into them.

The Jeep's right-side wing caught one guy in the hip and spun him violently sideways into the jagged rocks of the cave entrance with a crunch that Ben heard over the roar of the engine. The other one folded in half across the Jeep's bonnet and his head cannoned off the windscreen, and his body flipped right over them as they stormed out of the cave and into the night. Two for one. By Ben's count that made Takshak seven men down, including the guy he'd done for himself.

But the fight wasn't over yet, with a lot of heavily armed and very angry opponents left to deal with. The scene outside the cave looked like a war zone. The blown-up trucks and the bushes around them were still on fire. The Jeep's head-lights sliced into the billowing smoke and picked out flitting figures of the enemy running everywhere in disarray. Ben aimed the nose of the Jeep at one of them, who threw himself out of the way and went tumbling into a pile of wreckage. A near miss. Ben veered off and kept going.

Shots cracked out. Takshak's men were in full-on panic mode and firing wildly, but a lucky bullet could still find its mark. The Jeep's windscreen, already crumpled by the impact of the head of the man Ben had run over, shattered as a shot from behind just missed his shoulder. He kept his boot hard to the floor and the Jeep went lurching and bouncing down the slope and hit the rough terrain like a rodeo bull doing everything it could to shake off its rider. The steering wheel was juddering so badly in his hands that it was all he could do to hang on and not let his fingers and thumbs get fractured or torn from their sockets. Amal was getting a severe shaking in the passenger seat beside him. The five-point harness was doing its job, but the pain in his broken arm must have been terrible.

Ben clenched his jaw and kept going, dead ahead, as fast as he could get away from the cave and Takshak's remaining men. No mercy, no let-up. The engine screamed every time the wheels went airborne over a rise. Then the chassis would feel as though it was about to break when they came down to earth. Crashing over rocks, flattening bushes and small trees, pounding up blind inclines and skidding and slithering down sheer slopes, barely in control but still moving forwards. Bullets zipping by. Punching into the bodywork. The crackling chatter of fully-automatic gunfire hammering the night behind them.

The sound of something else, too. A heavy, deep, throbbing vibration that Ben could feel in his chest. It seemed to have come out of nowhere, building and intensifying within seconds from a subtle, distant pulse until it filled his ears and almost drowned out the noise of the Jeep. Just for a moment he eased his pressure off the gas, so that he could twist around and crane his neck back towards the source of the sound.

362

It was the rhythmic thud of rotor blades as a helicopter swooped down out of the night sky to hover above the foot of the hillside near the cave. Ben blinked at the hard white glare of the powerful searchlight that cut through the swirling smoke and swept the ground.

And that was when he knew that his timing hadn't been so far off, after all.

Chapter 61

Ben could count on the fingers of one hand the number of times in his career that he'd depended on the help of law enforcement officials, still less actively called in the cavalry. But the arrival of Captain Jabbar Dada's airborne police unit was a sight he was happy to see.

This was a big country and the arid hills and plateaus around Rakhigarhi covered a vast, sweeping area. Which was why Ben had conservatively reckoned on a three-hour time window to allow Dada to scramble his men together, refuel the chopper, empty out their armoury, tog up and make the long flight out here from base for the second time that day.

He'd been reasonably sure that a cop as gung-ho as Jabbar Dada would find it hard to refuse the prospect of a proper battle against some real, live bad guys. Who might or might not actually be dacoits, but that was the impression Ben had deliberately given his duty officer when he'd made the anonymous tip-off call to Dada's headquarters earlier that evening, using the satellite phone he'd taken from the limousine. No way he could have got regular mobile reception out here in the wilderness. But his smartphone was still useful to him in two ways, firstly because Dada's HQ number was still lodged in its call records, and secondly because even

364

without a signal it could give him GPS data accurate to within eleven feet of the target. He'd made the guy repeat back to him three times the coordinates of the alleged dacoit hideout, where he'd promised there would be all kinds of criminal activity taking place that night. If it was low-life bandit scum the captain wanted, he had only to roll in with his task force troops to be guaranteed a major score. Along with his name in the paper, and maybe a medal from the Director General of Police. Like offering a meaty bone to a hungry dog.

'Who is this? Who are you, please?' the duty officer had kept asking, deep suspicion in his voice.

'A concerned member of the public,' Ben had replied, before hanging up the call.

It had been something of a gamble, because the chance that the duty officer wouldn't even pass on the message was compounded by the possibility, slight but real, that Dada would decline to take the bait even if he did. Ben had been worrying about it ever since.

But now that doubt had been proved wrong. It wasn't quite the same as calling in the Chinooks of the Joint Special Forces Aviation Wing, the way he had been able to do back in the day. But it was good enough. The captain would get his moment of glory while Ben took the opportunity to get clean away with his freed hostage. A win-win situation for everyone except Takshak and the remnants of his gang, who suddenly had a whole new problem to deal with.

Ben let the Jeep roll to a halt and watched the chopper descend. Its searchlight tracked the running figures on the ground, caught like mice in the open. Its roaring down-draught was flattening the bushes and whipping up a dust storm. The flames on the ground were reflecting on its black and yellow livery.

But Takshak's men weren't going to run and hide, or give in without a fight. Dada was landing under fire as the crew stopped shooting at the escaping Jeep and doubled down on the new threat from the sky. Nor was Dada about to shrink away from a gun battle. Ben could see the captain's diminutive form hanging out of the side hatch of the chopper with his INSAS light machine gun clutched in one hand, spitting flame as he strafed the ground with bullets left and right. Both sides were taking damage. Ben could see the strikes hitting the chopper's fuselage. He saw one of Takshak's men lit up in the trembling white searchlight beam take a hit and go down in a spray of blood.

Amal yelled over the noise, 'What the hell's happening? Who are those people?'

Ben smiled. 'The enemies of your enemies are your friends. Looks like you have more of those than you thought, Amal.'

Under different circumstances Ben would have wanted to help in the fight. But there was little he could do with a pistol at this range, having left his rifle in the truck. And he wanted to get away from this place as fast as possible. Not least because Amal needed medical attention. He turned back to the controls and drove on, leaving the crackle of gunfire and the roar of the chopper behind him. The wild ride resumed. Jolting over the harsh terrain, ripping through vegetation, getting thrown about in their seats, Amal clinging on with his one arm, tense and silent with pain. They were close to the dry river bed now. Ben intended to retrace his steps back the way he'd come earlier, as far as Jind or Hansi where he was banking on finding a hospital. Then at last he could call Brooke and tell her the news that Amal was alive and safe.

They were getting away. His plan had worked out fine.

For the first time in a while, Ben was suddenly able to relax a little.

And then everything started to unravel.

The first thing that went wrong was the Jeep's fuel gauge, which Ben noticed with a start was reading empty. Except there was nothing wrong with the gauge itself. It was perfectly accurate and trustworthy. As Ben realised a moment later, when the engine began to splutter and die on the approach to the river bank. A bullet must have holed the tank or severed a fuel line. Ben swore and spurred the Jeep on as far as it would go. They made it to the top of the rise burning whatever few drops of petrol were left in the carburettor, and then the engine gave its last cough and died completely. They coasted to a halt in almost exactly the same spot as Kabir and his friends had been attacked.

Ben could still hear the sporadic crackles of the gun battle in the distance, blocked from view by the undulations of the terrain. The helicopter seemed to have landed. Dada was still mopping up the last of Takshak's men but it wouldn't take him long. Ben jumped out of the Jeep and grabbed his torch from his bag, crouched by the rear wheel, shone his light under and saw the bullet hole in the fuel tank. 'That's unfortunate,' he muttered.

'What do we do now?' Amal asked anxiously.

Before Ben could reply, the second thing went wrong.

Which was that the night sky in the distance suddenly lit up in a huge fireball that blossomed outwards and hurled flaming debris hundreds of yards into the air with a blast twice as loud as the exploding trucks.

Dada's chopper had just gone up in flames. Takshak's guys had put up more of a fight than Ben had anticipated. He should have known better than to underestimate his enemy.

'Ben? What are we going to do?' Amal repeated, panicky now.

'I have another car,' Ben said.

Amal glanced about him, craning his neck to see with his one eye. 'Where?'

'How do you think I got here? Stay put. I'll be right back.'

The exploded chopper was a fiery beacon in the distance. It would burn for a long time. As Ben left Amal sitting in the Jeep and ran up the rocky river bed he wondered what was happening out there. From this distance there was just no way to tell. If Dada or any his men were still okay they might be able to radio for assistance. If they'd been wiped out, it was because Ben had lured them to it. And Ben felt bad about that. Then again, what more magnificent end for the bandit hunter than to go down in a blaze of glory doing what he loved best?

Ben reached the overgrowth of thorn bushes where he'd hidden the Maybach, shone his light beam through the tangled mass and saw the dull glint of dusty black bodywork reflecting back at him. It was right in deep at the heart of the thorns. Nature's answer to barbed wire. Not much fun to dive into without a machete to hack a path. But he didn't have a lot of choice. His leather jacket protected his arms and chest as he waded in and used his elbows to force his way through, forearms covering his face, keeping his hands above the level of the thorns so that they didn't get lacerated to pieces. His legs got the worst of it. By the time he reached the car his jeans were pretty badly torn up and he was bleeding through them.

He clambered in behind the wheel. The limousine's luxury interior felt even more incongruous and ridiculous after the utilitarian off-roader. The engine fired up with a smooth purr at the first touch of the ignition. He turned on the lights, slid the transmission into reverse and toed the gas, and the limo backed out of the bushes amid a creaky scraping and raking of sharp thorns against expensive coachwork, like the rasp of fingernails on a classroom blackboard.

Once he was free he gunned the throttle and reversed the huge car quickly back along the river bed towards the dead Jeep. He'd almost managed to forget how badly the thing handled on rough terrain. Amal's uncomfortable ride wasn't over yet. Drawing up level with the Jeep he jumped out and opened up the rear Pullman cabin for his passenger.

'Hop in.'

Amal's jaw fell open at the sight of the Ray family limo. 'I can't believe you came out here in this thing,' he mumbled through his broken lips.

'I know you rich boys like to travel in style,' Ben said.

'I'm hardly rich. That's my family. It's not me.'

'Whatever.'

'I want to call Brooke. Tell her I'm okay.'

'Later,' Ben said. 'Let's get out of here first, and get you to a doctor.'

He helped Amal hobble out of the Jeep and into the back of the Maybach. Amal caught a glimpse of himself in the side mirror and groaned. 'Christ, I look terrible.'

It was a fair description. With six inches of chain manacled to his ankle, his arm in an improvised sling and a face like tenderised steak Amal might have been an escapee from some Third World slave labour camp. Ben said, 'I don't think Brooke will care what you look like, Amal. She just wants you home safe.'

'And I will be, thanks to you. I don't know what to say, Ben.'

'If I had lips like that, I wouldn't want to say anything at all. Do yourself a favour.'

'I just wish my brother was coming back with me,' Amal said in an undertone.

'I'm sorry, Amal.'

Ben shut him inside the car and was halfway back along its bargelike length towards the driver's door when he stopped. Turned to gaze across its roof in the direction of the western horizon. And stared. Not at the glow of the burning helicopter against the night sky. Something else had caught his eye.

The headlights of Takshak's sole surviving truck had just appeared over a rise in the distance and were bouncing and bobbing across the rough ground, approximately midway between the scene of the gun battle and the dry river bed where Ben was standing. Moving as fast as the terrain would allow. Growing brighter and larger every second.

Heading straight this way.

Chapter 62

The limo's rear passenger window whirred down and Amal's bruised, bloodied face appeared in the gap. He'd spotted the approaching headlights, too, and was staring at them in dismay through his one open eye. 'It's him.'

Ben was inclined to agree. Takshak was one determined individual, all right. There was no time to lose. The truck was coming on recklessly fast over the bad terrain, as though it had a demon at the wheel. It was hitting the rises and rocks so hard that its wheels were bouncing right off the ground and its front end was soaring skywards before crashing back down again, like the bow of a speedboat slicing over a choppy ocean. The headlights disappeared from sight as the oncoming truck attacked the bottom of the rise leading up to the river bank. Ben knew he'd be seeing them again soon, and much closer up.

Not good. Especially considering that he'd left his captured SLR with a full magazine in that damn truck, intending to come back to it later. The firepower advantage now belonged to Takshak.

Ben dived back in behind the wheel of the limo. 'Hang on tight,' he warned Amal.

'I am hanging on. Get us the hell out of here!'

Ben slammed the Maybach into forward drive and floored

the accelerator, and the twelve-cylinder biturbo engine spun the tyres on the rocky river bed. He started to slew the car around in a tight U-turn, intending to take them back the way he'd come, past the remains of Kabir's chopper and away in the direction of civilisation.

But it was a short-lived plan. Ben had been too slow, thinking he still had a few seconds in hand before Takshak caught up with them. With a blaze of light and a snarling diesel roar the truck came surging into view over the crest, then hit the downward incline and skidded crazily across Ben's path, cutting off the limo's escape.

Ben aborted his U-turn and twisted the car back the other way, its rear end swaying and swinging. The truck straightened itself up and came on in his wake, headlights glaring. The chase was on. It was an unequal match. Whatever advantages the Maybach possessed over its pursuer in terms of sheer brute horsepower, it more than lost in the traction contest as its smooth road tyres struggled to find a grip on the near-impossible surface. No amount of fancy electronics could compensate for its total unsuitability to these conditions. Ben reached the big overgrown clump of thorns half blocking the way ahead, pointed the nose of the car past their edge and ripped past. They were heading into uncharted territory now, because he had no idea what lay beyond this point.

Within seconds, the terrain became even worse. The river bed began to slope downwards, steeper, then steeper still, as the banks on both sides rose up to form smooth rocky canyon walls that lit up almost pure white in the headlights of the speeding, bucking car. Ben was only barely in control of the vehicle. The punishment it was taking would have destroyed its underside completely, if not for the armoured plate designed to protect it from bomb attacks. Ben didn't need to worry too much about things like UV joints or prop shaft or exhaust components getting pounded to pieces by rocks and boulders smashing into them. Instead he was worried about the wheels getting ripped clean off. Any second now, he fully expected to see one of them flying past his window and feel the scrape as the car slid onwards on its bare metal belly. Then the chase would be over fairly quickly.

The truck was gaining on them. Its headlights were filling the whole cabin. Ben snatched a split-second glance in the rear-view mirror and glimpsed the dark figure at the wheel of the truck. Then another silhouetted shape rising up behind the truck cab, clinging to the roof canopy bars to stand erect. A much larger figure. Huge.

Takshak wasn't alone. He had the seven-foot monster with him.

Then the giant silhouette was obscured by the strobe-light of muzzle flash, and a sustained burst of automatic gunfire rattled like hail against the back window of the Maybach. Amal let out a muffled yell.

Ben shouted, 'Get your bloody head down!' and Amal threw himself to the floor of the Pullman cabin, crying out again from the pain as he fell on his broken arm.

More gunfire hosed the back of the Maybach. The giant was shooting from a downwards angle. His bullets smacked into the glass and peppered the roof. All of which was theoretically resistant to small arms fire. But Ben had seen enough purportedly bullet-proof vehicles shredded to pieces in his time to take such claims with a pinch of salt. It was one thing to see the results of ballistic experiments the military carried out in safe, controlled conditions. Becoming a live guinea pig inside the test vehicle as it was hammered with high-velocity rifle fire at close range was something else entirely.

In any case those thoughts were the least of his concerns

as he struggled to keep the insanely jolting, bucking, slithering vehicle pointed in a more or less straight line without ploughing into the canyon walls either side of him. The nearside wing of the car glanced violently off a great smooth rock and one headlight suddenly went dark, making it even harder to steer a safe course. Then another sustained blast of full-auto SLR gunfire crackled from the roof of the truck behind them and Ben felt the limo's back tyres go as the rubber was shredded into ribbons.

Prem had said the car was designed to keep going for several kilometres even on four flats. They might just be about to put that to the test, too.

Amal was huddled on the floor of the Pullman cabin, clinging to a door handle for support. He screamed, 'Ben! Do something!'

The truck loomed up right behind them. Point-blank fire pounded the car roof and raked its flanks. The driver-side mirror shattered and fell limp from its mounting. The firing paused. Ben thought maybe the giant had run out of ammo. But that was little consolation as Takshak opted for another strategy.

The truck smashed into the back of the car. The wheel juddered in Ben's hands. He very nearly let the vehicle go into a skid from which it would never have recovered. Then the truck hit them again, with a crunch that resonated through all twenty-one feet of the car's length from stem to stern. Again, somehow Ben managed to get himself straightened up and jammed his foot down harder to try to widen the distance between the limo's mangled rear end and the front of the truck.

It wasn't working.

Then, just as he was thinking that things couldn't get any worse, they did.

One moment the car's single remaining headlight had been picking out the curves and contours of the rocks ahead and the canyon wall to one side, all smoothed out by the passage of the long-gone ancient river. The next, the rocks and the canyon wall suddenly vanished, and the path ahead appeared to drop away into nothing, and the car's headlight was shining its beam into empty blackness.

The part of Ben's mind that could rationally compute what was happening realised that once upon a time, thousands of years ago, the fast-moving river had carved this canyon out of solid rock on the approach to a giant waterfall. Now there was no water. Just a sheer edge as the river bed terminated without warning into a vertical cliff face.

But in the milliseconds that the trillions of chemical synapses inside Ben's brain had compressed all those logical conclusions into a flash of conscious understanding, it was already far too late to do anything but clutch the steering wheel in both fists and stare in horror through the windscreen as the nose of the car plummeted into a dizzying drop, and they went sailing over the edge.

Chapter 63

Down and down they went, the car slowly turning over and over as the blackness rushed up to meet them. Amal's panic-stricken yelling filled the cabin. Ben was just trying to hold on, even as he knew there was nothing to hold onto that wouldn't get pulverised and flattened at the precise same instant that the impact against the rocks below squashed his body into mincemeat. No point screaming about it. Of all the ways you could die, at least this was one of the quickest. And to have died trying wasn't such a bad thing.

Ben closed his eyes and waited. For how many more seconds, he didn't know, but it couldn't be many. They seemed to have been falling forever. How far down could the bottom be?

Then it came. The massive bone-jarring crunch that knocked the breath from his lungs. Something hit his head and his vision exploded into a brilliant white starburst and all kinds of strange memories seemed to stream through his mind. He saw Brooke's face smiling down at him through a drifting haze. Then her face broke up and became part of the blizzard of starry lights whirling around him. He was floating through space, or swimming through the deep water of an ocean. Now slowly bobbing up towards the surface. Consciousness gradually returning. He remembered the fall.

It seemed to have stopped now. Telling him that they must have reached the bottom. Which would mean he was dead now. Making it all the stranger when he found that he could open his eyes, and could move, and breathe, and felt a jab of pain in his head and through his ribs where his body had thudded into something solid on impact.

It was dark. Everything seemed oddly still and calm. He could hear the whistle of the wind and a trickle of cool breeze coming from somewhere below him. It took a few seconds longer for his dazed mind to begin to orientate itself. The solid object he'd hit with his chest was the car's steering wheel, which he was lying sprawled on top of with his head and shoulders jammed into the V-shaped angle between the windscreen and the dashboard. Except, for some inexplicable reason, the V was pointing vertically downwards, the force of gravity pressing his head tight against the glass. He was aware of a peculiar rocking motion, like the cradle in the nursery rhyme, gently swaying in the breeze. It was a restful kind of sensation. Not actually unpleasant. He was able to stretch his left arm out to the side, feeling around him, and his hand brushed against the rough bark of the thick tree branch inside the cab.

Tree?

The surreal realisation was what jolted him back to his senses. *What tree?*

He blinked a few times. It wasn't totally dark inside the car. Some dim moonlight was shining through the windows, and as his wits returned and his night vision focused, he understood. His present reality was better than being dead. But only slightly, and possibly not for long.

If Ben had been able to be present in this very spot thousands of years ago, he would have found himself at the heart of a massive torrent of water, endless tons of it crashing and foaming down the cliff as the mighty river surged over the edge of the drop. This land must have been a very different place then, lush and green and bursting with all manner of diverse life that could never thrive in the desert it had become now. Even after the water had dried up, the hardier varieties of flora had managed to cling on. And the tree that had sprouted from the side of the cliff, right where the gigantic waterfall had once been, was one of those. Its roots embedded deep into the sheer rock face, enabling the weight of its gnarled trunk to hang right out over the abyss, branches reaching upwards in search of light and rainfall. The tree had probably been slowly growing for a century or more. A fine nesting place for hawks and crows to raise their young, presumably, being impossible for egg-hungry predators to reach. And, in the extremely unlikely event of someone being foolish enough to drive a car over the edge of the cliff, the ancient tree provided a different kind of safeguard.

The branch that had arrested the limousine's fall had skewered the entire length of the limo, punching a hole the thickness of a man's thigh through the windscreen and passing all the way to the back window. Now the Maybach was literally dangling in mid-air, gently rocking as its five-ton weight flexed the gnarly old limb with lot of creaking and rustling of twigs and leaves.

It hadn't missed Ben by a wide margin. Another eighteen inches to the right, its tip would have speared right through him. The falling car might just as easily have missed the branch altogether, in which case no further miracles would have been available to prevent them from plummeting the rest of the way down the cliff. If Ben and Amal had been cats, they could have reckoned on having given up at least seven of their nine lives, in one swoop.

Ben struggled up off the steering wheel and managed to

get himself turned upright. Automobiles became a somewhat more cramped and awkward space to move about in when they were hanging nose-down. He craned his neck upwards and saw Amal above him, lying wedged against the steel, leather and wood bulkhead that separated the Pullman compartment from the driver's cab. The spearing tree branch had missed Amal by a wider margin than it had Ben; but all the same, it had been a close thing.

Knocked unconscious by the impact, Amal was just now coming round. His good eye fluttered open and gleamed down at Ben. In a muted croak he asked, 'Are we dead?'

'Apparently not,' Ben said. 'But I don't think we should tempt fate by hanging around here too long.'

As though to mark his words the tree gave a long, juddering groan and seemed to sag an inch or two. A small landslide of stones pattered down the rock face, pinged off the car's bodywork and disappeared into the abyss.

Ben was suddenly very aware of his movements. One sharp jerk, and the straining tree roots might just decide to tear free of the rock face. With great caution he unlatched the driver's door and eased it open. It was blocked from opening all the way by a neighbouring branch thicker than the one that had speared the windscreen. But he was able to wriggle his legs gingerly out of the gap and place one foot on the branch. He peered downwards. The bottom of the drop was still a hell of a long way below them, lost in darkness. He peered upwards and saw the lights of Takshak's truck shining out over the edge of the cliff far above him.

He'd almost managed to forget about that guy.

Ben slowly, carefully, placed his other foot on the branch to test his full weight on it. It would hold him, but the tree was making an awful lot of dire creaking noises that warned him things might not remain that way much longer. 'We need to get out of here,' he hissed up at Amal, keeping his voice low in case he could be heard from the top.

Amal's broken arm was obviously causing him terrible pain, but he refused to make a squeak of complaint as he gamely lowered himself into the driver's cab and slithered out of the door. Ben inched a little way along the branch to make space for him. 'Not scared of heights, I hope?' he asked softly as the chilly mountain breeze whistled around them.

'Only of falling,' Amal muttered in reply.

'Then don't look down,' Ben said.

Amal wasn't a heavy man, lighter than Ben, but the extra weight on the branch made it groan ominously. Another reminder that this was no place to hang around for too long.

Just then a strong torch beam shone down the cliff, searching back and forth. Takshak, trying to see where his quarry had ended up. The beam brushed the outer branches of the tree and then began probing closer in towards the rock face. It passed over the dangling car, hesitated and came back on itself, like a double-take. The light lingered over the crumpled bodywork and shattered windows, as though trying to find a way inside. Ben and Amal quickly sidestepped along their perch away from the car, hanging onto smaller branches for support.

Ben had seen something in the torchlight. A rocky ledge close to where the tree trunk jutted from the cliff face. It was wide enough for them both. There seemed to be a path winding down from it, but he couldn't be certain. The torch beam moved on and the ledge fell back into shadow.

Amal's broken ankle chain slithered over the rough bark. With only one arm and one eye, his movements were clumsy, and as he fumbled for support he lost his footing, teetered, and toppled off the branch.

One instant Amal had been there at his side; the next he was gone. Ben saw it almost too late. He dived after him. For a breathless heartbeat, he thought Amal was lost. Then saw that he'd managed to grab hold of a thinner branch on his way down and was dangling from one hand, his legs kicking and wheeling in empty space. His eye was open wide and he was gasping in terror. Ben lay flat against the coarse bark and reached down to him. 'I've got you.'

'I can't hold on. I'm going to fall!'

'No, you're not,' Ben said. He reached down a little further, straining his arm as far as he could. Not far enough. His fingertips were inches from Amal's hand.

The torchlight was suddenly on them. Ben blinked as the bright white beam shone into his eyes from high above. He heard the sound of faraway voices. Two men, or maybe three. Someone was laughing.

Then a booming rifle shot cracked out and a high-velocity bullet kicked splinters from the tree branch just five inches from Ben's shoulder. And another, which missed by a couple of feet and hit the side of the car. Takshak was taking pot-shots with his sniper rifle, but the angle was bad and the thinner branches above Ben's body were obscuring his aim.

Right now Ben had other problems. He could see Amal's hand strength was failing. His fingers were giving up the fight and letting go. Ben gritted his teeth and wrapped his legs around the tree branch and clung on with all his strength as he reached down a few more inches and grasped Amal's wrist. A second later, Amal would have lost his grip and gone plummeting to his death. Now his weight swung from Ben's hand. His kicking legs were making him sway like a pendulum. The branch was creaking and groaning. It sagged another inch. More stones and grit came loose and tumbled down into the dark abyss.

'Let me go, Ben,' Amal gasped.

'No chance of that.'

'It's okay. Really.'

'Forget it.'

'We can't both die. You can make it.'

'You think I'd go back to Brooke without you?'

'It's you she loves,' Amal said. 'More than me. It's always been that way.'

There had been a lull in the shooting, but only a momentary one as Takshak switched his sniper rifle for the SLR. Its chattering gunfire echoed out over the valley, raked the branches of the tree and snipped leaves from twigs. Several bullets thunked against the bodywork of the car. From somewhere deep within the tree trunk there came a crackling, splitting sound and it sagged another two inches. The dangling Maybach bobbed like a huge black fish on the end of a line.

The tree was going to rip out by its roots and give way.

Ben's hand was becoming numb and his arm felt as though it was pulling out of its socket. He said, 'Don't be a bloody fool.' And with all the strength he could muster, and a little more besides, he hauled Amal upwards and managed to clamp another hand on his arm, above the elbow. Inch by straining, gasping, sweating, agonising inch, he dragged Amal up onto the branch. He felt the two pistols slip from his waistband, saw them tumbling into the darkness. Too late to save those, but he was damned if he wasn't going to save Amal and bring him home to his wife like he'd undertaken to do. He would not fail.

Ben had him. He scrambled breathlessly to his feet. Grabbed a fistful of Amal's shirt and hauled him roughly towards the rock ledge just as another raking burst of automatic gunfire chewed up the tree bark and threw up a storm of splinters where Ben had been lying just moments ago.

The tree was going. A deep plaintive groaning became a frantic whining and snapping as its fibres parted and the trunk began to split and the roots tore free from the cliff. Ben and Amal only just made it to the rock face before it gave way. An avalanche of stones and boulders ripped free with it, tumbling down the cliff with a roar. Ben watched as the tree, with the car still skewered to it, went cartwheeling down and down until the blackness of the abyss swallowed it up and it was gone.

Chapter 64

They heard the impact as the car hit the bottom, a long way down. The rending, crunching smash of five tons of metal against rock echoed up the side of the precipice and rolled all around the valley.

Then silence. There was no more gunfire from above. Maybe Takshak thought that Ben and Amal had fallen to their deaths along with the tree. He'd almost been right.

Ben and Amal remained motionless on the ledge. A minute passed. Then another. Ben craned his neck upwards and listened hard for any sound or movement from the top of the cliff. He could no longer see the truck's headlights shining over the edge. The wind had picked up, a cold whistling breeze from the east. Over its sound he thought he heard the rattle of a diesel fading into the distance, but it was hard to be sure. He waited another three minutes, then five more. Nothing.

All through that time Amal sat crouched in a slump with his back against the rock face, lost in his own sullen thoughts. Ben could see he was in a lot of pain, and still in shock after his near-fall, and didn't try to initiate conversation.

After a full fifteen minutes had gone by, Ben was certain that the men were gone. The stiffening breeze had scudded the dark clouds away from the moon, illuminating the valley below them in a silvery light and allowing him, as he crawled as close as he dared to the edge of their rocky shelf, to peer over the precipice and trace the line of the path winding down towards the bottom. Far below them he could make out the dull glint of the wrecked car. 'I think we can make it,' he said to Amal, who was too morose to make any reply.

It was time to move on. Over the next two hours, working their way painstakingly slowly by the light of the moon, they followed the path's snaking route downwards. Here and there were traces of hoof prints and animal droppings that suggested the track had been created by wild goats, or some such creature. Apart from the few desiccated bushes that sprouted from the rocks the animal tracks were the only sign of life to be seen.

Amal was grimly taciturn as Ben helped him pick his way towards the bottom. It was a difficult trek, the pathway treacherous and extremely narrow in places and requiring all Ben's concentration, so that with the passing of time the earlier threat from the top of the cliff had become a fading memory. He wondered what Takshak was doing now. Perhaps already on his way back to the city, planning on recruiting more thugs to bring back out here to resume his treasure hunt. Or maybe he was still hanging around the vicinity, suspecting that Ben and Amal were still alive and plotting ways to catch up with them. He might be busy working his way around by another route to head them off when they reached the bottom. That wasn't a comforting thought, especially now that Ben had lost his pistols, along with all the spare weapons and ammunition that were still in his bag among the wreckage down there.

The two of them were three quarters of their way down the cliff by the time the first red glimmers of dawn were beginning to creep over the eastern horizon. Ben was weary and aching, thirsty and very hungry. He could only imagine how his companion must be feeling. Amal was shuffling like a zombie, dragging his oversized boots in exhaustion and often tripping as the short length of chain still attached to his ankle snagged in crevices among the rocks.

At last, they reached the bottom of the cliff, and were able to rest their tired bodies and get their breath. The foot of the ancient waterfall was a vast trench carved out of solid rock, smoothed like glass, dry as dust. Amal sat on a rock and nursed his broken arm. Ben left him to his silent suffering and hunted about in search of his fallen pistols, but all he found was a piece of splintered plastic grip panel from the Browning. His search led him to the twisted ruins of the car, which lay belly-up, its roof crushed flat, still snarled up in the remains of the tree at the foot of the ancient waterfall. There was no possibility of retrieving his bag. Their spare weapons and ammo, along with the sat phone, their only means of communication with the outside world, were hopelessly trapped inside. He'd have needed a cutting torch and a crowbar to get them out of there.

Giving up on the idea he returned to join Amal, who hadn't moved and was still sitting clutching his arm, gazing mournfully up at the cliff face that loomed overhead. Hard to believe they'd climbed all that way down unscathed. But that wasn't what was on Amal's mind. He muttered, 'You should have let me go. I nearly got you killed up there. I'm not worth that.'

Ben looked at him. 'That thing you said to me before, about Brooke. You're wrong, Amal. You couldn't be more wrong.'

Amal shook his head sadly. 'No, I'm not wrong. You know what I was thinking about as I was hanging from that branch? That if I'd let go, you'd have had to go home to her without

386

me, and then the two of you could have got back together. Because deep down, that's what she wants. She always has. I'm just the guy that got in the middle. We should never have got together.'

'Bullshit.'

Amal went on shaking his head, utterly miserable. 'I've known it from the beginning. I could never offer her what you could. I'm second best, always was, always will be.'

If Amal hadn't already suffered enough, Ben would have wanted to slap him. Instead he put a hand on his good shoulder and said, 'Don't you ever say that to me again, you understand?'

Amal shrugged Ben's hand away and winced at the pain the movement cost him. 'Why not, if it's the truth?'

'Because the past is the past. Because Brooke loves you and wants to get you home safely more than anything in the world. Forget about me. You're the man she's chosen to be with now. So act like it, and stop talking like a fucking idiot.'

Amal hung his head and said nothing more. Ben moved away from him. He found his cigarette pack in his pocket, crumpled and nearly empty. He lit up and smoked in silence. He regretted the surge of anger that had made him speak so harshly to his friend. The reality was that Ben couldn't stand to hear such painful words. It was like having his heart ripped out all over again.

When they'd rested a while, they set off. The arid valley stretched out seemingly to infinity, a barren desert of scratchy soil, bleached rock and prickly vegetation that snagged their clothing and wore them down. Death by ten thousand tiny cuts. Ben had to believe that if they kept moving, sooner or later they would surely find food, shelter, water, maybe even some basic medical assistance for Amal's injuries. He still had his wallet, with some cash in it. Nowhere near enough to procure transportation, but he'd steal a car or truck if he had to. It wouldn't be the first time, for sure.

The first hour of walking was slow. The second hour, it felt like they were going backwards. Four, five, and then six times Ben had to stop and wait for the seriously flagging, pale and weak Amal to catch up. The seventh time, he looked back and saw that Amal had collapsed. He hurried back to where he'd fallen. Amal's pulse was fluttery and shallow. Dehydration, hunger, pain and stress. Even the strongest man would cave in sooner or later, and Amal wasn't that guy. Ben gathered him up, the same way he'd done for Prem back in Delhi. *Come on, Amal, don't give up on me now. You're tougher than you think.*

Another hour passed. Amal was still so deeply unconscious that Ben got worried enough to stop twice and check his pulse. *Hang in there, Amal.* Ben kept going. He felt functional enough for now, but as the morning wore on towards midday and the sun beat relentlessly down from near its zenith, its heat seeming to suck the moisture out of every cell in his body and barely a tree or a tall rock anywhere to offer shade, he knew his strength wouldn't hold out forever.

If he hadn't been so weary, he might have heard the man coming before he stepped out into their path from the bushes.

Ben stopped. The man stopped too. They stared at one another, each equally surprised to have bumped into another human being in the middle of the wilderness. The Indian was bareheaded and wearing a long, white robe-like smock, and he was carrying a rifle on a sling over his shoulder, a battered old bolt-action thing dating back to a world war. Ben's first thought was that he was a member of one of the dacoit gangs that Jabbar Dada had told him infested these parts. Maybe even the same gang that had clashed with Takshak's crew. But then he realised his mistake. The guy wasn't dressed like a bandit, and he showed more fear than aggression. Bandits didn't go around with flocks of goats, either. Ben heard a ragged bleating sound from the bushes, and looked to see a dozen or so of the scraggy, curly-horned animals milling around back there, obviously a little agitated by the sight of a stranger. That was when Ben understood that the rifle was only there for protection against wolves, jackals or leopards, or whatever other nonhuman predators roamed the wilderness.

Ben knelt and gently laid Amal down on the ground. He stood slowly up, holding up his open palms to show the goat herder that he was no threat. He said, 'My friend needs help. I have money.'

The goat herder's name was Rishabh, and he spoke a little English. He was reluctant and suspicious at first, but then Ben showed him a sheaf of rupees from his wallet and Rishabh agreed to lead him and his sick friend to his village, which he managed to communicate in a combination of broken English and sign language was over *that way* – pointing south-east – and not too far. As a gesture of goodwill Rishabh reached into the folds of his smock and pulled out a small water bottle, which Ben gratefully accepted. He used most of it to moisten Amal's cracked lips and get him to drink, saving just a little for himself before offering it back to Rishabh. Then the goat herder beckoned them on and started off at a long stride through the bushes. The goats flocked after him, and Ben tagged along in their wake with the now semi-conscious Amal over his shoulder.

It was a longer hike than Rishabh had let on, and Ben was mightily thankful when the first dwellings came into view at the end of a narrow dirt road. The tiny village consisted of a few clusters of basic homes encircled within a rickety fence perimeter and looked unchanged for centuries, apart from a few strangely incongruous modern features like TV aerials. Some women in saris came out to meet them, and seemed more worried about the state of the injured man than the goat herder had been. One of the older women introduced herself to Ben as Ganika. She spoke good English and said she had been a teacher in Jind before her husband had died and she had returned to the village of her birth to care for her ageing mother.

'We have a small clinic, with some medical supplies,' Ganika explained. 'It is not much, but we can provide your friend with what he needs until you can get him to the civic hospital in Jind, to have his arm mended. Do you have a car?' Ben thanked her and said that no, he didn't, but that he'd manage to find a way.

'That is a shame. Because if you had had a car, you could have taken our other patient with you. He needs to get to the city as soon as possible.'

Ben was too tired and relieved to express much interest in the other patient. He followed her to the little adobe hut at the heart of the village that served as the medical clinic, and carried Amal inside. Ganika showed them into a minuscule sick bay with whitewashed walls and a pair of rudimentary but well-made wooden bunks, a table with a jug of water and some fruit, and a first-aid box with bandages and medicines. Then she hurried off, saying she'd go and find Pihu, the village nurse.

The sick bay wasn't unoccupied. Sitting on the other bunk was an Indian man, thirty-something in age, unkempt in a grubby T-shirt with a dark growth of beard. He was clearly the other patient Ganika had mentioned, and looked as though he might have been here for some time. He seemed very tired and thin, and his hollow cheeks and the shadows around his eyes gave the impression that he was recuperating from a long and debilitating illness. The man glanced up as they entered the room, unfocused and distracted, as if he'd been lost in a lot of glum thoughts.

Ben laid Amal, still half-unconscious, on the second bunk, then looked at the stranger, thinking he seemed oddly familiar. The man looked back at him, then turned his list-less gaze on Amal, and his eyes suddenly opened wide. He rose up with a shout of joy and amazement and came rushing across the room, which was only a few short steps.

'Amal! Amal! It's me, Kabir!'

Chapter 65

Ben's own amazement wasn't lagging too far behind. All this time he'd been prepared to give Kabir Ray up for dead, and now here he was. Maybe not in the peak of health, but most definitely alive. 'Careful,' Ben warned as Kabir went to grasp his brother's hand. 'His arm's broken.'

Kabir backed away a step, stood over the bunk where Amal lay and stared down in horror, taking in the bruises, the swellings, the blood. 'What happened to him?'

'I might ask you the same thing,' Ben said. 'There are a few people back in Delhi wondering what became of you. You're pretty much officially deceased, as far as most folks are concerned. Me included, until now.'

'And who are you?'

'Just a friend of the family,' Ben replied. His feet were aching from walking all that distance with Amal's weight on him. He sat on the edge of Kabir's bunk and bent down to unlace his boots.

'What's my brother doing here?'

'Looking for you,' Ben said. Which technically was over-simplifying, but he didn't feel like getting into the whole story just yet. He took off his right boot and rubbed his foot.

'Why's he all bruised up like this? Why's his arm broken?'

'Let's just say we ran into a little trouble on the way,' Ben said. He took off his left boot and rubbed that foot too. Feeling better already. He arranged his boots neatly side by side at the end of the bunk, soldier-fashion.

The sound of his brother's voice seemed to have stirred Amal awake. Suddenly alert, he sat bolt upright on his bunk. He blinked several times with his one good eye and his mouth fell open. He seemed to have forgotten all about his injuries. 'Am I dreaming? *Kabir?* Holy shit, it *is* you!'

The reunion of the brothers was an emotional scene that Ben watched from the background, full of questions but patient enough to wait. Amal was crying with happiness as Kabir embraced him. When all the hugging and joyful tears were done with, the village nurse called Pihu arrived to attend to Amal's cuts and bruises.

Her presence in the room hushed the conversation to a respectful silence. Ben watched as she opened up the medical kit, laid out her tools and efficiently got to work. She injected Amal with painkiller and antibiotics, then spent a few minutes cleaning up his face and examining his eye while the analgesic took effect. Then she stitched the cuts in his lips and the gash on his cheekbone and dabbed everything with antiseptic cream. She said she wasn't too worried about his eye, which would heal up fine. But she was more concerned about his arm, admitting that setting bones was beyond her skills. All she could do for the moment was splint the limb and exchange Ben's improvised leather belt sling for a proper one made of bandages. She did a fine job of wrapping up the arm and trimming the supportive dressing to a razor-straight edge with a pair of small, sharp surgical scissors. Never once while she worked did she enquire what had happened to Amal, or what he was doing in this remote area. If she had questions, she kept them to herself as she went about her duties with a kind of tight-lipped acceptance. Ben didn't know whether he was supposed to offer her money for her services. He chose just to say nothing for the moment.

Pihu finished up and then left. Then, at last, the three men were free to resume their discussion. Amal seemed more comfortable, though he was still very thirsty, pouring cup after cup of water from the jug and trying to drink as best he could with his stitched lips.

Kabir asked, 'Who did this to you, Amal? Was it the same bastard bandits who killed Manish and Sai?'

'They aren't bandits,' Ben said, mainly just to spare Amal from having to do too much talking.

Kabir looked at him. 'Tell me again who you are, exactly?'

'I told you, I'm a friend of the family.'

'Ben's a little more than that,' Amal said. His voice was slurry from the numbing effect of the drugs. 'He rescued me. Saved my life.'

'Rescued you from who?'

'The leader's name is Takshak,' Ben said. 'He's a killer and a kidnapper from Delhi. He and his men were holding Amal. They knocked him around quite a bit.'

'But why?'

'Because,' Ben said, 'when you start talking about giant fortunes of buried treasure sitting there ripe for the picking, you tend to attract that sort of bad company.'

Kabir's eyebrows furrowed. 'You know about the treasure?'

'I know all about your work. Haani Bhandarkar was able to tell me a lot more than your Professor Gupta. Though I'm sorry to have to tell you that Haani's dead too. Takshak's people got to him, by way of tying up loose ends back in Delhi.'

Kabir's face fell. 'Oh God.'

'Takshak found out that you let Amal in on the secret. He believed Amal could find it for him.'

'I don't understand. How could this guy have known what was said in confidence to my brother?'

'You know what they say,' Ben said. 'The walls have ears.'

Kabir looked baffled. 'You mean someone spied on me? Tapped my phone? How could they have figured out—?'

'It's a long story,' Ben said. 'I'll fill you in on the way home. Which is where we're headed asap. We can stop off en route to get Amal's arm patched up. Then you're going to have some explaining to do to your family and the cops in Delhi who'll be wondering how you suddenly managed to come back from the dead, and where you've been hiding all this time.'

Kabir motioned at the whitewashed walls of the tiny sick bay. 'Right here in this room is where I've been. And for most of the time I was asleep. In a coma, or the nearest thing to it. Pihu said it was a miracle I survived. Septicaemia is no joke.' He lifted the hem of his shirt to show them the ugly scar of a bullet wound in his right side, the edges of the flesh all puckered and discoloured. 'See what those bastards did to me? The gunshot missed my kidney by a hair's breadth. By good fortune it went right through me and clean out the other side.'

'Lucky,' Ben said.

'Luckier than my poor friends, anyhow. I only got away by throwing myself down that damn hillside. Dislocated my ankle in the fall. Those men came down the hill looking for me, but I managed to crawl away. I crawled for days. I don't even know how far. It was some children from this village who found me. By then I was very sick from the infection. I don't remember much about being brought here, or about the weeks I drifted in and out of consciousness. Just flashes of memory, like dreams. Sometimes it was Pihu who tended to me, sometimes Ganika. I'd be dead if it hadn't been for their kindness. It's only in the last few days that I could even get my head off the pillow, never mind stand up and walk around.'

'A few days is a long time,' Ben said. 'You couldn't have picked up a phone to let your folks know you were alive?'

'Easy for a Westerner to say,' Kabir replied. 'You obviously don't know a lot about our country. The telecommunications industry might do its best to look all modern and progressive to the outside world, but on the inside it's a shambles. Thousands of remote rural communities are still without internet or phone signal, and this is one of them. As soon as I was strong enough, I was planning to find some way out of here and get to the nearest town where I could call home. But this is a very poor village. The only motor vehicle I might have been able to beg, borrow or steal is sitting on bricks with a hole where its engine used to be.'

Ben said, 'Then maybe someone could have ridden their mule, or whatever, to the nearest town and alerted the authorities that you'd been found.'

Kabir shook his head. 'Again, you don't understand this country. These people live in constant terror of the dacoits. Bandit gangs pretty much rule this whole area. It's like the Wild West. They come into the villages whenever they please and help themselves to food, supplies, whatever money they can get their hands on, not to mention any young girl who catches their eye. Anyone who tries to oppose them is in serious trouble. When I was brought here with a bullet hole in me, the general consensus was that I must be just another victim of the dacoits, or maybe even one of them. There are turf wars all the time between rival factions. So not everyone in the village was too pleased about giving me shelter. There was a lot of worry about repercussions, if the dacoits found out the villagers were harbouring a member of an enemy gang. Or a potential witness to one of their attacks, who might go to the police with information. The last thing anybody wanted was to draw attention to my being here. They'll be very relieved when I'm gone.'

Now Ben understood why Pihu had acted so strangely tight-lipped and not asked any questions about the sudden arrival of a second battered and bruised newcomer to the village. And why Ganika had seemed anxious for their other patient to be driven to the nearest city as soon as possible. Whatever care and hospitality these good folks might be only too willing to offer strangers in need of help, they wanted no part of the trouble that had brought them here.

'Then their wish is about to come true,' Ben said. 'Because we're getting out of here, as soon as we've had some rest and food.'

'How?'

'You let me worry about how.'

'Fine by me,' Kabir said. 'I can't wait to get back to civilisation. But I won't be staying there long. As soon as I've got everything straightened out, it's my intention to come straight back here. I have unfinished business to take care of.'

'What?' Ben said. 'To repay Pihu and Ganika for helping you?'

'It would take more than money to reward them for their kindness,' Kabir said. 'I'll do everything I can for them, certainly. But that's not all I had in mind.'

'If you're planning on resuming the search for this great lost treasure of the Indus Valley People,' Ben said, 'I'd advise you forget about it and stay at home. You've got competition now, and not the kind that you want to tangle with.'

397

Kabir shook his head again. 'On the contrary, I can assure you that my plan is not to resume the search for the great lost treasure of the Indus Valley People.'

'No?' Amal said in his indistinct voice. He poured another cup of water and put it to his lips.

'No, brother,' Kabir said. He paused. Then a glow came into his expression and he couldn't repress a grin that quickly spread all over his face and chased away the dark shadows from around his eyes.

And he added, 'Because I already found it.'

Amal coughed up the gulp of water he'd been in the process of swallowing. Ben said nothing. The two of them stared at Kabir. Amal managed to splutter, 'You *what*? When?'

Kabir grinned even more widely. 'You see, I knew soon after we landed in the river valley that day that there was a problem with Trafford's map. I'd been so sure of myself at first. The coordinates were spot on, but the topography of the landscape didn't fit perfectly with what he'd drawn in his journal. There were hills that shouldn't have been there, and other minor discrepancies that made me start to doubt that we were in the right place. My guess was that Trafford must have been slightly out in his nav calculations. I hadn't factored in any margin for error when I converted his original figures into GPS data. Which was a mistake on my part. Potentially a disastrous one, if pure chance hadn't intervened.'

'What pure chance?' Amal spluttered. He was so incredulous that even his damaged eye was able to open wide.

'I told you I crawled a long, long way after I fell down the hillside escaping those men,' Kabir said. 'For two, three days I was totally lost, bleeding, dying of thirst, delirious and sick. But I've been studying that map so long it's imprinted on my brain. So when I found the second river valley, I knew for certain this time that I was in the right place.'

'There's a *second* river valley?'

'About a mile from the first,' Kabir said. 'And trust me, it's the one on the map. Every detail fits perfectly, down to the last rock and stone, allowing for a hundred and eighty years' worth of landslides and wind erosion. Which confirmed my suspicions that Trafford had got his geographic coordinates slightly wrong all those years ago. I can't blame him. The technology they had at their disposal in those days was still pretty crude.'

'So you're saying you think you know where the treasure is,' Ben said.

Kabir shook his head a third time, more emphatically. 'You're not hearing me. I said I found it. I've seen it with my own eyes. And I have a good idea how to get back to it from here. I've thought of little else since I woke up.'

Amal swallowed hard. 'What's it like?'

Kabir replied, 'It blew my mind. It's absolutely amazing. Like nothing anyone could have expected.'

But something else unexpected was just around the corner. Literally. Because at that moment, Pihu and Ganika appeared in the doorway and took a step inside the room. From the rigid looks on their faces, Ben knew instantly that something was wrong. Very wrong indeed. Another second later, he understood why.

Takshak appeared in the doorway behind them, pointing a pistol to the two women's backs. He shoved them hard into the room. Ganika stumbled and hit the little table with her hip, knocking over the jug. It fell and smashed. The medical first-aid box fell with it and burst open, spilling rolls of bandage and surgical tape and implements all over the floor.

399

Takshak took another step. He was smiling a wide, satisfied, victorious smile.

'Sorry for interrupting your conversation there, boys. Sounded like it was getting so interesting.'

400

Chapter 66

For a moment that seemed frozen in time, nobody moved. Ben saw the expression of pure hatred on Amal's face and was suddenly scared that he was going to fly at Takshak and get himself shot. He gave Amal a warning look, as clear as if he'd said the words out loud. *Don't even think about it.*

Takshak's triumphant gaze circled the room and landed on Kabir. 'Well, well. If it isn't the one who got away. Looks like I get a second chance with you, huh, Professor?' He gave a self-contented laugh and then turned his eye on Ben. 'And you. I can't seem to get rid of you, can I? You're like a disease that keeps coming back. Like syphilis.'

'I suppose you'd know all about that,' Ben said. 'Didn't your mother tell you not to mess around with goats?'

Takshak waved the gun in his direction. The diameter of the bore was nine millimetres across. The hammer was cocked, his finger was on the trigger and there was no doubt in Ben's mind that there was a round nestling in the chamber just waiting to be touched off. Takshak was standing eight feet from where Ben was sitting on the bunk. So near, and yet so far. The fastest and most highly-trained man alive wouldn't have stood the slightest chance of crossing that distance and disarming him. Especially from a sitting position, and with no boots on. Not good. Takshak was holding all the aces and all Ben could do was let the game unfold.

Takshak said, 'Let's see. Should I kill you right now, or can you be of any use to me? It's thanks to you I've lost most of my crew. Seems only right that you should take their place. Loading all that gold on the truck is more work than I feel like doing myself.' He thought about it for a moment longer, then swivelled the gun back to point at the two women. 'Your lucky day. Now let's all go for a ride. The professor's gonna show us the way.'

Ben motioned towards Amal. 'You don't need him. Let him stay behind.'

Takshak smiled. 'Right. So he can run to the cops.'

'He's not running anywhere,' Ben said. 'He's hurt.'

'How about I break his other arm, and both his legs?' Takshak said. 'Then he can stay behind. Deal?'

Ben said nothing.

Kabir said, 'You want the treasure? Fine, I'll take you to it. Right now. All yours.'

'There's a reasonable man,' Takshak said.

'But it's only fair to warn you, you'll have trouble fitting it in a truck. There's so much of it, you wouldn't be able to transport more than a fraction.'

'Sounds good enough for a start,' Takshak said. 'We can go back for the rest later. Let's go, boys, I'm getting impatient.'

Ben pointed at his feet. 'Can I put my boots on first?'

Takshak wagged the gun at him to say, 'Hurry it up.'

Ben reached out and slid his boots over from the bottom of the bunk. Kabir stepped between him and Takshak to help Amal stand up. Takshak shoved him hard out of the way. 'The little rat can stand up on his own.'

'I'm okay,' Amal said. Ben slipped on his right boot, then the left, and did up the laces.

Takshak marched his prisoners out of the narrow doorway in single file, like a little procession. The women first, then Amal, then Kabir, then Ben. It was hot outside. The afternoon sun was beating down hard on the village and most folks would have normally chosen to stay in the shade. But that wasn't the case, because it seemed as though the whole village, maybe sixty men, women and children, stood gathered in a small crowd outside the adobe hut, all wide-eyed and cowed and too terrified to speak. What was so frightening to them was plain to see. To one side of the crowd was the seven-foot giant, armed with the SLR rifle Ben had left in the truck the night before. To the other side stood the shorter, more compact guy Ben had guessed was Takshak's second in command, pointing Jabbar Dada's INSAS light machine gun at the crowd and looking as though he would love nothing more than to mow them all down.

Ben had just learned two facts. First, that Dada was dead, for sure. Second, that Takshak, the giant and the compact guy were the only surviving members of the crew. From sixteen down to three. But three was still plenty dangerous.

Takshak grinned at his men. 'Hey, Samunder, Hashim! Didn't I tell you we'd find these sisterfuckers? And look what I found.' He prodded Kabir hard in the side with his pistol muzzle, where his wound was. Kabir cried out in pain. Takshak said, 'The professor here says he found what we're looking for. He's gonna take us right to it. Happy days.'

'Sounds too good to be true,' said Hashim, the compact one with the INSAS.

'The professor's got more sense than to lie to us. Don't you, Professor? He knows that if he's just jerking our chain,

I'll take his rat brother apart piece by piece right in front of him before he gets it next.'

'What about that one?' Samunder said. He pointed a finger the size of a banana at Ben.

'Saving him until last,' Takshak said. 'He's going to make himself useful first.'

'You're going to kill us all anyway,' Amal said.

Takshak leered at him. 'Oh, sure I am. But once I get the treasure I'll be a happy guy, and happy guys are naturally generous. And so I'll be only too willing to make it quick and easy for you all. But if you make me unhappy . . .' He shook his head and whistled through his teeth. 'That's bad, bad news for you. And for all the rest of these nice people, when I come back to take out my crappy mood on them.'

'You know this doesn't get to happen the way you think it does,' Ben said to him. 'It never does, with guys like you.'

'Oh yeah? And why's that?'

'Because of guys like me.'

'You think you're good enough to stop me?'

'More than that,' Ben replied. 'I'm going to make it like you never even existed.'

Takshak laughed. 'Check this guy out. You've got some balls, that's for sure. Like the hero in the white hat, huh? Looks like I'd better watch my step around you. Tell you what. You're such a good guy, you won't want any harm to come to innocent hostages. Samunder, grab a couple of those women. We'll bring them along for the ride. Our hero here tries anything, he can watch while we cut their stupid heads off.'

Samunder slung his rifle over a massively muscled shoulder and waded in among the cowering villagers. He stood more than head and shoulders above the tallest of them. Reaching out with both enormous hands he grabbed two women at random. There were cries and gasps of fear from the crowd. One of his choices was an old lady, the other barely more than a girl, maybe sixteen and so frightened she looked about to faint. A brave little man with a moustache, presumably her father, protested and tried to grab her back from Samunder's grip, but he might as well have been trying to free her from the mechanical jaws of a concrete crusher. Hashim stepped up and smacked him brutally to the ground with his machine gun butt. Nobody else protested after that. Pihu and Ganika were hugging one another in tears.

Takshak was enjoying the show. He said, 'Hashim, why don't you go and bring in the truck?'

Hashim looked as if he'd rather finish off beating the little fellow's brains out with his gun butt. He responded with a surly nod and went off at a trot. A few moments later Ben heard the growl of the diesel, and then the truck came rolling into the heart of the village. By the light of day the black scorch marks and bullet holes were clearly visible all over its olive-green bodywork. It had taken a good few dents in the chase, too. But still functional. Hashim jumped down from the cab and went round to open the tailgate.

'You first,' Takshak said, pointing his pistol at Ben. There was nothing much Ben could do except comply. He clambered into the truck. Then Amal was herded aboard, and finally the two female hostages. The young girl was crying inconsolably. The old lady appeared quite unmoved by what was happening. Either she was some kind of sage possessed of infinite stoicism and selfless disinterest, or she'd simply lost her marbles long ago.

Turning to Kabir Takshak said, 'Professor, you ride up front with me and show the way.'

Takshak jumped up and took the wheel. Hashim jostled

Kabir into the cab from the other side and shoved him into the middle of the three-seat bench, with the gear stick between his knees. Then Hashim climbed in after him, watching him like a mongoose eyeing a snake. Samunder hauled his monster bulk into the back of the truck and closed up the tailgate. The giant didn't look like the Brain of India, by any means. But he wasn't as stupid as all that. There wasn't a moment when his SLR wasn't pointing in Ben's direction.

Then they were off. The truck rumbled away, leaving behind the crowd of villagers all weeping and moaning and consoling one another. Ben saw Ganika wave, a forlorn gesture of apology and good luck. He didn't know if he'd see her again.

Chapter 67

The drive from the village was long, dusty and uncomfortable. Kabir guided Takshak back along the same dirt road that Ben had walked with Amal. Before they reached the place where they'd met the goat herder, the truck turned off and cut eastwards across a landscape that was yet more of the same rough, arid, hilly terrain of which the entire region seemed to consist.

Ben sat quietly in the back of the truck, just biding his time while watching his travelling companions. Amal was slumped next to him, apparently lost in some very dark and brooding thoughts. Maybe he was thinking about Brooke. Whatever was on his mind, Ben was pretty sure the painkillers would be wearing off by now, and there was a good deal of suffering in Amal's immediate future.

The young girl had stopped crying. Ben wanted to catch her eye and make some gesture to let her know that everything would be okay. The old woman looked just as calmly dispassionate, gazing into space with no expression on her wrinkly nut-brown face, allowing her small wiry body to rock freely with the side to side motion of the truck over the uneven ground. Her thin, bony hands were folded in her lap. Wisps of white hair poking out from under her sari headscarf streamed in the wind as they rode along.

But mostly Ben was watching big Samunder. The hulk remained standing near the tailgate the whole way, his huge legs flexing with the bumps like a surfer's, one catcher's glove of a hand clutching the metal canopy frame and the other keeping hold of the pistol grip of his SLR, loosely pointed at the prisoners. Ben was still wondering how many bullets it would take to bring him down, if it came to it. The main problem being that Ben didn't have any.

Ben glanced forward at where Kabir sat wedged between Takshak and Hashim in the front cab. It struck him as odd that Kabir had agreed so readily to take them straight to the treasure. Something was up, but Ben had no idea what.

More than an hour of lurching, crashing, jolting journey had gone by when, at last, the truck rolled to a halt.

Ben took in the scene around him. If anything, the terrain was even worse here, though not by much. Everywhere looked the same. Rocks, dust, dirt, more rocks, a few thorny bushes and withered, puny trees, more rocks, and seemingly not a drop of moisture for a thousand miles in any direction. Though that clearly had once been far from the case. Way back in ancient history this whole region had been criss-crossed with sparkling blue rivers. He was looking at the sad remains of another of them, snaking and curving through the empty wilderness like a gigantic ploughed furrow in a dead field. In the distance beyond the dried-up river stood a series of sun-baked hills, arranged exactly as on Trafford's map. Kabir had been right.

The only question now was: *what had Kabir found here?*

Kabir said, 'Okay. This is about as close as we can get by truck.'

'You'd better be sure it's the right place this time,' Takshak said.

'I'm sure. Trust me, I know the map better than I know my own face.'

'I hope so, for your sake. Because you won't have a face left otherwise.' Takshak squinted at the barren landscape, as though he expected to see mounds of gold sitting there beckoning to him. 'So where's the mother lode?'

'Not far,' Kabir said. He pointed. 'You see that long, low escarpment to the south-east? Now, see those three big rocks, next to the old dead rohida tree split in half by lightning?'

Takshak reached under the truck seat and came out with a battered pair of binoculars. He spent a few moments focusing and scanning left and right, up and down, then said, 'I see them.'

'Now trace a line down from the middle of the three rocks, about thirty metres. See the vertical crack in the base of the escarpment directly below?'

'I see a split. Looks like ice made it.'

'You could be right. See the marking next to it?'

'I see some kind of graffiti some idiot put there.'

'No, you see an ancient archaeological relic of immense value in itself,' Kabir told him. 'An Indus Valley glyph. A symbol from a language that's so old and so secret, nobody understands it any more. Carved into the rock thousands of years ago to mark the location of something infinitely more valuable.'

'Is that where it is?' Takshak asked. He couldn't hide the trace of schoolboy excitement in his voice. His eyes were glowing behind the binocs, as though he were already counting the gold coins in his mind.

Kabir nodded. 'That's where it is.'

Takshak lowered the binocs, scowling. 'But we can't get the truck down there. The ground's too rough.'

'I know,' Kabir replied. 'That's why we need to walk it from here.'

'Glad we won't be shifting the stuff,' Hashim said, and jerked his thumb at Ben.

Kabir said to Takshak, 'Please, let my brother stay in the truck. He's in bad shape.'

'No chance,' Takshak said flatly. 'How do I know he won't drive off and leave us stranded in this shithole?'

'With only one arm?'

'No chance.'

Ben could have told Kabir to save his breath. He also would have liked to ask him a question or two. Such as what he was up to. There was something going on behind Kabir's eyes. Some private joke he seemed to be enjoying. Kabir had an agenda.

The three people from the front of the truck got out, and the five from the back got out, and they quickly arranged themselves into another single-file procession tracking across in the direction of the escarpment's base where Kabir had pointed out their route. A route to where, was still a mystery to all but him. He led the way with Takshak at his back, pistol in hand; behind Takshak, the young girl, ashen and miserable, and the old woman, who had yet to show a flicker of anything. The female hostages were followed by Amal, then Ben, then Samunder and Hashim riding shotgun. The late afternoon sun was still burning fiercely down on them. Amal was bent over like a man three times his age, clutching his arm and groaning in pain at every step over the rough, rocky ground. He stumbled, nearly fell, and stumbled again. Hashim pushed past Ben muttering a curse and was about to grab Amal by his broken arm when Ben blocked his way and dug two fingers into a nerve pressure point at the base of Hashim's neck. Not hard enough to cause serious debility, just a warning. *I don't need a gun to hurt you.*

Hashim backed up two steps, visibly shaken, and instantly pointed the light machine gun in Ben's face. A weapon that could cut a car in half, just a few inches away. Close enough to have taken it from Hashim and driven the butt down his throat, if Ben moved fast enough. But Ben was also close enough to Samunder's SLR to be certain of getting shot, if he made any rash moves.

Hashim snarled, 'What the fuck did you just do to me?'

'It's called the Dim Mak death touch,' Ben said. 'The reaction is delayed a bit. You'll probably go out like a light in about an hour from now.'

'I'll blow your head off, you touch me again.'

'How does it feel knowing you're going to die in this place?' Ben replied, his voice calm and level. 'Because one way or another, you're not leaving here. I promise you that.'

'Shut your mouth, asshole. Keep moving.'

Ben smiled to himself. Hashim was rattled. Rattled was good.

They trekked on. It took several minutes for the slow-moving group to reach the foot of the escarpment. The massive rock formation was some kind of spectacular geological wonder in its own right, multi-hued striations of blues and yellows and browns and reds showing the sedimentary layers that had built up over millions, probably more like billions, of years. Only in its relatively recent history had some unknown scribe carved the strange marking into its face.

The symbol was like no alphabet letter Ben had ever seen. The only things that came remotely close were the weird Indus Valley glyphs that Imran Gupta had shown him at the Red Fort Archaeology Institute in Delhi.

Kabir stood looking up at the ancient symbol like a devout believer gazing in awe at a religious icon. 'When I came across this, I knew I'd found it,' he said, shaking his head in wonderment. 'It's amazing. Even though I was half dead with pain and sickness, it gave me the strength to keep going.'

Hashim spat on the ground. He shouldered his weapon and fired a burst of fully-automatic fire at the carving. The roar of the machine gun echoed like rolling thunder over the valley. Chips and shards of stone flew off the rock. The young girl covered her ears and screamed. The old lady didn't seem to notice.

Hashim lowered the smoking machine gun and spat on the ground again. 'Not so fucking amazing now, is it?' Someone's ego had obviously taken a knock. Hissy.

Kabir stared in anguish at the pockmarked ruin that had been the Indus Valley glyph. 'Do you have any idea of what you've just done?'

'I have a pretty good idea what we're going to do, if you don't stop gabbling like a woman and lead us inside,' Takshak said.

The vertical fissure in the rock that had looked like a tiny crack was over ten feet tall. Much less in width. One by one, they slipped through. No problem at all for the young girl and the old lady. Nor for the slender-built Ray brothers, especially Kabir after his illness. Takshak, Hashim and Ben all had wider shoulders and had to turn sideways to slide through the gap. Samunder went last, and had the hardest time of all. Like trying to squeeze an elephant through a house doorway. Ben enjoyed watching him sweat.

The immediate interior of the grotto was only slightly wider, cool and dark inside. Takshak had brought three heavy steel flashlights from the truck for himself and his men. He shone his around him. 'So where is it?'

'We have to go deeper,' Kabir said.

'How much deeper?'

'You'll see. Give me your torch and follow me.'

Takshak reluctantly handed over his flashlight. 'Any tricks, you're a dead man.'

'Come on,' Kabir said. 'It's not much further.'

They kept going. The floor sloped one way and the other, hard to traverse. The way ahead gradually opened up. If the outside of the escarpment had been impressive, the inside was simply stunning. Ben had never seen such weird rock formations, of such vibrant colour. As it opened up further still, it felt like entering the maw of some gigantic mythological creature with jagged stalagmites and stalactites for fangs, some of them twice his height. The grotto smelled faintly of bat shit, but the air was surprisingly fresh, as though a current was circulating deep within.

Kabir stopped. Takshak almost walked into him. 'What?' he snapped.

'Do you feel it yet?' Kabir asked.

'Feel what?' Takshak was getting tired of playing this game. He just wanted his loot.

Ben didn't know what Kabir was talking about. He couldn't feel anything either.

'You'll see,' Kabir said again, and moved on.

The grotto wound its way deep into the rock, sloping more steeply downwards as it went. Ben was sure they must be some way underground by now. It was like delving into an old mineshaft, except one created millions and billions of years ago when dinosaurs wandered over the landscape above them, by the ravages of some prehistoric ice age, or the slow grinding slip of tectonic plates maybe, or some vast geological event powerful enough to rip vents in the very fabric of the earth.

Down, down they went. The torch beams scanning left and right, picking out crags and splits in the rock, more spectacular features, more incredible spikes hanging from the roof and jutting upwards from the ground. Ben had visited the famous caves at Lascaux in France. This place was on a whole different scale in terms of weird splendour. But he had other things to occupy his mind. He was supporting Amal, who could barely walk any more for the constant agony in his arm.

'It better be down here somewhere,' Takshak's voice echoed back at them from the front.

'Not much further now,' Kabir's voice echoed in reply. Then he stopped again. 'Close your eyes. Can you feel it now?'

Ben wasn't about to close his eyes while in close proximity to Takshak, Hashim and Samunder. But he could feel it. It was subtle, but he wasn't imagining it. A strange harmonic vibration that seemed to come from deep under his feet. From somewhere behind the harmonics, a soft continuous rumble, so low that it was almost subsonic. He couldn't begin to guess what was capable of making such a sound. He looked at Kabir. Amal was looking at him too, with the same expression of confusion. Even Takshak seemed to have lost his surly confidence. 'What the fuck *is* that?'

Kabir smiled mysteriously and said, 'Just a few more steps. Follow me.'

And just a few steps further through the rock tunnel, his words turned out to be true. Because when he'd said the lost treasure of the Indus Valley people was like nothing anyone could have expected, he hadn't been kidding.

Chapter 68

The vibration and rumbling that Ben had been able to sense just now were suddenly amplified a hundred times, to a rushing sound that filled his ears. He felt the freshness of moving air cool the sweat on his brow. Heard Kabir's voice raised over the strange noise, saying, 'Careful. Don't go any further. Two more steps you'll go right over the edge and it's a long way down.'

The eight of them had emerged onto a short and narrow craggy prominence that overhung a vast empty space, like a truncated bridge leading nowhere. Kabir stepped a little closer to the edge and shone his torch to show them.

Ben wasn't easily amazed, but the vastness of the cavern into which the tunnel had opened up was an incredible sight. The great domed ceiling arched high above them. Geological formations like gargoyles cast eerie shadows that trembled and flickered in the torchlight. The rushing sound was a continuous roar coming from below. Only one thing on earth could make that sound. It took Ben straight back to the days when he'd lived on the western Irish coast and spent many contemplative hours on his empty stretch of beach, gazing out to sea as the breakers rolled in to crash against the shore.

'Look.' Kabir directed the torch beam across the huge

space at the cavern wall opposite, some eighty or more yards away. Once upon a time, the prominence on which they were standing must have bridged the whole width of the chasm. Which was the only possible way to explain what Kabir was pointing out. Ben blinked as the pool of white light traced the contours of the same Indus glyph that had marked the grotto entrance. The carving had to be twenty feet high. More than just a marker. Like a symbol of veneration, designating a holy place. A shrine, or a temple. He shivered. The man standing next to him had probably been the first person in thousands of years to have taken in this sight. And now Ben was seeing it for himself. It felt strangely humbling.

Kabir raised his voice again and said, 'And here it is, people. The lost treasure of the Indus Valley Civilisation. The discovery that could have saved their entire civilisation from doom, if only they'd found it sooner. It was already too late to reverse their fate.'

Kabir inched forward as close to the edge as anyone would have dared, and shone the torch vertically downwards. He'd been right. It was a hell of a long way down. Ben peered after its beam and saw movement down there. Roiling and churning and swirling and foaming movement. Breathtaking in power. The great roar of the water filled his ears.

Kabir swept the light as far to the left as its beam could reach, to where it dissipated in the murk. Then did the same to the right. And Ben realised that what he was staring down at was the surface of a vast underground lake stretching for maybe hundreds of metres end to end. The reservoir had to contain a million tons of water. Maybe far more. He had no idea. It was cascading out under pressure in a great jet from a channel a few feet above the surface, a perpetual

416

waterfall driven by what must have been a virtually limitless source. No telling how far it had flowed to get here. Miles, Ben guessed. The overflow from the lake must then in turn be running off down natural drainage vents that carried it onwards, deeper still underground. So much water, sitting here for countless centuries, for millennia, locked inside its own natural cave system deep below the surface of the arid wilderness. The rock ceiling above them was so thick and dense that not a drop of moisture could seep upwards to quench the thirst of the land.

Now, suddenly, he understood everything. The same revelation that had struck Kabir when he'd made this discovery was also clear to him. It was the answer to the age-old enigma of what had killed off the biggest and most culturally advanced civilisation of ancient history. The force that had destroyed them hadn't come from within, like the overexpansion and social decay that had eaten up the great Roman Empire like a cancer. And it hadn't come in the shape of conquering invaders from the outside, in the way that had spelled the end for ancient Babylon. No, the long, slow, agonising demise of the Indus Valley culture had resulted from the inexorable cycles of nature. Once upon a time their land had been lush and green, fertile and bountiful and teeming with diverse life. It had sustained them aplenty for over fifteen hundred years, allowed their harmonious and peaceful civilisation to blossom into a long, happy peak of refinement that had been unique for its day. Perhaps unique in all of history.

But what Nature provides, Nature can also take away. It must have been such a gradual change that people didn't notice at first, when the rains stopped coming and the water levels began to ebb lower. Slowly but surely, maybe over hundreds of years, the moisture had receded from the earth.

The once-great rivers had become streams, then trickles, then turned to mud, and then to bare rocky trenches where lizards basked in the heat. The land had become crumbly and poor. The crops had failed. The livestock had perished. The people had begun to starve. Even the builders of the cities could no longer mix the clay and lime with water to make mortar, or fashion the bricks that had been a hallmark of their technical development when the civilisation was in its prime. Water, not gold or jewels or material wealth in any such crude forms, was their most precious commodity. They must have travelled far and wide in their desperate search for sustenance, as farmers watched their fields turn to dust and mothers helplessly witnessed their babies fade and die.

Little wonder that finding a sustainable source of water would have been the equivalent of the greatest mineral wealth discovery of their age, or any age. Whoever could restore life to the dying land would literally have been the saviour of an entire race.

Kabir had said it. By the time some intrepid Indus Valley explorer had stumbled on this subterranean lake, thousands of years in the past, it had already been too late to reverse the fate of a whole civilisation. It was a timeless lesson with as much relevance today as back in the mists of history. Little wonder that it had passed into myth and legend the way it had, only for the mystery to be unravelled all these millennia later.

'It's awesome,' Amal said, able to forget his pain for a moment.

But not everyone present could appreciate the momentous sight in front of them. Takshak's eyes were bulging and his teeth were clenched in rage as his vision of mountains of gold and endless riches suddenly crumbled and fell apart.

He pointed his torch at Kabir and screamed, 'No way! This can't be it! You're lying to me!'

Kabir should have been afraid, but he was smiling. Then his smile grew broader until it was plastered all over his face in a huge grin. Despite everything that was happening in that moment, mirth got the better of him. His laughter echoed all around the vast chamber, ringing out over the thundering roar of the water below.

'What the FUCK is so funny?' Takshak screamed.

Kabir was laughing so hard that he could barely speak. 'I told you you'd have trouble loading the treasure on your truck. You were warned, but you wouldn't listen. This joke is all on you, my poor pathetic friend.'

Hashim and Samunder were too stunned by the sudden catastrophic disintegration of all their dreams and plans to do anything but stare helplessly at their leader. Totally distracted. None of the three were paying any attention to Ben.

That was their big mistake.

Chapter 69

Ben stepped back into the shadows. Takshak was still raging at Kabir. Hashim and Samunder were still standing there in mute bewilderment, with no clue as to what to do. The old lady might as well have been in another world. Nobody was watching him, except the young girl. Her face was half-lit by the torchlight and wore a knowing expression, as though she could tell what he was planning. The first tiny flicker of a smile he'd seen on her curled her lip. He put a finger to his own, signalling her to stay quiet. She replied with an almost imperceptible nod to show she'd understood. She backed away a couple of steps towards the tunnel.

Ben bent at the waist and slid his right hand down the outside of his right leg. All the way down to his boot.

What happened next was inevitable. Ben had seen it coming, ten seconds before Takshak's fury and frustration finally boiled over. Now Takshak exploded. He made a savage lunge at Kabir with the torch, wanting to beat his brains out. Once Takshak had kicked off the violence, his men would quickly follow his lead.

Ben thought, *Not going to happen.*

And it didn't. Before Takshak got halfway through his backswing Ben was re-emerging from the shadows and coming up behind him with something clasped in his hand.

It was the item he'd palmed off the floor earlier while putting his boots on. Something small, hard and shiny, made of tempered steel and extremely sharp. Pihu's surgical scissors. Made for the purpose of helping heal the sick, rather than to cause harm. But the brutally simple truth of the matter was that, as with every manmade tool ever devised dating back to the primal beginnings of human evolution, all that divides the benevolent from the deadly is the intention of the user.

And Ben's intention was to end this, right here, right now.

He reached his left hand past Takshak's left ear and cupped his chin and rocked him violently backwards off his feet while simultaneously reaching around with his right and stabbing the open blades of the scissors into the flesh of Takshak's neck.

Another brutal truth, one that Ben had learned a long time ago, was that it takes only an inch or two of keen-edged blade to effectively and decisively end the life of another human being. Anything bigger was just a luxury. As long as it was sharp. The sharper the better. And Pihu's little scissors were like razors. Ben had already noted that as he'd watched her cut the bandages for Amal's dressing and sling.

Ben slashed Takshak's throat from left to right, all the way from ear to ear, in a single savage sawing motion that sliced through gristle and muscle and soft tissue. Takshak's left carotid artery went first, then the right a second later. The blood jetted out as hard as the gushing water below. It sprayed Kabir and soaked Ben's hands and filled the air with its coppery stench. Takshak let out a guttural howl of fear and struggled like a gazelle in the teeth of a tiger. But there was nothing he could do. It was all over for him before he'd even fully registered what had happened. Ben let go of him, and he crumpled forwards and crunched face-down to the stone floor.

Then Hashim and Samunder were screaming too, in a confusion of whirling light as the torch beams flashed and crisscrossed wildly all over the place in the darkness. Hashim's machine gun came up to point at Ben, but the weapon was long and clumsy in such a restricted space and Hashim had to wield the heavy gun one-handed so he could hold his torch in the other, which gave Ben more than enough leverage to easily deflect the muzzle. The gun rattled deafeningly but missed Ben by three feet. Ben swept his legs out from under him with a low scything kick, and Hashim went toppling over sideways. If there had been a stone floor under him, Hashim would have come down hard on his shoulder and ribs, and then Ben would have waded in with a series of savage kicks that would have pulverised his face and smashed his head in.

But there was no floor. Hashim went over the edge of the prominence. He hung there for just a moment, scrabbling desperately with his fingertips raking rough stone, and then he lost his grip and fell into space with a cry, spread eagled in mid-air like a free-fall jumper. He cartwheeled end over end and then hit the water with a splash, belly down. From that height it was like hitting concrete. The swirling current closed over him and sucked his broken body down into the depths.

Ben didn't see any of it. The instant Hashim went down, Samunder attacked. The giant might not have been too bright, but he was smart enough not to make the same mistake as Hashim. Throwing down his cumbersome rifle he came in with his huge fists and smashed a blow into Ben's chest that knocked him off his feet and almost sent him over the edge after Hashim. Kabir swung his torch into

Samunder's face and caught him across the bridge of the nose, breaking it with a crunch. Samunder roared and flailed out a huge arm in a backhand sweep and Kabir was flung hard against the rock wall. Amal let out a wild yell and tried to punch Samunder with his good arm. Samunder just flicked him aside and came stamping towards where Ben lay close to the edge of the drop, wanting to crush and trample him to death.

And that was when the old lady suddenly came to life. A thin bony hand slipped into the folds of her sari and came out with a knife that she planted in the small of Samunder's back. As though she'd been waiting all this time for the right moment to stick it to one of these men she perceived to be the hated dacoits who had long persecuted and terrorised her people.

It was like sticking a hat pin into a berserk gorilla. But it was enough to stop his charge. Samunder arched over backwards, reaching with both hands behind him to try to pluck out the knife. By then Ben was springing back up to his feet. His musings about how many bullets it would take to bring the big guy down had been answered. The number was zero. He closed in on Samunder and launched a stamping kick that drove his right kneecap in on itself. The leg folded the wrong way and Samunder went down on that knee with a bellow of rage and pain, lopsided like a listing building.

Then the other knee, with the same result. Now the big guy was evened up and his screaming mouth was chest high to Ben, covered in blood from his broken nose. Ben grabbed him by the hair and drove his head downwards and the solid ram of his own kneecap upwards simultaneously to meet in a savage impact midway, and felt Samunder's teeth crack, and what was left of his nose get crunched flat in a ruin of splintered bone. Two legs disabled, his face caved in; the

423

damage would have been enough to drive the fight out of almost anybody. Ben would have let it go then, given the option. Enough would have been enough. But with a guy like this, you didn't let it go. He was like a wounded bull, enraged past the point of no return. You had to finish it, or he'd finish you.

Ben kept a hold of Samunder's hair and dashed the bloody pulp of his face against the rock floor. Once, twice, three times, and Samunder was still screaming and struggling so Ben did it three times more. The guy's weight was unbelievable. Ben couldn't have kept it up much longer. But after six brutal impacts he was beginning to feel the fight go out of his opponent. With his last reserves of strength and energy Ben grabbed him under the arms and dragged him and pitched him over the drop. He stood on the edge and watched the huge body spin end over end and then break the restless surface of the water far below with a white foamy explosion like a depth charge going off.

And then it was over.

Chapter 70

The arrival of a beaten-up, flame-scorched, bullet-holed ex-Indian Army off-road truck at the civic hospital in Jind wasn't an everyday occurrence, least of all when it turned out that two of its passengers were the missing Ray brothers from Delhi, whom many of the medical personnel had read about in the news. Amal was whisked off in a wheelchair to have his arm attended to, while Kabir reluctantly submitted to a rigorous inspection of his healing gunshot wound and general state of health. The old lady and the young girl had long since been returned to their village, safe, sound, and sworn to secrecy.

Which left Ben alone and pretty much ignored by the nurses and doctors, and that was fine by him, despite a few minor injuries of his own. His muscles were stiff and sore all over, and his right shoulder joint still hurt from where it had come close to getting dislocated, and some of the thorn scratches on his legs had gone quite deep. He had a spreading purple bruise on his chest where Samunder had punched him, and his knee ached from having come into hard contact with the guy's face. Not to mention the torn and bruised knuckles on both his hands. But none of it was anything he hadn't gone through before, and in his estimation it didn't warrant suffering the indignities of a medical examination.

It had taken a good few hours to reach Jind and evening had fallen outside. Suddenly feeling very tired, he wandered the corridors of the hospital in search of a cup of strong black coffee, a payphone, and a cigarette vending machine, in that order, although of course the last proved to be too much to hope for. But the coffee was strong and black. He found a small dark waiting area off the main corridor near the reception foyer, which nobody seemed to be using. It had a view of the floodlit car park with the incongruous army truck in it, and the traffic zipping by in the street beyond. It felt odd to be back in civilisation again. He'd soon adjust. He always did.

He settled back in a bendy plastic chair facing the window and took his time sipping from his paper cup, enjoying a few minutes of peace and quiet in the knowledge that a whole bureaucratic shit storm was about to erupt as the news of the Ray brothers' return got out. When he'd procrastinated long enough, he drained the last dregs of his coffee, thought *here we go* and walked back out into the corridor to feed some coins into the payphone.

Brooke answered her mobile on the second ring, sounding breathless and anxious as though she'd been hovering over the phone all this time. 'Hello?'

'We're in Jind,' he said.

'Who's in Jind?'

'All of us.'

It took some explaining, by the end of which Brooke was crying and in a wild rush to get off the phone, saying she was on her way.

She was there in under two hours. Ben was working on his sixth large paper cup of black coffee and still resting his weary muscles in the empty, unlit waiting area when he saw the motorcade come speeding in off the street and screech

426

to a halt in the car park. Brooke and Samarth had come in his silver Bentley. In the rear sat a white-haired, well-dressed elderly couple whom Ben had never seen before, though he could guess he was looking at old Basu and Aparna, the Ray family patriarch and matriarch. Second in the convoy was an unmarked police car containing the familiar happy, smiling faces of detectives Lamba, Savarkar and Agarwal. Behind them was a black government sedan with Vivaan Banerjee of the Indian Foreign Office riding in the back, along with some clipped-looking white guy Ben presumed to be a British Embassy suit.

Unseen behind the glass of the dark waiting room, he watched the arrivals get out of their cars. Brooke was out before anyone else, all buzzing and jittery with agitation. Her hair was a mess, her face was tear-streaked, her nose and cheeks were red and she didn't seem to know whether to weep or laugh. A dishevelled Samarth stepped quickly from the driver's side of the Bentley and opened up the rear to help the elderly couple out. They were both in their eighties, and in different ways bore a strong family resemblance to their three sons. Basu and his wife were both as much aglow with excitement as could be expected of a couple who'd been catapulted from the crushing grief of losing two children to the sudden and totally unanticipated prospect of a joyful family reunion, all within the space of two hours.

Brooke led the way towards the hospital entrance at a virtual run. Samarth followed, holding his mother's elbow in one hand and a small travel bag in the other. His old father was weeping openly. The rest of the procession tagged behind in more sedate fashion, the cops smoking and looking sour, the government guys in restrained conversation together. Lamba paused to look uninterestedly at the truck. Then he moved on to rejoin his buddies, and the whole group were lost from view of Ben's dark window. Moments later, he heard the urgent patter of footsteps on tiled floor and the sound of raised voices as they entered the reception lobby.

He had little desire to spend the next several hours talking to the government suits, still less to get the inevitable third degree from Lamba's gang. That wasn't his main reluctance, however. A strange feeling inside made him prefer not to be present when Brooke was reunited with Amal. He stayed in the dark waiting area and went on quietly sipping his coffee. The voices and footsteps passed by his door and moved on. Minutes ticked by. Nobody came to look for him. He felt foolish and cowardly to be hiding like this.

A whole half hour had passed when he heard the creak of the door and turned to see a figure walk inside the waiting area. He'd been found.

The figure felt for a light switch, clicked it on, and the dark room lit up under bright overhead neons.

'There you are. I've been looking for you.'

It wasn't one of the cops, nor was it a government suit. To Ben's greater relief, it wasn't Brooke either. Kabir was smiling as he walked into the room. His thick black hair was neatly combed, and he was wearing a crisp new shirt and jeans. From the travel bag, Ben guessed.

'How is he?' he asked.

'He's fine. They've set the arm, and now they're waiting for the plaster to dry. He's been pumped full of God knows what and needs to rest for a good few days. My parents are with him now. Brooke, too. I spoke with her briefly a few minutes ago.'

'Is she okay?'

'Overwhelmed, I'd say. A lot of mixed feelings. Relief, elation, sadness, disappointment.'

'Sadness and disappointment about what?'

'I think that she kind of expected to see you here.'

Ben paused a beat. 'What about you?'

Kabir shrugged. 'For a guy who thought he was going to die today, not so bad. The doctors were actually pretty impressed with how well I've healed up. I'll soon put the weight back on and get fit again. But never mind me.' He eyed Ben inquisitively.

'Oh, I'm fine,' Ben said. Which was relatively true, in a physical sense. The strange mood he'd been in since seeing Brooke in the car park was still hovering over him.

Kabir sat in a bendy plastic chair next to Ben's, facing the window with the view over the car park. The journey to Jind had been fast and fraught, and they hadn't had a lot of time to talk until now. 'I never thanked you for what you've done,' Kabir said.

'I should be the one thanking you. If you hadn't sprung that surprise on Takshak I mightn't have had much of a chance. You gave me the edge I needed.'

'I figured you were up to something from the first moment they turned up at the village. I saw you pick up those scissors. I tried to distract him then, too, so he wouldn't notice. Then all the way to the place I kept wondering when you might make your move.'

'You timed it well,' Ben said. 'The rest just slipped into place.'

'Is that what you call it?'

'It is what it is. I don't like violence.'

'But you do it so well. I always thought my brother's friends were all a bunch of annoying writers and theatrical types. How wrong could I have been?'

'Where are the police?' Ben asked.

'Right at this moment? Hanging around outside Amal's

treatment room and being rather grumpy and impatient as they wait to talk to Brooke.'

'What will she tell them?'

'The same official version of the story I told them, when they cornered me just now. Which will also be the account Amal gives them when they speak to him. You can be sure of that. Namely, that Amal's kidnappers were all shot to death in the firefight with the local police following an anonymous tip-off. Tragically, it seems that none of the officers survived either. Whereupon Amal found himself wandering free and just happened to make his way to the same remote village where I'd turned up weeks earlier. Then the two of us just happened to find one of the kidnappers' trucks, and managed to get back safe. End of story.'

'Hell of a coincidence.'

'They'll just have to take it or leave it. The villagers will corroborate the story, if anyone even bothers to check. Personally, I think the detectives will be happy just to wrap the case up and move on.'

'So who called Brooke from the hospital?'

Kabir grinned. 'Why, I did, of course. We're family.'

'So they don't need to talk to anyone else?'

'As I understand it, you were never really officially here,' Kabir said.

'Not entirely true. I signed some papers for your Mr Banerjee.'

'Which can easily be unsigned. Or made to disappear entirely. Don't forget, we Rays are still able to pull a string or two. And there's certainly no official record to suggest that you travelled anywhere near Rakhigarhi. Why would you?'

Ben sat gazing down at the floor and said nothing.

'Something wrong?' Kabir asked.

'No,' Ben replied. 'I was just thinking about things.'

'I suppose you'll be thinking about going home soon.'

Ben nodded. 'No reason not to.'

Kabir glanced back over his shoulder, in the direction of the doorway. He stood up and put out his hand. 'It was good meeting you, Ben. I hope we meet again one day.'

'You're leaving?'

'No, I'm staying. I need to go and be with my family. It's not every day their son comes back from the dead. Besides, I think someone wants to speak with you in private.'

Ben turned to look. Brooke was standing in the doorway.

Chapter 71

Kabir left, and then Ben and Brooke were alone. Her face was less flushed than he'd seen it through the window. More composed. He stood up to meet her as she walked over to him. It felt to him like a replay of the day he'd arrived in Delhi. His heart was beating. He felt more nervous now than he had when he'd been in the thick of the fight with Takshak.

'I thought you were with Amal,' he said.

'I just left him. He's asleep now.'

'He'll be okay.'

'Thanks to you. Kabir told me what happened. This is just incredible, Ben. It's—' She shook her head, lost for words. 'Oh, God. Come here.' She pressed herself against him and wrapped her arms so tightly around his body that he thought he was going to suffocate. When she let him go at last, her eyes were full of tears again. She wiped them away with her hand.

He said, 'I'm glad I was able to do something right for you, for once.'

'Don't say that.'

'Kabir said the police were waiting to talk to you.'

She made a face. 'That Lamba's such an ass. I sent them away, told them I'd talk to them all they like once we're back in the city, but not before. I mean, give us some space, for

God's sake. Two hours ago we didn't know who was dead or alive.' She paused, then added, 'They don't know you're here, don't worry.'

Ben smiled. 'I'm not worried about them.'

'You want to get some air?' she said. 'I hate the smell of hospitals.'

They stepped out into the corridor and glanced left and right in case Lamba and his detectives were prowling nearby, but the corridor was empty. The two of them found a side exit and walked outside into the night. It was the perfect evening, warm and still, and the stars were out. There was a path running alongside the building, with a little lawned garden opposite. They walked in silence for a while, side by side, very close together.

Ben had so many things he wanted to say. He spent a long moment trying to find the right words. 'Amal told me—' Then he faltered. Maybe he shouldn't say anything.

But it was out now, and too late to take it back. Brooke looked at him. 'Said what?'

'When we were out there. He told me some personal stuff.'

She looked away. 'I think I know what. Did he tell you that our marriage isn't working?'

'Is it that bad between you two?'

She shrugged, then gave a sad nod. 'I admit, it's true. It's been breaking down steadily for a while now. Almost from the start. We should never have got together. We both know it.'

'I'm sorry. How come you never told me?'

'You mean, like, my husband's been kidnapped and maybe murdered, and by the way we were thinking of splitting up?'

'Are you?'

433

'It's been talked about. Neither of us has the courage to actually do anything about it. So we just keep sort of plodding forwards day by day, each trying to avoid the issue. Not a great strategy. I don't know how much longer it can drag on for.'

'I'm sorry,' he said again.

'What else did he tell you?' she asked.

Ben hesitated to reply.

'Did he tell you why? Because I was in love with someone else?'

'Was?'

'Am.'

Ben didn't answer.

They walked a few more steps in silence, as though too much had been said and they needed a few moments to let the dust settle before saying anything more. She asked, 'Are you going back home now?'

'Soon enough,' he said. 'I've done what I came here to do.'

'To Le Val?'

'It's the only home I have,' he replied.

'I loved it there so much. You have no idea how I miss it.'

The words on the tip of his tongue were 'It's not the same without you.' But he left them unsaid.

She stopped walking. Turned to face him, reached out and clasped both his hands in hers. 'Let me come with you. Just for a few days.'

He could see she meant it. 'You can't be serious. Your husband's in hospital. He needs you.'

'He doesn't really. He has his family all around him. And he'll spend most of the next week sleeping, anyway. What do I have to offer?'

'Oh, you know. Emotional support. Togetherness. Closeness. Camaraderie. Things like that.'

'The things we used to have,' she said.

He made no reply. Gently pulled his hands free and let them dangle loose by his sides, looking at her and thinking how exquisitely beautiful she was in the starlight.

'Let me come with you. If not right away, then after a week. Or two. Or three. I don't care. Just as long as I can spend a bit of time with you and remember how things were.'

He said nothing.

'Just as friends,' she said.

'If I were Amal, I'd need you.'

'But you're not. And he's not you, Ben.'

'But he needs you anyway. This is where you belong. With him, by his side.'

She sighed. A tear welled up and glimmered like an uncut diamond as it slipped down the curve of her cheek.

'He's a good man, Brooke. One of the best.'

'What am I supposed to do? I feel so confused. I'm lost.'

'You make it work,' he said. 'That's what you do.'

'You're going now, aren't you?'

He nodded. 'I'm going back to my life. You go back to yours.'

'Then I suppose I'll see you around,' she said quietly.

'See you around, Brooke.'

Then he did just about the most painful thing he'd ever done in his life. He turned and walked away. He kept walking until he reached the truck. He promised himself that he wouldn't look back.

Then when his resolve broke a moment later and he did look back, she was gone.

Ben fired up the truck and began the long journey home.

Read on for an exclusive extract of the new
Ben Hope thriller by Scott Mariani

House of War

Coming November 2019

PROLOGUE

Syria, 2015

The two men were the last ones still inside the ancient temple as the invasion force closed in. They had been racing against time in their desperate last-minute bid to rescue as many of the treasures as they could, but they'd been too slow, too late, and their efforts were futile. Nobody was there to help them. Everyone else had fled hours earlier, when the first death knell of artillery fire sounded in the distance and the terrifying rumours became reality. Now the battle was lost and the government forces trying to hold onto the ancient city in the face of withering attack had fallen into full retreat.

These preserved architectural splendours had graced the desert oasis for two thousand years, dating back to when the thriving city had been one of the major centres on the trade route linking the Roman Empire with Persia, India and China. Here the worlds of classical and Eastern culture had melded and blossomed for centuries. Right up until the present day, their noble heritage had remained as a source of beauty and wonder for the thousands of travellers who flocked there each year to marvel.

And now, on this terrible day that would be remembered for a long time, the ancient city was about to fall into the hands of the destroyers.

The two men knew the end was near. Even though their hours of labour had succeeded in moving the majority of the priceless artefacts to a nearby hiding place where they hoped they could survive, there was still so much to do, so many treasures to try to save. It seemed a hopeless task.

'We must hurry, Julien,' said Salim Youssef to his younger associate. 'They'll be here any minute.' He was trying to lift a magnificent Greco-Roman bust from its plinth, to place it on a trolley and wheel it outside to the already overloaded truck. But the artefact was far too heavy for his seventy-four-year-old arms to handle. He gasped and wheezed, close to a heart attack, but he wouldn't give up. For the last forty years the Syrian had been devotedly in charge of the preservation and cataloguing of the priceless antiquities in this place, which for him was as sacred and holy as a site of religious worship.

His companion was a Frenchman named Julien Segal, twenty-five years his junior, who had been closely involved in Salim's work for over a decade. He was based equally in Paris and the Middle East, and spoke Arabic fluently. A man known for his elegant dress style and cosmopolitan chic, he wasn't looking his stylish best at this moment, as he struggled and sweated to drag a six-foot Akkadian alabaster statue across the flagstone floor towards the archway near to which the truck was parked. Even inside the relative coolness of the temple, the August desert heat felt as though it could bake a man inside his skin.

'It's no use, Salim. We'll never make it. Everyone else has fled and we should do the same, while we still can.'

'You go, Julien,' Salim wheezed, still clutching his heart.

'I'm staying. I won't abandon these treasures, no matter what. This place is all I know and care about.'

'But they'll kill you, Salim.'

'Let those lunatic butchers do their worst,' the old man said. 'I'm not afraid of them. I have lived my life and don't have many years left. But yours is still ahead of you. Go! Save yourself!' He pulled the truck keys from his pocket and tossed them to Julien Segal.

The Frenchman was about to reply, 'I won't leave without you.' But the words died in his mouth as he turned to see the sight that froze his blood.

They were here.

Nine men had come into the temple's main entrance and now stood in a semicircle, watching them with detached curiosity. All ten were bearded and clad in dusty battledress, armed with automatic weapons. Their leader stood in the middle, with four of his soldiers each side of him. He wore black, in accordance with his rank as an ISIL commander. A holstered pistol and a long, sheathed knife hung from his utility belt.

That was when Julien Segal saw that three of the men were also clutching heavy iron sledgehammers in addition to their weaponry. He opened his mouth to speak, but his throat had gone dry.

Salim spoke for him. The old man stepped away from the bust he'd been trying to manhandle, and advanced towards the invaders, fists clenched in anger. 'You are not welcome here! Leave now!'

The commander in black stepped forward to meet him. He gazed around the temple's interior, looking at the statues and other artefacts that Salim and his colleague hadn't yet been able to remove to safety, and the vacant plinths of those that they had. His voice echoed in the stone chamber as he spoke:

'I am Nazim al-Kassar. You must be Salim Youssef, the curator. Tell me, old man. This place is looking quite empty. Where have you hidden the rest of these idolatrous pieces of trash you call art?'

'So you have come here to destroy them,' Salim said defiantly.

'This house of blasphemy, along with everything inside it and all that you have vainly tried to rescue,' said Nazim al-Kassar. 'It shall be razed to the ground, inshallah.'

'You will not! You must not!'

The commander smiled. 'These are the idols of previous centuries, which were worshipped instead of Allah. They have no place in the new Caliphate that will now rule this country for the rest of time. Allah commands that they be shattered and broken into dust.'

'Savages! Vandals! What gives you the right to erase history? You think you're doing Allah's bidding? Where does the Quran make such a command? Nowhere! I am also a Muslim, and I say that you bring shame and disgrace upon our religion!' The old man was seething with fury. Cringing behind him, Julien Segal was too terrified to utter a word.

The commander's voice remained calm as he pointed a black-gloved finger at Salim and replied, 'Old man, I will ask only once. You will lead me to where you have hidden the idols of this false divinity, so that the soldiers of the caliphate can consign them to the past, where they belong.'

'Then I belong there with them,' Salim said. 'I will die before I allow you to wreak your unholy destruction in this place.'

'So be it,' the commander said. 'What you ask for, you will receive.' He nodded to his men. Four of them stepped forward, seized Salim and Julien Segal each by the arms, and forced them down to their knees on the flagstone floor. The younger Frenchman knelt with his head bowed and shoulders sagging. Next to him, Salim Youssef refused to break eye contact with his tormentors and remained straight-backed, chin high.

The commander reached down to the hilt of the long, curved knife that hung from his belt, and drew out the blade with a sigh of steel against leather. Salim wouldn't take his eyes off him for an instant, even though he knew what was coming.

Julien Segal let out a whimper. 'For God's sake, Salim. We have to tell them. Please.'

'I'm sorry, Julien. I will not go to my grave knowing that I betrayed my life's work to these maniacs.'

The commander stepped around behind Salim.

Salim closed his eyes.

What happened next had Julien Segal burying his face in the dirt and crying in unbearable anguish. But the old man never made a sound. He faced his death with the same steely resolve that he'd shown throughout his life.

Moments later, Julien Segal felt the thump of something hitting the floor beside him. Followed by a second, heavier thud as Salim's decapitated body slumped forward to fall on the floor next to where the commander had tossed his severed head. Segal couldn't bring himself to look directly at it, and instead watched in horror as the blood pool spread over the floor, trickling into the cracks between the flagstones and reflecting the light from the arched window.

'Now it is your turn,' said the man called Nazim al-Kassar.

Chapter 1

The present day

It was a cold, bright and sunny October morning in Paris, and Ben Hope was making a brief stop-off in that city on his return from a long journey. The trip to India had not been a scheduled event, but then few things in his life were, or ever had been, despite his best efforts to lead the kind of peaceful and stable existence he might have wished for. It seemed that fate always had other plans for him.

All he wanted to do now was put the experience behind him, move on from it and get home. Home being a sleepy corner of rural France two hundred miles west of Paris, a place called Le Val, and he couldn't wait to get there. First he had some business to attend to in the city, which he fully intended to deal with as quickly as possible, partly since it was a rather dull chore that he'd put off for too long.

The first thing he'd done when his plane had landed at Orly Airport the previous evening was to call Jeff Dekker, his business partner in Normandy, to say he was back in the country and would be home by early next afternoon. Jeff was pretty well used to Ben's frequent impromptu disappearances; all he said was 'See you later'. The second was to call a Parisian estate agent he knew to talk about finally selling the backstreet apartment he'd owned for years and never used anymore. Back when he'd worked freelance and lived a nomadic existence, the place had come in handy as an occasional base camp in the city. It had never been more than a bolthole for him, and he'd made little effort to furnish or decorate it beyond the absolute basics of necessity. The pragmatic nature of military life was an ingrained habit that refused to die in him, though he'd been out of that for quite some years.

Whatever the case, the apartment had long since become surplus to his requirements. Though every time he'd been on the verge of putting the place on the market, as had happened on several occasions, another of those bolts from the blue would arrive to yank him off on some new crazy mission or other. Which, as he was all too aware, was just a reflection of the broader reality that every time he tried to do anything at all, some new crisis would loom up to divert him right off track.

Such was life. Maybe after another forty years, he'd get used to it.

But that wasn't going to happen this time, he told himself. This time he was going to see it through, get the thing offloaded and put the cash in his pocket, go home to Le Val and get back down to running his business. The eternally-patient Jeff, his long-time friend and co-director of the tactical training centre they'd founded and built together, might appreciate Ben's actually being around sometimes. Instructing the world's top law enforcement, security and close protection services in the finer points of their craft was a dirty job, but someone had to do it.

It was just after eight a.m. At ten-thirty he was due to meet with the property agent, a nervous-mannered chap called Gerbier who, Ben already knew, would spend an hour hemming and hawing about the difficulties of selling the place. First, because despite its theoretically desirable central location it was all but totally secreted away among a cluster of crumbly old buildings and its only access was via an underground car park. Second, because even at its best it had never looked like much on the inside, either, and needed decoration work to appeal to any but the most Spartan of buyers. And third, because right now wasn't a good time for the Parisian property market in general. Ben had to admit the guy might have a point about that. For months the city had been locked in increasingly turbulent civil unrest, boiling with constant anti-government protests that had sparked off over a long list of political and social grievances and seemed to grow more serious and violent each passing day. There had been mass arrests, the cops had started deploying armoured personnel carriers and water cannon, and there were no signs of things cooling down any time soon. Now the troubles had spread across the city into Ben's normally quiet neighbourhood. He had lain awake for some time the night before, listening to the screeching sirens and loud explosions of the latest pitched battle between rioters and the police. It had sounded like both sides meant business.

'Who can tell where this will end?' Gerbier had fretted over the phone. 'The city's falling into anarchy. Nobody's buying any more.'

How justified was Gerbier's pessimism, only time would tell. Ben had been up with the dawn that morning, as always. He'd laboured through his usual gruelling pre-breakfast workout of press-ups, sit-ups and pull-ups, taken a one-minute tepid shower, pulled on fresh black jeans and a denim shirt, scanned a few latest news headlines online, meditatively smoked a couple of Gauloise cigarettes while gazing out at the non-existent view for what might be one of the last times if he got lucky finding a buyer soon, then turned his thoughts to eating breakfast. Dinner last night had been a sandwich wolfed down on the hoof at the airport, and he was starving.

That was when Ben had realised that there wasn't a scrap of food in the apartment. Worse, much worse, the bare kitchenette cupboards contained not a single coffee bean.

And so here he was, heading briskly along the street, his scuffed brown leather jacket zipped against the chill and the third Gauloise of the day dangling from his lip, in the direction of a local café where he could get some breakfast. It was a five-minute stroll, but when he got there he discovered to his chagrin that the café had had its windows smashed in last night's disturbances and was shut for business.

The café owners weren't the only locals to have suffered damage from the latest round of protests. All up and down the street, storekeepers were resignedly sweeping up broken glass, nailing plywood sheets over their shattered windows, hauling out buckets of hot water to try and scrub away graffiti that had appeared overnight. Ben stopped for a brief conversation with Habib, who ran the little Moroccan grocery store and tobacconist's where he'd often bought his cigarettes. Habib expressed sympathy with the protesters but worried that his insurance premiums would sky-rocket if these riots kept up. Ben offered his commiserations, wished Habib good luck and walked on in search of breakfast. He still had plenty of time to kill before meeting Gerbier.

The signs of last night's troubles were all around. Though it hadn't rained overnight the roads and pavements were slicked wet, small rivers created by police water cannon trickling in the gutters and pooling around washed-up garbage that choked the drain grids. A recovery crew with a flatbed lorry were removing the burnt-out shells of three cars that had been torched by the protesters. Barriers and cones had reduced the traffic to a crawl as cars and vans and motorcycles threaded their way along streets still littered with riot debris and spent tear gas canisters.

As Ben walked along, he spied one of those rolling in the gutter and picked it up to examine it, just out of curiosity. It was the strong stuff, the real McCoy. Then again, the French riot police never had mucked about when it came to dispersing violent demonstrations. The warning on the empty canister said: DANGER – DO NOT FIRE DIRECTLY AT PERSON(S), AS SEVERE INJURY OR DEATH MAY RESULT. Ben had seen from the online news headlines that a couple of civilians had already been accidentally killed that way as the protests mounted. There was a good chance of more fatalities to come. One serious casualty among the police, and the government would probably send in the army.

Ben continued on his way, thinking about Gerbier's words and wondering where, indeed, it was all going to end. As he'd grown older and wiser he had come to understand that history was the key to predicting what lay in the future. As the saying went, those who failed to learn from the hard lessons of the past were doomed to repeat them. Paris had seen more than its fair share of revolutionary unrest in its time, and none of it seemed to have done much good. The big one of 1789 had kicked off much the same way as was happening now – and look how that ended, eating itself in an orgy of blood and severed heads and giving rise to the Napoleonic empire and rather a lot of even bloodier wars, followed eventually by a new monarchy to take the place of the old. Then had come the July Revolution of 1830, the one portrayed in the famous Delacroix painting that used to be on the old 100-franc bank note, depicting the topless Liberty wielding tricolour flag and musket as she led the people to victory, this time against the royal regime of Charles X. Same dubious result. Then just eighteen years later they'd been at it again, with the populist uprising of 1848 that had spilled enough blood in the streets of Paris to tear down the establishment once more and trigger the foundation of the Second Republic, which lasted exactly three years before the Second Empire turned the country back into a de facto monarchy.

And on, and on, through the ages and right up to the present. Round and round we go, Ben thought. An endless cycle of inflamed passion leading to disappointment, and resentment, and blame, simmering away and slowly building up to the next outburst. And for what? So much suffering and destruction could only deepen the rift between nation and state, while calls for reform would largely go unheeded and life would ultimately go on just like before. Sure, go ahead and protest about overinflated taxes and rising costs of living and the insidious encroachment of the European superstate and police brutality and human rights infringements and loss of personal freedoms and privacy and anything else you feel strongly about. All fine. Angry mobs ripping their own beautiful city apart, looting and pillaging, harming small businesses, terrorising innocent citizens, not so fine. Unless you really believed that a violent street revolution was the only possible way to change things for the better.

Well, good luck with that.

Those were all the things on Ben's mind as he walked quickly around the corner of Rue Georges Brassens and collided with a young woman who, quite literally, ran into him without looking where she was going.

He didn't know it yet, but fate had just launched another of those bolts from the blue at him.

Chapter 2

The woman crashed straight into Ben with enough force to
knock the wind out of herself and go tumbling to the pavement. It took Ben a moment to recover from his own
surprise. Though it hadn't been his fault he said in French,
'Oh, I'm so sorry,' and went to help her to her feet. He'd
become skilled at languages back during his time with Special
Forces, learning Arabic, Dari, Farsi and some African
dialects, along with various European languages. He had
now been living in France long enough to virtually pass for
a native speaker.

As she picked herself off the pavement he saw she was
more stunned than hurt. She was maybe twenty-five years
old and slender, wearing a long camel coat over a white
cashmere roll-neck top and navy trousers. Her hair was
sandy-blond and her face, if it hadn't been flushed with
shock, was attractively heart-shaped with vivid eyes the same
blue as Ben's own. She didn't look as though she weighed
very much, but it had been quite a collision. The little leather
satchel she'd been carrying on a shoulder strap had fallen
to the pavement and burst open, scattering its contents.

'Are you okay?' Ben asked her. She seemed too flustered
to reply, and kept looking anxiously behind her as though
she expected to see someone there. A couple of passersby

had paused to gawk, but quickly lost interest and walked on. Ben said, 'Miss? Are you all right?'

The woman looked at him as though noticing him for the first time. Her blue eyes widened with alarm. She backed away a couple of steps, plainly frightened of him. He held his arms to the sides and showed her his open palms. 'I mean no harm,' he said jokingly. 'You're the one who ran into me. Maybe you should look where you're going. Here, let me help you with your things.'

He crouched down to pick up her fallen satchel. Her purse had fallen out, along with a hairbrush, some hair ties, a book of metro tickets and a little black plastic case that said GIVENCHY in gold lettering. The contents of women's handbags had always been a bit of a mystery to Ben. He was also aware of the delicacy of the situation as he quickly scooped up her personal items from the pavement. She paid no attention while he retrieved her things, apparently too distracted by whatever, or whoever, she seemed to think was lurking behind her. When Ben stood up and offered the satchel back to her, she reached out tentatively and snatched it from his hands like a nervous animal accepting a titbit from a strange and untrusted human.

So much for being a knight in shining armour.

'You're bleeding,' he said, noticing that she'd scuffed the side of her left hand in the fall. 'Doesn't look too bad, but you should put some antiseptic on it.'

Still the same terse silence. She turned her anxious gaze behind her again. Pedestrians walked by, paying no attention. The traffic stream kept rumbling past in the background. A municipal cleaning crew was slowly working its way along the street towards them, gathering up last night's wreckage. A couple of pigeons strutted and pecked about among the debris in the gutter, apparently unbothered by whatever was frightening the woman. Then she quickly looped the strap of her satchel over her shoulder and hurried on without a word or another glance at him. Ben watched her disappear off down Rue Georges Brassens, walking so fast she was almost running, still glancing behind her every few steps as though someone was chasing her.

He shook his head. Some people. What the hell was up with her? The way she'd acted with him, anyone would think he'd been about to attack her. And who did she think was coming after her?

Maybe she was an escaped lunatic. Or a bank robber fleeing from the scene of the crime. Perhaps some kind of political activist or protest organiser the cops were trying to round up and throw in jail along with the other thousand-odd they'd already locked up. Ben looked around him and saw no squads of gendarmes or psychiatric ward nurses tearing down the street in pursuit. Nor anyone else of interest, apart from the usual passersby who were all just going about their business, the majority of them deeply absorbed in their phones as most people seemed to be nowadays, doing the thumb-twiddling texting thing as they ambled along and somehow managed to avoid stumbling into trees and signposts. It seemed to him that those without digital devices to distract them from their present reality were walking somewhat more briskly than normal, a little stiff in their body language as if trying hard not to take in too much of their surroundings and dwell at any length on the signs of the battlefield that their city environment had become.

One way or another, though, the Parisians had far too much on their minds to be worrying about some panic-stricken woman running down the street blindly crashing into people.

Ben shrugged his shoulders and was about to move on when he saw that the young woman had dropped something else on the ground. She'd been so distracted that she had failed to notice that her phone had bounced off the kerbside and into the gutter, where it was lying among the washed-up debris and broken bottles that the cleaning crew hadn't yet reached.

He picked it up. A slim, new-model smartphone in a smart black leather wallet case. The leather was wet from the gutter, but the phone inside was dry. There was no question that it hadn't been lying in the gutter for long, and that it belonged to the woman. He could feel the residual trace of warmth from where it had been nestling in her bag close to her body. In an age when people's phones seemed to have become the hub of their entire lives, she must have been in a hell of a preoccupied state of mind not to have noticed its absence.

Ben stood there for a moment, thinking what he should do. Further along the street he could see the striped red and white awning of a café-bistro that had obviously escaped damage and was open for business. His mouth watered at the thought of coffee and croissants and he was torn between the temptation of breakfast and the notion of going after the woman to return her phone. She was well out of sight by now, and could have turned off onto any number of side streets. He decided on breakfast and slipped the phone into his pocket.

The place was bustling and noisy, but there was a table free in a corner. Out of habit, Ben sat with his back to the wall so he could observe the entrance. A hurried waiter took his order for a large *café noir* and the compulsory fresh-baked croissant.

While he waited for his order to arrive, Ben sat quietly

and absorbed the chatter from other customers. Predictably the subject of the day, here as everywhere in the city, was the riots. A pair of middle-aged men at the next table were getting quite animated over whether or not the president should declare martial law, order the rebuilding of the Bastille prison, stuff the whole lot of troublemakers behind bars and throw away the key.

When his breakfast arrived Ben gave up eavesdropping on their conversation, took a sip or two of the delicious coffee and tore off a corner of croissant to dunk into his cup. A Gauloise would have rounded things out nicely, but such pleasures were no longer to be had in the modern civilised world. He went back to thinking about the strange woman who had bumped into him. What was she so frightened of? Where had she been running from, or to? He had to admit it, he was intrigued. And sooner or later, he was going to have to do something about the phone in his pocket.

Curiosity getting the better of him, he took it out to examine more closely. If the screen happened to be locked, there might not be much he could do except just hand it in to the nearest gendarmerie as lost property. But when he flipped open the leather wallet he soon discovered that the phone wasn't locked.

Which left him a number of potential ways to find out who the woman was and where she lived, allowing him to return the item to her personally. Ben was good at finding people. It was something he used to do for a living, after he'd quit the SAS to go his own way as what he'd euphemistically termed a 'crisis response consultant'. A career that involved tracking down people who didn't always want to be found, especially when they were holding innocent child hostages captive for ransom. Kidnappers didn't make themselves easy to locate, as a rule. But Ben had located them anyway, and the consequences hadn't been very pleasant for them. By contrast, thanks to today's technology, ordinary unsuspecting citizens were easy to track down. Too easy, in his opinion.

Feeling just a little self-conscious about intruding on her privacy, he scrolled around the phone's menus. There were a few emails and assorted files, but his first port of call was the woman's address book. She was conservative about what information she stored in her contacts list. There was someone called Michel, no surname, and another contact called 'Maman/Papa', obviously her parents, but no addresses for either, and no home address or home landline number for herself. But the mobile's own number was there.

Ben took out his own phone to check it with. Damn these bloody things, but he was just as bound to them as the next guy. He'd got into the habit of carrying two of them, one a fancy smartphone registered to his business, the other a cheap, anonymous burner bought for cash, no names, no questions. Its anonymity pleased him and it came in handy in certain circumstances. But for this call he used his smart-phone. He punched in the woman's mobile number. Her phone rang in his other hand. You could tell a lot about a person from their choice of ringtone. Hers was a retro-style *dring-dring*, like the old dial phone that stood in the hallway of the farmhouse at Le Val. Ben liked that about her. He ended the call and the ringing stopped. So far, so good.

Next he used his smartphone to access the whitepages.fr people finder website, which scanned millions of data files to give a reverse lookup. When a prompt appeared he entered the woman's mobile number and activated the search. Not all phone users were trackable this way, only a few hundred million worldwide. Which was a pretty large net, but still something of a gamble. If it didn't pay off, he still had other options to try.

But that wouldn't be necessary, because he scored a hit first time. In a few seconds he'd gained access to a whole range of information about the mystery woman: name, address, landline number, employer, and the contact details of two extant relatives in the Parisian suburb of Fontenay-sous-Bois a few kilometres to the east. If he'd been interested in offering her a job, he could run a background check to verify her credentials and see if she had a criminal record. If he was thinking of lending her money, he could view her credit rating. As things stood, he only needed the basics, which he now had. Piece of cake.

Her name was Mme Romy Juneau. All adult women in France were now officially titled *Madame* regardless of marital status, since the traditional *Mademoiselle* had been banned for being sexist. But her parents' shared surname matched hers, suggesting she was unmarried. Some traditions still prevailed. Ben guessed that the phone contact called Michel was probably a boyfriend. She worked at a place called Institut Culturel Segal, ICS for short. The Segal Cultural Institute, whatever that was, in an upmarket part of town on Avenue des Champs-Élysées.

More important to Ben at this moment was her home address, which was an apartment number in a street just a few minutes' walk from where he was sitting right now, and in the direction she'd been heading when they'd bumped into one another.

Given the time and place where he'd met her, on a weekday morning just a short distance from where she lived, it seemed safe to assume that she hadn't been going to work. Maybe she had the day off. Whatever the case, it was a reasonable assumption that she'd been making her way home. From where, he couldn't say, and it didn't really matter. If she was heading for her apartment, there was a strong likelihood that she'd have got there by now, considering the hurry she'd been in.

Ben scribbled her details in the little notebook he carried, then exited the whitepages website and punched in Romy Juneau's landline number. As he listened to the dialling tone, he thought about what he'd say to her.

No reply. Perhaps she hadn't got home yet, or was in the bathroom, or any number of reasons. Ben ended the call and looked at his watch. The morning was wearing on. He needed to be thinking about finishing breakfast and heading over to see Gerbier at his offices across town. Romy Juneau would have to wait until afterwards.

He was slurping down the last of the delicious coffee when his phone buzzed. He answered quickly, thinking that Romy must have just missed his call and was calling him back. His anticipation soon fell flat when he heard the unpleasantly raspy, reedy voice of Gaston Gerbier in his ear.

The estate agent was calling, very apologetically, to cancel their morning appointment because his hundred-year-old mother had started complaining of chest pains and been rushed off to hospital. It was probably nothing serious, Gerbier explained. The vicious old moo had been dying of the same heart attack for the last thirty-odd years and false alarms were a routine thing. Still, he felt obliged to be there, as the dutiful son, etc., etc. Ben said it was no problem; they could reschedule the appointment for next time he was in town. He wished the old moo a speedy recovery and hung up.

There went his morning's duties. Ben couldn't actually say he was sorry to be missing out on the joys of Gerbier's company, and he was in no desperate hurry to sell his place. With a suddenly empty slate and nothing better to do, he decided now was as good a time as any to play the Good

Samaritan and deliver the lost phone back to its owner in person. Given the nervous way she'd acted around him before, so as not to freak her out still further by showing up at her door he'd just post it through her letterbox with a note explaining how he'd found it. And that would be that. His good deed done, he could wend his way back to his apartment, jump in the car and be home at Le Val by late afternoon.

Ben munched the last of his croissant, paid his bill, and then left the café and set off on foot in the direction of her address. The sky was blue, the sun was shining, the day was his to do with as he pleased, and he felt carefree and untroubled.

He had no idea what he was walking into. But he soon would. He was, in fact, about to meet Mademoiselle Romy Juneau for the second time. And from that moment, a whole new world of trouble would be getting ready to open up.

House of War

Coming November 2019

DEEP SOUTH. DEEPER SECRETS.

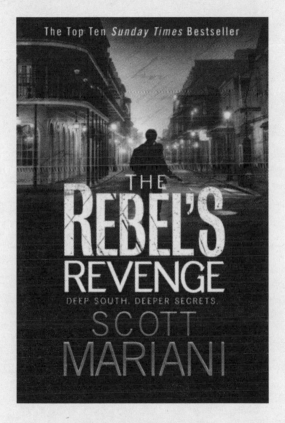

The Top Ten *Sunday Times* Bestseller

THE REBEL'S REVENGE

DEEP SOUTH. DEEPER SECRETS.

SCOTT MARIANI

LOUISIANA, 1886.
The courageous act of a slave girl changed
the course of the American Civil War.
Now, over 150 years later, could it change the
course of Ben Hope's life?

**DON'T LET THEM GET INSIDE
YOUR MIND . . .**

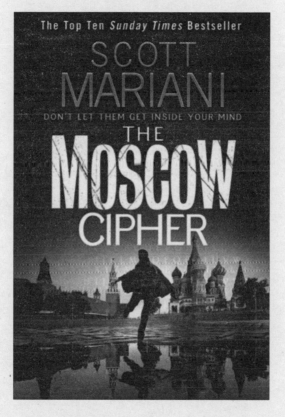

'If you like your conspiracies twisty, your
action bone-jarring, and your heroes impos-
sibly dashing, then look no farther.' MARK
DAWSON

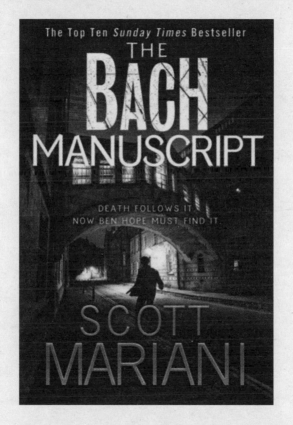

THE HUNT IS ON . . .

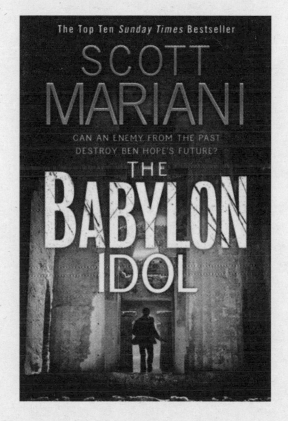

Don't miss the action-packed *Sunday Times* bestseller.